House of
Blues

HOUSE OF BLUES

A SKIP LANGDON NOVEL

JULIE SMITH

FAWCETT COLUMBINE • NEW YORK

A Fawcett Columbine Book
Published by Ballantine Books

Copyright © 1995 by Julie Smith

All rights reserved under International and Pan-American Copyright Conventions. Published in the United States by Ballantine Books, a division of Random House, Inc., New York, and simultaneously in Canada by Random House of Canada Limited, Toronto.

ISBN 0-449-90936-0

Manufactured in the United States of America

For Linda Buczek,
because this is her favorite

ACKNOWLEDGMENTS

The wonderful folks at Arnaud's provided invaluable expertise on the restaurant world, and Chef Kevin Davis even lent me his knives. My heartfelt thanks to Chef Kevin, Rick Mayeaux, Ross Miller, Norman Henry, and especially to Jane and Archie Casbarian, who let me spy on them to my heart's content.

NOPD Captain Linda Buczek gave generously of her time, energy, and imagination, as did Lieutenant Bob Italiano, Sergeant Jimmy Keen, and Detectives Wayne Rumore, Tony Caprera, and Joey Catalanotto.

Help came from many other kind New Orleanians, including Betsy and Jim Petersen, Kit and Billy Wohl, Janet Plume, Debbie Faust, Chris Wiltz, and two writers whose excellent books I relied on: Bethany Bultman, author of *New Orleans*, my favorite guidebook; and Carol Flake, author of *New Orleans: Behind the Masks of America's Most Exotic City*.

Thanks to them all and to David Ramus, Earl Emerson, Susan Berman, Becky Light, Steve Holtz, Sandy Pearlman, Jon Carroll, and Captain Ronnie Jones of the Louisiana State Police Department's gaming enforcement division.

The fictional restaurant herein—Hebert's—isn't based on a real restaurant, but the proposed casino is very real. At this writing, there's no plan for an important restaurant in the casino and therefore there's been no infighting of the sort described in the book.

In Louisiana, though, it's never over till it's over.

House of Blues

1

In New Orleans, as in many American cities, crime is Topic A. The annual murder rate is somewhere around 400 and climbing. In addition, 2,000 people who do not die are shot each year.

The detectives assigned to Homicide say there are no fistfights anymore.

The police, as is traditional in America in the nineties, where people talk of little but crime, are overworked, understaffed, and paid more like schoolteachers than CEOs.

White people blame black people. Many carry guns.

Blacks, many of whom are among the 2,400 killed or wounded annually, feel as if they are under fire in more ways than one. They also incline toward firearms.

The economy, which was hit hard from the oil bust, is still in disarray, but there is hope. The world's largest casino, soon to be built, may create employment and draw the sort of tourist the city so desperately needs— the sort that starts with F, soon parted from his money. That is, the casino is soon to be built if the wrangling over every tiny detail connected with its building and operating is ever settled.

The petty scam is so much a way of life throughout the state that the natives shake their heads and tell the tourists, "Louisiana doesn't tolerate corrupt politicians; it demands them."

In one gubernatorial election, a candidate perceived as a dangerous racist ran against one of such unsavory reputation that a bumper strip urged good liberals to "Vote for the crook; it's important." Indeed, the winner himself remarked that one-armed people had been unable to vote for him, since his supporters needed one hand to hold their noses and another to pull the lever.

Yet despite crime and corruption, New Orleans remains arguably the most beautiful American city; the most gracious; the most charming.

It is also the most eccentric. Walker Percy, one of its most revered writers, noted that here "the tourist is apt to see more nuns and naked women than he ever saw before," the combination being the intriguing part. But eccentricity has its perils: Louisiana has the usual drunk-driving laws, and New Orleans more than its share of drunks—yet drive-in daiquiri stands abound and flourish.

On the other hand, the city's justly famous flamboyance is also its best feature. As the neighborhoods change, as the Crips and Bloods get bigger toeholds, as more and more middle-class mamas start to pack pistols, this at least remains a constant. The drag queen is welcome here, as is the voodoo queen, the queen of vampire fiction, and the Queen of Carnival —as long as none of them bore anybody.

Like Mexico or the Caribbean, the city is an odd mixture of the up-to-the-minute and the archaic—with a good deal more emphasis on the latter.

Yet perhaps even that is changing. A local publication recently lamented that people hardly ever say they're going out to "make groceries" anymore.

Only rarely now is a sidewalk referred to as a "banquette."

Still, "neutral grounds" continue to divide the streets, and a Mardi Gras trinket remains, not a string, but "a pair" of beads.

And some of the old customs survive. It used to be that everyone cooked red beans and rice on Monday because this was wash day—you could put your beans on and go about your business. Though the washing machine made the custom obsolete, some of the restaurants still observe it. In at least one august and unlikely household, that of Sugar and Arthur Hebert, it was revived some years ago.

Owner-operators of Hebert's ("A-Bear's," the menu tells tourists), a restaurant where the dish has never been served, they convinced themselves at some point that they enjoyed nothing so much as the simplest of fare after a week of serving up Creole delicacies, and fell into the habit of consuming the dish during their weekly family dinners—on Monday, because the restaurant was closed then.

Hebert's was one of the city's finest restaurants—of the sort called "Creole," meaning the kind of sophisticated, French-style cooking native to the city rather than the country. In the bayous, it is sometimes thought, is where you'd find the cuisine called "Cajun," unless you went to a city restaurant specializing in it—K-Paul's, for instance. In reality, however, many Cajun-style dishes are found in fine restaurants like Hebert's. Creole cooking is such a mixture of styles and cultures it can't really be classified.

An excellent book on New Orleans notes that, "In each bowl of gumbo served in Louisiana today, there is French roux, African okra, American Indian file, Spanish peppers, Cajun sausage, and oysters supplied by Yugoslav fishermen, served over Chinese-cultivated Louisiana rice."

Red beans, however, essential as they are to the city's cuisine, are humble enough that you'd more likely find them at neighborhood restaurants than on the menu at Antoine's—or Hebert's.

● ●

Why? thought Sugar as she dished up beans one balmy evening in June. *Why, when we could be having a nice crab salad? Why, week after week, red beans and rice, nothing else? Ever.*

Why?

Because Arthur wants it. Everything's that way.

Why did the termites nearly eat the restaurant? Because Arthur wouldn't believe it was happening. Why did we almost lose Nina? Because Arthur's such a snob he wouldn't speak to her at first.

"Mom, can I help you?" It was her daughter, Reed.

"It's done now." Sugar could have used her twenty minutes ago.

Eighteen-month-old Sally was already at the table, rocking in her high chair, straining to get out.

Reed's husband Dennis was trying to talk her out of it.

Arthur was opening champagne.

That was Arthur's little irony. He might eat red beans and rice, but he always served an excellent wine with it. Tonight they were having champagne because there were things to celebrate.

He filled the glasses.

"A toast," he said, "to la deuxieme Hebert's—a triumph against terrific odds."

"May our luck hold," said Dennis.

Arthur gave him a look that said, *What do you mean "our"?*

"Hear, hear," said Sugar, to smooth it over.

"We did it," said Reed. "I don't know how, but we did it."

"May you never have to sit through another board meeting."

"I'll drink to that."

A dozen restaurateurs—some old, some new—had fought for the concession at the casino. An elegant restaurant was called for—something in the New Orleans tradition—and it had to be a name brand, something the tourists would recognize. Hebert's was certainly in the running, but it was in competition with bigger names—huge names like Antoine's, Arnaud's, Brennan's.

Yet it had won.

Hebert's had won. Reed's relentless research and planning, her constant dogging of the board, the endless nights she'd put in planning the restaurant, then planning her strategy, had paid off.

She was a prize, Sugar thought. Surely the pride of the Heberts. It was a miracle, and she'd pulled it off.

"We have something else to drink to," said Dennis, his grin slightly crooked, a little unsure.

"What's that?"

"Arthur's sixty-fifth."

Reed said, "Happy birthday, Daddy."

"We already did that."

"Let's do it again."

"Let's don't."

Oh, don't be an old coot. Sugar didn't say it, but she was mad; she hated it when he put Reed down. And putting Dennis down was putting Reed down.

You'd think that with Sally and everything, he'd have simmered down. But he gets more and more irascible. I wonder if he's depressed? Doesn't Alzheimer's start like this?

Despite his ill nature, everyone drank to Arthur. Sugar served the plates, as she had every Monday since she could remember.

Sally protested.

"What is it, baby?" said Reed. "What's the matter? Mmmm. Red beans. Yum. Sally's favorite, hmm?"

Arthur seemed embarrassed. "Hey, Dennis," he said. "There were these three black guys, Jackson, Leroy, and Clarence. And Leroy says to Clarence, he says—"

"Daddy, please don't." Reed's face said she'd just seen a car crash; her voice sounded desperate.

"Oh, Reed, take it easy—I haven't even said anything yet."

"I can tell this is going to be the kind of joke I don't like."

"Well, la-di-da, Miss High and Mighty. You always have to have everything your own way, don't you?"

Reed looked at the table, embarrassed.

"You just have no sense of humor." He paused, but no one spoke. "Do you?"

"I just don't see why you have to tell racist jokes."

"I am not a racist and you know it, Reed. Dennis doesn't mind. Dennis likes my jokes, don't you, Dennis?"

Dennis bared some teeth, but Sugar wasn't sure it was exactly a smile.

"Look, I pay my employees better than anybody in the Quarter, don't I? And I hire blacks. You know I hire 'em. Look at my second-in-command—not only black, but a woman. I give the best benefits of anybody around too. You watch out who you're calling a racist."

"I didn't think that joke was going to be appropriate, that's all."

To deflect the two of them, Sugar said, "We certainly had a good crowd over the weekend."

"Reed put in twelve hours on Saturday," said Dennis. "Sally was beginning to wonder if she had a mother."

Arthur smacked his lips. "Hell, she should have gone home. Doesn't do that much anyway."

Reed's voice was small. "I try."

Sugar knew he didn't mean it—Reed had been more or less running the restaurant for years; it was just the way he talked.

"Anyway," said Reed, "you can relax soon. It'll all be up to me."

"God help us."

"Know what I think I'm going to do? Have the place painted cream—like this room, like your dining room—and put in a lot of mirrors."

"No, you're not. We've got a winning formula—why mess with it?"

"Some plants too. I'd just like to update it a little; freshen it up."

"You mess with Hebert's, I'll update you, young lady."

Far from being daunted, Reed smiled; he was just being Arthur. "I think the wait staff is a little short too. We've never had waitresses—I'd like to hire some women."

"No!" It was a roar. "You don't have waitresses in a place like Hebert's. You have waitresses at lunch counters."

Sugar spoke up: "Oh, Arthur, take it easy. She's just excited. There has to be a period of adjustment, you know; when a new person takes over."

At his birthday party the previous Friday, Arthur had officially announced his retirement, passing the torch to his daughter. Since Reed had worked in the restaurant from the time she was a teenager, had gone to Cornell to learn how to run it, had eaten, slept, and breathed Hebert's all her life, it was her big moment in the spotlight—the culmination of her training and her life's work.

"Anyway, Reed's been full of plans for three days—the only thing is, they're different every hour."

Reed seemed not to be listening. She said, "Daddy, what would you think about getting a decorator in? Maybe you're right. Maybe I shouldn't try to do it myself."

"You're not getting any decorator in."

Sugar had had enough. "She can do what she wants, Arthur. Reed's in charge now."

"Well, I don't think she's up to the job."

"You should have thought of that before you gave it to her."

"I didn't give it to her, I was just talking."

For a moment there was a stunned silence. Dennis broke it. "What do you mean you didn't give it to her?"

"Can't an old man get drunk and sentimental? I was in a real good mood about Hebert's II, and anyway, it was my birthday."

"Dad, are you saying you don't want me to take over the restaurant?" Reed's voice was like feathers—insubstantial, barely brushing the air.

"That's what I'm saying."

Dennis said, "Hey!" Anger shot from his eyes.

"But you gave me a legal document. I'm the CEO now."

"I want it back on my desk by tomorrow morning."

"You can't be serious."

"Reed, you're too immature to be running a business. We'd be broke in two weeks with you at the helm."

"What are you saying?"

"I've already said it loud and clear. I was drunk, I didn't mean it, and that paper means nothing either. I'm not retiring and you're not taking over."

"You can't do this to me! You just can't play this kind of game. To me, it isn't a game at all. All my life, I've worked for you, and now—" She stopped and flung out both arms as she struggled for words. One of them caught Sally's dish, on its high-chair tray. The dish flipped onto the child's chest and fell back onto the tray. Hot beans dripped into Sally's lap.

She howled.

"You idiot!" shouted Arthur. "For Christ's sake, Reed, you don't have the sense God gave a marmoset. Look at that poor child. Don't just stand there—get that hot food off her before she has to be rushed to the hospital."

Dennis reached for Sally, giving Reed a look that said he wished he could do more. "It's okay, baby, you're all right," he cooed, wiping at the red-brown mess with a white linen napkin.

"Just look at that," said Arthur. "Her clothes are ruined." There was a curiously satisfied note in his voice.

Sugar went to the kitchen and plucked Reed's house key off its hook; they lived only blocks apart and were in and out of each other's houses constantly. Each had a key to the other's. "I'll go get her some clean overalls."

Sugar slipped out easily, hardly noticed. She thought of driving, but found she really wanted to walk. It was three blocks there and three back —about a twenty-minute walk. Daylight saving time had kicked in, so there was plenty of time before dark.

True, they were in the heart of the Garden District, a high-crime area, but kids were still out playing; people were watering their lawns, coming home from work. Though it was the Heberts' weekend, it was still Monday for everyone else.

It should be safe enough now, and she needed the break from her family. That and the fresh air. She took some deep breaths. The city was a little like a sauna, but there was a breeze. It was going to be a heavenly, velvety, subtropical evening.

Flowers were in bloom.

Sugar painted flowers.

This was her hobby and her art. She had wanted to work in the restaurant, but Arthur hadn't wanted her; had tried volunteer work, but had had the sense of being interchangeable with everyone else who was doing it. She had to find something that was uniquely hers, and she had happened to take a course in watercolor.

And that was it. She loved the softness of the colors and the softness of flowers; the two belonged together.

She had tried other things, but she hadn't been good at them. Figure drawing was beyond her. Landscapes were tedious.

Flowers were her. They went with her personality, and her name.

She was nicknamed Sugar for a reason—in her peaches-and-cream blondness, she had reminded her parents of nothing so much as something yummy for dessert. Her dad had told her that a thousand times.

Pink was her favorite color.

Flowers were her delight, and her symbol. They were endlessly fascinating, with their pistils and their stamens, their petals and their sepals, their stems, roots, xylem, and phloem; she was in heaven when she was surrounded by flowers and paint.

What's wrong with Arthur?

What does he think he's doing?

Sugar banished thoughts of the ugly thing happening at her table. She wanted to be away from all that for a while.

But she couldn't stop herself.

Maybe he wants Nina to run the restaurant.

And maybe he just can't stand to give up control.

"Hey, Sugar." Mary O'Connor was on her way to her car.

"Hey, Mary. Your yard looks nice."

"You know, I just thought you'd want to know. I was in Hebert's the other night and it took an hour for the entrées to come. It was a delicious dinner, but don't you think that's ridiculous? I just thought you'd want to know."

"Thanks, Mary. I appreciate it."

"Well, actually, some of the vegetables were really underdone. I don't mean al dente, I mean barely warm. Raw, to tell you the truth."

"The chef is breaking in some new help; I'll speak to him about it."

"Well, I knew you'd want to know."

She'd have to remember to tell Arthur. Or Reed. Who knew who was going to run the restaurant? The players seemed to be changing drastically.

Sugar was much more in the mood for flowers than for complaints about Hebert's. Right now there wasn't that much in bloom, at least on this street. There were some hibiscus and some roses, though—some gorgeous double yellow hibiscus. They'd be fun to paint. She didn't usually work with tropicals—something about them seemed a little too easy, like long summer days with nothing to do. She preferred a more complicated flower, like these double blooms.

A kid came barreling down the street on his bike, pedaling so fast his feet looked like an eggbeater. He was giving it every ounce of energy he had, pouring it on as if that were all there was to life, moving your legs and feeling the breeze in your face, your heart pounding in your chest until it hurt. Sugar could remember doing that, and for a moment bemoaned the dulling effect of age, regretted that she'd never do it again nor want to. Though she could remember the act, she no longer had the slightest notion what it was like to have that kind of energy.

As she drew closer to Reed and Dennis's, she walked more slowly, enjoying herself, glad to be away from the oppression of the house.

Of Arthur.

What's wrong with me? she thought. *He's my husband but I can barely stand him anymore. The older he gets, the surer he is that he's right. Which is all he wants to be.*

She didn't think at all about how the problem with Reed would be resolved—she wasn't interested. She thought only about Arthur. She thought he had been horribly unfair to Reed, given the hard work she'd done for the restaurant. But fairness entered into few of Arthur's decisions. He wanted what he wanted, which was to be right, and to be in control.

She wondered what had made him think for a moment about giving up control of the restaurant. He had said he would run Hebert's II, and that he couldn't do both. But it would be like Arthur to die trying.

Do married people ever really like each other, or is it always this way? He doesn't like me or he wouldn't have other women. And I haven't liked him since . . . when?

Since the time the children started coming, probably. You fall in love and then you have children and you lose all sense of everything but that, and then one day you look across the table and you think, "What am I doing with this jerk?"

● ●

Reed's house was beautiful, even bigger and better-restored than Sugar's own. Reed wasn't much of a gardener—had only a few perennials blooming—and the house was plain white with green shutters; Sugar would have done something more imaginative with it.

But it was freshly painted and graceful, a Victorian with a wonderful huge front porch supported by Ionic columns.

The front yard was enormous. Two giant oaks grew there, dwarfing a small forest of bananas.

Sugar entered the yard through the small iron gate and walked briskly up to the porch, finding the view before her very pretty indeed.

She fit the key in the lock, turned off the burglar alarm, and relocked the door. Just as she headed up the stairs, she heard the phone ring. Was it quickest to dash up the stairs or race down and try to catch the call in the kitchen? She opted for the kitchen and got there just as the phone stopped ringing.

"Hello?" she said, but Reed's voice on the machine floated above hers, saying she wasn't home but the caller could leave a message.

Sugar would have hung up, but the caller had heard her. "Hello?" said a man's voice. "Reed, is that you?"

When Reed's alter ego had stopped speaking, Sugar said, "It's Sugar Hebert, Reed's mother. Can I take a message for her?"

"Why, Sugar, how are you, dear lady?" She tensed at something forced in the voice, something falsely hearty. "This is Milton Foucher, Dennis's father. It is a pure delight to hear your voice."

"It's good to hear yours too, Mr. Foucher." She had met him once—at Reed and Dennis's wedding—and she was quite sure she wouldn't recognize him if he walked in right now.

"How have you been, Sugar?"

"Just fine. How've you been? And Mrs. Foucher?"

"Oh, as fine as frog hair, Sugar. We are doing splendidly. Indeed we are."

Why couldn't he talk like a normal person? Hadn't he ever heard of contractions? Sugar was about to ask him if she could take a message, but he said, "We heard Hebert's was awarded the concession for the casino restaurant."

"Yes, we got it."

"Well, congratulations on that. We are very very proud of you." Sugar fought to keep her snobbery under control. A part of her knew that Milton Foucher was a polite (if pretentious) man who'd had too many children too late in life and that he had suffered a lot—mostly due to his youngest, Dennis.

Another part of her didn't want to admit she was related to him, even by marriage.

"Thanks a lot, Mr. Foucher; I appreciate that. Could I—"

"We were so happy for you when we heard about it. That is a very important plum for you."

"It's going to keep us all pretty busy, I expect."

"I only wish Dennis had gone into that business"—his voice was full of regret—"but what can you do with youngsters? You have to let them do what they want to do—there's no help for it, is there?"

"There sure isn't." She hoped her voice didn't betray the bitterness she felt.

12

"Well, I had better not keep you. I have some sad news for Dennis."

"I'm afraid he isn't here right now. Could I give him a message?"

"Well, if you would, please. Tell him Justin is not expected to live out the week."

Sugar searched her memory. Was Justin a relative? "I'm sorry to hear that," she said.

"This thing is a terrible waste." Sugar could almost see him shaking his head. "A terrible, terrible waste."

"I'll be sure and tell him."

Hanging up, she looked at her watch and hurried to get the overalls. She'd been gone nearly twenty minutes, and it would take her ten more to get back if she hurried instead of getting into conversations and peering into everyone's garden. She hoped they wouldn't still be yelling when she got there.

She raised a hand to set the alarm, but couldn't remember the combination, punched out with such dispatch when she came in. Now her mind was a blank. She had to sit down and focus till it came to her.

She walked briskly back, but when she saw a pair of teenage kids with reversed baseball caps coming down the street, she crossed and circled a block that wasn't on the way. She'd probably lost five minutes, with one thing and another. She was starting to feel guilty.

She picked up her pace.

Finally, arriving slightly out of breath, she remembered she hadn't brought her purse, had simply picked up Reed's key and hurried out.

Feeling silly, she rang her own doorbell and waited. It was probably a full two minutes before she realized no one was coming. Glancing around for Reed's car, she didn't notice it at first, wondered if Dennis and Reed had gotten so mad they'd stalked out.

But in that case why hadn't they come home?

She marched to the side of the house and turned over the rock under which she kept an extra key. Letting herself in, she felt for the first time a slight sense of foreboding; the lock didn't give at first, not until she'd turned the key a few times. Could it be the door hadn't been locked? Had she unwittingly locked it herself, then had to fiddle to unlock it?

"Arthur?" she called. Getting no answer, she turned from the hall into the dining room, where her family should have been.

Instead there was blood.

Red on the cream walls, splashed as if a kid had filled a balloon with blood and fanned his arm in a great and joyous arc to empty it. But it was as if he'd done it sitting on the floor. The blood was low on the wall, and above the splashes, there was a bloody handprint. Blood was also pooled on the floor.

Blood. Like something in a movie. Or on television; an event in someone else's life.

The heavy mahogany table had been upended. China, silver, and beans had spilled every which way, and chairs were overturned, though not Sally's high chair, which was empty.

Arthur lay on the floor, faceup, eyes open, white shirt soaked red. There was blood on his pants too, at the groin.

The house was so still Sugar's breath sounded like screaming.

2

• •

"**M**rs. Hebert? I'm Skip Langdon."

The woman on the porch looked blank. She was as ordinary a woman as Skip had ever seen, though she was trying—she had on a lot of makeup and her dishwater hair had been highlighted and permed. She was a little overweight, not much, really, just slightly round, and wore expensive pink slacks with a sleeveless white knit top to which small pearls had been sewn at the neckline.

"Yes?" she said, as if unable to comprehend why strangers were invading her house.

"Detective Skip Langdon. I'm from Homicide."

"Oh, I see."

Skip had arrived with her platoon, all in the same car, because there weren't nearly enough unmarked cars to go around. They must have looked terrifying, a six-foot-tall woman and three men in suits, advancing like a phalanx. Skip was talking because she had caught the case, meaning it was simply her turn—she'd been next on the list when the call came. She gestured for the others to go in—she'd interview the witness, they could divide up the other chores.

Rather than sad, the woman seemed bewildered and scared out of her

15

mind, though she'd had a little time to calm down. The district officer had arrived first and had called Homicide. All Skip knew was that Sugar Hebert had arrived home to find her husband shot dead in the dining room.

Hebert said, "They're gone. All of them. I only left for twenty minutes."

"Shall we talk in the car?" Hebert looked as if she could stand to sit down.

"Yes. Please. They said I couldn't stay in the house."

"I'm sorry."

"Well, not that I'd want to." They were side by side now, and something passed over Hebert's face that could have been a memory—of her dead husband, perhaps.

Another car arrived—Paul Gottschalk from the crime lab and Sylvia Cappello, Skip's sergeant. "Can you tell me what happened?"

"We were having dinner—my husband and my daughter, along with her husband and their little girl. Somebody spilled something on Sally and I went to get her clean overalls. When I came back, it was like it is now. Blood everywhere, and Arthur—"

"The other three were gone?"

"Gone! Disappeared into thin air."

Slowly, Skip drew the story out of Sugar Hebert—how the family had dinner every Monday, how they had recently celebrated Arthur's birthday and he had announced his retirement, but tonight had reneged; how they had fought, the other three, though this one didn't participate. How she had been gone only twenty minutes—thirty at the most—and had come home to find her world in shards.

"Did you touch anything?"

"No. Not even Arthur. I couldn't stand to look at him; it was too . . . that wasn't my husband down there. I just sort of crab-walked to the nearest phone and called the police."

"And where was that phone?"

"In the hall."

In the house. So she *had* touched something. "Did you call anyone else?"

"My son Grady. But he wasn't home."

"Would you like to call him again?"

"I left a message." She looked around, as if she expected Grady to be in the car.

The obvious explanation, it seemed to Skip, was that the argument had escalated, someone had pulled a gun—probably Dennis—and shot Arthur. Then Reed and Dennis had fled with their daughter.

"Excuse me a minute," she said, and radioed for a district car to check Reed and Dennis's house.

She turned back to Hebert. "Do you know anywhere else they might go?"

"Not really." She looked uncomfortable.

"Are you sure?"

"Well, Dennis's parents live here. But they'd never go there. Why would they?"

"What's their address?" When she had it, she radioed for a check there as well.

"Do you know," she said when she was done, "if Dennis carried a gun?"

"I know he didn't. He and Reed were dead against guns."

"So Reed didn't either."

"No."

"What about your husband? Did he keep a gun around the house? In case of intruders?"

Skip heard running footsteps and looked up to see a young man approaching, his face white, hair disheveled. "Mother? Mother, what's going on?"

"Oh, Grady." Sugar got out of the car, extended her arms and fell against her son, letting out what she'd been holding in. She sobbed against him for a while and then she said, "Oh, Grady, I was only gone twenty minutes."

"What happened?"

Briefly, she told him. Getting out so she could hear the woman, Skip listened carefully, but it was the same story Sugar had told before.

She found Grady a weedy young man, tall and too thin, as if he smoked a great deal and ate little. He had on a white shirt so old it was gray, and a pair of jeans that had been worn a few times since their last washing. He wore glasses and his hair was greasy.

Skip introduced herself, staring at his face, assessing him. Like his mother, he looked bewildered, still putting pieces together.

"What happened here?" he asked. "Where are Reed and Dennis?"

"Maybe you have some ideas."

"Me? Why would I?"

"What did your mother's message say?" Skip wasn't sure why she asked

17

the question; it was something about the breathless, pale way he'd arrived.

"It said, 'Your father's been murdered. Come as soon as you can.' "

"Did it really?" She found it hard to believe Mrs. Pretty-in-Pink had been so cold.

"Well, it got my attention." Grady smiled a little nervously, aware he was apologizing for his mother.

"Perhaps you can help us."

But he glanced at Sugar, who was now weeping quietly. "I think I need to call someone to help with Mother."

"I'm afraid you can't use the phone till the investigation's finished. We don't seal homicide scenes, but we won't be out for a long time."

"Oh, God, she's going to need a place to stay." He turned to his mother. "Mother, did you call Nina?"

Hebert shook her head.

"I'm going to get her to come over." He left in as much of a flurry as he'd arrived in.

Glad to get out, probably, Skip thought. Something about him didn't strike her as intensely filial.

She and Sugar got back in the car. "How are you feeling?" she asked.

"Kind of numb. I wish Reed were here."

"Tell me about her."

Sugar looked dumbstruck. "Tell you what?"

"What she's like. Where she'd go if she needed a safe haven."

"A safe haven?" Sugar pondered, as if unsure what the words meant. "That just isn't Reed. People would come to *her* to be safe."

"Does she have friends?"

"Nina. The woman my son's calling. She works for us at the restaurant —she's kind of Reed's assistant."

"You mean her secretary?"

"Oh, no. I mean her right-hand woman. She was Reed's maid of honor."

"Does Reed have other friends?"

Sugar thought. "Not really. She's pretty busy with Sally and Dennis and the restaurant and everything."

"How about Dennis?"

"Oh. Well. His business partner. They run a nursery—Dennis likes plants. Like his mother-in-law."

"Ah, you like plants."

"Flowers. I paint them."

"Tell me something, Mrs. Hebert. If you were someone outside the family, how would you describe Dennis and Reed?"

"A lovely, hardworking young couple. Absolutely devoted to their little girl. Arthur would never give Reed credit . . ." Her eyes flashed and her voice started to rise, but she stopped. "I guess that's family business."

Skip let it go for now. She could afford to be patient; before she was done, every secret the Heberts had, every scrap of "family business," was going to be picked over and examined.

"Could you do me a favor? Could you step outside with me and point out your car? And Arthur's and your daughter's?"

"There's mine over there. And Arthur's in the driveway."

"I'd like you to show me Reed's."

Sugar opened the car door. "I'll try."

It was dark now. But when she noticed, apparently for the first time, that most of the neighbors were outside, she retreated back to the car. "I don't think I'm up to it. Is that all right?"

"Sure." Skip could get Grady to do it. "Do you have a picture of Dennis and Reed?"

"Inside—shall I go get it for you?"

"I can get it."

"It's on the little table in the living room."

"How about one of Sally?"

"In my purse—on the table in the foyer."

Skip found the purse, checked it for weapons, and asked Paul Gottschalk to photograph and dust it. While he did that, she went in to get a good look at the dining room, to fix the crime scene in her mind, and then found the picture of Dennis and Reed.

It was a wedding picture that showed only faces—Reed's radiant, surrounded by tulle, Dennis's a little daunting. Reed was a classic southern beauty, natural-looking, with straight brown hair and straight white teeth —teeth whose straightness had not come cheap, Skip imagined, but the orthodonture was worth it.

Dennis was another matter. His features were very distinct, his lips generous, his eyes intense. He had a little baby fat, like the young Brando, that softened him, made him slightly vulnerable. But there was something brooding about him.

Heathcliff, Skip thought; but a man who liked begonias—or whatever he had at his nursery—didn't fit the stereotype.

For now, she left the photo, giving Paul a little time to get it dusted.

She went back to Sugar. "May I borrow the picture?"

19

"Of course." But she hesitated.

"For the investigation," Skip said, and Sugar nodded. "May I see the one of Sally? And could you check your purse to see if anything's been stolen?"

Quickly, Sugar checked her credit cards, checkbook, and money. "Everything's here," she said, and drew from her wallet an Easter snapshot of a pretty towhead in a pink dress. She was holding a basket of eggs.

"Can you tell me what they were all wearing? And their heights, weight, eye color—all that?"

To Skip's surprise, Sugar's lip started to tremble. She tried to control her face but lost the battle. An anguished rasp escaped her, not quite a sob. "Sally!" she managed to gasp. "She must still be wearing the dirty overalls."

Skip said nothing for a few minutes, but the information trickled out: Dennis was dark, Reed was light; he wore jeans, she wore a summer dress with sandals, and Sally wore beans.

Skip wondered what else there was to get. She repeated Sugar's earlier statement: "Reed and Dennis really hate guns."

"Hate them. Feel strongly. Arthur tried to give Reed a little gun to carry around—you know how dangerous it is in the Garden District—but neither of them would hear of it. They said they didn't want to live like that." She turned away for a moment. Gazing back at Skip, she said, "Of course, Arthur had a lot of opinions."

Once more Skip heard a clatter. It was Grady, back with a handsome young woman in tow, a black woman, though probably she'd describe herself as Creole. She was barely beige in color, and she wore her straight hair in a low-riding ponytail.

"This is Nina Phillips. She's our director of sales at Hebert's."

Before Skip could shake hands, Sugar had repeated her performance with Grady—fallen upon Nina Phillips's neck, wailing.

"That's right," said Nina. "Grady's told me everything. You just go on and cry."

It was a good time to talk to Grady. While Sugar wasn't listening, Skip asked him the same question she'd asked his mother. "Tell me a little about Reed and Dennis."

He pondered a moment. Finally, he said, "The couple of the nineties. She's the brains of the operation. Also the brawn."

Skip smiled. She didn't think he was nearly done. "How so?"

"God forbid anyone should call me a feminist—they shoot guys for that in some parts of town—but, look, he's got it easy, she's got it hard. She brings home the bacon and then she cooks it; after changing into some diaphanous frock and also changing the baby, of course. I guess it's like that apocryphal old woman said: 'I makes the livin' and he makes the livin' worthwhile.' "

"I gather you don't think much of your brother-in-law."

"Oh, completely wrong. Fine fellow. Charming fellow. Anyone my dad hated can't be all bad."

Skip's heart speeded up.

"But don't get too excited." He shrugged. "There weren't all that many people he liked."

"Your dad had enemies?"

Grady looked startled. "The kind who'd kill him, you mean?"

Skip nodded.

"Well, I never thought of it that way. He was irascible. You don't kill people for that, do you?"

"You tell me."

"Tell you what? Tell you I did it? What is this?"

Skip said nothing.

"Look, some thug broke in here and killed him. What could be more obvious?"

"In that case, what happened to Reed and Sally and Dennis?"

Grady's face, so facile, so obviously trying to betray no emotion, went slightly pale again. "I don't know. I don't want to think about it."

Neither do I, she thought. The Heberts were a prominent family. She didn't know how much money they had, but it might seem reasonable to someone that they'd pay a good-sized ransom for a kidnapped member. Perhaps Arthur's murder was the result of a kidnap gone wrong. But then, why take the remaining three when one would do?

Because they knew the kidnapper's face.

Which doesn't bode well for their future.

Sugar was beginning to come around again, talking quietly to Nina. Skip addressed the younger woman: "Do you know if Reed or Dennis had a gun?"

Sugar said, "I *told* you—" but Nina interrupted, smiling, shaking her head. "They wouldn't be caught dead with a gun. Neither one of them. Dennis—um, lost a relative once. . . ." She let her voice trail off, apparently thinking of something too regrettable to mention.

"I already told you that," Sugar said; it sounded a lot like a whine.

"How about Arthur?"

"Arthur?"

21

Skip nodded.

"Arthur had a gun."

"Where did he keep it?"

"In a safe in his office. Here, I mean. In the room he called his office."

"Would you mind telling Mr. Gottschalk? Our crime lab man."

"Of course not."

Skip smiled sweetly at Sugar. "Will you be all right alone?"

Sugar looked a little disoriented, as if things were moving too fast for her. "I guess so. You mean tell him now?" She put a hand on her chest.

Skip couldn't tell if she was faking or not, but she nodded at Grady. "You can go with her if you like—just to the porch. An officer will meet you there."

She wanted some time with Nina. "I feel for them," she said, nodding at Grady and Sugar.

Nina simply shook her head, as Skip had seen dozens of friends and relatives do when confronted with death.

"Have you worked for them long?"

"A few years."

"I gather from Grady the old man was difficult."

She shrugged. "Grady's not so easy himself."

"And Mrs. Hebert?"

"Complicated. I feel sorry for her."

"Why?"

"Arthur treated her like dirt, for one thing. For another, she's got some real little emotional knots."

"What sort?"

"She doesn't really have a lot of self-esteem." Phillips thought a moment. "And I guess she thinks she can get it by pretending."

Nina had a maddening way of throwing out enticing generalities that made little sense initially. "Pretending what?" Skip asked.

"Whatever. It varies."

Skip still didn't get it, but she couldn't stay there. There was too much to cover in a hurry. "Do you know the family pretty well?"

To her surprise, Nina snorted. "I'd say so. Grady and I were an item once, God help me." She paused here. "Reed and I are best friends. And Dennis is my cousin."

"Dennis! But I thought—" She stopped, but Nina made her complete the sentence. "I thought he was white."

"Oh, he is, I guess. He's from a white branch of the family, anyway. We didn't grow up together—I didn't even know about the Fouchers; the white ones. Dennis looked me up when we were already grown." She snorted again. "He wanted money."

"Was this before or after you knew the Heberts?"

"Before. He introduced me years later. What you have to understand is he was a different person then. He was an addict."

"I see."

"Oh, there never was any harm in him; not a bit. He's a gentle soul—a very sweet man." She stopped and stared at the wall. "Lord, lord."

"What is it?"

"I was just thinking how much he and Grady are alike. Passive. Sweet, but ineffectual."

Grady hadn't struck Skip as sweet, but she kept her mouth shut.

"No wonder Reed and I hit it off so well. We're like mirror images, one black, one white. Otherwise, we could be twins. Well, no, not exactly, I'm more of a rebel than she is.

"Good lord, Goody Two-Shoes is more of a rebel than she is.

"But how we're alike is—we're real obsessive. Can't rest till everything's done; and done perfectly.

"But her daddy criticized everything she did, and to tell you the truth" —she dropped her voice—"her mama's not much different. Reed never steps outside the lines they draw, and in the end she can never really believe she can do anything very well. But of course she's a whiz. Terrific mother, great cook, runs her house, runs the restaurant, supports Dennis in his little venture."

"A nursery, isn't it?"

"Yeah. That's what I mean about him being a gentle soul. Loves his plants to death." Something in her voice sounded like contempt.

"Reed sounds like she's wound pretty tightly."

Nina shrugged. "I guess. She's so busy being nice to everybody you wouldn't notice."

Paul Gottschalk came out, trailed by the two Heberts. He said, "The gun's there all right. I'd be surprised if it's been fired."

Skip nodded. "Thanks, Paul. I'm going to leave you folks now." She wanted to examine the crime scene. "But Mrs. Hebert, I need you to walk with me through the house when we're done, to see if anything's missing. Are you thinking of staying with friends?"

"I might just stay at Reed and Dennis's house—I don't think they'd mind, do you?" She looked at Grady, holding her hands at breast level, rather like a prairie dog. She was beginning to look tired and very frightened. Skip thought the shock was starting to wear off.

Grady said, "My hovel certainly isn't suitable."

"Do you think you could maybe. . ." She let it hang, clearly not wanting to ask her son for something.

Grady looked meaningfully at Nina, and Skip realized he wanted her to come to his rescue. Nina ignored him. Finally, he said, "Yes, Mother, I'll stay with you," speaking not nearly so gently as the circumstances called for. To Skip, he said, "Can I take her there and bring her back when you call?"

"Sure, but one last thing. Can you point out Reed and Dennis's car?"

"Of course."

He and Skip walked up and down the street. "It's not here."

"It's not?"

"It's a beige Mercedes sedan—do you see one?"

She didn't. She handed out her card, told everyone to call immediately if they saw or heard from Reed and Dennis, then said good-bye and went into the house.

The district officers who'd checked out Reed and Dennis's, and Dennis's parents' house, reported no sign of any member of the Foucher family. Skip put out a bulletin for them and their car, asking officers who spotted them to contact her immediately.

Because it was her case, it was her job to stay with the body till the coroner took it away. She was standing in the dining room, staring at the carnage, when Paul Gottschalk joined her. "What do you make of it?"

"I give up. You?"

"Well, I've got a theory. We'll have to see if it checks out, but here's what I think. He was shot first in the right leg—in the groin, actually, and the bullet hit his femoral artery. Blood spurted all over the floor, and the impact threw him back and twisted him toward the right, toward the wall, where he touched his hand to the wound, then to the wall to steady himself." He pointed to the handprint.

"Then more blood spurted all over the wall—that's why it looks like a knife fight in here. And then he turned around, he might have even walked a couple of steps, and that time he got shot in the chest."

Skip nodded, about to say something, but Gottschalk, strange bird, simply walked away looking satisfied.

When the body had been removed, Skip called Sugar to come examine her house. Nothing was missing.

● ●

The last step was to canvass the neighbors, a task she dreaded. People in the Garden District, with its mansions and its private patrol service, were probably the most frightened of crime in the whole city. She didn't want to look at their dilated eyes and tight lips as they pressed her for details, as they wrung their manicured hands and begged her to tell them how to protect themselves.

She didn't have the least idea how to reassure them, and right now she didn't have time either.

As it happened, the neighbors on the right were on vacation, according to their own right-hand neighbors. The ones on the left had been out at the time of the shooting, and the ones across the street had been closeted in their air-conditioned house.

Two doors down, however, on the Heberts' side of the street, a Mrs. Gandolfo did think she'd heard a shot, had even peeked out through her curtains. She called her neighbors, the Heberts' left-hand ones, and getting no answer, dialed the Heberts. A young man answered and said everything was fine and he hadn't heard a thing. Reassured, she'd given up.

"When you peeked out," Skip said, "did you notice any cars parked in front of the Heberts' house?"

"Not really," said Mrs. Gandolfo. "No more than usual, anyway. Maybe a beige one, I guess, or white. And there might have been another one, but I really can't remember anything about it. You know how your mind registers something, but you don't necessarily know what?"

"Can you say anything else about the beige one?"

"No. No, I can't. Except it might have been kind of small."

A Mercedes sedan was at least middle-sized, in Skip's view.

3

Pulses pounding a wild tattoo in her ears, the wheel slick from her sweat, Reed drove the Mercedes like a sports car, finding it clumsy on the turns.

My fault, she thought. *Dennis could do this better. Oh fuck, oh fuck, anybody could.*

Blind with her own tears, she tried not to think, just drive. Oddly, the streets were nearly deserted, or the Tercel might have hit another car. She might have as well; a cop might have stopped either one.

But it was a lazy night in the Big Easy—everyone was home from work and staying in, it looked like.

She thought she could remember these words: "If anybody follows me, I'll shoot them through the head, I swear to God I will."

But she wasn't sure. At the time, the words hadn't even registered. Nothing had. Thought had taken a holiday. Reed simply acted on automatic pilot.

Her feet had worked. It was that simple.

She had given chase, seen Sally thrown roughly into the Tercel, as if car seats hadn't been invented, and gotten there too late. The car door was locked.

Reed was getting flashbacks of the scene, as if they were part of a dream. In her mind she saw herself as she couldn't have in real life: tearing out the door, nearly falling down on the front steps and pausing to right herself, losing precious milliseconds, tugging at the car door, through the window seeing Sally's small blond head hit the door on the other side, calling out her name—*Sally!*—before hearing the Tercel's ignition. The key had been left in it, ready to go.

Reed had had to grapple for her own extra key from under the right fender, a tiny delay that had made the difference. Then began the chase, Reed still on automatic, just doing what she had to do to get her child back. She paid no attention at all to where she was being led, what neighborhoods she went through, where she got on the expressway—she just drove; and now these scenes had started flashing, perhaps the first sign of sanity returning.

Could this really be she, Reed Hebert? What did she think she was doing?

She thought she should stop and call the police, but she knew she wasn't about to. She might not be able to find a phone booth. If she did, 911 might be busy; might not answer right away. She'd lose the Tercel.

What if she had stayed at her parents' and called the police from there? That was the only sane thing to do, but she hadn't thought of it; hadn't thought anything at the time, had simply been the burden her feet were carrying. But it now occurred to her that she wouldn't have known anything about the car if she had, not its color or model or license number, all of which she knew now.

So I must be doing the right thing.

She neither believed that nor disbelieved it. It was just something to think while she drove.

They were near Bayou St. John, she noticed.

She thought: *This isn't right. What the hell are we doing here?*

She realized that she thought she understood why Sally had been taken, but a place like this didn't begin to enter into it. Gentilly. The posh, nouveau part, about two blocks from near-slums.

The Tercel stopped in front of an enormous house, an absurdly huge house, as big as any on St. Charles Avenue, built of gray stone and surrounded by a fence of iron bars standing dignified as deacons. A group of men walked out of the gate and turned left on the sidewalk.

The Tercel driver got out of the car and, clutching Sally, raced to the gate, now being closed by a man in a suit who still managed somehow to look like a servant. Sally was screaming: *"Mommy! Mommy! Mommy!"*

Reed certainly wasn't going to bother to park. She simply abandoned her car in the street. As she rounded it, she found herself staring straight into the eyes of one of the men in the little group, who had all turned toward the screams.

It was Bruce Smallwood, whom she knew from her pleadings before the casino board. With him was Lafayette Goodyear, another member of the board, and she thought a third was Barron Piggott, a colleague of theirs, but she couldn't be sure.

Thank God.

She closed her eyes for a second, in relief or silent prayer. "Bruce! Lafayette! Help!"

None of them moved.

Men she had been to lunch with, sat across a table from. Smiled for.

Barron had even tried to grab her thigh, but she'd seen it coming and crossed her legs.

The kidnapper was screaming above Sally: "Goddammit, let me in. Get Mo. Tell Mo I'm here, goddammit. Who the fuck do you think you are?"

The entire group of able-bodied men, civic leaders, stood as if nailed to the spot, looking as frightened as she was.

If her child were to be rescued, it was up to her.

She reached for Sally, but the kidnapper's body was in the way. She closed her fists and began beating that body as hard as she could—the shoulders, the back, the kidneys, she hoped. But she didn't feel the slightest yield.

"Give her back to me, goddammit! Sally, baby, it's okay. Mommy's here. Everything's going to be—" She couldn't get the last word out. She had intended to say "fine," but she was out of breath. And besides, she hadn't the heart. She didn't believe it. Woefully, she looked again at the group of men.

One had broken from the group, Lafayette, the only black one, who was running toward her, finally moving his fucking ass.

But the gate swung open and the kidnapper fell away from Reed.

Startled, she swiveled and saw that two men had pulled the kidnapper through the gate, Sally kicking as hard as she could.

They pulled Reed in too.

● ●

Grady drove his mother to Dennis and Reed's, Sugar sitting quietly instead of running her mouth as usual, eyes facing front; no drama. That puzzled him, but he was thoroughly undone when she climbed the stairs without a word and retreated, dazed, to one of the guest rooms. Following with her hastily packed bag, he watched her turn on the television and lie down on the bed, all her clothes on and no expression in her eyes. He had never seen her like that, and the shock moved him to solicitude.

"Mother? Mother, can I get you anything?" His voice sounded oddly meek to his own ears.

Sugar didn't answer.

She wasn't the sort who had to be cajoled. She wanted what she wanted, and it was always the same thing—lots of attention, someone to listen to her, to rant to even if they finally yelled back. She would cry and fall apart, but she would always provoke the same situation again—they'd listen till they couldn't take it anymore, they'd yell back at her, anything to get her out of their face, and then she'd cry and fall apart again. She craved human contact like a child who'd been raised by wolves, and it was usually about as smooth for her.

She sometimes liked a nip at bedtime, for soporific purposes, she said. "Shall I get you a drink?"

"I don't really think I care for anything." She sounded unconvinced.

"How about some Bailey's Irish Cream?"

She loved that stuff, probably because it tasted like dessert.

"All right," she said, as if doing him a huge favor.

He raced down to look for some, relieved to be doing something; anything.

There wasn't any.

When he came back upstairs, he saw that she'd taken off her shoes, which he took for a good sign. "Mother, I'll have to go out and get some. Will you be all right for a minute?"

She looked at him. "I guess so." He thought perhaps she was afraid.

"Are you sure?"

"I guess so."

He had to get out of there. "I'm putting the alarm on. Don't worry, no one can get in."

He had in mind to go instantly to the House of Blues, but in the end he couldn't bring himself to run out on her. For one thing, he had to take her back for the damned house check.

He got the liqueur and returned to find the phone ringing: the cop asking them to come back. He took his mother home, brought her back, and then utterly amazed himself, the way he spoke to her—the way a good son was supposed to; the way he never did.

"Now, Mother, I want you to undress and get under the covers while I pour us a little drink. Will you do that for me now?"

He thought he saw a flash of surprise in her eyes, but she didn't say anything.

"I'm gonna close this door now, to give you a little privacy. When I come back, we'll have a nice drink together. Will you get in bed for me now?"

She nodded.

He took a while opening the bottle and finding glasses, to give her time to obey. When he knocked on the door, she said, "Come in," and this time she was tucked in. She still had her makeup on, but he wasn't going to quibble.

"Good, Mama. You need to get some rest." He hadn't called her "Mama" since he was twelve.

The television hummed in the background, and he was suddenly afraid she would see the news and that his father's death would be on it. "Let's turn this off, shall we?"

He poured her a drink and handed it to her. He poured himself one and sat on the stool that went with the dresser. He had no idea what to say to her. She was the one who talked—talked and talked and talked, much to the discomfort of everyone around her. His relationship with her consisted of fending her off.

Finally, she said, "Do you think she killed him?"

"Who?"

"Reed."

"Reed?" He would have been as shocked if she'd said Hillary Clinton. "Why Reed?"

"What he did wasn't right. All that child ever wanted in her life was to run that restaurant—that and please her daddy. And he took everything away from her."

Grady felt a tingle. *Oh, God, another lovely evening in the House of Blues.*

The House of Blues was a club, one of several in various cities, but still the biggest thing to hit New Orleans since the casino was voted in. It was artfully funky and low-down, full of Louisiana native art. Its sound system had probably cost millions. Its acts were top of the line. It perfectly captured the city's idea of itself, every college student's fantasies, every baby boomer's memories, and managed somehow to be the exact club Grady would have built—any music lover would have—if he just had unlimited funds. Grady went there a good three times a week, every time he got to feeling depressed.

But he had first been attracted by the name. He'd always been disappointed that there wasn't really a House of the Rising Sun. When he was about twelve, maybe thirteen, he'd spent a lot of time thinking about the song's second line: "It's been the ruin of many a poor boy and, Lord, I know I'm one."

He found the song unspeakably romantic and somehow true; true in a way he couldn't put his finger on. He never thought of it as a bordello, just as a house in New Orleans, like the first line said.

The name House of Blues, the melancholy the phrase evoked, hit him the same way, made him think of the old song. But there was something more, something like the twist of a knife, and it excited him. It inspired him, gave him ideas he'd never had before.

He had written a lot of nonfiction, pieces for *Gambit* and *New Orleans Magazine*, and now he'd begun to write short stories about vampires. If Anne Rice could, why not Grady Hebert? The metaphor—the love that devours and kills, the sucking of blood, the sucking, sucking, sucking till there is no juice left—had spoken to him as a teenager. At least that was the way he grandly put it now, as if it were a metaphor.

The Undead seemed appropriate to the city, he thought, and so he had tried his hand.

But he wasn't sure about these vampire stories of his. He had sold a couple, his first published fiction, to horror magazines, and that was a thrill—not only for its own sake, but it had delighted him to tell his parents, to watch their confused reactions. His father, of course, had belittled them, as he did everything; Sugar had tried to be nice, but in the end she couldn't conceal her distaste. Grady thought perhaps he felt a bit of the same thing.

He wanted to write something more real.

He had found himself thinking of his own childhood home, Sugar and Arthur's home, as the House of Blues, of the Hebert dynasty as having its own name, a name like House of Atreus, House of Tudor, House of Hanover.

And he had known that he would write about The Thing. Not to be published, perhaps, but it was something he would do.

When he had done it, he would be like Clea in *The Alexandria Quartet*, the artist who painted well only after she lost her hand.

He too would have an artistic breakthrough. Why this was so he didn't know, any more than he understood why Clea had.

He knew that he had to do it, he was excited by the idea, thrilled in a macabre way, but he also knew he could not. And so he went night after night to the House of Blues and let the music flow through his body, cleansing him.

• •

Sugar told him the story, told him what Arthur had done to Reed, how he had taken back the restaurant from her.

Reed's world, Reed's life, her worldview, had always made Grady despair.

This nearly made him cry.

It touched him in a way that his father's death had not; or had not yet—he knew that would hit him in the end. This was more accessible, this insult to Reed, this slap in the face.

But no, he didn't think she had killed her father. That was the last thing he thought. He told his mother he suspected some thug had done it—someone who had conned his way into the house.

"But why?" said Sugar. "Nothing was taken."

Why. He hadn't thought about why; in a way, he was as numb as Sugar.

So they could kidnap the others and hold them for ransom.

But he didn't say it.

Wait a minute. Someone drove Reed and Dennis's car away.

He said, "They probably meant to strip the place, but Dad got out of hand. You know how he is. And then they got scared."

"I think I can sleep now," Sugar said. "How he was, you mean."

They had demolished nearly the whole bottle.

He left her and went to the House of Blues. He liked to stand there nursing a beer in a plastic cup, swaying; letting the music pulse through him. It was a good way to empty his mind, forget his life and his failure, forget the way he missed Nina; forget his father's death, his mother's odd quiet.

Buddy Guy was playing. Grady should have been a zombie, blitzed on the music and alcohol, but his brain was still functioning.

Or maybe you could call it that. He was having something that might be called a thought, but perhaps it was just a feeling.

He never got what he wanted.

If it was a feeling, it was guilt.

I was supposed to be Reed.

That made him angry. Snatches of derision came back, seduced him from the magic of Buddy's flashing riffs.

"Be a man."

"Gracie . . . oh, Gracie"—singsongy here—*"are you wearing your lacy underpants?"*

"Stand up and do what you have to do . . . no, you don't *have a choice. You're an Hebert . . ."*

"Reed can do it better. Are you gonna be outdone by a girl?" At this point his father would let his wrist flop and affect a falsetto. *"Grady Hebert. Faggot writer. Excuse me—unpublished faggot writer. La-di-da-di-da. I guess little Reed'll just have to do your job."*

Grady worked every summer as a prep cook in the restaurant, and loathed every second of it. He spent his days chopping vegetables, the heavy chef's knives leaving bruises on the inside of his forearm. He peeled potatoes, he cleaned, swept, and mopped, he cored and scored, he made stocks, he peeled shrimp until his fingers wrinkled, he cracked crabs, he cut and ground meat, and he learned to make forty gallons of gumbo at a time.

Why was kitchen drudgery more masculine than writing? He'd struggled with that, and he hated himself for it. Now, of course, and even then, deep down, he knew his dad's taunts meant nothing. They were just bullying. But they had left their mark.

He was sweating, and it wasn't just from the press of the crowd.

Why can't I think of something nice about him?

He ordered another beer, and tried.

Really tried.

Another memory came back: his dad flopped down in his chair, watching television, his tie not even loosened, smelling of the day's sweat, grunting, not answering if the kids spoke to him. "He's tired," Sugar would say. "He's just too tired for y'all right now."

But Grady had found that if he sat on the floor underneath the arm of Arthur's chair, his dad would eventually touch him on the head, tousle his hair. Grady had asked Evie to stroke his hair, and later Nina, and other women.

He felt his face go red; he hadn't put all that together.

But that was nice, wasn't it? When he touched my head?

He could remember the warmth and strength of his dad's hand. It gave him a slightly fuzzy feeling; or maybe that was beer on top of Bailey's.

I wonder if I'll miss him?

And then another vignette: Arthur walking around Hebert's, dressed in a dark suit, white shirt, perfect tie; immaculate, his thatch of white hair giving him a Walker Percy distinction—the platonic ideal of the southern gentleman.

The main dining room was a palace to Grady's eyes then: the prisms of the chandeliers caught the light and sent it back to the silver, lined up so perfectly on the white linen.

The dark wood of the chairs, the tiny tiles of the floor, the poufs of the window shades, the waiters' tuxedos—it was stately, yet so reassuring, so warm, like a comforter covered in satin. When his parents took him there, he was a prince in his dad's castle.

Arthur was king.

He moved smoothly around the dining room, greeting everyone, sometimes sitting down, telling a joke, touching the men's shoulders. He was grand; he was regal. Grady was proud to be his son.

Later, all that had looked phony and he had learned the word glad-handing, which he had said once with a teenager's contempt, and only once. His father had struck him.

His mother had been no help: "It's what puts bread in your mouth, you idiot. Of course it hurt his feelings."

They were that way with each other, forever explaining each other's points of view, complaining that he could never see anything but his own.

But he was never permitted to have one.

Don't get into that, Grady old boy. Go back; go back to ten or twelve.

He saw his father, gliding about the dining room, everyone smiling at him, and he got the fuzzy feeling again.

That's it, Grady, stay with it. Stay with it now and see if you can feel a human feeling. You're supposed to be sorry when your father dies. If you can't, you'll never eat garlic again.

He was drunk enough to look in the mirror above the bar, to make sure he could see his reflection.

All right, it's there. You're not Undead yet.

But if you're alive, why don't you feel anything?

Actually, you do. Admit it, why don't you? Your throat's closing on you.

Oh, God, he never had a chance to be a person. He died without having the least idea.

Finally, he felt the tears. Automatically, he stole another glance in the mirror, to see if they showed. It was way too dark, of course, and he would have felt silly if he hadn't got distracted.

There was a blonde standing behind him, in a black dress. A gorgeous skinny woman with hollows in her cheeks, a little wasted-looking.

He whirled. "Evie?"

The blonde smiled. "Leslie."

He was surprised that he had said it aloud. She didn't look that much like Evie. Her eyes were brown and had the glow of health in them. Evie's were blue-green, slightly washed-out.

Tragic.

The last time he'd seen her, her hair was dirty and hung in hunks, as if it had broken off in places. She was wearing filthy jeans and a halter, so that her thinness showed, her wrecked, pathetic body—her ribs, her shoulders, fragile as fish bones. He had tried to keep himself from looking at the insides of her elbows, but he couldn't help himself. One of them was horribly bruised.

That was five years ago.

4

• •

Sugar was wrong about being able to sleep. She was too mad. Her fists clenched and her neck got stiff she was so mad.

She had tried to make the marriage work. For thirty-odd years she'd tried, but Arthur was determined not to have a marriage, even though legally he did and even though he lived with her.

She wanted closeness, she wanted to really know him, but he wanted to keep her as far away from him as possible. He did it a number of different ways—staying at the restaurant all the time, being short with her, even downright nasty when he felt like having other women.

Getting himself killed.

I hope you're satisfied, Arthur. She held her teeth tight together.

She was pissed because now it was never going to work, she was never going to have the marriage she wanted. All those years of praying, out the window.

Goddammit, God, I ruined my knees for nothing.

He was a bad father—she was always having to explain his behavior to the children—and he was a bad husband. He hadn't slept with her in twenty years. That is, he hadn't made love to her; he slept with her every night and acted so goddamned pious.

His lady friends came right into the restaurant, right in there with their little giggling girlfriends, their gay gentlemen friends, their mothers. Whenever Arthur comped a woman and her daughter, everyone knew. She'd seen it herself at least once. He said the mother was someone he worked on a committee with and he owed her because she'd voted right. He thought that was how the world worked, and he expected Sugar to buy it too.

Votes bought with *pommes de terre soufflés.*

What a small mind.

And what a liar, when all along he was sticking it in the daughter, who might as well have had the word "floozy" tattooed on her cleavage.

That was years ago, but there was always someone. She heard him on the phone, whispering, whispering all the time.

God, I hate the bitch. If she comes to the funeral, I swear I'll snatch her bald-headed.

She'd learned the phrase from a maid she once had who, in the end, she had also wanted to snatch bald-headed. She turned on her side, furious.

She'll probably wear black, maybe a veil; maybe she'll tell people she's Mrs. Hebert.

That had happened before. She knew somebody it happened to. The man wasn't a bigamist, the mistress was nuts, that was all.

I don't care.

I don't care if everyone in the city knows. It reflects on Arthur, not me.

She was crying.

She sat up in bed, surprised.

What the hell am I going to be by myself? I've been with Arthur all my life.

A key rattled. "Reed? Dennis?"

She struggled into her robe, forgetting slippers.

"It's Grady, Mother. I went out for a while."

She hadn't heard him leave. Maybe she had slept briefly.

"What time is it?"

"Late. Can I get you anything?"

She pattered downstairs. "Grady, I've been thinking. It's outrageous the way your father treated me."

"What?"

"Listen. What's done is done. But now we have to get rid of Nina. I can't take her crap anymore. The woman has to go. And if she comes to the funeral, I'll ask her to leave. I will, Grady, I swear it." She could feel the tightness of her lips; she liked the feeling.

37

Grady plopped in one of Reed's aqua-covered chairs, hands at his sides, keys slipping out of his fingers. He looked tired.

"Nina?" he said. "Why are you mad at Nina?"

"Because she's your father's mistress, that's why. You know that as well as you know your name."

"Nina?" he said again. He seemed slow tonight. She wondered if he was drunk.

"Of course Nina. She has been for years."

"Mother, Nina's black. Have you forgotten Dad hated black people?"

"He didn't hate Nina."

"He more or less did, actually. Reed brought her in, and he only put up with her because she's so damn good at what she does he couldn't do without her. He paid her about half what she's worth, and Reed couldn't do a thing about it."

"She got what she wanted."

"Which was what? A fat old racist who farts in bed? Mother, get serious. She wouldn't look at Dad if he were the last man on earth."

"I can't believe you're talking to me this way. Your father's dead and this is the way you're talking."

"A very good point, Mother. My father's dead. My sister's missing. My niece is missing. My brother-in-law is missing. My mother can't stay in her own house because it's got blood all over the walls. Good God, why are you making up stories about Nina? Haven't you got anything better to think about?"

"You're drunk."

"Well, frankly, I think that's more appropriate to the situation than crazy accusations cut out of whole cloth."

"What am I supposed to think about, if not my husband's extramarital activities?"

"I don't know. How about the funeral?"

"Oh. The funeral. When should we have it?"

"Well, I think under the circumstances, it can't be right away."

"What circumstances?"

"Dennis and Reed. Sally." She heard tight, cold anger in his voice.

"Well, don't get mad at me."

"Sorry."

"Grady, what am I going to do?"

He was staring at his watch. He looked up, surprised, perhaps at the fear in her voice. "Do about what?"

"All day. What am I going to do all day?"

38

He spoke gently. "You don't have to do anything. Friends are going to come, with food. They'll take care of you. You get to rest for a while."

"I'm not like that. That's not who I am."

"Now, Mother—"

"I'm a doer."

He stood up. "What would you think about going back to bed?"

"You go. I can't sleep."

She sat down on a silk sofa that never, though there was a baby in the house, showed the slightest bit of wear.

Without Reed and Arthur, who'll run the restaurant?

She felt a flutter of excitement as the answer came to her.

Miss Nina is going to be in for a little shock.

●   ●

Skip shaped her body to Steve Steinman's and slipped an arm around his waist. He stirred, pulled on the arm to bring her closer. "What time is it?"

"You don't want to know."

"Mmmmm."

He'd been with her almost a week, and he was going home soon. She began to rub his back.

He said, "How about a heroin dealer?"

"What?"

"For my project. A profile of a heroin dealer."

"Are you awake? Does this mean I can turn on the light?"

"I guess I am."

She groped for the table lamp. "There isn't that much heroin here. Only in spurts. It's all cocaine. Mostly crack."

"A really nasty crack dealer."

"I can't think where you'd find one. They're usually such sweethearts."

He said, "I won't ask what you've been out on."

But of course he was dying to know—he was trying to be discreet.

"You'll read about it in the paper. You know Hebert's? Somebody walked into the owner's beautiful Garden District home and blew him away during dinner. Three others missing."

"Kidnapped?"

"God, I hope not. Considering how this isn't going to help anyone's nerves, even without that."

"Paranoia—for my film. White urban paranoia."

"Why not?"

39

"No good. No real excuse to come back to New Orleans—I could do it anywhere."

"It's worse here."

She wanted him to come back. He lived in Los Angeles, and she was missing him more and more lately. She had let him walk out of her life a few months ago, or rather, had provoked a fight with him, out of her own insecurity.

And then he'd walked out.

She didn't realize how big a hole he was going to leave. How big an ass she'd been.

Stupid and cruel. It hurt to apply the words to herself, but they were true and she knew it and she couldn't think about it without feeling her face go hot.

How could I?

To this day she wasn't sure. She just knew she'd been scared to death and acted out of panic.

In the end, she flew to Los Angeles and begged, something she could never have imagined she'd do. She had simply turned up at his door, having no idea whether or not she'd be welcome.

He didn't say a word, just broke into a smile of such unmistakable delight she'd laughed, and he hugged her so hard she felt petite for once in her life.

He was a film editor now and very successful, but he missed his first love, the one he'd had before Skip—making his own documentaries. Hence, urban paranoia.

"How about a day in the life of a cop?"

"I don't know if you could really capture the passion." She captured a part of him.

"I'm sure you're right. Police work is so exciting."

"But sweaty."

"I could rise above that." He was starting to. "The only thing is, I don't know enough about it."

"Maybe you could find a cop and just—you know— pound a confession out of her."

"With a blunt instrument?"

"It's a thought."

He shook his head. His hand closed around her breast. "Maybe I'd just squeeze the truth out."

"She might have to frisk you for weapons."

"What would she do if she found one?"

"Put it in a real safe place."

● ●

She awoke refreshed.

The night before, after canvassing the neighbors, she'd checked the hospitals and even run rap sheets on Reed and Dennis. Neither had a record, despite Dennis's drug history.

What remained in the way of background checks were calls to Eileen Moreland, Skip's friend at the *Times-Picayune*, and to Alison Gaillard, known privately to Skip as proprietor of Gossip Central.

The only clips Eileen could find involved nothing more exciting than Hebert appearances at charity functions, and Reed and Dennis's wedding. There wasn't even a clip file on Grady.

"No problem," Skip said to herself, dialing with delicious anticipation. "Alison will dish the dirt."

Alison could come up with amazing stuff even when a family was obscure. The Heberts were nearly as visible as the Neville Brothers— she'd know everything down to the hairdressers Reed and Sugar went to.

"This is Alison," said her machine. "John and I are having our first vacation since the baby was born. You're crazy if you think I'm saying where we are."

Skip actually held the phone in front of her face and stared at it. "Well, damn you, Alison Gaillard."

When she'd recovered from the shock, she decided to go see Nina Phillips, who'd already been a good source and probably had a lot more in her.

She was shown through a couple of heavy swinging doors, around a corner or two, and into a complex of offices—three or four, it looked like. Probably one each for Arthur, Sugar, Nina, and the chef.

Nina was on the phone, ordering the day's supplies. Sugar was sitting beside her, making her life miserable, as far as Skip could see.

Nina indicated a chair. "A case of almonds," she told the phone. "A case of anchovies; two cases beef base, two cases lobster base; one case crab boil; four tubs Creole mustard; ten cases vegetable oil; four sacks rice; twenty-five sacks rock salt."

She hung up and, without looking at Skip and Sugar, made another call. "Hello, Mr. Daroca; Nina at Hebert's. I need four cases of shrimp, please, sir; a hundred pounds of crawfish; fifteen pounds of alligator;

fifteen pounds of frog legs; five gallons of oysters; seventy pounds of pompano fillet, and . . . let's see, I think that's it." She paused to listen for a minute. "No. No crab today."

Sugar shook her head violently.

"Just a minute, Mr. Daroca."

Sugar said, "What do you mean no crab? We have nine crab dishes on the menu."

"Jumbo lump crabmeat's eighteen-fifty a pound."

"So? Pompano's nine-fifty. Would we serve tilapia or drum as the catch of the day? Of course not—a restaurant of this caliber serves pompano."

"If I bought crab at that price, we'd have to charge so much for it, no one would order it."

"Well, can't you get imitation crab?"

"Your husband always said, 'This is *Hebert's*, Ms. Phillips. You order crab remoulade, it better be crab.' "

"We'll just do half and half," said Sugar. "Nobody'll know the difference." Her expression said she was absolutely confident no one had ever had such a clever idea.

"Reed tried that about five years ago. You know what happened? The chef walked out."

"Can't we just get a new chef?"

Nina closed her eyes and picked up the receiver again. "Mr. Daroca, I'll have to call you back." She glanced briefly at Skip, apparently deciding she didn't mind if she had a witness. "Sugar, you've had a bad shock. I know you must feel you have to take up the slack, with Arthur and Reed gone, but you've really got to give yourself a break. You shouldn't be here, stressing yourself out at a time like this." She brushed hair off her forehead. "God knows I wouldn't be if I had any choice."

"Nina Phillips, don't you patronize me."

"I'm not patronizing me, I'm just trying to do what's best for the restaurant right now."

"It's not your restaurant."

Skip wondered how Nina was going to answer that one. Sugar was apparently one of those people who specialized in the unanswerable. Her own mother was one as well.

Nina brushed at her hair again. "Sugar, honey, I know you want to do what's best, but you have to remember, your husband was raised in this business. Reed went to Cornell to learn how to run a restaurant; I've had five years' experience here, and five before that over at Dooky Chase's.

You can't just walk in one morning and take over a multimillion dollar business."

Sugar looked as if she couldn't decide whether to destroy the room or cry. It was a small child's anger and hurt Skip saw on her face.

She must have been some mom, Skip thought. *A giant-sized four-year-old.*

Nina's voice was very gentle. "Now, I'm going to talk for a minute with Detective Langdon. When I'm done, I need to be able to make my groceries."

Sugar looked briefly at Skip. Her eyes were furious, but the hurt and humiliation in them far outstripped the anger. She turned and left on noisy high heels, yet Skip thought "stalked out" too dignified a term for her exit. She thought she heard a sniffle as the older woman passed.

Nina was too frustrated for discretion. "She's like a five-year-old. She suddenly decides she's something she isn't, and no one can tell her different. Life's been pretty easy for a couple of years, ever since she became an artist—never had a lesson in her life, but at least she didn't bother anybody. Now she's an expert on the cost of crab—can you imagine?"

"Sorry it's a bad time, but I really need to ask you some questions."

Nina was suddenly all business. "Of course. I apologize for all this."

"First of all, do you mind if I have a look around Mr. Hebert's office?"

Nina hesitated. Was it her call? Skip could almost hear her wondering. Finally, she sighed, evidently deciding she was in charge. "Go ahead. But I'll stay with you."

As Skip began going through papers, Nina reached for the phone and dialed. "Grady Hebert," she said. "Your mama's been down at the restaurant creating havoc. If you don't keep her out of here, there's not going to *be* any Hebert's."

She hung up, presumably having vented her spleen on a machine.

Skip searched quietly, found nothing that meant anything to her. When she was satisfied, she said, "I'm puzzled about something. Mrs. Hebert isn't acting very bereaved. How did she and Arthur get along?"

Nina thought about it. "I guess they more or less hated each other. But she probably still misses him."

Unless his death was a hit. It wouldn't be the first time.

"I've got to tell you, this is how she is, though. She runs around in circles so she doesn't have to sit down and think about anything. The more upset she is, the crazier she makes everyone else."

"I really came to talk about Dennis. You're pretty sure he's really off drugs?"

"He's a pillar of AA. Has been for years." She glanced quickly at Skip. "Believe me, I'd know if he was using again. Reed would tell me. And she wouldn't put up with it for a minute. That was part of the deal when they got married."

"It seems like a pretty odd match."

Nina shook her head vigorously. "Oh, no. Reed got him off drugs— does that tell you anything?"

"Should it?"

"She's the classic codependent; just *loves* helping out. I should know. It's a common complaint."

"What drugs did he do?"

"Heroin."

"Coke?"

She shook her head. "Don't know. Only know about the heroin. And alcohol; lots of it."

"It's hard to imagine." Skip had blurted it; she instantly regretted it.

"What do you mean? You're a cop; you've seen it all."

"Reed sounds like such a competent woman. It's hard to understand the attraction."

Nina sighed. "Well, there are books and books on it. Or you could go to Al-Anon, if you're really that interested. She's a dynamo, and he needs one to get him going."

"He's weak, you mean."

"I guess so." She hesitated. "I don't know if you can really say a person who's kicked a habit like that is weak. But he's certainly no ball of fire."

"Do you know what his old haunts are? Places he liked to hang?"

"I never asked, to tell you the truth."

"Who would know?"

"Well, you could go see his family."

"I'd like to meet his business partner as well."

"Ah. The lovely Silky Sullivan."

"I beg your pardon?"

Nina nodded. "Uptown girl. You know how they go in for nicknames. She must have been Susan or something and next thing you know she was a horse."

Skip couldn't help smiling. It really was a very New Orleans name— there'd once been a cop named that, an Irish Catholic who converted to Judaism.

She got the necessary addresses and phoned the Sullivan-Foucher enterprise—known as Lush Life—but got no answer. The Uptown girl now lived in the Faubourg Marigny, in a charming double shotgun newly painted light blue with teal trim.

No one answered Skip's ring, but she persisted. It was a good five minutes before a woman in jeans came to the door, dirt up to her elbows.

"Sorry," she said, when Skip had identified herself. "I was out in the back. I'm so upset about Dennis I took the day off. Come with me, will you?"

Sullivan walked the length of the house and stepped into the backyard, where she found a hose and washed off the dirt. She was nearly as tall as Skip, who was an even six feet, but Sullivan was a good deal thinner. She was lanky and angular. Skip couldn't banish the impression that she had the feel about her of a thoroughbred—that her name, probably applied when she was a baby, had somehow come to fit. Her short hair was brown and shiny—indeed silky; her skin was porcelain.

"How can I help you?"

"You know what happened last night?"

"I know Arthur was killed and everyone else is gone, if that's what you mean. I'm nearly out of my mind." Skip thought her eyes grew wet as she spoke.

"You're close to the family?"

"To Dennis. And of course Sally's adorable, but I hardly know Reed. I mean, she's always been very nice, I guess I've known her since Icebreakers"—seventh grade subscription dances—"but we never had much in common."

"And Dennis? How do you know Dennis?"

She turned slightly pink. "I'm not supposed to say."

Skip said, "AA. I know about that."

"He was the one who got me into it. He really helped me a lot. I mean —a *lot*." She shrugged. "We were both into plants, so we finally went into business together. Oh, God, what's going to happen to me now?"

Skip wondered what their financial arrangement was. "Did Dennis put up the money?"

"No. I did. But he's indispensable—I can't run this thing without him. I've been on the phone all day—do you have *any* idea what happened over there? At Arthur and Sugar's?"

This was Skip's least favorite kind of a question. "Sorry, it's under investigation. I really can't discuss it. Tell me—how has it worked out? Your business, I mean?"

"Well, it's only been a few months. But so far, fantastic. Just being around Dennis is like—I don't know—being born again."

"That's pretty strong."

Sullivan had been examining one of her plants. She turned to stare at Skip. "I must sound crazy. Let me start over. I come from a family of macho men—everybody's got to prove how big and mean he is. There's a sweetness about Dennis; a sort of quiet gentleness that's the most soothing thing I've ever been around."

She's in love with him.

Skip said, "You'd never guess it from his picture."

Sullivan laughed. "I know. You should see him—piercing, scary eyes; and that brooding look. There was an Irishman in the woodpile somewhere. I know because half the Sullivans have it. Only they don't just look violent—they are."

"Have you heard from him, Silky?"

Sullivan stared at her quizzically. "I'd have told you if I had."

"Where do you think he is?"

"You think I know? I'd go get him if I knew."

"Tell me about your business arrangement."

"I put up the money because I had it. We pay ourselves salaries, but any profit above that goes to me until I'm paid off. After that we split."

"How about insurance?"

She shrugged. "We've got some."

"Any life insurance?"

"Life insurance? Why on earth would we need that?" Skip didn't speak for a moment, and Sullivan apparently realized the irony of what she'd said. "Oh, God." She brought one hand to her mouth and bit it.

When she'd gotten control, she said, "We don't have life insurance."

"Dennis probably knew some pretty questionable characters when he was using. Maybe you know them too."

"Are you kidding? I grew up on First Street. I did my drinking where it was socially acceptable."

"Did he tell you about his other life? As an addict?"

"Not much." Something in her face closed down.

"Look, I'm trying to find him."

"Detective, I can't help you. If I could, I would, but I really can't. Sober people usually don't talk that much about that part of their lives—the thing they've left behind."

"I thought that was what AA meetings were all about."

"I could tell you what Dennis went through emotionally—if that's what you mean. But I wouldn't. We have a saying: 'What we hear in the rooms stays in the rooms.' "

"I'm more interested in the people he knew then. Who he hung out with and where."

"I'm sorry. I really don't have the least idea."

Skip handed her a card. "Let me know if you think of anything."

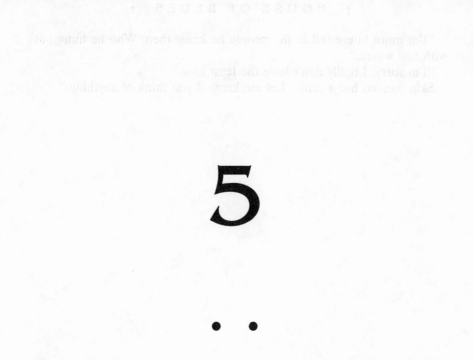

5

Dennis's parents lived in an old neighborhood near Mercy Hospital, perfectly respectable but not prestigious—"yatty," a friend of Skip's called it; full of the working-class whites known as "yats" to white-collar New Orleanians.

The family homestead was a neat house that could have used paint but wasn't yet an eyesore. It looked as if its owners cared but had put off painting for a year too many. In the yard were bushes pruned into roundish shapes, suggesting attention; so the peeling paint was probably a function of economics. The house was a bungalow style with trellislike ironwork pillars that held up the porch. Four steps led to a little waist-high gate of the same fanciwork—perhaps there had been a dog once, but there was no barking now, so it seemed an oddly superfluous luxury. At the rear of the porch there was an old-fashioned screen door. It was a peaceful structure that reminded Skip of small houses in sleepy country towns.

When she identified herself, Mrs. Foucher drew in her breath. "He's dead. Dennis is dead, isn't he?"

"Oh, I'm so sorry. I didn't mean to frighten you. We have no word of him yet. I'm just here to ask you some questions. I'm trying to find him."

Mrs. Foucher had a tissue in her hand that she had squeezed the life out of. She was overweight and her face looked as if it was probably sad even when no one was missing or dead. "Truly? I thought he was dead. Milton, I thought he was dead."

Her husband said, "It's all right, Josie. It's all right now." He put an arm around her shoulder and turned to Skip, holding open the screen door. "Come in, dear lady. Permit me."

The formal, old-fashioned mode of speech sounded strange to Skip's ears.

They're such ordinary white people, she thought. But the town was full of families like this—some members "white," some "black." Mrs. Foucher was the lighter, with gray-streaked brown hair, and her husband had darkish hair, also graying, which he wore with a moustache.

Skip was surprised that both the Fouchers were home, though it was a Tuesday. Perhaps they were out of work, or one of them was. Or perhaps Dennis's father had stayed home to await news of his son. "Could we give you some coffee? You are a blue person," Milton said. "I know you understand how Josie feels. We are happy to have you in our house."

He used no contractions and he enunciated each word, speaking in discrete phrases and projecting so strongly that if he'd been a preacher he could have reached every ear in the congregation without benefit of microphone. She wondered if he was a lay preacher who just liked to practice; also whether he was a raving lunatic.

"A blue person," she ventured. "Is that what you call a policeman?"

"Oh, hardly. I would hardly call a young lady a 'man' of any sort. Accuracy is my passion, and I do not make mistakes so easily avoided."

He and his wife had now led her into a cramped and dreary kitchen, still smelling of breakfast. Skip refused coffee, but joined them at a table under a hanging light fixture that threatened to decapitate anyone who moved too fast.

Josie was silent. "A blue person," Milton said, "is a person of compassion, someone who feels for other people, who is kind and who wants to please. Josie is one as well. I myself am a green person—a scholar, something of a recluse, an intellectual, someone who loves studying above all else."

In spite of herself, Skip was fascinated. "Is this your own system or someone else's?"

"Well, we green people are indeed the creative ones—the inventors, the scientists. But this is not my handiwork. It is something I learned in a seminar. I attend every seminar I am able. I also read constantly. But

49

never fiction, of course. No, sir, I am interested only in facts." Here his voice rose as if he were either angry or in the pulpit, making his most vital point. "Only facts!" he raged, and his face turned red.

He lowered his voice. "If there are no facts, I do not have interest. I do not watch television for any reason."

"Are there other colors?"

"Of course. The world could not survive without gold people. These are the doers; the movers and the shakers."

"I see. Which one is Dennis?"

An odd expression came over Milton's face. Skip could have sworn it was confusion, but Milton didn't seem the sort who went in for that. He recovered quickly.

"He is not intelligent enough to be a green person. He does not do enough to be a gold person. I would say that he is a blue person except that he does not listen. No system is perfect."

Skip turned to Josie and smiled. "I wonder if you've heard from him since yesterday?"

"Of course we have not," said Milton. "If we had, we would have mentioned it. Dennis was always a hellion. He skipped school more often than he went, he associated with unsavory individuals, and he smoked marijuana. I was obliged to whip him at least three times a week. Quite often, he even failed to come home—he stayed out all night with fringe-element friends."

Milton had curly hair and looked like a laborer of some sort. Skip had never in her life heard anyone—especially anyone who looked like him—talk this way.

"Worried us to death," said his mother. "And such a smart boy. He finished two years at UNO, did you know that? But then he disappeared and didn't come back for a while."

"Somehow or other, he managed to meet Miss Reed Hebert. Neither Josie nor I will ever have the slightest notion how he did it. She civilized him as no one else had been able to do. We watched her turn him into a different person altogether. At this moment, a good friend of his is dying of AIDS—a neighborhood boy, two blocks away. *This* neighborhood. AIDS.

"This young man is as red-blooded as I am. He contracted this disease by using needles. That is correct. In this neighborhood. I stress that this boy is not a homosexual—this thing could have happened to Dennis. It did not because of Reed Hebert."

He set his lips in a grim line, and Skip wasn't sure she didn't hear regret in his voice. She thought he had probably predicted it and hated to be proved wrong.

"As it happens, I was talking to Mrs. Sugar Hebert when the kidnap occurred. I had called Dennis to tell him about his friend Justin—the boy who is ill—and Mrs. Hebert answered the phone."

"What kidnap, Mr. Foucher? What did you mean by that?"

"That is what happened, of course. Surely the police have figured this out."

Josie said, "Did he mention green people like to control things?" Skip thought she was trying to be playful, but it wasn't working.

As always, Milton ignored her. "We will soon be receiving a ransom note—that is, Mrs. Hebert will. These people could not get a cent from the Fouchers." His voice was smug.

"This friend—Justin. Could you give me his address?"

"You wish to visit Justin? What on earth for?"

"I want to see Justin and any of Dennis's other friends."

Both the Fouchers looked furious—Skip couldn't think why, but she thought it had to do with the control Josie had mentioned. Blue person or not, she shared her husband's world, and very likely his reality. Perhaps they wanted to be the only sources, the world's greatest living experts on Dennis Foucher, dope fiend.

"We will be glad to comply," said Milton, "with anything the police desire. However, we know of no other friends of Dennis's."

His anger was so strong, so naked, she found it uncomfortable remaining in the room even long enough to get Justin Arceneaux's address.

If I lived with these two, she thought, *drugs might seem very attractive indeed. In fact, they do right now.*

She also found herself thinking new thoughts about Reed—most of them respectful. Boys from families like this one simply did not marry into Uptown families.

How on earth had Reed met Dennis? And, more important, how had she found the courage to bring him home?

There must be a little outlaw in her, Skip thought, and she liked that. But she thought it must be deeply buried; it certainly didn't jibe with anything else she'd heard about Reed.

As she was leaving she said, "Can I ask you one thing? Do you know Nina Phillips?"

Milton Foucher turned red. "I don't believe I do."

"She works at the restaurant. Says she's your cousin."

"Dennis probably told her that. I am afraid the boy does not know the meaning of veracity. If he were here right now, I swear I would whip him again."

Skip sneaked a look at Josie. Her face looked as used-up as the crumpled tissue she clutched.

• •

Justin Arceneaux's family and friends were gathered in the living room, as if he'd already died. A buffet table in the dining room was piled high. The sadness in the air was like a heavy fog on the river.

As Skip entered the house, she wanted to run, or claim to be an Avon lady, to do anything but state her business.

How can I say I'm a cop? This is the last thing they need now.

When she spoke, she heard the stress in her voice, the slight loss of focus, the disorientation anxiety bred. "I wonder if I can speak to Justin," she heard herself saying, and was ashamed at the arrogance of it. Why should she, a stranger, claim some of his last minutes?

"He's very, very ill," said his mother. "In fact, he isn't expected—" The sentence stopped and a sob came out.

"I wouldn't ask if it weren't extremely important. It's about Dennis Foucher."

"Dennis?" She looked puzzled. She glanced around the room. "Dennis isn't here."

She probably hadn't read a paper that day, or even turned on the television.

"He's disappeared. Along with his wife and daughter."

"Dennis? But Justin hasn't seen him in years." She looked as confused and forlorn as if Skip had accused her son of a crime on his deathbed. Treason, perhaps, or multiple murder.

"I'm very sorry to disturb you like this." She had already said this, but she figured Mrs. Arceneaux was hearing selectively. "I wonder if you could just ask Justin if he'll see me."

Skip hoped he wasn't asleep. She didn't want his mother waking him.

Mrs. Arceneaux came back looking as if the folds of her face were being dragged down by invisible weights. "He says he'd like to see you. But he's very, *very* ill—in fact, it's the second time we've thought he'd be dead before morning. They go real, real slow with AIDS—you just can't tell—but he's still got his mind." She nodded. "He's got his mind. He can talk if he can just—you know, he's hardly got any energy at all."

Skip rose and let herself be led to the bedroom, feeling as if she were marching to her own death. As they walked down the hall, Mrs.

Arceneaux said, "Now, don't be shocked. He weighs about eighty-four pounds."

The curtain of bereavement, the fog, had settled on Skip like a thick mesh she could not squirm out of.

The first thing she saw was the metal tree for Justin's IV, and then she saw the people in the room. First a young woman sitting by the bed, ramrod straight, alert as a sentry. Her hair was white-blond, short and wavy, her face thin and gaunt, but Skip could tell that was from strain. She was extraordinary-looking, this young woman, someone who'd turn heads in this city of beautiful women. But she was stiff and tired, nearly frantic under her calm, with the effort of holding herself together.

Next a little girl, also blond, lying on the floor, her dress flipped up so that her panties showed, feet in the air, one hand out to her side, touching a toy dinosaur, stroking it but not looking at it. Instead looking at Skip without interest. Obviously beside herself with boredom, having been here for hours, or days perhaps.

And then there was Justin himself. Later Skip could remember almost no details except that his hair was a sandy color, that he had freckles and that his eyes were like holes in a sunken face. Despite his mother's warning, the shock of seeing someone so wasted nearly rendered her speechless. He had on no pajama top, so that she could see paper-thin skin, skin like plastic wrap, stretched over a frame that looked too small to belong to a man.

"Hello," he whispered. "This is my wife, Janine. And my daughter."

Skip thought he had meant to say his daughter's name, but decided to save his breath. He grimaced as if it hurt to talk, but Janine said, "It's the sheet. It hurts his feet, and his shoulders sometimes. It's caused by a deadening of the nerves that makes him supersensitive."

"I know what that is," said the little girl. "It's called neuropathy." Skip thought that was a fact the child was much too young to know.

Janine stood up and swabbed Justin's mouth with what looked like a giant Q-tip. She slipped something between his lips that must have been an ice chip.

Skip walked a step closer, not wanting to invade his space, but not sure she could hear from a distance. She said again that she was sorry to disturb him, and she told him Dennis was missing. This time she said nothing about Reed and Sally; it was somehow too grim.

"Dennis," said Justin. "He was always a needle freak. We shared. But he got through okay." The words came slowly, one by one, painfully. His lips looked as if he'd spent weeks in the Sahara—this was not normal chapping, something much more extreme. When he spoke, Skip could see that the inside of his mouth was dead white, tongue and all, as if he had no blood left.

Skip waited a moment. "If he were really in trouble, does he have a friend he'd go to?"

"Me. Me, man."

"Has he been here? Has he phoned?" It sounded ridiculous, but she had to ask.

"I don't know," he whispered.

Janine turned pouched and swollen eyes on her and shook her head. "If he's in trouble, he'd go to Delavon."

"Delavon?"

"His dealer."

"You mean Delavon's a friend—or he'd go to make a buy?"

"To get fucked up."

"He's been clean for a long time."

Justin shook his head, or rather turned it on the pillow once or twice. "Don't know that Dennis. Only know the other. He needs the warm hug; gotta have the cocoon."

"I beg your pardon?"

"Dope."

"What kind?"

"Only one kind. He hated coke; couldn't stand that wiry feeling."

"Heroin?"

Justin was quiet, as if the question didn't deserve an answer.

"Where do I find Delavon?"

"Treme. No last name. I know Dennis. He'd go to Kurt's too." The words came slowly, each one an effort.

"Who's Kurt?"

"Not a person. A bar."

"Can you tell me where?" She felt like an officer of the Inquisition.

"Dumaine. Near Rampart."

"Thanks. Anything else?"

Justin closed his eyes and again rotated his head.

"Thank you," Skip said, and she said it again, this time whispering. Janine looked at her, not changing expression. The little girl had turned over on her stomach.

She looked about four or five, and no doubt her mother thought she didn't understand what was happening, or that her father needed her now —or more likely, since she'd known about his nerve problem, that it was

54

better for her to face it. Skip wondered how many years on a shrink's couch she would spend as a result of this experience, or if she would simply forget it, bury it, and suffer depression the rest of her life.

She wondered too if the girl and the woman carried the virus.

Even outside, in her own car, she could not escape the fog of misery. She went back to headquarters to talk over the case with her sergeant, Sylvia Cappello, who threw a file down hard as Skip walked in. "Shit!"

She looked in the direction of an officer who was just leaving. Maurice Gresham.

"What's wrong?"

"Goddammit, another piece of evidence is missing. I'm so damned tired of the little things that happen when—" She stopped, but stared in Gresham's direction, pointing him out.

"What, Sylvia?"

"Too much shit happens here, that's all. We're about to serve a warrant, nobody's home. We lose a little piece of evidence and it turns out somebody"—again she stared at the space where Gresham had been—"checked it out and, what do you know, they *lost* it."

Cappello was far more upset than Skip had ever seen her. What she was saying bordered on unprofessional, and Cappello was never unprofessional. She was a by-the-book cop who thought before she spoke, and right now she was bad-mouthing one of her officers to another.

Skip tipped her chin at the now-invisible Gresham. "You think he's dirty?"

"Who's not in this goddamn town? You read the paper? You notice how just about every day some relative of some politician turns up on the payroll of some casino? Everybody's taking kickbacks, everybody's got a scam, everybody's looking out for their friends—it's got to the point where no one cares. One day you can be a front-page scandal, the next day you get elected to high office—or more likely appointed because you've got a buddy."

"Why don't you just get him transferred out?" She avoided saying Gresham's name.

"You think he's the first one I ever had? Or the only one now? What if I did get rid of him? There'd just be another. Or a swarm of them, like cockroaches. Skip, I can't take this anymore. I swear to God I'm getting out."

Skip sat down, feeling as if the breath had been knocked out of her. "Getting out? You mean quitting?"

"I mean quitting and moving out of town and probably out of the state." She paused. "Maybe I'll go to law school."

Skip was speechless.

"You know what this casino means? It means several billion dollars are up for grabs. That's *billions*. In permits and hotels and restaurants and jobs and parking lots and every piece of the pie you can think of. You think this city and this state were crooked before, it was just a warm-up for the kind of scrambling that's starting now. I don't want to raise my kids in a place like this."

Skip was vaguely aware that Cappello had kids, but it was nothing they ever talked about. She never thought of Cappello as someone with a personal life, just as a police sergeant—and about the best cop Skip had ever worked with. If she quit, it would leave a gaping hole in Homicide.

But she could see what the sergeant meant. Skip knew Gresham was dirty. She knew there was nothing Cappello could prove, nothing she could do about it except try to keep him out of certain cases.

But since she didn't know who was paying him, and what cases involved his employers, it was hard to do that.

Then there was the problem of overhearing—Gresham could know things and dole out tips with almost no effort.

There was nothing the sergeant could do, and Gresham was only a symptom. The dirt, the buying and selling, the scamming, could wear on you; it wore on anyone who worked for the city and tried to do a good job. It wore particularly on police officers.

"Oh, hell, you're right," Cappello said. "I'll get him transferred out."

Skip decided to wait till later to talk to her about the case. She was feeling a lot like one of Justin Arceneaux's relatives—so stressed out she'd come unfocused. She didn't trust herself to give a good accounting right now.

But Cappello said, "How's the heater case? Every lieutenant in the building's called." A heater case was one the brass cared about—any case, said the more cynical, involving a white person.

Skip ran this one down for her.

Then she ran unsuccessful records checks for "Delavon," both as a first and a last name. Since it was near lunchtime, she called Narcotics without much hope, but her pal Lefty O'Meara answered with his mouth full. "Lefty. If I'd thought you'd be there, I'd have come up to see you."

"If you thought I wasn't here, why'd you call?"

"Hope springs eternal. Who do you know named Delavon?"

"Nobody. Who's he supposed to be?"

"Big-time dealer. Heroin, maybe."

"Not much of that around."

"I hear Delavon's got some."

"Trust me. There ain't no Delavon."

She trusted him, but she thought there was. It was just that O'Meara probably knew him as something like George Boudreaux, or "Tiny," maybe—no last name.

She sat at her desk and stared at the phone. She needed human contact, but not with Cappello right now—with someone who wouldn't depress her.

She called her friend Cindy Lou, hoping to snag her for lunch. But there was no answer.

She called Steve for impromptu cheering up—but her own machine answered.

She called her landlord and best friend, Jimmy Dee Scoggin, but got his secretary; he was in court.

Feeling disoriented, almost dizzy, she went out to get a sandwich, which she consumed without tasting, thinking of the way Justin Arceneaux's bones pushed at his skin.

6

• •

Treme was a black neighborhood, poor but at least not one of the ancient, pathetic, falling-down housing projects that breed crime like roaches in New Orleans. Most murders these days were in the projects. Many cases—Skip thought most, but maybe it just seemed that way—involved juveniles who didn't care whether they lived or died. She had known thirteen-year-old crack dealers who had to hide their stashes from their mothers—and not because they feared punishment.

Treme was itself falling down in places, but it still had dignity; its residents didn't have the beaten-down feel of people from the projects, still seemed to take joy in life. The Municipal Auditorium was here, historically the site of the two biggest Mardi Gras balls and now the site of the city's temporary casino.

The auditorium was on the edge of the neighborhood, just across Rampart Street from the French Quarter, and the real estate agents all predicted the casino would vastly alter the character of the Quarter near Rampart. It already had, to some extent. Even without it, merely in anticipation, property values had shot through the roof. A healthy Hollywood community had settled in, and almost none of the old Creole town houses were still on the market, having been snapped up by investors and speculators. On one side of the street prosperity had already arrived.

But no one thought the Treme would change. Broken windows were common here. Paint peeled. Wood rotted. Formosan termites chewed.

On another case, Skip had met a prostitute who lived in the French Quarter at the time, had since moved to the Iberville Project to be with a man, and now lived in Treme. She was a sometime informant; though, if the truth were told, she didn't really know much.

But she had a daughter, and Skip felt sorry for her, gave her little cash gifts now and then. She hadn't heard from her in six or eight months, had simply one day found a note with the prostitute's new address on her desk —Jeweldean kept in touch. She might not know how to find Delavon the dealer, but she was a perfectly good place to start.

Skip found her building, a once-proud Italianate town house that didn't look too bad now—a ten-thousand-dollar paint job, a few little repairs, and new plumbing would probably have made it close to livable.

She rang the bell and a woman came out on the balcony. "Who's down there?"

"Hey, Jeweldean. It's Skip Langdon."

"Langdon. What you want, girl?"

"Let me in, would you?" Skip was starting to feel conspicuous—as if she had on one of those jackets with POLICE in two-foot yellow letters on the back.

Jeweldean's little girl was lying on the living room sofa, watching television, covered with a cotton blanket and looking far too sad for a child not yet in school. Skip hadn't actually met her before, her dealings with Jeweldean usually taking place on the phone or after the girl was asleep.

"This is Tynette," Jeweldean said. "Say hello, baby."

The child complied, seeming barely able to get the word out.

"Le's go in the kitchen." When they were out of earshot, she said, "We went over by my mama's for Easter and Tynette got shot."

"Shot? That little girl?" Skip knew it happened all the time, but this girl was so small it shocked her—small and the child of someone she knew.

"We moved out of the projects 'cause of all that mess, but we *had* to go see my mama. She live over in St. Thomas"—another project—"and Tynette was playin' jump-rope. The shootin' started and she didn't know what to do. The other kids run away, but Tynette too scared. Poor little baby, you should have seen her lyin' in the courtyard, still wearin' her Easter dress, blood all over that pretty yellow skirt, on her white shoes,

little legs and everything. Her grandmama bought her that dress."
Jeweldean's face was stoic, her voice steady.

*Her life is so different from mine. She's been living with this for so long,
she can't even cry anymore.*

"How badly was she hurt?"

"Bad." Jeweldean nodded, as if trying to convince herself. "Pretty bad.
She's gon' be okay though." She nodded some more. "She can walk, and
tha's more than my cousin's baby can. He was shot when he was twelve
years old; he seventeen now and he ain' never walked another step.
Tynette can walk. She be fine."

"How do you get her to the doctor?"

"Biggie take us sometime. Man I been seein'. We manage." She flung
her head back, proud; not wanting to say more. Holding something back.

But that was what Skip wanted. It gave her an opening. "You might
need to take a taxi sometime," she said, and pulled a couple of twenties
out of her purse, half of what she had at the moment. "Better be prepared."

"I sure do thank you," Jeweldean said.

Skip thought she heard a slight sigh behind the words, which came out
low and slow, not the way Jeweldean talked at all. She was embarrassed,
which in turn embarrassed Skip. "I need some information."

"I thought maybe you did."

"But the money's not for that. That's just for Tynette."

Jeweldean looked unbelieving, but expectant.

"Is there any heroin around?"

"Well, *I* sure don't know. Why you think I'd know?"

"You know a guy named Delavon?"

Jeweldean's pupils dilated. "Oh, Delavon. Well, if anybody'd have any,
it'd be him."

"Where can I find him?"

"You crazy, girl? You go mess with Delavon, you get yourself killed."

"Dangerous character, huh?"

"He as soon cut you up as say hello."

Skip shrugged. "I'll chance it. I've got to ask him something."

"*Ax* him? Oh, ax him. Honey, you don't *ax* Delavon. Delavon *ax you.*
He like a king, you know? He don' answer to *nobody.*"

"Well, I'll be sure to say 'your majesty.' "

For some reason, Jeweldean got tickled. "Girl, girl. You're somethin'
else, you know that?"

Oh, can it. I'm a cop. She waited for the giggles to subside.

"You ser'ous about this?" said Jeweldean.

Skip nodded.

"Well, maybe Biggie do somethin'." She paused hardly a second and hollered, "Biggie! Biggie, come on out."

In a moment, a wiry little dude snaked out of the hallway, someone whose nickname was clearly ironic. He was about five-feet-six and may have weighed 130 pounds with his shoes on. He wore running shorts and matching tank top, in black and violet. His athletic shoes were open, with their tongues hanging out, laces dragging.

"Biggie, this Detective Langdon; Ms. *Skip* Langdon. You know her?"

He nodded. "I heard about you." He meant from Jeweldean.

"She need to find Delavon."

"Delavon! You don't want to mess with no Delavon."

"Sho' she does," said Jeweldean. "And you gon' help her find him. *And* you gon' stay with her, make sure she all right." She turned to Skip and held out her hand. "But you give the money to me."

She held out her hand for it. But Skip said, "I don't think we should do it that way. It's too dangerous for Biggie."

Biggie cocked his head. "You ain' worried 'bout me. You white po-lice."

Jeweldean raised a hand as if to hit him. "Biggie! Don't you talk that way to her."

Skip shrugged. "Jeweldean says he'd as soon cut you up as say hello."

Biggie was nodding to himself, tiny little nods, sizing her up. Finally, he said, "I'm gon' make a phone call, see if we can work it."

Ten minutes later Skip and Biggie were outside, walking down the street, looking fairly conspicuous, a six-foot white female, dressed for business, and a kid-sized black dude, now in a pair of baggy pants, but still wearing the tank top, cool as you please.

Almost immediately Skip heard gunfire—two shots, that was all. She jerked her head around; it had come from a falling-down brick apartment building from which screams were now emanating. Automatically she crouched, reaching for her radio. She called in a 10-28 for emergency clearance and quickly gave the location of the gunshots. "Stay here," she said to Biggie, and broke into a run.

"Hey!" He sounded outraged. "You can't go in there. Hey!" He ran after her and grabbed her arm. "You crazy, you know that? Hey, white po-lice, you crazy!"

He wouldn't have grabbed her if she'd been a man, she was pretty sure of it. She shook him off and kept running, uncertain whether to bang on the door or slither to the side and try for the back. But the problem was solved when a kid about seven came running out the door, and she caught it before it closed. She raced up the first flight of stairs, hearing commotion just above her.

She reached the second landing, gun drawn, to find a young man, about seventeen probably, down and bleeding, people gathered around, someone working on his leg.

"Police! Who shot him?"

Silence.

She sighed, lowered her gun, and once again delved in her purse for her radio.

A half-dozen cars converged in minutes, with lots of officers to deploy, but she had no description of the shooter. He was just "some dude" that, oddly enough, no one had seen and no one knew. It was an hour before she had the scene cleaned up, and when she emerged from the building, she harbored a dim, distant hope that Biggie would still be waiting for her.

But of course he wasn't. Nobody was on the street except some gangster leaning against a fire hydrant.

There was nothing to do but go back to Jeweldean's and start over. She waved good-bye to the driver as the last police car left.

The leaner caught her eye. "I hear you lookin' for Delavon."

"Yeah. I am."

"I take you to him."

No way she was going off with a strange man without backup.

"But you gotta be blindfolded," the man said. She was struggling not to laugh when she felt her elbows grabbed, her purse ripped off her shoulder. She was cursing herself for an idiot, getting her purse snatched like some tourist, when someone slipped a blindfold over her eyes. She was being held tightly now, unable to kick or struggle, and she realized that it had taken at least four strong men to immobilize her.

The three she never saw had been soundless. There wasn't a thing she could have done.

Somehow, the knowledge that she hadn't done anything wrong, that her predicament wasn't her fault, calmed her.

Curiously, they hadn't gagged her. And why should they? If the spectacle of a blindfolded woman being dragged down the street didn't elicit anyone's sympathy, cries for help weren't going to either.

"Where are we going?" she said.

"You be quiet now," someone answered. She thought she might as well.

They put her in a car, in the backseat, one on either side of her, each holding an arm. The air was thick with the smell of sweat.

And fear. Hers.

Her legs were free, but she couldn't see the point of struggling now; at the other end was soon enough.

They drove for a long time, and she talked to herself, told herself silent stories about curious ways to get to interviews—anything to avoid thinking like a victim.

When they stopped, someone said, "We at Delavon's. You be quiet now."

The psyching-up had worked—she had an odd feeling, almost of trust. This thing was so preposterous she felt it had to be merely a show of force, a posturing and flexing of muscles; that they wouldn't harm her.

She heard a metal door clang, and they walked her up two flights of metal steps. When they opened another door and took her blindfold off, it was as if she'd come by magic carpet, so exotic was the scene.

She had thought she was in one of the projects or maybe one of the scruffy apartment complexes that dotted certain areas, New Orleans East in particular. They were nasty slums on streets with names like Parc Brittany or Poplar Lane; brick fourplexes, some of them, some made out of wood, with porch roofs falling off, everything falling off.

But she was in a room too big for a place like that, unless someone had knocked a few walls down. And the furnishings were wrong. There were Oriental rugs everywhere, good ones, she thought, though she couldn't be sure, overlapping so that every inch of floor was covered. The walls were hung with fabric—a heavy, dark brocade with plenty of gold in it. A different fabric covered the ceiling in poufs, the way kids like to hang parachutes—something shiny, a taffeta perhaps, in deep burgundy woven with gold.

There were no windows that Skip could see—presumably they had been covered as well.

Near the back of the room was a sort of raised platform, on which a large chair had been mounted. The wall fabric, the dark brocade, had been draped over platform and chair. A man sat on the chair, a smallish, wiry black man who exuded energy as exuberantly as a stage actor. He had on a skullcap, loose-fitting shirt, and harem pants of gold-woven taffeta, a lot like the ceiling fabric, except that it was purple, yellow, and bronze.

Continuing the harem motif, no fewer than three sinuous young
women lounged on the floor, all black, all sporting long, Egyptian-style
ponytails, and all wearing halters and harem pants, clearly run up by the
same mad designer who'd contrived the man's outfit.

Skip would have laughed if she hadn't been so busy trying to keep her
jaw from dropping. And if there hadn't been something sad about it all.

She couldn't shake the feeling that if she pulled up the gorgeous car-
pets, she'd find a plywood floor, maybe covered with linoleum.

That if she looked in the women's eyes, she'd see despair.

That if she ripped down the window coverings, she'd look out on buildings so poorly constructed the gutters, the roofs, anything that wasn't part
of a wall would be hanging by a thread; or perhaps she'd see gorgeous old
Greek revival buildings, now shells, like the ones in Central City along
Baronne and Carondelet, deserted, their windows boarded up.

"You be the tall one," said the man. "I been hearin' 'bout you."

"I guess you be Delavon."

"*Don't* you mess with me." He brought a hand down flat against the
arm of his chair. Because of the padding, it didn't make much noise, but
perhaps it wasn't meant to intimidate. Skip read it as a simple loss of
temper.

"You know how I got here." She couldn't bring herself to say the word
kidnap. "Who's messing with who?"

Delavon sat up on his makeshift throne, dignified, back in control. He
held up a hand like a traffic cop. "Let's don't get off on the wrong foot,
tall one. Peace in the valley, man. I brought you here for two reasons, first
one bein' I gotta thank you."

"Thank me for what?"

"Nothin' happens Delavon don't know about. He know what you done
for Jeweldean. Today and other times. Hey. I gotta get you to sign my
guest book." He spoke to one of the houris. "Kenyatta."

The woman, whose outfit was mostly yellow, rose without using her
hands, like a dancer, and walked to a small table of white rock or concrete
shaped like an Ionic column. On the table was a book covered with green
leather. Kenyatta beckoned.

Skip stood her ground.

"Go on," said Delavon.

Kenyatta offered her a pen and a clean page.

"Every celebrity get their own page," said Delavon. "Can't have you
knowin' what other white po-lice been here; now can I?"

"I don't feel like playing games right now."

"Aw, go on. Do it for Delavon. Maybe I do somethin' for you some-day."

"Maybe you will." Skip signed "Scarlett O'Hara," and turned back to Delavon. "What's the other reason?"

"You tell Delavon."

"I'm gettin' lost here. If you brought me here for two reasons, you must know what they are."

He leaned forward and touched his chest, a wronged man. "I just want to help you, that's all. Just want to he'p you. You tell me what I can do for you, I do it."

Suddenly, she realized she could say "Find Dennis Foucher," and he would. But she'd owe him for the rest of her life.

"Why would you help me?" she said.

"I been hearin' 'bout you. I know who you are."

It was possible. With more than four hundred murders a year, and thirty-five detectives to work them, Skip ended up with about fifteen cases a year. Most of them involved drugs; many, teenagers. Any or all of them might involve Delavon's gangsters—or his friends or sons; maybe his enemies. He could have heard of her.

"What have you heard?" she said.

"I heard you treat people nice. With respect."

"I try to."

"And I heard you he'p out Jeweldean now and then."

"So you want to do me a favor."

"Tha's what I said, idn't it?"

She felt silly, standing in her linen slacks and T-shirt like a supplicant before a king. She wanted to regain control. "Okay. Come on down to headquarters with me."

He slapped his chair arm hard. "I tol' you not to mess with me!"

Good. He'd lost it again. She struggled to hold back a grin. "I'm not messin' with you. I thought you wanted to help."

"You got somep'n to ax Delavon, you ax him *here*."

"You know a guy named Dennis Foucher?"

"I know Dennis."

"I'm wondering if you've seen him in the last few days. Or heard from him."

"He was in a shootout, now wadn't he?"

"That I can't say. Maybe you know."

"Nooooo. Delavon don't know nothin' 'bout that. Don't know *nothin'* 'bout that."

"Have you seen him, Delavon?"

"No, sir, Delavon hadn't seen 'im. And why hadn't I seen 'im? 'Cause Dennis prob'ly be needin' some illegal drugs, that's why. And Delavon don't fool with that shit."

Right. You probably run an orphanage.

"I know that Dennis Foucher. He a hard-core heroin addict. I know what they like. They get clean, then they want that sweetness back; they want them lovin' arms aroun' 'em jus' like it used to be. But you know what? It never is like it used to be. He gon' cop some dope, he gon' decide somethin' wrong with the quality, he gon' complain; he gon' make life miserable for somebody. But then he gon' buy some more shit, 'cause he gotta have that feelin', like bein' wrapped in cotton candy. Warm spun sugar, man."

Delavon was staring into space, carried away with his own poetry, probably seeing it in Old English script on a thick white page, one of many, bound in red leather.

"Sounds like you know a lot about it."

"Delavon know these assholes. Look at me. I'm tryin' to make things better for people. People come to Delavon, I do 'em favors. They think I be involved in illegal activities, but tha's not who Delavon *is*. I made some good investments, I got some money, and I know things. Right now I know the man your boy makin' miserable. He be Turan."

"Turan who?"

He hit the chair arm again. "I don' know *nothin'* 'bout no last names. How come you white po-lice always has to have last names? Turan. Tha's all you need. Turan a mean dude, you ain' gon' like him a-tall. But he the only dude in town got any smack right now. Your boy Dennis, tha's what he into—and I know he is—he gon' find Turan."

Oh, sure. One guy in town's got heroin. Tell me about it.

She said, "Where am I gon' find Turan?"

"You use yo' famous skills as a white po-lice detective."

"Come on, Delavon. I didn't come all this way for nothing."

For some reason, that struck Delavon as funny. When he was finished laughing, he said, "Smart girl like you. You find him, all right."

"Shall I tell him Delavon sent me?"

Delavon laughed, emitting a kind of high-pitched giggle Skip found inappropriate to royalty. "Yeah. You tell him that thing."

"I'll do that." She glanced behind her. Her escorts were standing on either side of a brown-painted door, the only surface in the room that wasn't decorated.

Delavon said, "I hear Turan work for Gus Lozano." Some said the mob was more or less dead in New Orleans; but Lozano was still operating, as close as the city got to a crime boss.

"That so?"

"Some funny rumors goin' 'round about Gus. What you white po-lice know about it?"

It occurred to Skip that maybe she'd been taken to Delavon so he could ask this question; he had the ridiculous idea she could tell him something useful—and would.

Though she hadn't heard the funny rumors, she looked Delavon straight in the eye. "He's on his way out."

Delavon nodded. "Yeah. That what we hear too."

He made some kind of tiny hand signal—Skip was barely aware of movement—and once again she felt her elbows grabbed. The blindfold was slipped in place.

When it came off, she was back in Treme, at the exact spot where she'd been snatched. One of her guides returned her gun. "You be careful," he said. "Streets full of badasses."

7

• •

She planned to go to Kurt's that night, the bar Justin Arceneaux had mentioned, but she couldn't see doing it before nine or ten, giving the regulars time to filter in. A good thing because she had dinner plans. All the people she loved best—two of whom didn't care that much for each other—were getting together.

The two who didn't get along were Steve Steinman and Skip's best friend and landlord, Jimmy Dee Scoggin ("Dee-Dee" to Skip). From the moment Skip met Steve, Jimmy Dee had considered him a rival (though Dee-Dee was ineligible by dint of sexual preference). Steve had sensed his dislike and returned it.

But things were starting to change. For the first time in years, Dee-Dee had a lover, and with Layne as a buffer, the four of them could get through a double date with perfect civility. Tonight there would be five, including their friend Cindy Lou Wootten, sometime police psychologist. Despite her white-bread name, Cindy Lou was black; and despite her *Vogue*-model appearance, she knew the darkest secrets of the human heart, including such nuances as how to handle Frank O'Rourke, the homicide sergeant whose life's work seemed to be making Skip miserable.

They were going to Irene's, the Italian place down the street. Skip was looking forward to it like a kid—after the humiliating events of the day, she needed diversion.

She was slipping on a silk tank top when she heard Steve mumble something.

"What?"

He walked into the bedroom. "Sorry. I can't get used to this place. I thought you were two feet away."

"It's better, though, isn't it? You can get a beer without bumping into me."

"I kind of liked that aspect." He looked around. "But I have to admit this is rather grand—I never saw a slave quarters this big."

Skip's old apartment had been one room—one small room—hardly big enough for two people to have a drink in. But Jimmy Dee had taken it back when he decided to adopt his dying sister's two kids and convert the entire Big House, as they now called it, to its former use as a one-family home. He'd given Skip his own beautifully restored slave quarters at her old rent, and she was in the process of converting it from the quintessential bachelor quarters to an airy oasis of plants and art—or as much art as she could afford.

Only now they called it the garçonnière.

The kids were from Milwaukee, and Dee-Dee wanted to protect them from the city's brutal history.

"Well, Dee-Dee knocked out walls. They probably had two or three families in here." She shook off the thought. "Let's not dwell on it. I'm sure it wasn't fun, but at least no one could be bothered haunting—they were all too glad to get out."

"Maybe the ghosts just don't like the color." Skip had painted her living room cantaloupe.

"Does that mean you don't like it?"

"Don't be so insecure. Of course I like it."

"What were you saying when I didn't hear you?"

"I said it's not too late. We could change our minds and go to Hebert's."

"Let's skip that, shall we? I've had kind of a hard day." Exactly how hard she wasn't about to say. "Let's go get the boys."

Layne hadn't yet arrived, and Jimmy Dee was still getting dressed. Eleven-year-old Kenny barely looked up from his television show. "Hey, Steve. Hey, Skip."

"That's Auntie Skip, Buster." Skip leaned over the sofa to tickle him. His body jerked slightly, but he didn't turn around to smile at her.

Getting ignored, she thought, was probably an improvement. There'd been a time when he was so eager to please he'd probably have jumped up and stood smiling, standing on one foot and then the other, under similar circumstances. His sister Sheila, on the other hand, had been such a tough customer at first that Jimmy Dee started to regret he'd ever even thought of fatherhood.

Now they were both more relaxed: Kenny ruder, Sheila more polite.

Sheila came down the hall her favorite way: off to a running start, sliding the final third in her sock feet. She was nearly fourteen and dressed like a grown-up when she felt like it. She'd probably act like one when she was seventy-five.

"Auntie Skippy," she said.

"Oh, can the 'Aunt' if I have to be Skippy."

"Why do you want to be called that, anyway?"

"It makes me feel loved."

Sheila rolled her eyes. Kenny didn't deign to respond.

Steve said, "What are you two having for dinner?"

"Uncle Jimmy said we could order from the Verti Marte. But boy, is Geneese mad—she made greens."

"Y'all are so cruel," said Skip.

Kenny turned around, on his knees on the sofa. "Yuck. I *hate* greens." He was much more animated than when he liked something.

All to the good, Skip thought. *He's settling in a little more every day.*

Sheila was getting on her mark, ready to slide back down the hall. "Hey, Steve," she said. "Why don't you change your mind?"

"About what?"

She didn't answer until her run was over and she was about to come out of the slide. At the last minute she turned briefly back around. "Going home."

She disappeared into her room.

Steve turned to Skip with a pleased smile: "Well, how do you like that?"

But Jimmy Dee had appeared in time to hear the exchange. "Hey, if you're not Uncle Jimmy, you can't be all bad."

"I heard that," Sheila shouted. "You know what? You're right."

The bell rang, Cindy Lou came in, and instant replay began, Kenny ignoring her, Sheila flitting in and out while they waited for Layne. It was funny, Skip thought, how much attention children demanded the first few years of their lives and how hard adults strove ever after to get their attention.

"Kenny's getting pretty relaxed," Cindy Lou said as they were headed down St. Philip Street. "He's not such a little people-pleaser any more."

Skip saw Jimmy Dee and Layne exchange glances, the way parents do, and for some reason she found it touching. Mostly, she was glad Dee-Dee had a friend. Her landlord was fifty-something by now, a distinguished gentleman—if slightly short—with graying hair, extremely popular with the ladies, most of whom didn't know he was gay. Layne was younger—thirty-five, she imagined—and balding, with glasses and an intellectual bent, a puzzle-constructor by trade. ("Cool," Sheila had said when she heard that part, and Layne was an instant family member.)

Skip said, "What's wrong?"

"What makes you think something's wrong? Except the little prince is now a little brat. You need something else?"

"I saw that look."

"Tell them," Layne said. "At least tell Cindy Lou. She might know what to do."

Dee-Dee looked at Cindy Lou, and Skip could see him make a decision. "After we're seated."

There was a half-hour wait at the restaurant, but when they'd finally secured a table, Cindy Lou pushed it. "Okay, Dee-Dee. Lie down on my couch."

"Kenny's started wetting the bed."

Cindy Lou sipped her wine. "How old is he?"

"Almost twelve."

"He must be upset about something."

"Now why would you say that? His dad deserted the family, his mother died six months ago, and he's living in a strange city with a weirdo uncle who's dating a man. Can't he just roll with the punches?"

Cindy Lou laughed, but she kept at him. "I think he should be in therapy."

"He's *in* therapy."

"With all due respect," Steve said, "I don't know what I think about that."

Skip was flabbergasted. "About what?"

"About therapy. I'm sorry, Cindy Lou, I know it's your job."

She shook her head. "Uh-uh. I'm a research type. I'm paid to have opinions, not listen to people's problems."

Cindy Lou seemed fine, but Skip couldn't shake the feeling Steve had insulted her; and she was confused about this odd opinion of his—whatever it was.

"What's your objection to it?" she asked.

"I don't see how just talking is going to solve anything."

Cindy Lou sipped again. "Well, it's kind of a complicated process. But one thing—it can't hurt."

"Yeah, but does it *do* anything?" The speaker, to Skip's further surprise, was Layne.

She glanced at Dee-Dee, who looked uncomfortable and a little undecided, as if he had half a mind to join that camp as well.

"Well, it's all we have," Cindy Lou said. "Besides, it works now and then."

"Works how?" asked Layne.

"Makes people feel better. That's the point, isn't it?"

"I thought the point was to keep the kid from soaking the sheets."

"If he's doing that, he's unhappy. Unless it's something physical." She raised an eyebrow at Jimmy Dee.

"It's not. We had him checked out."

Steve said, "You want to make him feel better? I've got a great idea."

"What?"

His face took on a maddeningly smug look. "I don't think I'm saying. But this is a great idea; trust me."

"Oh, God. Count your fingers and toes."

"I just need to take him on a little field trip. Okay, Dad?"

Jimmy Dee nodded. "Sure, what's the harm?"

Skip hadn't been in therapy herself, but it hadn't occurred to her to discount it. She'd go if she needed to, she'd always thought.

Cindy Lou looked at her, amused. "A lot of men feel this way. Haven't you noticed your women friends complaining about it?"

"I guess not."

"Oh, well. They do. They say men are in denial, have no self-knowledge, and aren't willing to open up—you never heard that?"

"You're my closest woman friend, and you never talk like that."

"Well, the kind of men I pick, you can't expect much."

Everyone laughed a little nervously. Cindy Lou had the worst taste in men of anyone in New Orleans; she'd once dated the still-married father of a friend of Skip's, and that wasn't even her worst idea.

"Who're you seeing now, Lou-Lou?" Dee-Dee was obviously ready to leave the heavy subject of his kids.

"What's this Lou-Lou crap?"

"Payback for Dee-Dee."

Steve said, "Lou-Lou. I like it."

She made a face at him. "I'm seeing Harry Connick, Jr."

"He's married."

"That's what makes it so much fun."

"Come on. Who're you really seeing? And why didn't you bring him tonight?"

"Well, this one's nice. I'm not kidding—he's really nice; and he's kind of an old friend. I knew him back in Detroit."

Skip perked up her ears. A nice one? That was good, but it probably wasn't the whole story. Others had been nice—just sons of her bosses or husbands of her neighbors. "What's wrong with him?" she said.

"Now, y'all can't make fun of him; I mean that."

"Okay, we won't. Why didn't you bring him?"

"He gets tired easily. He was in an accident."

They were silent.

"It left him paralyzed; from the waist down."

For a minute Skip thought this was one of her jokes. But Cindy Lou was looking down at the table. "I'm sorry," Skip said.

"We dated in high school. I guess I'm still in love with him."

Steve reached for Skip's hand and squeezed it. She was grateful to be with him, however briefly. She knew Cindy Lou would get over this man —she got over all of them—but what she was going through had to hurt. And what Dee-Dee was going through was no picnic either.

For just a second—one tiny fraction of time—Skip's life was going right. She wished she could dip the moment in amber and preserve it forever.

And she thought she ought to knock on wood.

Holding the moment as long as she could, she waited awhile, till the others had ordered coffee, and went off to Dennis's bar.

Kurt's was a neighborhood-type saloon that could have been anywhere in New Orleans—the type beloved by its customers for reasons not apparent to the newcomer, dark and characterless. The sort where serious drinkers could get down to business in peace. As it happened, it was in the French Quarter, a fact that gave Skip a little hope. Maybe its clientele would be slightly more accessible, the atmosphere a little less inviolate than that of most neighborhood oases.

After a quick glance around for Dennis, she bellied up and asked for a Coke. The bartender was a handsome man, ruddy and Irish-looking, but now a little too heavy and starting to gray at the temples. She had the feeling she knew him from somewhere. She watched him awhile.

He was good, jollying folks, keeping up conversations at different ends of the bar, yet remaining constantly in motion as he filled drink orders, seemingly without effort. He was precise and controlled, much like a dancer. She was waiting for an opening but she was in no hurry. There was plenty of time; no reason to push things.

When he brought her a refill, he said, "Hey, big girl, we know each other?"

"Maybe. You look really familiar."

"You don't know who I am?"

"My second grade Sunday school teacher?"

"Come on. You can do better than that."

The man at the next stool, an older man Skip had barely noticed, put a hand on her arm. "This here's Donnie." He slurred his words pretty badly.

"Hi, Donnie. I'm Skip."

"You still don't know who he is?"

Skip shook her head.

"From—you know—that show."

Donnie named a television show from way back, before Skip's time, but one of which she'd seen reruns. There was a character on it named Donnie, a cute little kid, maybe ten or eleven.

"Oh, *Donnie*. The kid."

"My real name's Phil." The bartender smiled as if he couldn't be happier.

It had entered her head from time to time, when she thought her life wasn't going fast enough, to wonder what became of child athletes and child stars. Something about Phil, about his too-ruddy face, once known to nearly everyone in the country, now seen only by a few drunks in a dark room, made her feel slightly panicky. She couldn't pinpoint the reason, thought it might have to do with the notion of change, things not being what they used to be, but she couldn't see how that applied to her life.

He was staring at her, still smiling, and she saw what was required. "I remember you. God, that was funny, that time you got locked in the closet with the dog."

"You can't even imagine how hot it was. Doing that scene."

Maybe I shouldn't feel sorry for him. Here's a guy who's got something in common with every person he meets. Maybe his life is wonderful.

But she couldn't shake a feeling of melancholy. When they had passed enough pleasantries, she said, "You know a guy named Dennis Foucher? Used to come in here pretty often."

"Man, what a coincidence. He was here last night. Comes in, like no time has passed instead of five years, gets shit-faced, and then I read in the paper he's wanted for murder or somethin'."

Skip showed him her badge. "He's not wanted for murder. We just want to talk to him."

"*You're* a cop?"

"*You're* Donnie?"

"Everybody's got to be somebody." Phil laughed as if it were the funniest thing in the world. When he had wiped away the tears and returned to relative sobriety, he leaned close and touched Skip's elbow, conspiracy marked on his features.

"You're not the only one lookin' for him tonight." He pointed with his jaw. "That's Toni in the white T-shirt. She left with him last night."

Toni was sitting alone in a booth facing the bar. She was staring at Phil, as if expecting him to produce Dennis, and apparently saw him point her out. She got up and came forward, bringing her drink, a glass of white wine. Her gait was unsteady.

"Hello," she said. "Did we just meet?"

"I hear we're looking for the same man."

"Oh?" Toni was a slight woman, dark and hungry-looking, a little wiry, but full-breasted and apparently proud of it. Her T-shirt was tucked into black jeans that emphasized her small waist and hips or, more properly, the way they contrasted with her chest.

"For different reasons," Skip said, and identified herself.

Toni's eyebrow shot up. "Why don't we have a drink?" She turned and sauntered back to the booth. Skip picked up her Coke and followed.

Toni reached across the table. "Let me have your hand."

"I beg your pardon?"

"Give me your palm. Then we'll talk."

Oh, well. It's not like I've got a pressing appointment. She stuck out her hand, palm up. Toni took the hand and studied it.

"Your life line's okay, you have a good family life. There are two important men in your life, and that may cause you some trouble." She paused, as if taking a deeper look. "But here's the thing—you're on a journey right now, you've got to go through some doors, you're going from one level to the next as you travel downward. And you're going to suffer." She looked up, into Skip's eyes.

Skip felt her heart speed up. She didn't believe in this, but she was susceptible to the power of suggestion.

Toni looked half blitzed. "The ways of the underworld are perfect and may not be questioned."

"What?"

"At each door, you're going to suffer a loss. I've got to tell you something. There's danger all around you."

"I'm a cop." Skip snapped out the words, angry; Toni was spooking her.

"Listen to me. This is the most dangerous thing you've ever done. But you can't stop now. The ways of the underworld are perfect."

"What's that supposed to mean?"

"What do you think it means?"

"I don't know. The underworld. I don't know—in a way it's where I live. I see the worst side of the city, but let me tell you something—if it's perfect, we're all in trouble."

"Uh-uh. It's not about that."

"What, then?"

"It may be about Dennis. It may have something to do with all that."

Skip remembered Toni's unsteady gait. She wasn't slurring her words, but Skip figured alcohol and an eccentric view of the world had probably combined to produce gibberish that was best ignored.

"You've already suffered a loss, haven't you?"

She thought of Delavon's velvet-footed thugs and laughed. "Yeah. Of my dignity."

"It will get worse." She reached out again. "Let me see the other hand."

Skip complied, figuring it was a small price to get her to talk about Dennis.

"You have a formidable enemy. A very evil enemy. And she's female." Toni cackled. "Maybe it's yourself."

The things she'd said about Skip's personal life were true, but Toni had probably just made lucky guesses; either that or said the same thing she always said. Skip was damned if she was going to give it any credence. "Tell me about Dennis," she said.

"He was here last night. Phil told you."

"You met him then?"

"Met him?" She seemed to find that hilarious. "Met him? I've known him ten or twelve years. He walks into my life, walks out, back in, back out. Then he gets married and I don't see him for years, and then here he is again. Same place, same time, same line."

"Did he tell you anything about his life?"

"You mean about his father-in-law getting killed? Not a goddamn word —Phil told me, I never even saw a paper. All he talked about was his nice wife and his adorable kid. You wouldn't have had the faintest idea there was anything wrong."

"Was he drinking?"

"Oh, heavily. I guess that was a clue."

"What did he say about Reed?"

She looked puzzled. "Who's Reed?"

"His wife. I thought he talked about her."

"He called her 'my wife.' I never thought about it. I just assumed he married Evil."

"Evil?"

"That's what I call Evie. His girlfriend when I knew him. Her daddy was some big shot—owned a restaurant or something, but Dennis never said which one. He's the one who was killed, I guess."

Skip produced the wedding picture of Reed and Dennis. "Is this she?"

"Yes." But she grabbed at the picture. "Let me see that. I don't know. She used to be blond and she was skinnier. Sure looks like her, though."

"Dennis didn't talk about what happened yesterday?"

"No. Believe me I'd remember—knowing what I know now."

"Did he seem okay?"

"Okay?"

"Did he have any injuries?"

She laughed. "I'm the one with injuries. All inflicted by the same damn man."

"How'd he look after all that time?"

"Oh, great. Same old Dennis."

"There wasn't anything unusual about him?"

"What do you mean?"

"Did he have blood on him?"

"Omigod. Blood. No, he didn't have blood on him. He was just the same as always. Even dressed the same—T-shirt and jeans. He's got a great rear end. Some things never change."

"Is this a place where you and Dennis used to meet?"

"Oh, sure. I've been a regular all the time I've lived in the Quarter. And he used to be too."

"So he probably came here to find you."

"Are you kidding? He came here to get shit-faced. I just happened to—" She stopped and drummed her fingers on the table. "Oh, wait a minute. Now that I think of it, he might have wanted me for something. Oh my God, I think I've been had."

I guarantee you you have.

"See, he didn't want to make love with me. I don't think he even wanted a place to stay, especially. I invited him to come home with me, just like I always did, so he did. But he—"

"Wait a minute—can I ask something? How'd you get to your house?"

"Walked. Why?"

"I just wondered what he was driving."

"Don't know." She shook her head, impatient to get on with her story. "Anyway, he came home with me, but he kind of argued about it—he didn't want it that bad. Then when we got there he just sort of crashed on the sofa, and he was gone before I got up." She shrugged. "Story of my life."

Skip was about to say something, but Toni had an announcement to make. "Boy, am I pissed."

"I don't blame you. But what do you think he wanted you for?"

"He wanted to know where he could score."

"Ah."

"So I told him about Maya's. Just use my name, I said; no problem— Maya'll take care of you. Shit! He's probably there right now. The bastard."

"Maya's?"

"Yeah, Maya's—party, party, party, all the time party. God knows what Maya's into—but let me tell you, she hangs with some major creeps. Not exactly southern gentlemen, if you know what I mean."

"How's that?"

"Well, once I went in the bedroom, looking for a bathroom, and the door closed behind me. I just had enough time to see I was alone with two guys before the light went out." She stopped and sipped, building suspense.

"So what'd you do?"

"Screamed." She shrugged. "It worked, but Maya was a little put out."

"How mad at Dennis are you?"

"Pissed as all hell. Wouldn't you be?"

"I can think of a great way to get even. Why don't you take me over to Maya's?"

A smile played at the corners of Toni's lips. "Maybe I'll just do that."

"Let me make a phone call."

Suddenly Toni seemed much more alert than Skip had imagined. "Uh-uh. I might take you—I just might do that. But no one else." She drained her glass, and Skip wasted not a moment.

"Let me get you another drink." She gestured to Phil, and then she changed the subject for a while. When Toni had drunk half her wine and slowed down a bit, she brought up Maya's again.

"Listen, Toni, I can't go there without backup. How about if they stay outside? Just you and I go in?"

"Goddammit, okay!" She made a fist and brought it down on the table. "I'm going to get that bastard for what he did to me."

Skip wasn't sure what he'd done to her. Nothing much, it sounded like. But Toni was the kind of drunk who lost track of such considerations. Skip hoped she stayed loaded long enough to get her to Maya's.

People had brought food to Reed and Dennis's, and Nina had sent some from the restaurant. Grady and his mother had sat down together, but neither of them had really eaten. Sugar did not talk about Arthur, about her loss—even about Reed and Sally. She talked only about Nina, how she was ruining the restaurant, how she couldn't do anything right, how nasty she was to sweet Sugar, herself a paragon of behavior and business sense.

That was okay for Grady, it was more natural—it was the Sugar he was used to and for now preferred to the passive one, the strange one of the night before.

She was with some friends now, friends of Arthur's. Sugar didn't really make friends, and she and Arthur had so little in common they didn't have couple friends. Yet people had come over, and Grady was grateful. He had no idea how to take care of his mother, had never seen the possibility he'd need to. He'd devoted his life to protecting himself from her.

Grady had brought his computer over—a small notebook that it had taken him a long time to be able to afford. He was upstairs now, practicing his own peculiar brand of therapy—the one thing that had gotten him

80

through so far. He found that when he wrote, when he created his own universe, he left this one behind. He had problems with his father, a whole lot of problems, but he did not want to think of what Arthur's death meant to him.

What had happened to Reed and Dennis and Sally was another matter. In his heart he didn't feel they were dead, and he was feeling less and less sure they'd been kidnapped, because there'd been no ransom demand, and it had now been more than twenty-four hours. He and his mother had carefully left telephone messages at both their houses, so there'd be no problem getting in touch. And there was always the restaurant—anyone could call there.

If they weren't dead, what? He didn't like to think about it, what that might mean. And he thought it odd that his mother wasn't trying to find them, wasn't bending everyone's ear with cockeyed theories as usual. Instead she had turned her attention to the restaurant, and to Nina, her newly declared enemy. There must be a reason for that. And Grady thought he knew what it was. She had fears about Reed and Dennis—the same ones he had.

He wanted to stop writing about the vampires, to branch out, to write about reality. But how to go about that? The thought of it made his stomach flop. Writing was important, it was necessary, it was his obsession.

It scared him to death.

When he really thought about it, writing was like a vampire. It caressed you, it wrapped its treacherous arms around you, and it sucked you dry.

No, no, no, it isn't like that. A vampire would suck your blood and cast you aside. Writing ensnares you; it keeps you; it won't let you go.

Like Sugar would if anyone would let her.

But writing is the good mother.

Right.

So do it.

An idea came to him, simply to do a writing exercise rather than a finished, publishable product. Just to let his mind go wild and see what happened.

He started writing what appeared to be a children's story:

● ●

Once upon a time, there was a little boy named Bill. Bill lived on a strange planet with some people he wasn't too sure about, but it wasn't all that bad a life.

Children were allowed to do anything they wanted, especially climb as many trees as they liked, and keep lions as pets. Or tigers, if they chose, but Bill preferred a nice lion because you could get a good grip on its mane when you rode it.

They ate nothing but fruit and spaghetti and sometimes pizza, so no one had to cook very much and no animals had to die. The spaghetti hung from certain trees that grew in a grove, like Spanish moss hangs from certain trees here. Sometimes the people asked the neighborhood giraffes to reach up and get it or, when it grew low, they sent the children out on their lions for it.

Sauce for the spaghetti came down from a mountain, in a sort of waterfall, and the people caught it in barrels. That happened once a week, and every week the sauce was different—sometimes you got tomato, sometimes pesto, sometimes Alfredo or primavera.

Flying saucers made out of pizza dough blew through now and then. The people caught them in nets they put in the tallest trees and plants. You could put the sauce from the waterfall on the saucers and make a very fine pizza if you didn't mind not having any cheese. Which no one did because they never heard of it.

It would have been a very good life if it hadn't been for the Evil One. Bill found out about the Other Side when he was sent out to pick spaghetti and couldn't reach it—someone had come along and trimmed each strand an inch or two, maybe three, just enough so a boy standing on a lion couldn't reach it.

He was flabbergasted—so flabbergasted he squeaked in amazement, causing his pet lion to bolt, which caused Bill, in turn, to fall off him, onto the jungle floor. The ground was usually soft with vegetation, so he wouldn't normally have been hurt, but there was a hard root right under him, from the spaghetti tree he'd been trying to pick. Bill hit his knee on the root and knocked some of the skin off. He'd never in his life had an injury. Such things were very rare on his planet and he didn't know what to think.

He was terrified—so terrified he set up a howl that sent all the elders of the town flying to his aid.

Then he was embarrassed—so embarrassed it made him feel a way he'd never felt before—a nasty, red, jagged kind of way that made his throat close and his cheeks hot.

He learned later that he was angry—so angry he made his hands into fists and started hitting people; and kicking people.

In turn, that made some of the elders angry and they hit him and kicked him back.

A buzzing began among them. He heard words he didn't know. "Evil, evil. The Evil One. Evil One."

Finally, one of the oldest women, the one they called the Wise Woman, held him and patted his back and soothed him until he felt better.

When he got home, he told the people he lived with what had happened to him, and they said the same words he had heard in the spaghetti grove. "Evil. The Evil One," they said.

"She planned it that way," they said. "She cut the spaghetti short so that no one could harvest it, and she is devilishly clever. Do you see what she did? She made sure that whoever tried to harvest the spaghetti would be standing right over a root, so that he would fall down and knock the skin off his knee. She must be punished."

Bill didn't understand at all. "I don't see how anyone could do that," he said. "There are thirty spaghetti trees in the grove and every one of them had short spaghetti. How could she know I would be under the one with the exposed root? And how could she know my lion would bolt? And how could she know that if it did, I would fall off it?"

"You ask too many questions," they said. "Elders know things that you don't."

And that was all they would ever say.

But that night he heard terrible shrieks and screams that turned the planet into an ugly and fearful place. He dreamed about crawling things with many legs and writhing things with forked tongues and winged things with fur and fangs.

He woke up hot and exhausted and asked the others what the sounds in the night had been.

"Oh, that was the Evil One," they said. "We punished her."

That was not the only time he heard those screams. He heard them many times after that, always when something went wrong on the planet.

Once the barrels that caught the spaghetti sauce had been slightly moved so that some of the sauce fell on the ground and could not be eaten.

He found out later that the man whose job it was to set the barrels said the Evil One had moved them.

Once, one of the children who couldn't yet swim fell in a river and almost drowned.

He found out later that the child's mother said the Evil One distracted her, so she couldn't watch her child.

Once someone burned a pizza he was making.

He knew he was not supposed to ask questions, but that time he was simply too puzzled to keep quiet. "Was there a punishment last night?" he asked.

"Why, yes, there was," said the people he lived with.

"Did they punish the man who burned the pizza?"

"Of course not," they said. "The Evil One was punished."

"But surely it was the man's fault about the pizza," said Bill. "Why did they punish the Evil One for that?"

"Because it wasn't the man's fault," they said. "It was the Evil One's fault. She turned up the heat when he wasn't looking."

"Why would she do that?" asked Bill.

"You ask too many questions," they said.

●　　●

Grady was thrilled when he was done, sure he was finally getting somewhere, that this was a breakthrough at last. However, when he read it over, he thought, Fine. Good statement of the problem. But no resolution.

●　　●

Heavy curtains covered the windows, and the lights were kept on, so that Reed couldn't tell whether it was day or night.

The television was on as well, and Reed had been given some books and magazines to read. One hand was free; the other was handcuffed to the chair she sat in.

The room itself was beautiful, or nearly so—but perhaps it was just a beat off. The ceilings weren't quite high enough for the heavy period furniture, and most of the pieces were reproductions. Still, they had been chosen with care, almost certainly by a decorator. The carpet was thick and the curtains were expensive brocade—gold, not Reed's favorite color, but undeniably rich-looking.

The mantel was genuine—something that had probably been bought at auction—and so was the clock that stood on it. Above the mantel hung a dark, brooding European painting of some sort; nineteenth century, Reed thought. It had probably cost plenty, and it cast a pall of gloom on the room.

It was a room that was meant to impress, and in that it succeeded, with its ostentation if nothing else. A room you'd be thrilled to get in a bed and breakfast, say, but not one you'd necessarily want to live in—and certainly not one in which you'd wish to be handcuffed to a chair.

She was not gagged. Thinking it might help and certainly couldn't hurt, she'd screamed loud, hard, and long, to no avail. It occurred to her that the room must be soundproofed, though why it would be was beyond her.

She had nothing but questions about this situation.

A hand had gone over her mouth the minute she stepped in the gate at this house, the house where she'd followed the kidnapper.

Once inside the gate, she could see there was a porte cochere behind the wall, and cars parked there. The place was lit up as if there were a party going on, and Reed could hear voices. She was dragged to a side entrance, following the kidnapper, she thought, but she'd lost sight of Sally and could no longer hear her.

It came to her that someone was holding Sally's mouth, just as hers was being held, and the thought made her break out in a sweat, followed by a fury she couldn't contain. She whipped her shoulders back and forth and tried to kick, but the man who held her was too good—she couldn't get near him. She let her knees bend, so he'd have to drag her, but he said, "Don't make me hit you. It'll give you an awful headache," and she saw the wisdom of that.

She was taken to a back stairway, and from there she could see the kitchen, which appeared to be full of caterers hard at work. The others were stumbling ahead of her, but she still couldn't see or hear Sally.

Then she was in this room, and for a while she had been gagged as well as handcuffed. Perhaps, even if the room were soundproofed, it leaked a little. She was left here, in the dark, alone, not knowing where her child was, for an hour or two, she thought, probably until the party was over.

And then a woman came into the room, a woman of about sixty, she thought, or perhaps seventy, a stunning beauty; but terrifying. Her hair was a steely color, streaked with white so becomingly it might or might not have been natural. It was thick, and cut so that it waved and pouffed in ways Reed had seen before, that made her envious of those born with thick curls instead of fine silk.

The woman wasn't black or Creole, Reed thought, though she couldn't be sure. She was Mediterranean perhaps, but who could say in this city where anyone could be anything?

She wore a black dress with expensive jewelry and lots of it, some of it diamonds. Her face was longish, very elegant. Her mouth was red, her makeup flawless.

She was perfectly groomed, perfectly tailored, perfectly in control—a perfect dragon lady. A perfect aristocrat.

She could be a high-up corporate executive, or perhaps an ambassador from some sun-drenched country.

Or maybe she was just a department store buyer who knew how to dress.

"Who are you?" the woman asked.

"Who are you?" Reed retorted.

The woman did something with her chin, and a man, the one who had found Reed at the gate, tossed the woman a document. "No purse in the car. This is all there is."

"Dennis Foucher," read the dragon lady. "Who are you?"

Reed realized the document was Dennis's car registration.

"I don't see why I should tell you that. Where is my little girl?"

"*Your* little girl?"

"Of course my little girl. Goddammit, what's going on here?"

"Perhaps you can tell me." The Dragon did the unexpected; she smiled. "How did you come to be here?"

"How did I—" Reed stopped and looked around, speechless, gripped by the absurdity of the thing. And then the words poured out, as if she couldn't talk fast enough.

The more she talked, the grimmer the Dragon's features became.

When Reed was nearly finished, when she was at the part where she had leapt from her car, she saw a way to make an ally of the Dragon. It was the New Orleans way, the way that always got you through. "We have mutual friends," she said breathlessly. "I saw people I know leaving your house." She was beside herself in her relief. "Bruce Smallwood and La-fayette Goodyear. Barron Piggott. I saw them leaving your party."

Reed thought the Dragon flicked her eyes at the man, but otherwise she remained impassive. "I don't believe I know them," she said.

"Oh."

The Dragon said nothing.

Reed let a moment go by and then she began to plead. "Where's Sally? Where's my child? Please tell me my baby's all right."

The woman looked annoyed, as if she couldn't stand having her time wasted this way. "Of course she's all right." There was something differ-ent about her voice; it was still very definite, but a little softer.

But her face remained hard as a peach pit. She left without speaking again, and as Reed remembered the scene, she could hear the click of the Dragon's heels.

But that was impossible, the carpet was inches thick.

She didn't know how long ago that had been, but she had had two meals since then; a day must have passed, or nearly a day.

She couldn't hear anything, even telephones ringing. Not once did she catch a child's voice, even a faint high cry.

Where is Sally? What's happening to her?

The questions came up and up again, but Reed never saw harm as coming to her child, couldn't, in her heart, imagine her hurt.

She was unable to watch television or read the books and magazines; instead she thought about having Sally back, about what their life would be like when this was over.

Would Sally be scarred? Would she have nightmares? She might be afraid of people from now on, and loud noises; she might be clingy and whiny. Oh, poor, poor thing, who had been so innocent—it was so unfair.

Nothing untoward had happened to Reed. Her life as a child had been idyllic, perfect. Except for one thing, of course. How could she have forgotten?

She was transported to another room where she'd been a prisoner, a place that made her sweat and writhe to think of, where everything was white instead of gold.

Quickly, she wrenched herself out of it. She thought about her father, how he took her to the restaurant and showed her things; how he called her his "little smart girl."

She had made him a cake when she was six.

When she was a teenager she was already working at the restaurant, already planning to go to Cornell to learn how to run it. The thought of him—his smile when she did something right, his big, heavy features, the way he spoke so softly when her mother yelled at her—all that was so sad now.

She had nearly forgotten him in her fear for Sally.

Was he dead? Could he really be dead?

She hadn't seen, she had left too soon, but the answer weighed heavy inside her.

Yes, he was dead. Her dad was gone.

She cried for him now, and for her daughter, but furtively, feeling guilty and inept; worried that the Dragon would catch her.

9

Maya's house was actually an apartment not far from the bar, a large apartment with high ceilings and big rooms. Skip could see only the first two, which had once been double parlors and now seemed to serve much the same purpose. The furniture was minimal but effective. An ancient sofa had been draped with some sort of covering to make it presentable, yet a table with a wonderful antique lamp stood next to it.

It was dark, what light there was coming partly from candles, partly from very dim bulbs. All the lamps were of lacy metalwork like the ironwork on the city's balconies.

There was a table in the second room, which might sometimes have been used as a dining room—though Skip doubted it—and there were a few chairs in both rooms. The drama came from the lamps and from the walls, which were decorative by virtue of exuberantly peeling paint. A few darkish paintings hung, probably found in thrift shops.

The peeling paint may have been left that way on purpose, and the dim light, the dark paintings, were certainly for effect. But if the idea was to create a storybook den of iniquity, there were two even better effects—a slight scent of mildew under a few layers of incense, and a thick coat of dust over every surface, including the floor.

On the mantel was an altar of sorts. There were flowers and a few leaves, and a couple of framed photos, one of Marilyn Monroe, another of Tom Cruise, the logic of which was lost on Skip. There were also Mardi Gras beads, a ceramic figure Skip couldn't identify, and five or six of the colored candles poured into glass and marked for success, riches, or various saints that can be found in occult stores.

What Maya was into wasn't instantly clear, other than drama, drugs, and, very likely, some informal version of prostitution. The phrase "coke whore" came to mind.

There were a lot of people in the two rooms, ten or twelve at first glance; which one was Maya, Skip couldn't tell. What she could see was that this was a very hip scene, and biracial, which probably indicated musicians hung here. That and a couple of instrument cases. There was a good sound system, too, currently playing music with a lot of fairly subtle percussion.

The women were all young, thin—maybe a little too thin—and wearing something figure-flaunting. From what Skip could see in the dim light, they were fairly attractive, as Toni was, and had a kind of hungry look about them, as if they were looking for something but not quite sure what.

The men were less attractive. But how they fit into the world was a little unclear. They weren't young professionals. Some were probably the suspected musicians—the black ones, maybe. Others could have been waiters or bartenders or hairdressers, or small-time hustlers and thugs, or people who had smallish jobs for performers or clubs. A lot of them had a hanger-on kind of feel to them; an uneasy posturing.

Like the women, they seemed hungry, on the make; Skip wasn't sure for what, and she wasn't sure they knew.

For the most part, they were older than the women. Some were overweight, some muscular, some had a tough, streetwise look that Skip wasn't crazy about. One of them, Skip was willing to bet, paid for Maya's apartment.

A group was sitting in the living room, mostly on the floor around a coffee table. One of the women wore an unbuttoned blouse, revealing her bra. A couple of loners sat in corners, probably too loaded to socialize.

A few people stood around the table in the dining room, as if there was food there. One couple were leaning against a wall, going at it fairly heavily.

Toni said, "Damn. He's not here."

"Could he be in a bedroom or something?"

89

She shook her head. "Trust me. That's not what he's into. Let's go find Maya."

She led Skip to the dining room group, plucking at a woman in black jeans and a black, tight-fitting garment that might have passed for a T-shirt if it had been shaped remotely like a T. It was mostly Lycra and shaped a lot like the woman inside it.

"Maya, meet a friend of mine."

Maya was one of the too-thin ones. Her body looked fine in the outfit, but her face was a little gaunt, her chin and nose a little sharp, giving her a raw, unfinished look. Her hair was brown and thick, but slightly bedraggled.

However, Skip's attention was instantly riveted not by Maya, but by the woman she was talking to. It was Tricia Lattimore, her best friend from McGehee's, the exclusive private school her parents had sent her to.

Tricia had moved to New York and dropped out of Skip's life for a while. When she came back, she hadn't called. Skip found out she was back coincidentally, from the bartender at the place where Tricia waitressed.

Tricia said she hadn't called because she had a drug habit; but now she was over it.

She wasn't over it anymore.

Skip felt her face flush in fear that Tricia would blow her cover.

Just as her ears were starting to ring with panic, Tricia nodded very slightly with her chin, as if to say that was all the acknowledgment Skip was going to get. Maya didn't introduce them, but Skip said, "Hey, Tricia."

"Hey, girl." That wasn't a way Tricia normally talked.

"You know her?" Maya said, ignoring Toni and Skip. Guests were probably supposed to be prescreened.

But Toni was impatient. "Look, we don't want anything. I'm looking for Dennis—you know that guy I sent you?"

Maya was suddenly cold. "I don't think I do."

"You know. I called you about him. Has he been here?"

"Toni, you're drunk." Maya turned her back.

Skip said, "Look, he's my brother-in-law. He left my sister with two little kids." She brought out the picture, but Maya shook her head.

"I haven't seen him."

Casually, she turned to Tricia. "Have you?"

"I might have."

"Can we talk?"

Tricia nodded, and slipped out of the conversational circle. She and Skip fell back toward the wall.

Skip said, "Don't blow my cover, okay?"

Tricia nodded again, seemingly in shock; probably very loaded.

"Do you know this man?"

Tricia shook her head, still not saying anything.

"Ah. So you wanted to talk to me. I'm sorry to see you here."

Tricia looked as anguished as if she'd been caught stealing.

"Will you leave with me?"

"I can't. I haven't—" She stopped.

"You haven't scored yet."

But why not? Skip wondered. *Why not just plop her money down and get out?*

Because she doesn't have the money.

She probably has to go to bed with somebody to get her drugs.

Skip hesitated, but only for a moment. She didn't want to support a drug habit, but there were worse things. She dug in her purse. "Do you need money?"

"No. Of course not."

The light was too dim to tell for sure, but Skip had the impression Tricia's color had changed.

Her hand closed around a wad of bills. She extracted it and pressed it on Tricia. "Don't argue, Tricia. Just take it. Please."

They had been talking softly, but Tricia took a breath and Skip could see she was going to yell; it was too late to stop her. "Leave me alone, goddammit!" She threw the bills in Skip's face.

Mortified, Skip bent automatically to retrieve the money and heard a ragged sob. It was followed by a loud, "Oooooh, God!" and then Tricia was a crying machine.

She had her face down, one hand at her mouth, and Skip was trying to decide if she ought to hug her, and if so, how to do it, when Maya said, "Okay, Toni, that's it for you. Take your friend and don't ever come back. Tricia, you too."

Toni started to protest, but Maya said, "I mean it. Out."

That seemed a fine idea to Skip—the sooner the better—but she hung back a moment, as if stunned by what was happening. She wanted to see which of the men would come forward to police the eighty-sixing.

Maya turned to her and Tricia. She put an arm around Tricia's shoulders and started to guide her out. "Let's go, ladies. That's enough for tonight."

Skip glanced around. The guests were frozen in a silent tableau, watching the action. No one seemed about to participate.

She followed.

Tricia was talking low now, pleading. "Maya, I'm really sorry I lost it. Let me go out and get a breath of air and I'll be fine. I'll be back in five, okay?"

"Another time, babe. This isn't your night."

They were at the door now, Toni already outside, Maya more or less pushing Tricia out, and Skip behind. She felt movement at her back and turned around to see a man in black, dark and, at the moment, extremely unhappy-looking. Probably the one who really ran things here.

Skip said, "I'll take care of her," which caused Tricia to give her a look of flat-out hatred, but Maya stepped aside.

Skip guided the still-dazed Tricia down the steps and looked at her, about to offer to take her home. "Goddamn you, Skippy Langdon!" Tricia hollered at full capacity. "Goddamn you!"

Toni said, "Shhhhh," rather helplessly. She looked as if she'd been slugged with a crowbar.

"Come on, Toni. Let's get her out of here."

"You are not getting me out of here. I'm not going anywhere." Tricia was yelling and sobbing at the same time.

A black man stepped out of a parked car. It was Jim Hodges, Skip's backup. He only looked at her inquiringly, letting her know he was there, but giving her the option of ignoring him. She shook her head slightly; absurd though it seemed even to her, she didn't want to upset Tricia any further.

She spoke very softly, patting Tricia's back. "Hey, Trish, it's okay. Come on, I'll take you home now. Everything's okay."

"I can't go home. Don't you understand? I can't leave here. I've got to have what I came for." She sat down on the pavement and began sobbing hysterically.

Skip looked helplessly at Toni. "Listen, she's an old friend. You go on home. I'll take care of her."

But Tricia yelled, "No! Toni, help me. Where else can I go?"

Skip said to Toni: "Go." And she went.

Tricia lay down and started to roll around. "Oh, goddammit. Oh, nooooooo. Nooooooo. Oh, goddammit, noooooo."

Now there was no choice. She said, "Jim, let's get her out of here." When they bent to pick her up, she kicked and struck out with her hands.

Jim said, "You stop that now, or we gon' have to hurt you," and Skip winced.

"She's a friend of mine, Jim. If you get her legs, I'll get her arms."

He held her legs down while Skip handcuffed her. It happened so fast it was done before Tricia realized it. She turned wild eyes on her friend and hollered in amazement. "Skippy!"

"Let's get in the car."

She put up no more resistance. When they were all three in the car, Tricia in the backseat, crying softly, Skip said, "Tricia, what are you on right now?"

She shook her head violently. "Nothing! Nothing! That's the problem."

"What do you need?"

"Why do you want to know? So you can get me some?"

"I want to know if you're about to go into shock. Let me see your arms." At least she could check for needle marks.

"Oh, forget it. Nothing's wrong with me a little crystal won't fix."

Methamphetamine. Skip wasn't sure what would happen if she didn't get some. She said to Jim, "Let's take her to Charity."

"You don't have to do that. I'm fine."

For now, she looked fine and sounded fine.

"You weren't fine a minute ago."

"I got upset, that's all."

"You're sure you're okay?"

She nodded. "Yeah."

Skip had walked over to Kurt's. She said, "Jim, I'll take her home if you'll drop us at my house."

"No problem. I'll take y'all." She'd been pretty sure he'd say that. Jim was a sweetie—one of her favorite officers to work with; she knew he didn't want to leave her alone with a woman this volatile, and she was glad of it. Tricia might behave in front of a stranger.

Skip looked at Tricia. "What's your address?"

"I don't want to go home."

"Where do you want to go?"

"Here."

"Tricia, I'm talking to you as a friend, not a police officer. I'm worried about you. If you go in there right now, something might happen. Maya's got some not very nice friends. They wouldn't think twice about beating you up if you make another scene."

"That's none of your business."

Skip sighed. "I guess you're right."

She got out of the front seat, let Tricia out, and took the handcuffs off. Immediately, Tricia started to kick her. "Fuck you! Fuck you, fuck you, fuck you! How dare you handcuff me? Fuck you!"

Skip had her turned around and under control before Jim even managed to get out of the car. She pushed her up against it and cuffed her again, aware they were putting on a show for Maya and her pals.

When all three were again in the car, she said, "Okay, Jim, let's go to Charity."

"Don't want to go to Charity! Goddammit, you can't take me to Charity!"

"You listen to me, Tricia Lattimore. You just assaulted a police officer. I could take you to jail if I want to. Do you understand what you did?"

The jagged sobs started again. "Oh, goddammit. Oh, goddammit. I need Darryl. Oh, please, goddammit; take me to Darryl. Please, please, Skippy."

Darryl Boucree was Tricia's best friend, the bartender at the place where they both worked. Skip knew him well.

"What's his address? He's Uptown, isn't he? Jim, I'll take her."

"He's moved." Tricia gave them an address on Mandeville, in the Faubourg Marigny.

Jim didn't say a word, just started driving.

The house was an unusual one for the neighborhood, a raised cottage with a front porch, larger than most. Skip saw it was a double. She rang the bell on the left, and in a moment Darryl answered. He was a light-skinned black man, handsome, but that wasn't the main thing—he had a whippety kind of energy, a fast, easy charm that Skip found close to irresistible. She could see a glow in the living room, probably from candlelight. He must have a date.

"Skip. This isn't a good time."

"I've got Tricia. It's a long story, but she's way under the weather. I almost had to arrest her."

He looked as if she'd slapped him.

"Sorry to ruin your evening." She hoped she didn't sound sarcastic, but she was so unnerved she wasn't sure.

Darryl was someone important to her. He was not only a bartender, he was also an English teacher, a musician, and a member of a family she knew and liked a lot. Once, they had made tentative moves toward dating, when she wasn't sure where her relationship with Steve was going. Jimmy Dee adored him and so did Kenny. Sheila was frankly in love with him.

Skip couldn't bear to have him think ill of her.

He said, "But what are you doing *here*?"

"She wouldn't go home. She—" She stopped, unsure what to say next.

He must have seen how upset she was. "Let's go get her."

When Skip let Tricia out of the car and took the cuffs off, she began the hysterical sobbing again, but this time on Darryl's shoulder.

He looked at Skip over Tricia's wracked body and his face was inexpressibly sad. She had seen him look that way before, and it always had the same effect—it made her want to press him to her breast.

A woman stood on the porch, a young black woman, also light-skinned, with long, brownish, curly hair. She was in silhouette, but Skip had the impression she looked like a movie star.

She got back in the car.

"Are you okay?" asked Jim.

"There's nothing wrong with me a little crystal wouldn't fix."

"I'll take you to Charity."

He took her to Steve.

10

• •

Grady had gone home for a few hours to write and to get more clothes, and since his mother had company, to be away from her for a while. He was pleased with the children's story he'd written—not that it was anything he would ever be able to sell (or would even want to), but it was fiction and it wasn't about vampires, and it was a start. Toward what, he wasn't sure; maybe just away from the damned Undead. He was realizing more and more how sick he was of their everlasting blood lust.

With his father dead on the dining room floor and most of the rest of his family missing, vampires seemed a trifle superfluous, a sort of playing at gruesomeness. It came to him suddenly that he was truly done with them—that there was no going back—and that surprised him. All he had written was the tiny exercise about the planet where spaghetti grew on trees, and he had no plans for anything else. Yet he knew in that moment —when he said good-bye to the vampires—that there would be something else. He just didn't know what.

That was frightening. Writing was safe because it wasn't life. If he didn't know what to write, he couldn't write now, and if he couldn't write, how could he keep reality at bay?

There's the House of Blues, of course. And alcohol.

But if I stay out late and drink, then I won't feel like working tomorrow.

The thing was, he wanted to get on with it, he wanted to do it, whatever it was.

The only thing to do is gut it out.

He turned on his computer and sat in front of it, a quote he had once heard flitting through his head. It was a recipe for successful writing: "Sit staring at paper until drops of blood form on forehead."

If that's what it takes, I'll do it.

But his mother came over.

Nonplussed, he let her in. "Are you all right?"

"I just wanted to see if *you're* all right."

"Why wouldn't I be?" She never came to Race Street.

"I don't know. You know how I'm kind of psychic sometimes. I thought maybe you were feeling a little down."

"Can I get you something? I have tea and beer."

She seemed to consider. "Maybe just some water."

He got her water and himself a beer, which might interfere with the writing, but it didn't look like that was happening anyway. "Mother, you know I'll be over there soon. You should have waited for me. You're moving around too much for someone who's—um, bereaved." He was shocked at himself—shocked that he couldn't even say "lost her husband" or "widowed."

"People are supposed to come to you," he said.

"Well, I was kind of passing by."

"Nina told me you were at the restaurant today. Don't you think you should leave that alone for a while? I don't see how you can even think straight with all this going on."

"Well, Grady, somebody's got to do it—a restaurant just doesn't run itself."

"Mother, no one expects you to be down there right now. And Nina's got years of experience. She can handle it."

"Grady, I'm going to ask you something. You know I don't intrude on you and your relationships—I'm always *very* careful about that—but I'm going to ask you something about Nina."

Oh, Lord. Here we go.

"Why does she hate me? What possible reason does she have to treat me like she does?" Here, as Grady had known she would, Sugar teared up. He went to get her a tissue.

"I'm sure she doesn't hate you, Mother."

"Yes, she does. It's evident in all her dealings with me. She treats me like I haven't got good sense."

"She's got a lot on her mind right now, with Dad and Reed gone."

"She ought to think about the fact that I'm her boss."

"You're her boss?" Grady hadn't even begun to consider that.

"I'm your father's heir."

"But Reed—"

"Reed's not here, Grady."

"Well, look, I wouldn't worry about Nina. She does a good job and you shouldn't let her get under your skin."

"I don't think she's doing such a good job. I went in there today and she wouldn't even order crabmeat! Can you imagine Hebert's without crab? People are going to quit coming if they try to order all our famous dishes and they get told they don't even exist."

"Mother, the dishes exist, we just don't have them every day."

"I think she was just being contrary. She doesn't like me, so she has to contradict everything I say."

Grady had gotten Nina's phone message about Sugar: "If you can't keep that woman out of the restaurant, there's not going to *be* any Hebert's."

He said: "You've got to remember she has a lot of experience. I think my inclination would be to defer to her."

"Well, I wouldn't mind deferring if she just wouldn't be so mean to me. She hates my guts, Grady, and I don't know why." She was getting teary again.

"Mother, you always have an enemy. No matter where you end up, it's always somebody." He regretted it the minute he said it.

She looked utterly bewildered. "What do you mean by that?"

"Nothing. I'd appreciate it if you wouldn't talk to me about Nina, that's all. I think you know how I feel about her."

"No. I don't."

"You know we saw each other for a while."

"You're still in love with her."

Glad to have distracted her, he tried for an answer that might elicit her maternal concern, a bonding sort of answer that might also have been true, he wasn't sure. "I guess I am," he said.

"Well, she isn't in love with you." There was malice in her voice, all the nasty triumph of a child delivering a hurtful riposte.

He felt the usual anger rise up, felt the way he was used to feeling when she said something mean, but it was only a flash.

It's just how she is, he thought, if not with resignation, then with something close to it; with something approaching calm. Perhaps his father's death was having the effect deaths are supposed to have, that of making much of life seem trivial.

He wasn't about to respond to the content of what she had said, and couldn't think how to answer the tone. Perhaps his silence told her she had gone too far, that she ought to backtrack. She said in a softer voice, "Into each life some rain must fall."

He hated her clichés. Again he didn't answer.

"I've been unlucky in love too, Grady. It was one of my greatest sorrows when your father turned against me."

Oh, no.

"It was love at first sight, you know. He was so different then."

"Mother, please don't tell me."

Tears flowed out of her eyes, as much on cue as if he'd turned a faucet. "I don't have anybody to talk to. My own son—"

See a shrink, dammit. But he said, "It's just painful, that's all. If you really need to talk, go ahead."

Wimp.

"We met on a blind date—did you know that?"

He shook his head, stunned that he hadn't known it, that it wasn't a piece of family mythology. His parents had never talked about such things.

"I was a senior at Sacred Heart and he was already in college. He was a junior at LSU, home for Christmas vacation. I couldn't believe someone like me got to go out with someone like him."

Grady's curiosity was piqued. "What were you like?"

"Well, I was naive."

"What else?"

"I guess I was pretty."

"Come on, Mother—you *had* to have been pretty."

"Well, I was considered rather . . . pretty."

Suddenly he saw her through his father's eyes: blond with big tits.

"And he was . . ."

"Worldly?"

"More than that."

"Well, what?"

She looked uncomfortable. Finally, she shrugged, apparently deciding there was only one way to say it. "He was Arthur Hebert."

"What did that mean?" He thought he knew full well.

"There was nobody like him in New Orleans. When I saw him in that coat and tie, hair slicked back, so tall and everything, I thought I'd swoon. We went to a fraternity party, and I had my first drink. Can you imagine? I just never dreamed I could marry somebody like that. Then when the children were young . . ." She stopped and started to cry again. This time he waited her out, wondering about her odd reference to "the children"—probably she was talking to herself more than to him.

"We were so happy, Grady. You can't imagine how happy we were. You were the cutest little boy and your father just loved you so much. And then a few years later, I don't know, this mean streak came out."

She had never talked like this. He said, "You saw it too?"

"Saw it! Of course I saw it. He started treating me like a servant."

"Oh. Did he change toward other people?" Meaning himself.

"Other people? How should I know? All I know is one day we were in love and the next day he hated me. He just turned against me, right in midstream."

"When was it, do you remember?"

"I don't know when I first noticed it. It must have happened gradually. All I know is one day I woke up and I had no husband."

"Do you think it had anything to do with what happened?"

The Thing.

They never spoke of it. Grady's heart pounded.

"What do you mean 'with what happened'?"

"You know. At the restaurant that day; that time. On Sunday." *Don't make me name it.* He couldn't; he was quite sure he couldn't get the words out.

"Oh. No, of course not. In fact, we were close for a while after that, and then he went back to treating me like dirt again. He just turned against me, that's all. One day, he up and turned against me. My own husband."

She could probably get a golden retriever to turn against her—or at least she could convince herself that it had.

"And then he turned you against me," she said.

"What?"

"My own children. I know the way he talked about me. What am I talking about? Usually he did it in front of my face. He made you hate me."

"Mother, you know that isn't true."

She was sobbing, sunk in such a swamp of self-pity it would take a crane to pull her out of it.

"Do you think *Reed* hates you?"

"Once he turned against me, then he just didn't care, that's all. He had all the mistresses he wanted—slept with everybody in town and didn't care who knew it."

"Did he?" Grady had never heard a whiff of it, and he didn't like to think of himself as naive.

"Well, if you didn't know, that's a blessing, that's all I can say about it. I've been thinking about what happened the other night, Grady."

"What happened the other night." A new euphemism for those madcap Heberts.

"He did the same thing to one of his women that he did to me—and she killed him for it. But she didn't think Reed and Dennis and Sally would be there, so she had to kidnap them."

Was this possible? If Arthur was a philanderer, he supposed it was, but most of Sugar's stories were cut from whole cloth. And he didn't want to say it, but he thought killing the Fouchers would have been a better solution than kidnapping.

"See, she thought if she kidnapped them, then it would look like some kind of mob thing or—you know—something criminal."

Grady hooted involuntarily. "Not that," he said, for a moment almost enjoying himself.

Even Sugar saw the humor of it. She smiled. "Well, you know what I mean. A cover-up." Her cheeks were flushed with the thrill of the chase— Sugar liked nothing better than to be on the trail of some crackpot theory or other.

"Who do you think the woman is?"

"Whoever he just dumped. How hard could that be to find out?"

Grady suddenly saw how much mischief she could make if she took it into her head to do it. "Mother," he began, "you've really got to cool your heels."

● ●

Sugar drove back to Reed and Dennis's alone, stewing.

Grady wanted to write for a while.

Write. Sure.

The great artist was going to spend the evening kidding himself as usual.

How dare he try to talk me out of trying to find out who killed my husband? If not me, then who?

She was good at this—when her children were sick, she always knew what was wrong with them before the doctor did. If Grady cried a certain way, for instance, she knew he had an ear infection. Being a mother was detective work—figuring things out.

Who does he think he is, trying to lecture me? He could never do anything right—Arthur always had to help him. And now that he's grown up, he'll never amount to anything.

Her mouth set in a hard line as she realized she was for the first time facing the truth about her son: Grady was a ne'er-do-well.

I'll always have to help him, always have to be Mama, just like it always was. My little boy's not growing up. Ever.

Her mouth relaxed. This was something she knew how to do, something with which she was comfortable.

He was such a precious little boy, and absolutely the apple of his daddy's eye. But we spoiled him, I guess—he just doesn't think it's up to him to make his own way in the world.

Nina must have dumped him because he's so worthless. He's always going to need my help. Always, always.

He's never going to find a woman of his own.

• •

Grady was trying to get her on paper, but he didn't think he understood her well enough.

What drives her? What's she about?

Don't try to answer that. Just tell her story.

But what was her story? What could have made her so insecure? So paranoid.

Was something medically wrong with her? Was there a chemical imbalance? Something like that seemed the only explanation.

Just tell what happened when. Like that time we went to Florida.

He was six at the time and he had dived happily into a swimming pool, only to feel the horrible sensation of last year's bathing suit coming off his bottom. The elastic, rotten from drying in the sun, had snapped on impact. He cried out but, being underwater, swallowed a bucket or so of water. He came up coughing; drowning, he thought.

He panicked, not knowing what to do next.

So he started crying, crying and coughing at the same time, not really caring whether he drowned or not, just afraid he wouldn't get his trunks back before it was too late.

"What is it, son?" his father had yelled, and about that time arms had closed around him, and he realized he was being rescued—by a heavyset woman his mother's age.

"No!" he screamed. And he fought and kicked, because if she pulled him out, everyone would see him naked.

"Goddamn brat," she said, and let go.

His father laughed. Sat on the side of the swimming pool and laughed while Grady coughed and struggled. Later, he said it was because Grady's trunks had come floating up and he'd caught on to what the problem was.

But while his father laughed at him, Sugar had dived in and pulled him out, apparently not even noticing he was naked. "No! No!" he yelled, and again kicked and struggled, but she was a mom saving her kid and she wasn't letting go.

Once she got him out of the water, he jumped back in again, sure he was blushing all over, crying as if he'd broken all ten toes.

His dad was still laughing his head off.

Grady held onto the side of the pool so tightly his fingers turned white, but he was crying too hard to ask for his trunks, and his dad was laughing too hard to mention them.

Sugar, furious and bewildered that he'd wriggled out of her grasp, was yelling at him: "Grady, what's wrong with you?"

Finally, another swimmer saw the trunks, grasped the situation, and gave them to Sugar, Grady still being too upset to be distracted.

That afternoon, Sugar took him shopping for a new bathing suit, and as they were leaving the store, he nearly fell down on the escalator, but Sugar grabbed him.

"What's wrong, Grady?"

"I stumbled."

"Why did you stumble?"

"I don't know. I just stumbled."

"Well, there must have been some reason."

"I just stumbled, Mama."

That night when the family was together, she told the story of Grady's falling and asked Arthur if he had any opinions. "You're the expert," he said.

"I just don't understand it," she said. "He's never done that before."

The more Grady thought about the incident, now, his computer before him, the more confusing he found it. Some of it was predictable—his father's cruelty, his mother's strange thought patterns—but he couldn't see that writing it down was going to solve anything.

However, he had a deal with himself.

He sat.

And then he wrote.

As long as he wrote he was fine, but when he stopped to think about it, he got so anxious it was nearly all he could do not to reach for a beer to calm down.

He understood these things—the confusion; the anxiety. He was used to them. What he didn't understand was how it was possible to be like Reed.

Never confused. Impatient with those who were.

Perfect.

Why couldn't it have been me?

11

• •

First thing in the morning, Skip trooped up to Narcotics, where she found her pal Lefty O'Meara chewing on his habitual unlighted cigar and just hanging up the phone. A smear of shaving cream decorated his right ear.

"Hey, Skip. You're gonna make me work—you've got that look."

"I just want to know if you know somebody. Heroin dealer named Turan."

"Oh, Turan. He's dealin' boy? I thought he was into girl."

"What's going on here? Am I in Vice or Narcotics? This guy's not a pimp, he's a dealer."

Lefty laughed. "Funny, ain't it? I heard some guy make a buy like that the other day—'two boys and one girl.' 'Member, you heard it here first."

"Girl's coke?"

"Yeah, I guess. Turan used to be a girl kind of boy. What's this heroin shit?"

"You're supposed to be the expert."

O'Meara shrugged. "Who knows about these dudes? Come on, let's get his record."

They moved over to the division's one computer and O'Meara fed the

105

monster a name: Turan Livaudais. It spat stats: Turan had a lot of arrests and one conviction; from the dates, he'd been a bad actor all his life, which, according to the sheet, was only twenty-four years along.

"Let's see the address," said O'Meara, and frowned. "Nah, that can't be right. I've got to make a couple of calls. I'll call you in ten."

"Thanks, Lefty. I really appreciate it."

"By the way, did you ever find Delavon? I axed around—couple guys heard the name, but nobody knows who he is."

"We talked, but I forgot to get a list of his aliases."

She was sure O'Meara'd get the address; it was the kind of cop he was. He was still a patrolman, had probably never even taken the sergeant's test, or maybe couldn't pass it for one reason or another. But he was one of the best policemen in the department—competent but not flamboyant. If he said he'd do something, he would.

She spent the next hour on the phone, calling everyone she knew who knew who anyone else was who might know anything about Dennis, or drugs, or even Reed. It was a highly tedious and unproductive exercise, but it had to be done.

About ten o'clock, desperate to hear a friendly voice—and also needing to talk about something—she called Cindy Lou and asked her to lunch. She was just starting to wonder what had happened to Lefty when he called.

"Hey, I got your address. Sort of."

"What's this 'sort of'?"

"Iberville Project. That's the best I can do. He deals out of the Conti Breezeway, always after ten o'clock at night—could be any time, like one A.M., two A.M., you never know."

"Oh, happy day." She was already exhausted from her late evening at Maya's.

She had gotten past that, and was thinking how conspicuous she was going to look, hanging around the Iberville, when O'Meara said, "You know about the Tidewater Building?"

"Know what about it?"

"You can see everything in the Iberville from the roof."

"Lefty, you're a prince. I owe you one."

She got some coffee and hit the streets with the picture of Dennis and Reed. By twelve-thirty she was hot and discouraged. She headed for the Thai restaurant where she and Cindy Lou were meeting.

Cindy Lou was a little late and, by the time she arrived, a bit bedraggled, unusual for her. "Too damn hot," she said. "I should have stayed in Detroit."

"I hear it's lovely in summer too."

"I think I'm having a beer."

"What's wrong? Something's wrong."

"Nothing's wrong." She spoke so sharply Skip said nothing. "Yeah, something is. I had a message on my machine last night. He's going back to Detroit."

"The guy? The one you like?"

"It wouldn't have worked out, right? How could it? I mean, no sex; come on."

"It seems a little cold to leave a message."

Cindy Lou pointed a manicured finger at Skip. "Thank you." She studied the menu a moment. Skip didn't bother. She always got whatever crawfish dish was on the menu—today, eggplant and crawfish.

"I mean I never expected it to work out," said Cindy Lou. "That's not my thing."

"You just hate feeling like chopped liver."

"Thank you."

They gave their orders and sipped tea. Skip considered the virtues of letting Cindy Lou talk it out, but on the whole she figured there wasn't that much to say—it was about the shortest duration of any of her friend's relationships, which were notorious for their brevity; therefore, despite the ancient connection, it had probably been no more than a spark.

"Listen, Lou-Lou—first of all, do you hate being called that?"

"I kind of like it, actually—but don't tell Jimmy Dee."

"Good. Look, I've got to tell you about something."

"The case? Things didn't go well last night?"

"Things went a lot better than I hoped—I met someone who'd seen the person I'm looking for; and better yet, sent him to a sort of upscale crack house, which she took me to." She broke off and shuddered. "Thoroughly revolting scene."

"You didn't find him, I gather."

"No, but I did find someone."

"Uh-oh."

"I need to talk to you about it, but the thing is, it's kind of a touchy subject."

"Hey, I'm the police shrink. It's okay to talk to me."

"The problem is, this is personal."

"Oh. A friend."

"Yes, but that's not the problem. It's that her dad's a former friend of yours."

"Oh, my God. Tricia Lattimore." In a moment of ridiculously poor judgment, even by Cindy Lou's standards, she had dated Tricia's still-married father. It had been one of her longer relationships, and as far as Skip could see, she'd cared about him. "Her dad told me she had a drug problem."

"She did, but she was supposedly over it. I ran into her at the Monkey Bar—the place where Darryl Boucree works."

"Oh, yeah. The Butterfly Man."

"Oh, Lou-Lou, he is not." For reasons Skip couldn't fathom, Cindy Lou had taken a dislike to Darryl on grounds that he was lightweight. "He works three jobs and supports his kid; he brings over presents for Sheila and Kenny. He's a perfectly decent guy."

Lou-Lou sniffed. "I know him. He's a type."

"Anyway, Tricia was waiting tables and looking fine—she told me she'd had a habit and she was over it."

"Either she lied or she couldn't stay clean. What's she doing?"

"You mean what drug? Crystal, she said. And a lot, I guess. She acted kind of crazy."

"So she'll be doing some kind of downer as well—could be alcohol. Probably is, with something else. Valium, maybe."

"You mean she's got three different addictions?"

Cindy Lou shrugged. "It's all part of the same thing. She's in deep. Her dad used to worry like crazy about her."

"Yeah, well, me too now."

"Do you know the statistics? They say in AA you have to be sober three years before you have an even chance of staying that way."

"But she's such a wonderful person. She's a writer."

"I thought she was a waitress."

"She isn't published yet."

Cindy Lou snorted. "Why do you suppose that is?"

"Come on, Lou-Lou. Help me. You know the family situation—"

"I know it's fucked up."

"Should I call her dad?" She hesitated. "And her mom? Isn't there something called an intervention?"

"I don't know, Skip; I just don't know. Or let me put it another way—I know things you probably don't; things her dad told me. I don't think intervention's a good idea."

Skip was dying to ask her what she knew, but she had no business knowing and Cindy Lou wouldn't tell anyway. She sighed, overcome by a sudden feeling of hopelessness. She said, "Okay. Let's talk about my case."

Cindy Lou looked relieved. Because she was a consultant to the New Orleans Police Department, Skip was free to tell her anything she wanted, and to ask for her assistance.

When she had run down the case, she said, "Dennis was supposed to be a pillar of AA too."

"Well, he had a shock."

"Do he and Reed seem an odd match to you?"

Cindy Lou looked placid. "Of course not. Codependent and druggie. What could be more perfect?"

"That's what Nina said."

"She sounds like a smart cookie."

"But Reed sounds so damned perfect. It just seems like she wouldn't let herself be with someone like that."

"You forget—he isn't 'like that,' or at least he wasn't. She reformed him—evidence of her very perfection."

Skip felt oddly unsatisfied. "People are weird."

"You're not kidding. If they weren't, I'd be out of a job."

That tickled Skip. "So would I."

"Uh-uh. People are bad. That's what keeps you employed."

"Miss Cynical."

"Don't get me wrong, they're good too. Usually both things in the same body."

"Usually?"

"Okay, always. It's the ones who don't cop to the bad part who keep you in business. Most of us know what evil lurks—and we control it. But if you decide you deserve what you can get by dealing dope or maybe you're some kind of missionary, or even that you're above all that, and what you do is okay because other people deserve what they get, then you're dangerous."

"Delavon."

"Who's that?"

"Somebody I hope you never meet—because he's so truly rotten to the core, you'd probably fall desperately in love."

"Uh-uh, I don't like criminals; just creeps."

"And the utterly unavailable. With any luck at all on my part, Delavon's going to get fifty or so years someday—what could be more perfect for you?"

Cindy Lou smiled. "I have to admit it has merit."

●　●

Skip was dog-tired on account of her late night at Maya's, and she could feel another all-nighter in the works. She wanted to go home and get some sleep, but it was time to report to her sergeant.

Cappello was glad to see her. "Skip. Making progress with the heater case? I'm still gettin' calls."

Skip raised an eyebrow. "Joe?" Joe Tarantino, their lieutenant.

"No, not Joe. Just a bunch of assholes who're probably on the take and need somebody to make them look good. Can you believe this stuff in the paper?"

"What stuff? I didn't see the paper this morning."

"Not one, not two, but three great items. First, the policeman O'Rourke's platoon arrested for murder. What a department. Then the vice squad hearings."

Several members of the vice squad were accused of raiding French Quarter joints, then when all the strippers and barkers were outside, helping themselves to the contents of the cash registers.

Skip winced. "I hate that one a lot. Not just bad and stupid, but crude."

"Then there's this new stuff about that security firm run by our favorite high-ranking officer. You know: the one with the fancy cars and the Armani suits."

Skip named him. "What about his firm?"

"It seems he got booked in by some production companies making movies here and they say he charged them for equipment the department normally lends out."

"But the city got the money, of course."

Cappello laughed. "Oh, sure it did. And that wasn't the whole thing—they also claim he overcharged them for people's hours, and what really fries me, that he booked officers to work on those jobs who were scheduled to be working for the department at the same time."

"A little double-dipping; very Louisiana."

Cappello snorted. "Don't you ever get tired of this shit?"

Skip sat down, nonplussed once again at Cappello's frustration. "Well, yeah, I get tired of it. But we don't even know if that one's true. Nobody's proved it, right?"

"Skip, Skip, Skip. In what other city does this kind of stuff even come up?"

She didn't know what to say that would make Cappello feel any better.

But the sergeant was on a roll. "I bet half the cops in this building are on the take."

"Oh, come on."

"I mean it. You've got to remember the mob *started* here."

"A lot of Italian-Americans would dispute you on that."

"Oh, hell, I'm Italian myself. What I'm saying is, we've got a history here. This casino business has stirred things up like I haven't seen since I came on the job. When the bottom fell out of oil, nobody had any money and no way to make any. Now there's big bucks in town; big things at stake. The state was crazy to say they'd keep the mob out. Maybe the operators aren't mob, but the town's suddenly crawling with characters you wouldn't want to meet in a dark alley."

"Hey, that reminds me. I met this unsavory dude who tells me Gus Lozano's on his way out."

"Mr. Kingpin? No shit?" She shrugged. "Well, it makes sense. There's a lot of new guys in town, all of them probably wanting hunks of Gus's pie. Anyway, what's the difference? The new guy might not be named Gus, but he'll be his twin brother. He'll buy some cops and we'll have to work with 'em. Sleeping with the enemy as usual."

Skip tried to think of something to say.

"I've got to get out of here," said Cappello. "I don't know how long I can take this."

"Uh, you want to know about the heater case?"

"Oh, yeah. Work."

"I found someone who's seen Dennis." She ran it down for the sergeant, and told her what she planned to do that night—go find Turan.

"Take Hodges," said Cappello. "He's good and steady."

"Why not? We had a good time last night."

She went home, hoping Cappello would pipe down sometime soon. It wasn't that she didn't sympathize with her; it was that she didn't like her talk of leaving. Skip liked being on Cappello's platoon, and there were other sergeants she didn't much care for—like Frank O'Rourke.

Oh, well. She could get transferred out as easily as she could leave. So could I for that matter.

Every time a new mayor got in, there was a new superintendent, and sometimes there was one in between terms if he embarrassed the department too badly. Each new superintendent did what he pleased; seemingly random transfers had happened before and could happen again.

Skip had stepped in the shower that morning without washing her hair, forgoing beauty in favor of extra sleep. But after a day in the sauna that was New Orleans in summer, it was a mop of wet nasty curls she couldn't wait to deluge. After that a nap would go down well, alongside Steve Steinman if he was home.

But when she opened her door, a great, fanged, snarling beast leapt at her.

Steve said, "Napoleon! Easy, boy! Hey, it's okay." But he seemed to be somewhere in Kansas and there was a large dripping muzzle in Skip's face, a hot smelly one, and jaws that clipped together every time the creature barked, which was about eight times a second.

She had already stepped back involuntarily, past her own threshold, and now stood in the courtyard, which the beast seemed to be willing to concede to her, as long as it could have the house.

"Napoleon. Hey, boy. That's Skip; our good friend, Skip. Hey, boy, take it easy now."

The thing was a German shepherd, she saw now, and she also saw that Steve was holding it by the collar. She had heard barking when she arrived, she realized that also, she just hadn't put it together that it was in her house.

"What the hell is that creature doing in my house?"

"You're mad?"

"Mad? Wouldn't you be if you came home and found the hound of hell in your living room? Which is probably now covered with hair and God knows what else."

"He's for Kenny. Easy, boy. Hey, Napoleon. She's a friend, okay? Skip, hold out your hand so he can sniff it."

"Are you crazy? That thing just tried to kill me."

"Well, I admit that was a little disconcerting. Maybe you remind him of someone."

"He reminds me of somebody too. Cerberus. The Hound of the Baskervilles. The monster in every movie I saw before I was ten."

The dog was starting to calm down, but Skip was having a delayed reaction. She felt slightly shaky, and didn't want to admit it.

"Nice dog," said Steve. "Go say hello to Skip."

"Listen, how about if you take him for a walk while I go in and take a shower? Then you can leave him in the courtyard while you tell me what the hell this is all about."

"Well, uh . . ."

"What?" She was almost inconceivably tired, it was ninety in the shade, her hands were still shaking, and she was getting madder by the minute.

"He just pooped in the kitchen."

She brushed a handful of sticky curls back from her face and started silently counting, but she only made it to three. If she ever got this mad on the job, she hated to think what could happen. "You take that creature out of here, and by the time I get out of the shower he better be Rin Tin Tin and you better have my kitchen clean."

"Okay, okay. I just have to get his leash."

As she wasn't about to walk by those fast-snapping teeth, that meant she had to wait another century or two before she could go into her own home. When she did, the smell of fresh dogshit greeted her.

She stayed in the shower about half an hour—at any rate, longer than she ever had, because the water was starting to go tepid, which it never had before.

When she came out, she pulled on a light cotton robe and lay down on the bed, feeling slightly better, especially since she heard sounds that sounded like cleaning up down below.

In a while Steve joined her. "I'm sorry. I didn't know you didn't like dogs."

She sat up. "I don't like dogs? Excuse me—there's a big difference in not liking dogs and being attacked in my own home."

"He's for Kenny. For that little problem he has."

She was bewildered. "What?"

"He needs a friend. So I got him one—a nice fuzzy one."

"Wait a minute. You think you can cure Kenny of bed-wetting by siccing Cujo on him? What do you plan to do—*scare* the piss out of him?"

"I just think having a dog will make him feel secure."

"Haven't you noticed that animal is vicious?"

"He just doesn't like you, that's all."

"Doesn't like me! He nearly tore my throat out. Well, look, let's say for a minute that he's just the most precious little pooch and Kenny loves him to death. What do you think Jimmy Dee's going to think?"

"Jimmy Dee?"

"Yes, Jimmy Dee. The kid's uncle and guardian. Have you noticed how absolutely fabulous he made that house, just for those kids? How do you think he's going to like the last of the timber wolves leaping up on the dining room table and scarfing the pasta?"

"Jimmy Dee," Steve said again, as if he'd just heard of him for the first time.

"Did you get that thing from the pound?"

"Yes. Why?"

"Okay, well, Kenny's going to ask that too. So here's how it's going to go—assuming we don't have to pump Napoleon's stomach to get Kenny out. Meaning this is the *best* case scenario.

"Kenny and Napoleon fall in love. But Jimmy Dee says he can't have the dog. So then he knows Napoleon's got to go back to the pound, where he's going to meet a horrible end. How do you think that's going to make him feel?"

"God, you're being nasty."

She was, and she knew it. But somehow she just couldn't stop. "Nasty! I just came home to a mouth full of teeth and a kitchen full of shit. Anyway, I can't get over how thoughtless you were about this."

"Thoughtless! Nobody else is doing anything for Kenny."

"That isn't fair and you know it."

"You have the nerve to tell *me*—oh shit, listen."

Skip heard children's voices. "Where'd you put Napoleon?"

"In the courtyard. Tied up. Don't worry."

By now the dog had set up a racket. Without another word, Steve went tearing downstairs. Skip stopped to pull on a pair of shorts and a T-shirt.

She arrived in the courtyard to find a young man on the ground with Sheila bending over him, Steve holding Napoleon and looking grim, and Kenny staring wide-eyed, holding out a hand for the dog to sniff.

Napoleon's tail began to wag. A pink tongue came out and licked Kenny's hand. Gaining confidence, Kenny began to pet the dog's massive head. Napoleon snuggled into the caress as if he'd died and gone to heaven.

Sheila said, "You're sure you're okay?" and began helping her friend up.

The boy looked as if he had the flu.

"What's happening?" said Skip.

Sheila put a hand on her hip, outraged. "He attacked Emery."

Emery. Sheila's new boyfriend—or what passed for a boyfriend in the eighth grade. She'd better try to make amends, Skip thought, and held out her hand. "I'm Skip. He doesn't like me either."

The boy managed a weak smile, but Sheila scowled.

Steve had by now let go of Napoleon's collar, and Kenny was caressing his chest and back, petting him all over as reverently as if the dog were a unicorn with whom he'd been granted an audience.

Emery continued to stare round-eyed at the animal. Finally, he blurted, "I think I'd better go home."

"But Emery," Sheila said, and her eyes locked with his. She saw the futility of protest and stopped in mid-whine. "I'm sorry this happened." She sounded so polite and grown-up, Skip was bowled over.

Sheila walked him back to the street, and when she returned, she hissed, "What is that animal doing here?" Her eyes meant war. Skip couldn't believe this was the same Sheila who only the night before had asked Steve not to go back to California. Now she hated him.

Steve glanced guiltily at Skip. "He's a provisional pet. I mean, he *could* be a pet if Uncle Jimmy agreed."

Kenny stared at Steve like an actor in one of those movies in which island natives think a shipwrecked man is god. "You got him for us?"

"Well, a boy needs a dog, don't you think?"

Sheila said, "Do you know what you just did to me? I'm probably never going to see Emery again." Tears were starting.

Steve grinned. "Napoleon really didn't like him, did he?"

She started to sob. "I didn't want a dog, I wanted a cat."

Kenny stared at her, astonished.

"I don't see why I can't have a cat."

A voice came from the side of the house. "Anybody home?" They heard metal against metal as Jimmy Dee unlocked the gate.

Napoleon started barking as if the Huns were invading. Steve grabbed his collar again.

They heard Sheila say, "Uncle Jimmy, if Kenny can have a dog, why can't I have a cat?"

"If Kenny can what?" Jimmy Dee came into view and proved the third person that day who reminded Napoleon of someone. The dog strained against his collar until he choked, slobbering, barking, growling, and showing his shark-sized teeth once again. Skip prayed Steve would be able to hang on.

"This is Kenny's?" said Jimmy Dee.

Kenny said, "Isn't he beautiful?" and Skip wished fervently that she'd die in the next two minutes.

Steve did lose his grip, and Napoleon launched himself toward Jimmy Dee rather like a Patriot rocket, but he stopped about an inch away from Dee-Dee's face.

Showing the famous grace under pressure, Jimmy Dee, unlike Skip and

Emery, did not lose his cool. "Would someone," he said, "please call the zoo?"

Kenny understood instantly that heaven, which had arrived so unexpectedly, was about to be snatched away. He sank down on the flagstones and simply stared at the ground. Skip thought she'd never seen anyone look so miserable.

When she thought things couldn't get any worse, he said, "He's going to die, isn't he?"

12

• •

Jim Hodges was quite a bit older than Skip, which could have intimidated her but didn't—hadn't, right from the start. Skip was young, she was from Uptown, and she already had an enemy in Homicide when she was transferred in. Because Frank O'Rourke never missed an opportunity to make her feel green, incompetent, and out of place, she was wary at first, had been wary a long time—but she'd always been okay with Hodges.

He wasn't a great conversationalist, wasn't the kind of cop who loved to tell stories and jokes—in fact, he didn't socialize much, even in the office. It might have been because he was one of the few black officers in the detective bureau. Or maybe he was just that way. Cappello was; so was Skip herself.

"Do the job and go home," Cappello had told her once. "Don't take it with you. You'll be a better cop for it."

Whatever the reason, Hodges was one of the best—cool, quick on his feet, there when you needed him. Skip found him a genuinely nice man as well—a kind man. But maybe that just went with being a consummate professional; thinking about his partner's needs; the needs of the people he dealt with on the job.

117

Most policemen were on the job because they wanted to help. It was the number one reason they gave for becoming cops. Skip's reasons had been different, had much more to do with the fact that the work simply suited her, suited a six-foot woman with a lot of energy. But she figured Hodges might fall into the helper category. He was a tough cop, but he was still a gentle man.

Working with him was like having a twin, a part of yourself that knew what you needed before you did. She hoped she was as good a partner as he.

When they had scrounged a car—not the easiest thing these cheeseparing days—Jim said, "What are you thinking? We going over to the Tidewater roof?"

"Now how'd you know that?"

"I've been around awhile. You forget that?" He laughed. "Yeah. I've really been around awhile."

Skip laughed too. "Oh, come on. You're just a youngster."

The Tidewater was on Canal Street, and Skip was astounded by the view it afforded. The only thing was, they were too far away to see anyone's face, especially in the dark.

So what to do? Head in if they saw a white man? She didn't think they could even tell at this distance, and she knew they wouldn't have enough time to get there.

"This isn't going to work," Hodges said.

"You're telling me."

"I'm going to have to go in there."

Skip sighed. "Yeah."

"Damn good thing Cappello gave you a black backup."

"Oh, who needs you? I could have come in disguise."

"Yeah. Some cornrows and pancake; that'd prob'ly do it."

He laughed at the silliness of it.

She said, "You got a pocket phone?"

"Yeah. You?"

"I'll get one—let me use yours."

He produced his and she dialed Jimmy Dee. "Dee-Dee, do me a favor, will you? Lend me your cute little phone."

"What's wrong? That jerry-built cop shop doesn't have any?"

"Are you kidding? It took us half an hour to find a car that works. Put it in a cab and send it to the Tidewater building; could you?"

"Okay. But the monster's got to be out of here by noon."

"Steve or Napoleon?"

"Hey, the dog can stay if you'll send the other one back."

"How's Kenny?"

"Put it this way—I've got clean sheets at the ready."

She hung up, feeling glum; Steve had probably made things worse.

While they waited for the phone, Jim said, "How do you want to work it? How about I go in and loiter while you wait in the car? Seems pretty straightforward to me."

"I don't know; I'm starting not to like this. You're supposed to be *my* backup."

"Yeah, but there's a little problem. You're white po-lice. Face it, Skip. It's the only way to play it."

"We could both stay in the car."

"We can't park close enough to see what's going on. Turan's going to be in the Conti Breezeway, but that doesn't mean Dennis has to walk in from the street. He could enter the project at one of the other breezeways, for instance. Or he could drive in."

The Iberville's "breezeways" were park areas between rows of red-brick buildings now grim with age and abuse and neglect—and memories, probably, and the busted-up dreams of busted-up families, or families that had never happened, that had started out as pregnant teenagers and grown into young mothers of three or four, strung out on crack and turning tricks to get it.

Children should have played in the breezeways, and did, sometimes. They should have functioned as village greens. But dealers dealt in these open spaces, and blood flowed there. Almost every day the *Times-Pica-yune* reported the body of a young black male found in the courtyard of one of the city's projects. If someone wanted to kill you, he had a clear shot here.

Once you were actually in the breezeway, you were a sitting duck. This was Skip's problem with the plan. She really thought about the "disguise" she'd suggested so facetiously, but people would never have left her alone, would have tried to talk to her. She'd have been made in about thirty seconds.

"What are you going to say? Who are you?"

"Are you kidding? I'm looking for James. My brother. Let's stop here a minute."

He pulled up at a convenience store on Rampart. "Wait for me."

Skip waited, annoyed at the way he seemed to be taking over her assignment. He came back with a bottle of Thunderbird. "You drive awhile."

Skip took the wheel while he perfumed himself. He was wearing jeans and a dark T-shirt, but his hair was short and neat. At least he didn't wear glasses.

"James, he stay at Placenta house. You know Placenta? She stay over there, don't she?"

"Jim, give me a break. Nobody's named Placenta."

"I swear to God. I heard it in Schwegmann's the other day. Little four-year-old kid."

"It's an urban myth, like Nosmo King."

"The kid named for the No Smoking sign? That's my nephew."

"Listen, I don't care if you did hear it in Schwegmann's. Rename James's girlfriend just this once. Please?"

"Okay, she Magneeta. Magneeta, she stay with her nanan, and her name, uh, let me think . . . I think her nanan named . . . uh . . . ain't she the lady stay over there? You know, the one with all them kids? She 'bout this high and she got a real pretty smile."

"Magneeta. Holy shit. Magneeta."

"You just white po-lice. What do you know?"

"Jim, I don't like this."

"Here's a good place. Park here."

She knew it was a good place; he didn't have to tell her to park. But the longer she didn't park, the longer she put off his getting out of the car. For the first time in her life she had a bad feeling. She didn't even want to look for Dennis. She wanted to go home and forget the whole thing.

But she didn't say it to Jim, because they were grown-up police officers and they were going to do their job.

She parked. "Got your phone?"

"Got it."

Jim was out of the car, and in another minute he was gone; out of her sight.

This could take hours. How the hell can he do the Magneeta routine for hours?

She thought of what he'd say if she asked him: "I'm a pro."

That made her laugh—the whole Eddie Murphy zaniness of it. Actually, this wasn't like the usually dignified Jim. She remembered that he used to work Narcotics and realized why he was so eager to get in there—he was having the time of his life.

She began to relax a little.

She rethought strategy. They could wait here forever for Dennis, who might not ever show. Or they could just talk to Turan.

But what would that do? Even if Dennis did make a buy, how the hell would Turan know where to find him? It's not up to a dealer to find his clients, it's up to them to find him.

She was in a funk of indecision and doubt when the phone rang. For some reason, she punched the "Indiglo" feature on her watch: it was nearly midnight.

"Call for backup. Something's going down."

"Dennis?"

"Two guys with AK-47s. Stay where you are."

"The hell I will."

She called for backup and got out of the car, knowing she probably shouldn't if he said she shouldn't, but she couldn't be sure—the situation could change from second to second.

He'd had to get off quickly so she could call headquarters, and now she couldn't call him. A ringing phone on a Thunderbird-soused raver just wasn't going to cut it.

It was dark in the breezeway. She could see in only a little way. She couldn't see Jim or anyone who might be Turan; certainly could see no one with automatic weapons. They must have cut through to another courtyard.

Someone fired.

She saw orange flames; the noise was like war. More flames on the other side of the breezeway—then someone running. The first shooter.

She heard Jim call, "Halt! Police!" and her heart sank.

Drawing her gun, she started running toward the shooter, who was running toward her. He turned around and fired—at Jim, presumably, and then he turned her way again. Something hit her from behind. She went down, her gun flying from her hand, and she knew it was over.

The man who had hit her—butted her with his head, was her guess—had stopped to take a look at her. She saw his face, clearly, and was surprised that he was terrified. And about sixteen.

A young scared-shitless kid, with the power of life and death over her.

Sirens were getting loud, nearly upon them, the backup she'd called for.

The kid didn't even stop for her gun, just took off after the shooter. She recovered it herself and yelled for Jim.

No answer. She called him on her cute little phone—still no answer.

She found him at the back of the breezeway, a bullet in his chest.

But he was breathing.

She talked to him all the way to the hospital, told him he'd be fine, to hang on, that his wife would be there soon, that he had to stick around to see her.

They went to Charity, where she'd been so many times on other shootings, and where she'd been taken herself once or twice. It was utterly familiar territory, and yet right now a nightmare landscape.

"Room Four," she heard someone say. "Room Four now!" That was the trauma room.

"You can't go with him," a woman said, a nurse probably.

"I'm going."

The nurse shrugged.

Skip was okay about blood as long as it wasn't in a hospital; she didn't know if she could trust herself to stay on her feet in here, and she might be in the way. But Jim needed someone to hold his hand.

I don't want him to die alone. She was shocked at the thought when it came, had no idea that was on her mind.

"You won't die," she told him. "You're not going to die."

I'll die if you die. You can't die.

A piece of her would; she knew it as well as she knew the river was wet. She'd never be the same if he died.

Oh, shit, why Jim? Why couldn't it have been O'Rourke?

"I really have to ask you to get out of the way. You can stay in the hallway if you like."

The man who spoke was in his early twenties, she thought, but he must be a doctor. Other people were in the hallway, lots of them—they came from all over the hospital to watch a Room Four.

Okay, she couldn't hold his hand, but she could stay close. She could send him healing wishes or something.

In the end, she couldn't find the energy in herself to will him to heal, just to keep living, which he did, which he kept on doing, until finally they sewed him up and took him upstairs.

There were policemen in the waiting room, and a black woman with them, with two children, about ten and twelve, a boy and a girl.

When the policemen rustled, the woman realized instantly who Skip was, and rose. "I'm Dionne Hodges."

Skip thought that if she had to categorize this woman in one word, it would have been "pleasant." She was average height—about five-feet-five —and a little plump, so that her cheeks and chin were rounded. Her hair was about ear-length, styled for business. She could have been anything— schoolteacher, receptionist, high-level executive; her clothes might have given a clue. But at the moment she was wearing shorts and a T-shirt, probably just pulled on when she got the call about her husband.

She didn't introduce the children, and Skip was glad. She didn't want to look at their faces too closely, to see their fear and misery, to have it remind her of her own. Dionne seemed a little ragged, but at least she was still in one piece.

Skip said, "Did the doctor talk to you? Jim's holding his own."

Dionne breathed deeply. "No, he didn't. This is the first I've heard."

"Well, they didn't stop to fill me in, but I think he's out of danger for the moment. They took him upstairs." Anxiously, she swiveled her head. Where was the doctor? Skip felt strongly that this was no job for a cop, particularly one as utterly exhausted as she was.

"What happened?" asked Dionne

"Maybe we should talk privately."

"Why?"

Because I don't want to talk about it in front of his children. What's wrong with you?

Dionne seemed way too distracted to catch on. Skip was trying to formulate an answer that might fly when another woman approached the little knot of policemen. She was black as well, wearing white slacks, a little taller, a little older than Dionne, and accompanied by two girls who looked to be juniors or seniors in high school—they were probably a year apart.

"Excuse me," she said, "I'm Jim Hodges's wife. Do you have any word?"

"Oh, shit," said Dionne, and Skip turned to look at her, alarmed.

But Dionne showed no signs of fainting or flying into a rage. A tear floated slowly out of each eye and she whispered something: "I should have known."

Skip felt lead in her chest. She could go no further, couldn't say another word to Dionne or anyone else for a long while. She walked briskly out the emergency entrance and stood there gulping air.

13

The back of her neck was clammy when she awoke after three hours' sleep. She had given her statement to Cappello and then gone back to the Iberville—with other officers—and they had spent most of the night trying to turn up anyone who'd heard or seen anything.

Nobody had. Not only that, nobody knew Turan Livaudais, or had even ever heard of him. They surely hadn't seen him or anybody else selling drugs in the Conti Breezeway that night or any night.

That morning, she awakened feeling vulnerable, almost panicked. Her first real thought was: *Steve: Is he here?*

He was.

Her second was: *Jim: Is he alive?*

She knew she could call to find out, but she didn't want to deal with it over the phone. She hardly felt up to brushing her teeth.

She pulled on a peach-colored blouse and a pair of white pants that made her think of Jim's second wife—or first, probably; she seemed the older one.

Oh, God, even if he makes it, his life's not going to be worth living. Why'd he do a stupid thing like that? A smart guy like Jim?

Love, I suppose. It makes everyone stupid.

124

She felt for Dionne and for the other woman too—she hadn't stayed long enough to get her name—and for all the Hodges kids. There might be eight or ten of them for all she knew.

She envisioned scenes with both women trying to hold Jim's hand during his convalescence; and others—worse ones—in which both of them dumped him.

Today, she thought, she could look at mug shots. She'd gotten a good look at the kid who hit her, and there was something distinctive about him—his lower lip was larger than the upper, and hung down slightly, as if his mouth were open.

She entered the detective bureau with trepidation, but everything sounded okay. There wasn't any unusual silence. "Any word on Jim?" she said to the desk officer.

The woman shrugged. "Not yet. Someone's waiting for you." She pointed with her chin at the little waiting area. Tricia Lattimore was there, in a linen outfit, more dressed up than Skip had ever seen her.

"Skippy, I just wanted to apologize."

"Tricia, that was some scene. I was pretty worried about you."

"It was horrible what I did—attacking my oldest friend. Listen, I'm really sick about it. I just wanted you to know that."

"Well, I know it wasn't you that attacked me. That was the drug. And that's why I'm so worried about you." She knew the repetition was a little schoolteacherish, but she couldn't stop herself.

"I knew you would be, and I didn't want you to worry. That's another reason I'm here. I want you to know I don't do crack. I don't even do crystal, except once in a great while. I was just in a mood."

Oh, sure. "You better be careful with that stuff."

"Oh, I am. I never touch crack for any reason—and the other stuff . . . I don't know, I just get a whim now and then."

"I thought you were in AA."

"Did I say that?"

"Maybe not. Maybe you just said you used to have a drug habit—so I assumed it."

"Oh, AA—they think you can't *ever* do it."

"Thanks for coming by, Tricia."

"Skippy, listen, I'm really sorry. I just wanted to tell you."

"Thanks. I appreciate it."

"We should get together sometime."

"Sure." *During Lorena Bobbitt's presidency.*

Skip went in, got herself a cup of coffee, and called Charity. Jim was still on the critical list.

Well, hell. At least he's alive.

Next, she looked at mug shots, and found a pretty good candidate—a nineteen-year-old named Augustine Melancon. The kid she'd seen looked younger, she thought, but she'd only gotten a glimpse.

She went to find Cappello. "Sylvia, I found a kid who looks like the one I saw."

"Skip. Did *you* have a bad day yesterday."

"Not as bad as Jim."

"I swear to God if he dies I'm out of here. I can't stand this fucking crap." Cappello almost never swore.

"I'm feeling pretty down. I don't know if it was worth it, what we did. What were our chances of finding Dennis, anyway?"

"For Christ's sake, don't start, Skip. Until Jim got shot, that was our biggest case of the year. Are you kidding? Arthur Hebert, who's about as important to this town as Aaron Neville, was gunned down in his dining room. Good God! Do you know how much pressure Joe's been getting to put every guy in Homicide on that one? You know why he hasn't? Because there's nothing for them to do. You had exactly one lead and you followed it. You did what you were supposed to do."

"I forgot it was a heater case. On some other case, understaffed like we are, it would have been a waste of manpower—even if nobody got hurt. Doesn't it strike you there's something wrong with that?"

"You're damn right it does. That's just the kind of crap I'm talking about when I say I'm getting out."

"Where are you going, Sylvia?" Skip thought she might as well face reality.

Cappello had been scanning papers on her desk even as she ranted. She looked up at Skip through round, horn-rimmed glasses that Skip thought quite elegant. "Going? I'm not going anywhere."

"But I thought you just said—"

She smiled. "I'm just letting off steam, that's all."

"Well, at least there's some good news today."

"But if I had anyplace to go, I'd go there."

"Listen, I've got to go see a thug. Who can I take with me?"

"Can't it wait? Everybody's out right now. You think we had a heater case *before*."

"This dude gave me Turan's name."

"Oh—I'll get somebody."

"Never mind. I'm not exactly sure where to find him. Let me do some work on that first."

Cappello lowered her eyes again. "Okay."

"I almost forgot. The kid I found the mug shot of—can we schedule a lineup?"

"You make it sound so easy—you know where to find him?"

"No. But I figure with all the manpower we've got on this, somebody'll get him by noon. Not me, though. Delavon's my special little project. The kid's name is Augustine Melancon."

She went back to her desk, and found a message from the desk officer: someone else to see her. Sugar Hebert.

Puzzled, she went out to the anteroom. "Mrs. Hebert? You wanted to see me?"

"Could we talk a few minutes?"

"Sure. Come in." She led her into Homicide.

Sugar's eyes strayed to a sign someone had posted: THOU SHALT NOT KILL. Skip sat her down. "What can I do for you?"

Sugar looked distinctly uncomfortable—and seriously out of place; but downright good for a woman who'd just lost her husband. She wore a white silk suit with a black silk rose pinned to the chest, and a black straw hat. Skip wondered if the hat and the flower were meant for mourning.

"I think I might have some information for you."

Skip smiled, invitingly, she hoped. *You probably don't even know we've got a cop on the critical list. Would you please spit it out and get out of here?* She kept smiling, even nodding her head in encouragement.

Sugar fidgeted. Finally, she said, "I think I might know who killed my husband."

Skip went right on smiling and nodding. "Oh?"

"Arthur's girlfriend would have—well—a motive, right?"

"Arthur's girlfriend?"

"Yes."

"I don't think you mentioned her before." *And I'm going to strangle you.*

"I was too ashamed to talk about it. Well, and I guess I didn't really know for sure. I mean, I couldn't face facts. But I've been thinking about the way he'd suddenly hang up the phone when I came into the room; or if I picked up, not knowing he was talking, I'd hear a woman's voice—and he'd get mad and tell me to get off."

"What makes you think this meant he had a girlfriend?"

"Well, it wasn't the *first* time." She acted insulted, though why, Skip wasn't sure.

Because I impugned her detective skills?

Probably not. Just general defensiveness. I wish I could feel sorry for her, but there's something about her . . .

"Do you know the woman's name?"

"Anne. That's all I know. Sometimes I'd hear him call her that."

"And why do you think she had a motive?"

"Well, you know. He wouldn't divorce me." She tossed her head like a teenager, dislodging the hat a little. "Isn't that the usual thing?"

Skip said, "I'll check it out."

Seeing her out, she thought, *This is a woman with too much time on her hands.*

Or else, that's what she wants me to think.

Still, it had to be checked. She called Nina Phillips. "Did Arthur have a girlfriend?"

"Not that I know of, and I worked with him pretty closely. May I ask why?"

"Mrs. Hebert seems to think he did—someone named Anne."

"Oh, Anne. Oh, for heaven's sake. That's just like Sugar."

"I beg your pardon?"

"Anne's his lawyer; Sugar probably heard them on the phone or something."

"Anne who?"

"Ebanks. Anne Ebanks."

"Thanks a lot."

Skip hung up shaking her head. Sugar was a piece of work, but what kind, she couldn't be sure. The one thing that looked obvious was that her idea of mourning was a bit on the unconventional side.

Now how to find Delavon? Nothing to do but go back to square one.

She headed once again for Jeweldean's run-down apartment.

"Hey, it's me again."

"I'm a night worker; haven't you heard?"

"I've got something for Tynette." She had stopped and picked up a stuffed toy and a book; she'd also gotten an extra fifty out of the bank.

Jeweldean came to the door clutching an ice pack to her head.

Skip said, "You don't look so good."

"I got mugged last night."

"Oh, God. The whole city's gone crazy."

"What you talkin' 'bout? I'm not the first hooker ever got mugged." She let Skip in and took her into the kitchen. "Some kid was waitin'. Soon as I turned around to unlock the door, he hit me with something and grabbed my purse."

"How do you know it was a kid?"

" 'Cause who else pulls that kind of shit? It was some baby crackhead knew I'd be home late. Fact, I think I know whose kid it was."

"That's so sad. To have to be afraid of your neighbors."

"Who's afraid? I'm not afraid. I'm gettin' me a purse phone is all—from now on, when I'm comin' home, I'm callin' Biggie and he' gon' be out here waitin' for me. Any kid messes with me, Biggie blows him away."

"He's got a gun, does he?"

"Now don't be axin' impertinent questions. Anyway, it prob'ly won't happen again. Biggie might have already had a talk with somebody or other. This is some neighborhood, you know that?"

"They all are."

"Yeah, you right. But a thing happened yesterday nearly broke my heart. My friend Lanita, lives downstairs, lost her boy 'bout two weeks ago—he was shot down not all that far from here."

"My God." Skip's mind was reeling at the matter-of-fact way Jeweldean accepted violence as a fact of life.

"Two days ago they arrested some kid lives down the block, turns out it's Lanita's best friend's boy. So yesterday the friend was over here cryin' and carryin' on, sayin' she hoped it wasn't gon' ruin their friendship, just 'cause her boy killed Lanita's. Now tha's pathetic."

"Things are getting out of hand." Skip was aware of a depression within her that was always just beneath the surface, that had nothing to do with her own life; it bubbled to the top on occasions like this, when it was brought home to her how truly out of hand things were getting.

Cappello's right, she thought briefly.

"Here's some things for Tynette," she said, thrusting them into Jeweldean's hand.

"You go give 'em to her yourself. She be glad to see you."

Reluctantly, Skip went into the living room, where the little girl lay on the couch. She had seen a lot of misery lately and it was starting to get to her—Justin Arceneaux, Tynette, Jim.

But the little girl smiled. Tynette *was* happy to see her; and she was so thoroughly delighted with the stuffed monkey Skip had been unable to resist, and the book about the rain forest, some of which Skip read to her, that the depression started to lift.

She heard Jeweldean making phone calls. When all was quiet in the kitchen, she went back in. "You think Biggie could get me to Delavon again?"

"Sure don't. Why?"

"I need him bad. Look. Maybe I could talk to him."

"He ain' here." Jeweldean was momentarily sullen. Skip thought she didn't like the idea of Biggie's consorting with Delavon.

"Here's all I ask. Just have him tell Delavon I want to see him—he can name the place and time, I don't care." She put the fifty on the table. It would buy the favor and then some. She was counting on the lagniappe to soften Jeweldean's heart.

Jeweldean didn't answer.

"You take care of that little girl," Skip said, and left. Almost the minute she hit the sidewalk, two kids stepped in front of her. One of them had a knife.

"Oh, shit."

One of the kids, the one without the knife, held out his hand for her purse. She slipped it off her shoulder, but instead of handing it over, she swung it so it smacked him in the groin. The one with the knife lunged, but she smacked him too. Because her gun was in the purse, both hits were a lot harder than the average mugger had a right to expect.

"She's a cop, guys," a voice said. Jeweldean's, from her balcony.

The two kids took off.

Skip knew she could call in a 27-64—attempted armed robbery—but it would only be a waste of time unless she could find out where the kids lived.

"Hey, Jeweldean," she yelled. "You know those punks?"

"Uh-uh. They just some kids."

"Come on. They must live around here."

"I don' know 'em. Why I got to know 'em?"

Skip was pretty sure she did.

14

She fumed all the way back to the office, partly at her bad luck in getting mugged, partly at Jeweldean for protecting the punks.

She wasn't even sure Jeweldean was going to give Biggie the message about Delavon, much less that Biggie would deliver it if she did, or that Delavon would call if *he* did.

What a shitty, shitty day, she was saying to herself as she walked into the detective bureau.

The minute she stepped in, she realized it had just gotten a lot worse. The quiet she hadn't noticed that morning had fallen. People's faces looked contorted. One man was wiping his eyes.

Cappello walked out of her office, her face a grim white mask.

"Skip . . ."

"Jim died."

"We just got the call."

Skip nodded, to show that she had heard, and walked to her desk on legs of Jell-O. She sat down, feeling a strange distance between herself and the world, as if the air had solidified, so that it formed a barrier around her.

She wasn't going to cry. There was no question of that at all. She didn't even feel sad, just vaguely miserable, as if there were news of war from far away.

What she had to do was make herself believe this. Understand that Jim Hodges no longer existed, that she wouldn't be joking around with him, wouldn't be working with him anymore.

She thought of Jim's two wives and four children—and how they were going to feel. His death seemed cataclysmic to her, yet out of reach, ungraspable.

Nothing she seemed to be able to do was helping her wrap her mind around it. Thinking didn't work at all—she couldn't think.

She thought of saying something over and over to herself, something like "Jim is dead," to make it sink in, but she couldn't bring herself to do it.

She simply sat at her desk running her hand through her hair again and again, disoriented, her mind a blank.

"He wouldn't be dead if it weren't for you, Langdon."

At first she didn't think she'd heard right. She knew the voice. It was the voice of a man who was perfectly capable of saying that, but she couldn't believe he actually had.

"Didn't you hear me, Langdon?" Frank O'Rourke was standing over her now, too close, invading her space.

She only stared, unable to answer, still uncomprehending.

"You stupid bitch. If it weren't for Joe Tarantino, you wouldn't even be in Homicide—you'd be back in some district, where you damn well belong."

She felt her mouth fall open, was unable to close it.

"I got no idea in hell why Joe puts up with you—his idea of affirmative goddamn action, I guess. And now your incompetence has finally gotten somebody killed, just like it was bound to. How does that make you feel, Uptown rich bitch?"

Skip stood, noticing her legs were still like Jell-O, and struggled briefly to keep her balance. And she smacked him in the jaw.

Or rather, she noticed that she had.

She hadn't meant to do it, couldn't remember moving her arm, just felt the sting, as if she'd suddenly recovered consciousness, and found herself staring into the furious eyes of O'Rourke, but for only a split second. He hit her back. The blow landed on her jaw and knocked her over, so that she sat down hard on the floor.

Three men were now holding O'Rourke, she saw, and she felt someone grab her shoulders from behind. She heard shouting:

"Hey, cut it out, you two."

"Goddammit, O'Rourke."

"Oh, shit."

Crowd noises.

Joe Tarantino, drawn by the commotion, emerged from his office: "What the hell's going on?"

Someone, a voice in the back, said, "O'Rourke hit Langdon."

Joe lost it. "Goddammit, Frank, that's it. I'm getting you transferred out of here, and suspended if I can. That's it, I swear to God."

"Wait a minute, Joe. We've known each other for twenty years. Yeah, I hit Langdon. She hit me first."

"Oh, sure she did. Big nasty Langdon's always picking on poor pitiful you. You childish sonofabitch—you're like some playground bully with Langdon. Even if she did hit you, which I do not believe, I'm sure she had a damn good reason." Even in her state of suspended animation, Skip realized what a remarkable thing Tarantino had done—he'd flat-out lost it. He'd reprimanded O'Rourke in front of the entire unit, and he'd taken one officer's side against another. The irony was, O'Rourke didn't deserve it.

"I did," she said.

"What?"

"I did have a damn good reason and I did hit him first."

"*What?*" Tarantino was turning red, beginning to be embarrassed at what he'd done; also, she thought, to realize he'd been made a fool of.

But he said, "Now you're protecting him? For God's sake, Skip. Cappello, did she hit him first?"

There was a long pause. Skip sensed Cappello hesitating, making up her mind, though she had absolutely no doubt what the answer would be. Cappello was a by-the-book cop, scrupulously fair. She probably didn't like O'Rourke, but she was far too professional to say so; and Skip had a pretty good idea the sergeant did like her. But she'd never lie about a thing like this.

"No," Cappello said. "She didn't."

No one else said a word.

Tarantino spoke more quietly now. "Okay, okay, everybody's upset about Jim. But let's try to act like professionals, please. Frank, I'll talk to you later. Langdon, come into my office."

She followed him in and sat down.

"Okay, what happened?" he said.

She had no choice but to lie, or put Cappello in a bad spot. "He insulted me, and I guess I didn't rise to the bait well enough. So he hit me."

"Why'd you say you hit him?"

She was confused, couldn't think fast enough. She was still trying to compose an answer when Joe said, "You've got some friends out there, kid."

"Do I?" She was reeling, trying to figure out what had happened, why everyone was willing to let O'Rourke take the rap for her crime. "I think—"

"Never mind. It doesn't matter."

What she thought was that it was nothing personal at all, that O'Rourke had provoked the incident, and that in the interests of a kind of skewed justice, they thought he should be the one punished for it.

She appreciated that, and in her heart of hearts she agreed with it. But she was the one who had thrown the punch, and she didn't feel right about someone else getting blamed.

"Look, I'm not going to pursue this," Joe said. "Forget it. We're all upset. But you know something? You look terrible. I know you haven't had much sleep the last couple of nights, and your face probably hurts. Go home and put some ice on it. And get some sleep."

"Thanks, Lieutenant."

Something had to be done before she left. She'd rather get a suspension than do it, but there was no alternative. She walked over to O'Rourke's desk, but he didn't look up.

"Frank, I'm sorry I hit you."

He still didn't look up.

"I don't feel right about it. I owe you one."

He lifted his head with a jerk and she watched his face become suffused. He didn't speak, obviously trying to hold in his bile for once.

She left, feeling isolated by his hatred. Even though everyone in the unit had stood with her against him, something that should have warmed her, she felt cold.

No one knew exactly why he hated her. Because he hated women and he hated anyone from Uptown—because his wife had dumped him—these were the easiest explanations, but they didn't seem like enough.

She must symbolize something for him, or perhaps she had a scent, so subtle no one could consciously smell it, but that some people experienced on some level, and that made them hate her.

Skip, get a grip, she told herself. *You're just depressed because of Jim. Oh, Jim. I forgot about that.*

A wave of something washed over her, something stinging that she recognized as sorrow. The shock was wearing off.

She drove out to the West End, to look at the lake. She sat there, in her car, and thought about Jim, intermittently, between sessions of going blank again, feeling the way she'd felt before O'Rourke had spoken to her. She thought mostly about how kind Jim was, and that surprised her. If anyone had asked her to describe him, she'd have said first that he was professional and competent, second that he was kind. But the part of him that was human, not the cop part, was what stuck with her now.

He probably married both those women because he couldn't stand to hurt either one's feelings. The thought made her smile. And then she had one that she'd been smashing down: *It could have been me.*

Face it, it could have.

You can get killed on the job. You know it when you start, but then you forget.

You can die.

Oh, shit. I want to go home.

What she wanted was company—specifically that of Steve Steinman. She wanted to feel his naked body against hers—his chest hair, his hard thighs, his heat. She wanted sex not so much as a couple of arms around her.

He wasn't home, and for some reason that set her off: she cried at last. And then she slept.

She was awakened by the phone.

"This your lucky day." It was Delavon.

"With all due respect, Delavon, it's not my lucky day." *How the hell did he get my home phone number? Jeweldean doesn't have it.*

"Uh-oh. Thought you wanted a meeting."

"I do. Where and when?"

"Why you in such a bad mood?"

"You probably know already. You know my home phone number."

"Delavon know all, see all."

"Where're we meeting?"

"You comin' alone?"

"Of course not—do you think I'm crazy?"

"Hey, you asked to see *me*. What you scared of?"

"Okay, okay, I'm coming alone."

"Tha's more like it." He gave her an address.

In the mood she was in, she would have loved to go alone, but that was too dicey. She reached Cappello at a crime scene.

"Damn. I'm missing one?"

"I know you're all torn up about it."

"I need backup. I've got a meeting with the guy who sent me to Turan."

"Can it wait an hour?"

"I don't think so. This dude's pretty capricious."

"We're having some problems here—I can't spare anyone."

"Hey. This is about Jim."

"I know, but here's the situation. O'Rourke wasn't in the office when we left. I don't know where he was, but he might be back." She let a beat pass. "But that's crazy. I don't see you two working together right now." Skip could almost see her shaking her head.

"Hey, I'm a pro. I can live with it. What's he going to do? Not do his job just because he hates me?"

"I can't send him." They were both sergeants. "It'll be up to him. And I'm not exactly in his good graces right now."

"Sylvia, this is about Jim."

"I know. I'll call you right back. Look, I've got some good news."

"You've got to be kidding."

"Fazio brought in Augustine Melancon. The kid whose mug shot you picked."

"No!"

"Swear to God—the bad guys don't win all the time. Lineup's tomorrow at four. That okay with you?"

"Sure." She gave Cappello the address Delavon had given her and then brushed her teeth, hoping the morning-time ritual would somehow make her more alert.

She was pulling on white pants when the phone rang: "He's on his way. He'll park in front of the building."

"Tell him to come get me if I'm not out in fifteen."

The building was in a part of Gentilly where there weren't all that many white people, which could make it hard for him, she thought. But he was there, in a beat-up car she recognized as one of those assigned to Homicide. He was scrunched down, hunched over, and wearing a baseball cap.

What a weird job, she thought as she climbed the steps. *Here I am, entrusting my life to my biggest enemy. And the amazing thing is, I actually trust him.*

Delavon answered the door himself. "Hey, Tall Beauty." He had changed her nickname; not a good sign, she thought. A little flirtatious; presumptuous.

"Hey, Short Ugly."

He laughed. "Now you know you don't mean that. Come on in."

It was a Sharper Image kind of apartment as far as it went—all chrome, glass, and leather, but very sparse. Skip didn't see any sound equipment, which she thought strange. The kind of man who'd have this kind of furniture would have a fancy stereo system.

"You heard what happened last night?"

"You get right down to business, don't you? Can't I give you a drink or something?"

"A policeman was shot, Delavon."

"Now ain't that too bad."

"He died."

"Um-um." He shook his head in mock sorrow.

"He was black. African-American. Do you care at all?"

"Hey, 'member we talked about Gus Lozano?" The mob boss.

"I remember. Who shot my partner?"

"Now, how would Delavon know a thing like that?"

"I think you set me up, asshole. You sent me there. Was I the one who was supposed to get whacked?"

Delavon found a piece of furniture to smack. That seemed to be his style. "Jim Hodges's death was a accident!"

"Now, how would Delavon know a thing like that?"

Delavon laughed. "Delavon know everything. More'n you know, I bet. Bet you don't know Gus Lozano's dead."

"I don't give a shit. Jim Hodges is dead."

"You real sure you don't give a shit?"

She wasn't. She was already starting to regret having said that. She had a moment to think about it while Delavon answered his cellular phone.

"Well, now that's mighty int'resting," he told the caller. "I think this be lesson time." He hung up and looked at Skip inquiringly, almost benignly.

"Okay, okay. Tell me about Lozano."

"All I know is he's dead, if you believe the word out on the street. New guy prob'ly killed your partner."

"Oh, come on. Turan was too small-time for that kind of crap."

"Mob be everywhere. Don't you know that?"

"It is not, Delavon. The mob's practically dead in New Orleans."

"Ah-ha. Now you gettin' to the crux of the matter. Mob practically dead—Gus Lozano *actually* dead. Think those two facts be related?"

"Probably not." She didn't think the mob was going to have somebody killed for inefficient business practices. Stealing, yes. But not incompetence.

"Prob'ly *so*. New guy's takin' over lots o' little operations. Gon' be runnin' much tighter ship." He shrugged. "What I hear, anyway. Hear he flexed muscles last night. Turan got real unlucky; your partner got in the way."

Skip was pretty sure the person she'd seen was no Mafia enforcer. He was certainly not Italian, and probably not even an adult. But to keep the conversation going, she said, "Who is this new guy?"

"Thought maybe you'd know."

"What'll you trade me for it?"

"Might have somethin' for you. But don't call me, I'll call you."

Skip stood up. "You'd *better* call me if you've got something. A cop got killed, Delavon—have you grasped that yet?"

He smiled again, the genial host seeing his guest to the door. "Hey, I heard about your run-in with that babe over at Maya's place."

"You're just everywhere, aren't you?"

"I sho' try to be."

"Then you must know where Dennis Foucher is."

Delavon made a show of looking at his watch, which was a Rolex, Skip noticed. "Well, no, not at this precise moment. But I sold him some shit about a hour ago."

Skip wheeled. "Goddamn you, Delavon." She had no idea whether it was true or if he was playing with her.

"Hey, I can't be everywhere at once. How'm I s'posed to know where somebody is I saw a hour ago?" He paused. "But listen, I'm a good guy. You want me to find him for you?"

The man was maddening. "Yeah. I want you to find him for me. 'Cause you're a good guy and a damn good citizen. Because virtue's gonna have to be its own reward, you know what I mean?"

"Miss Tall One, you think you hot stuff, don't you?" His features had become a hard and nasty mask. "You think you get anything you want just 'cause your daddy a doctor. Well, let me tell you somethin', girl. You got a few things to learn. Things don' work that way. You think this where I live? This idn't where I live. I had to borrow this place from a friend. Had to leave my bi'ness and come over just to satisfy you. And Delavon don't like being inconvenienced.

"So you see you owe me already. You owe me just for comin' over here."

It was all she could do not to blurt: *How the hell do you know what my daddy does?*

15

When she came out of the building, O'Rourke wasn't in his car. She had been inside only ten minutes—he wouldn't have come for her yet, and she would have passed him if he had.

She knew he wouldn't have left for a trivial reason—whatever else he was, O'Rourke was a good cop; even Joe Tarantino wouldn't put up with him if he weren't.

He'd been made.

She remembered Delavon's phone call: *"Well, now, that's mighty int'resting. I think this be lesson time."* Delavon's life was probably full of interesting discoveries that called for painful "lessons," but she was pretty sure this one involved her. He'd gotten a little nicer—right after he hung up the phone—no doubt luxuriating in the knowledge that he had the upper hand for the moment.

Without stopping to call for backup, she headed for the rear of the building. Delavon would leave that way, she felt it; he'd expect her to wait for backup, and he'd be long gone by the time it arrived.

He wasn't there, but O'Rourke was, stomped and beaten, maybe dead. "Dammit, O'Rourke, don't be dead."

He had a weak pulse. "Okay, hang on. You're going to be fine." Reluctant to leave him, she shouted until somebody looked out a window.

"Call 911," she said. "Get the police and an ambulance."

She noticed she was holding O'Rourke's hand, and she continued to hold it until he woke up in the emergency room.

He said, "Langdon. Goddammit, am I going to live?"

"Of course. You're too ornery to die. But just in case, can I ask you something?"

"What?"

"How many wives have you got?"

"I'm too ornery to get married." He had gotten married once, to a police officer; she was the one who had dumped him.

"What happened?" she asked.

"Couple assholes pulled me out of the car and beat me up. Took my badge and gun."

Delavon, I'm going to get you.

She had left the district officers to get a description of Delavon's car and any available eyewitness accounts, but she knew they weren't going to turn up anything. Even Jeweldean, her friend, wouldn't identify the neighborhood mugger. No one here was going to turn in a heavy-duty gangster.

She headed for the assessor's office, where she learned the building was owned by a Reginald Vicknair, who lived in Pontchartrain Park, a high-end black development. He had an office on Gravier Street.

Arriving there, she saw that it was occupied by a well-known law firm.

Vicknair was as she expected—dignified, middle-aged, in every way comfortable-looking; perhaps a little smug. He wore glasses and a smile that seemed practiced. "How can I help you?"

"I need to know the name of one of your tenants."

"May I ask why?"

"Certainly. A police officer got beaten up outside the building."

"And you suspect my tenant?"

"Let's say I need to talk to him—or her."

He sighed. "Very well. What apartment?"

"Seven."

His eyebrow went up. "Mr. Smith."

"First name?"

"John."

"I see. What does Mr. Smith look like?"

"Black, about twenty-nine or thirty. Medium skin—darker than mine, say. No scars or anything. Perfectly nice-looking fellow. Medium—uh, height and weight."

He could have been Delavon.

"By the way, how does he pay his rent?"

"He's only been there a couple of weeks."

"What else do you know about him?"

"He has a nice car, I remember that—a Lexus, I think. That was one reason—I hate to admit it—I didn't check his references. He had nice clothes, a nice car, and he was clean-cut. I thought he'd be fine."

"What does he do for a living?"

"I can't remember, but I can call my wife. Those records are at home, of course." He got his wife, made the request, and said to Skip, "He's a salesman. For a company called Amglo Products."

"Address?"

He spoke to the phone. "Honey, is there an address?" He scribbled something and handed it to Skip. "I'm getting a sinking feeling," he said. "Let's look it up."

It wasn't listed.

Skip glanced at her watch. It was about five. By the time she could get back to Gentilly, people would have started getting home from work.

She knocked first on Mr. Smith's apartment, but got no answer. Then she talked to everyone else in the building. No one had ever seen Mr. Smith, not even when he moved in. His next-door neighbors had never heard anything either.

Skip remembered how there hadn't been a sound system, how Delavon had been called on a cellular phone. It was her guess there wasn't any Mr. Smith, there wasn't any Amglo Products, and Mr. Vicknair's tenant, whoever he was, wouldn't even be back for his furniture.

She had no way back to Delavon, except Biggie. But if she took Biggie to headquarters and sweated him, he wouldn't talk and she'd lose him as a semi-informant. She wasn't willing to do that yet. She had one other hope: O'Rourke might be able to pick out a mug shot of one of his assailants.

She went home exhausted, remembering that she hadn't seen Steve all day, that he'd be there for her.

But he wasn't.

The house was empty and seemed dark, though the evening was bright. She had been thinking about Jim on the way home, and the tears were near the surface. As soon as she put her key in the door, realizing the house was empty, she relaxed enough so that a sob rose up out of her.

Blinded by tears, crying loud now, she wanted nothing except to get in the shower, perhaps to wash her grief away.

She threw off her clothes as she climbed the stairs, and slipped behind the shower curtain, turning up the hot water, even though it was June, and stood there until she was cried out.

Opening the bathroom door, she thought she heard a noise. "Steve?" The noise came again, almost like a cry. Pulling a terry-cloth robe around her, she found her gun and crept down the stairs. The noise was coming from the kitchen, pretty steadily now, and she was beginning to have a suspicion; the gun was making her feel silly, but she kept it anyway, just in case.

She opened the kitchen door and something soft touched her leg. Her suspicion was correct—another animal. Not Napoleon because he would have barked; probably a lion cub or a ferret—small but potentially destructive.

Actually it was another dog—or at least a dog-to-be. At the moment, it was little more than a handful of white fur with one black eye and one black ear.

"Oh, you angel," she blurted, putting her gun on the counter and reaching down for the puppy. It was shaking. "Oh, Mama's widdle baby's terrified; never seen a great big ol' gun before. Poor widdle baby animal."

It settled into her hand as if she really were its mama. She was just getting it calmed down when the door burst open. "Hellooo-oo," Steve singsonged.

He never does that, she thought. *But hold it—I don't do babytalk either.*

The kids—both Sheila and Kenny—were with him. She had a moment of thoroughgoing gratitude that they hadn't come home in time to catch her.

"Did you find Angel, Auntie?" Sheila was beaming, as if she'd been chosen class president. "Isn't she the sweetest? Come to Mama, baby." She reached for the puppy.

"Angel. That's what I called her."

"She's *my* dog." Kenny grabbed for her too. Angel yelped.

"Hey. Hey," said Steve. "She's nobody's dog yet. Don't forget about Uncle Jimmy."

Kenny's attention wandered to Skip's gun. "Hey. Were you going to shoot her or what?"

Skip pocketed the gun. "I thought she was Napoleon."

She regretted it as soon as she'd said it. Kenny's eyes brimmed at the memory of the big dog.

Setting down a grocery bag of pet supplies, Steve ruffled his hair, causing Skip nearly to gasp. She'd never seen him do such a thing. When he'd arrived a week ago, he'd been pretty much of a dyed-in-the-wool child-hater. This dog thing was having a weird effect.

"Hey, champ, Napoleon's going to be okay. I promise. Nothing bad's going to happen to him."

"How dumb do you think I am? They're going to kill him."

"No, they're not."

"I'm not *stupid*."

"They don't kill dogs that get adopted. Napoleon got adopted."

"Oh, *sure* he did. Like you'd really know all about it."

"Well, I should. I'm the new owner."

"What?" Skip and Sheila spoke together. Kenny's mouth dropped in wonder.

Steve shrugged sheepishly at Skip. "I guess you'll never come visit me again, huh?"

"You adopted that dog?"

"Had to. They were going to kill him." He leaned against the counter with something that resembled a swagger.

It worked like crazy with Kenny. "You did? You really did?"

"Uh-huh. Bet *you'll* come visit me."

"Can I? Hey, Skip, can I?"

"What, and leave Angel alone?"

"Aren't we forgetting something?" Sheila spoke severely. "We still have the James Scoggin hurdle." She still had possession of the puppy, which was starting to wriggle out of her arms.

"Where is Napoleon?" Skip said, wanting to make sure he wasn't anywhere close.

"Oh, they're keeping him a few more days. I paid for his vaccinations and all. Besides, they love him at the shelter. Nobody wanted to off him. Shall we unpack? See, some nice puppy food, a water dish—"

"I'm going to put the gun away." She pulled on some clothes while she was at it, crossing her fingers that Jimmy Dee would let them keep the puppy. He had twin soft spots for Kenny and Sheila, but she just didn't see him opting for a pet that was bound to systematically destroy his carefully decorated abode.

Hearts were going to break, she thought.

Let's face it, including mine. I really fell hard for the little dickens.

She had a thought as she came back down the stairs: "Hey, Steve, she's not a border collie, is she? She looks kind of like one."

"Why?"

"They're murder. They herd you and all your neighbors. And they have to run a lot. Also, they're smarter than most humans. I find that an unsettling quality in a dog."

"Nah. She couldn't possibly be one." He tweaked the puppy, distracting her from Kenny's shoelace, which she was enthusiastically masticating.

"By the way, how come you're babysitting? Did Jimmy Dee go out or something?"

"I don't think so. He's making cannelloni for Layne. When Kenny saw it, he said such rude things I felt sorry for Uncle Jimmy and offered to take the kids to McDonald's."

"I did not!"

"Well, the look on your face said it all. Anyway, I brought them over here and cast my evil spell first. We were kind of hoping you'd be back in time to go with us."

"I got delayed." She hoped her face didn't betray too much, but it must have told him something.

"How's Jim?"

She shook her head briefly, telling him to shut up. "Let's take Angel over to the Big House."

"Okay," said Steve. "Everybody ready?" He was a regular dad all of a sudden.

"Kenny, you take Angel," said Sheila. "You can be last."

It was uncharacteristically generous, but Skip figured she had a reason —she had a flair for drama.

"Uncle Jimmy! We've got something to show you."

He and Layne were in the living room having coffee. "Hey, everybody. What took you so long?" They were twin souls of civility. Skip didn't want to think about how a dog could disrupt the momentarily peaceful household.

"We had to make some stops," said Sheila.

"Where's Kenny?"

"He's bringing up the rear."

"What are you showing me?"

"Kenny's got it."

Here goes, thought Skip. *His last normal moment. After this, everything changes.*

"Oh, Kenny, you can come in now." Sheila hummed the wedding

march. Skip and Steve joined in. Catching on, Kenny came in haltingly, in time with the music.

"Oh, my God, it's a puppy. Kenny Ritter, you get that creature out of here this instant."

"But she's beautiful," said Sheila.

"The only thing worse than a big dog is a little dog." Kenny held the puppy to his uncle's face, which she obligingly licked.

"Help, I've been kissed by a dog."

"Look how cute she is."

"She had the audacity to *lick* me."

Layne said, "My God, that's the cutest thing I ever saw in my life."

Dee-Dee glared at him. "Et tu, Brute."

"Oh, for Christ's sake, James—quit camping it up and look at her. Is that a face you can resist?" He held his hands out for Angel, who came to him with full tail wags. "Ohhh, look at the widdle thing. How can big ol' mean Jimmy Dee say no to a little ol' ball of fur like this?"

"I can't stand it! You're all disinherited—including you, Aphrodite." Meaning Skip.

"Aphrodite," said Sheila. "Maybe we should call her that instead of 'Angel.' "

Layne said, "How about Elsie? I had an aunt named that."

"I'm leaving." Dee-Dee stood up. "Wait a minute, what am I doing? *She's* leaving." He pointed portentously at the wriggling furball. "I mean it, Kenny. *No dogs.* Period."

He sounded so intractable that even Skip felt herself shrinking slightly. Worried, she glanced at Kenny. He was fighting his disappointment, but it was winning. His face twisted, a horrible, cracked half scream escaped his throat, and tears began to stream.

To Skip's amazement, Steve stepped forward and put an arm around the boy's shoulders. "It's okay, son. You can come to my house and visit Napoleon. Anytime you want, honest."

"Major grouch," said Sheila, almost in wonder, as if she were witnessing a spectacle of some sort.

Layne handed the dog to Jimmy Dee. "You can be so heartless sometimes." He was fumbling in his pocket for something.

Dee-Dee stared at the tiny black and white face. "You are pretty cute, you know that?" He patted her. She wagged her tail and wiggled. He looked at Kenny, whose face had now taken on a pathetic hopefulness. He handed her to him.

"Okay, you can keep the damn dog."

145

Both Kenny and Sheila began doing war whoops, which terrified Angel so much she began yipping. The noise was so shrill Skip was tempted to cover her ears, but she didn't want to take any chances with Uncle Jimmy's largesse.

"What is it, Layne?" asked Steve.

Layne had now found a handkerchief and appeared to be crying into it, moved to tears by the happy domestic scene. He sneezed. "I think I'm allergic to her."

146

16

• •

When they were alone, Steve found Skip's white terry-cloth robe, pulled her T-shirt over her head, and held the robe for her. "Let me take off your jeans."

She stood still while he wriggled them off.

"Now. Tell me about Jim."

She felt her mouth go funny on her. When she could control it, she said simply, "He died."

"I'm sorry." He held her, not saying anything, and it occurred to her that there were no suitable platitudes when a policeman was killed. You couldn't say, "It happens," or "Every cop knows the risks," or anything else that would remind the officer you were trying to comfort of her own mortality.

Her fragility, Skip thought. *Sometimes I think we're all just hanging on by threads.* "There's more," she said. "O'Rourke blamed me for it in front of everybody."

"So he's dead too, of course."

She surprised herself by laughing. "Well, he is in the hospital."

She told the story with an exuberance that surprised her, and when it

147

was over, found herself wandering inevitably back to her grief. She ended up crying in Steve's arms, inordinately grateful that he was there.

He pushed her back against the pillows and loosened the belt of the robe, so that it fell away from her. "We're alive," he said, and kissed her, and then kissed her breasts.

He kissed her and stroked her a long time in a quiet, sensuous way that was almost like a massage. She put a hand between his legs, just to see what was happening, and found him hard. Her mood changed in an instant from languorous to passionate.

She unzipped him lazily, thinking of ways to prolong the moment, but he was having none of it, and as it happened, that suited her too. She wrapped her legs around him as he buried himself in her, and in that moment life seemed so sweet she actually felt she tasted it, like honey on her tongue.

●   ●

The next morning she woke up feeling as depressed as she ever had been in her life.

As she got dressed, she realized she had no plan for the day. She tried to think what to do.

Jim had died and a new life—albeit a canine one—had come to her. This was both the cruelty and the beauty of nature. She could have gotten into "giveth and taketh away" if she'd thought in those kind of terms.

Something was nagging at her, nibbling at the edge of her consciousness.

Old stuff, new stuff, dead stuff. You're going crazy, Skip baby. You didn't invent the life cycle, you know.

So why can't you get it out of your mind?

An image came into focus. A baby, from the photograph Sugar had shown her. Sally.

Skip's stomach turned over.

Where is she?

Is she with her mother?

Where the hell is that kid?

Dead?

She felt sweat break out on her forehead, the back of her neck prickle.

I lost the whole day yesterday.

She couldn't shake the feeling of panic, of time running out.

At least Dennis isn't dead; that much we know. So why would Reed and Sally be dead?

Where the hell are they?
Kidnapped? Hiding from something?
Me, for instance.
Nothing made sense. All the stories she could think of to tell herself seemed preposterous.

Feeling desperate, unable to calm down enough to make her palms stop sweating, she spent the morning taking Dennis and Reed's picture around to every fleabag hotel in town. Different clerks worked different hours, of course, but the picture had also been in the paper. If either was staying in a hotel, there might be gossip: *Is that those two? I don't know— looks like him, but I don't think it's her.*

However, Skip encountered nothing of the sort. By lunchtime she was no closer to Dennis, Reed, or Sally. But there was still an avenue to follow up. She went over to Remoulade, the Arnaud's spinoff, and bought some Shrimp Arnaud to get her through the afternoon. She had a few oysters as well.

For June, the Quarter seemed pretty crowded. Everyone had on shorts and walked slow. Everyone's hair was damp. She wasn't thrilled about plunging into the heat again, but sitting still was a worse option. She just had a feeling something bad was going to happen.
Something bad's already happened.
And she knew, in her heart, that that was what was causing the feeling, that nothing had changed except her.
It's the way it is after an earthquake—you don't trust the ground anymore.
She walked over to the law offices of Anne Ebanks, Arthur Hebert's lawyer.

Ebanks was cursed with bounciness. She was about fifty-five, about five-feet-four, and about 140 pounds. Her knees were too plump for it, but she was wearing a miniskirt. She moved fast. Skip would have bet a thousand dollars she was a fabulous Cajun dancer—anyone with that much spring in her step would have to be.

She had dark hair, worn short and rather puffy, and flawless skin. She wore an ordinary, Ann Taylor kind of suit, and plenty of good gold jewelry, but the hoops in her ears were just a hair bigger than the average lawyer would probably think of. Skip got the feeling her life outside the office was a whole lot more interesting than her law life.

She led Skip to her office and moved some papers off a chair so her guest could sit. "Sorry the place is such a mess. Housekeeping never was my thing."

"It looks fine to me."

"Does it? These other assholes keep their little cubicles so neat you'd swear they were in the army. What can I do for you?" She fixed Skip with a pair of eyes that were green, like her own. She had an open, friendly face.

"I need to talk to you about a client."

"Arthur Hebert? I figured you'd be along sooner or later. Not that I can tell you anything, except that he was a hateful old coot. Probably anyone who'd ever spent five minutes with him wanted to kill him."

It wasn't professional, but Skip was laughing, partly at the silliness of her mission, partly at Ebanks's outspokenness. "Have you always felt that way about him?"

"Are you kidding? Did you ever meet the man? What a poisonous old bigot."

"I'm surprised you'd represent anyone you felt that way about." And somewhat surprised she'd talk that way about a client, though Skip had to admit she found it refreshing.

"Oh, he hated me too. We were stuck with each other, out of loyalty to my husband, who was Arthur's lawyer all his life until he died of AIDS last year. Arthur always pretended he thought it was a heart attack. God, he was an awful man. He grew up with Carleton—who was quite a bit older than me—and Carleton always said I was way too hard on Arthur— that he was trapped.

"Trapped by his God, first of all—he thought he just had to be religious, when he was really a brutish old bastard who didn't have a spiritual bone in his body. But most of all trapped by being an Hebert—life was running the restaurant, and you didn't ask questions about it.

"Of course, Sugar just made him feel more trapped than ever—she never saw anything like him in her life. Had a blind date with him while she was at Sacred Heart and married him just as soon as she could get herself pregnant. Poor man never knew what hit him."

"Is she the jealous type?"

"Now that I wouldn't know. I don't really know her personally."

"She seems to have the idea that you and Arthur were lovers."

"Lovers!" She hooted. "Lovers!" She leaned back in her chair and laughed until she actually had to wipe away tears. "Oh my God, I'd rather go to bed with Ross Perot. Can you imagine what kind of little skinny thing he's got down there? Oh, my God. Lovers! Let me tell you something—I'm sure the only thing he ever loved was his damned restaurant."

Skip laughed. "Are you saying you weren't lovers?"

"I'm saying if he'd touched me, I'd have broken out in hives." She checked her skin, as if the mere thought might cause eruptions.

Skip was trying hard to retain a professional demeanor. Anne Ebanks was lively, bawdy, and funny—somebody she'd love to be friends with. But she might be a liar. Fighting hard not to smile, she said, "You were his lawyer. Do you know if he had any enemies?"

"He had *hundreds* of them. I'm sure his wife must have thought the world of him—there's no accounting—but aside from Sugar, I can't think of a soul who could stand him."

"I meant the sort who'd have reason to kill him."

She opened her arms, causing a great jangling of bracelets. "Cast of thousands."

Skip waited, trying to set a tone: *This is no time for horsing around.*

"But I don't know of any who actually threatened his life." Ebanks spoke more quietly, perhaps having gotten the message.

"I'll try to make my next question as general as I can—were you and Arthur recently working on something requiring long, confidential phone calls?"

Ebanks swiveled jerkily, raising an eyebrow; the effect was curiously like a stage double-take. "Why, no," she said, sounding unsure of it.

Skip was silent, giving her time to process it.

"So there were phone calls—that must be where she got that ridiculous idea." She drummed pink, perfect nails, staring into space. "Another Anne, maybe. Anything's possible, but I can't imagine who'd put up with him." She refocused on Skip. "Oh, yes, I can—somebody young and dumb. These old coots can always get them.

"Tell me something—why can't women? I'd just love a strapping young creature myself, wouldn't you? Oh, no, you're young, you've probably already got one. I'd like a zookeeper, say; someone who's kind to animals. I've got plenty of money and tons of energy—why can't I have one?"

Skip gave up the struggle not to laugh; Ebanks probably carried on this way in court, and maybe at funerals. "I'm sure you'll get whatever you want. Mind telling me about the will?"

"Arthur's?" She inspected her perfect nails. "I guess I can. It hasn't been admitted to probate yet, but it became an operable legal document when he died. Sure, I can tell you—simple usufruct, with the children as naked owners. Don't you love the way we talk in this game? It means Sugar, as usufructuary, can use the property till she dies or remarries; after that, it goes to the kids." She shrugged. "How conventional can you get? I'm falling asleep just thinking about it."

Skip left, feeling buoyed by the sheer exuberance of the woman. From what she'd heard of Arthur Hebert, Anne probably wasn't kidding around—he just didn't sound like her type. She was right about somebody young and dumb—if Arthur had a lover, it was almost certainly someone like that.

Or someone young and grasping.

She hit the streets and showed her pictures at more hotels, once again striking out.

Then she headed back to the office. It was nearly time for the lineup. Two of the men in it had prominent lower lips, like the kid she'd seen at the Iberville. Two others didn't, and these she quickly eliminated.

The first two were the right height and build; in fact, they looked so much alike they could have been brothers. She searched both faces, looking for nuances she remembered, clues that would jog her memory.

But in the end she couldn't be sure. She beat her fist against her face, out of pure frustration. "Sylvia, I hate this. Those guys look so much alike, it's a good thing they're dressed differently."

"Does either of them look like the right kid?"

"That's the hell of it—they both do."

"Damn."

"Yeah."

"Melancon's got a very nasty record. He's a damn good candidate."

"Well, I'd pick him out if I only knew which way to point."

Skip was instantly sorry for the sarcasm, but Cappello was unfazed. "Do me a favor, okay? Would you please get some sleep tonight?"

Steve was home when she got there, in the courtyard with the kids and Angel. They were playing a game she thought was a poor idea, which seemed to involve letting the puppy chase everyone and bite their ankles.

"Hey, Skip."

"Hey, Auntie."

"Hello, everybody and their animal." They paid her no mind as she crossed through. She went upstairs and threw on an oversized T-shirt and a pair of Steve's shorts. When she came back down, Steve was in the kitchen, stirring a pitcher of lemonade. "Look what I made you."

"What happened to the kids?"

"Uncle Dee-Dee called them. He's getting to like the dog, by the way."

"Who wouldn't? He just had a hard time making up his mind to say good-bye to his expensive furnishings. Now it's done and they'll all live happily ever after." She accepted a glass.

"Let's go out to the courtyard."

There was a metal table and chairs outside, and the merest hint of a breeze.

Watching Steve sipping his lemonade, wearing shorts exactly like the ones she had on, so comfortable here, she felt a twinge.

"What?" he said.

"Oh, nothing. I wish you could stay longer, that's all."

"Well, so do I, but now I've got the damned dog to rescue."

"Napoleon."

"I let him down and he's an ex-dog."

"How terrible." She let the corners of her mouth turn up.

"Try not to cry. Anyway, I'm still trying to think of a project that'll get me back here."

"Did we talk about kids who get shot? Tynette's so pathetic; and you could find lots of others, I'm sorry to say."

"I don't know if I could take it, I really don't."

"Have the Mardi Gras Indians been done?"

"Probably. Anyway, I'd like something a little dark, a little—you know —illuminating of the urban condition." He looked embarrassed.

"I can see that."

"Know who I'd really love to interview? That Delavon of yours. 'Portrait of a Sociopath'—do you like it?"

"He already thinks he's a star. Don't encourage him."

"I mean it."

She could see by his expression, which was almost pleading, that he did. "Well, you can forget that idea. If I ever get hold of him, I'm going to make sure he doesn't get out of jail long enough to talk to his fans."

"Fans! I beg your pardon—how irresponsible do you think I am?"

"This is a really great opportunity for an argument—"

"Look, you jumped on me. I don't really think—"

"—but I'm way too tired." She stood up. "Anything you say, dear. Time for my nap now."

"I'll make dinner."

"You will?" He'd never done this before.

"Sure. Me and the Verti Marte." The local deli.

"Good night, sweet prince."

When he woke her, hours later, she saw that she hadn't undressed, and she could barely remember lying down. "Skip, wake up."

Vaguely, she recalled the last thing he had said to her. "Is dinner ready yet?"

"Dinner was hours ago—mine was, anyhow, but I didn't have the heart to wake you. You've got a phone call."

"Who?"

"Tricia."

She grimaced.

"I think you'd better take it." He handed her the phone.

"Tricia? Is that you?"

"Skip, I've got him."

"I beg your pardon?"

"I've got Dennis."

She sat up. "You what?"

"Come on, goddammit. I'm on Esplanade." A beautiful street, but not a safe one. "He came to Maya's—I followed him for you."

"I'll be right there."

She jumped out of bed, reaching for shoes, badge, radio, cuffs, and gun. "Back soon," she said to Steve, and left without even combing her hair, which was probably so matted from sleep she looked like a bag lady.

She double-parked in front of the address Tricia had given her. Her friend was there, looking slightly the worse for wear. Skip didn't know whether Dennis had a gun or not, couldn't predict what would happen if he came out. The thing to do, she thought, was scope out the scene a little and then get some backup.

But first, get Tricia out of there.

She remembered the scene from the other night. *If only she's not too loaded.*

Suddenly, Tricia pointed. "There he is!"

A figure just emerging from the side of the building broke into a run.

"Stay where you are," she yelled to Tricia, and took off after the runner, radioing as she ran. When she had given her location, she shouted, "Halt! Police!" aware that in shorts and T-shirt she didn't cut a very impressive figure.

He paid no attention.

"Halt or I'll shoot." Of course she couldn't, couldn't even fire a warning shot.

It occurred to her to yell his name, but she thought that might make things worse. There was nothing to do but catch him.

He was running away from the river, into ever darker and more dangerous territory, but right now she was about the most dangerous thing around.

Feet, fly, she commanded. *Come on, feet, do it.*

She thought he was slowing, and poured on a little more speed. He *was* slowing. The gap was closing.

He's been to Maya's, and his drug of choice is heroin. If he's fucked up, I'm surprised he can run at all.

She felt confident, drawing on the reservoir of energy her nap had created. It was almost fun, pounding down Esplanade at top speed in the middle of the night.

She could hear him breathing now.

"Give it up, Dennis," she said, and he couldn't resist looking around, shocked to hear his name. Her heart raced as she recognized the face in the picture she'd been carrying.

He tried to speed up, but the backward glance had finished him.

This is going to hurt, she thought, and threw herself down in a tackle. He managed one more step before he went down, and she fell full on him, not even scraping her bare legs on the pavement.

He tried to fight, but she pulled her gun from the back of her shorts: "Don't even think about it."

She identified herself.

"Am I under arrest?"

"I need you to come to headquarters with me. You're a suspect in the murder of your father-in-law."

"Forget it."

She shrugged. "Okay, then. You're under arrest."

She cuffed him and read him his rights. Now how to get him to headquarters? She couldn't see frog-marching him back to her car. However, a figure came into view—Tricia, screaming and crying, who hadn't heeded her admonition to stay put.

Just what I need.

By now people were starting to peek out their windows, the boldest even venturing outside.

She heard a siren, and then a district car came into view. An officer started to open the door, but seeing a wild woman with a gun, quickly jumped back inside. "It's okay," she shouted. "Langdon; Homicide. I need help with a suspect."

Gingerly, the young man—very young, she noticed—opened the door again.

"Let's get him in your car."

Looking as if he might cry, he walked forward, apparently still not convinced she was a police officer. "For Christ's sake, my badge is in my pocket. Reach in and get it."

He relaxed and helped her wrestle Dennis into the car.

"I've got to check the building he came out of. Can you call for another car?"

"Here comes one."

Sure enough, another district car was arriving.

"Okay, take this guy to Homicide, will you? Say he's Dennis Foucher, and they'll know what to do till I get there."

"Dennis Foucher! You've got to be kidding."

Without answering, she went to Tricia, who had thrown her arms around a tree and appeared to be howling at the moon.

"Trish? Come on, babe. It's okay; I'll take you home in a minute."

Tricia let go of the tree and transferred herself to Skip, getting her wet with tears and slobber. "Oh, Skippy, I fucked up again."

Skip didn't know whether she meant by getting loaded or by shouting when Dennis came out.

"Everything'll be okay."

"Ohhhh, Skippy."

Skip broke the grip Tricia had on her shoulders. "Can you walk? That's it; that's good. All you have to do is get to that car—you can wait there a few minutes."

"I'm not getting in any police car."

"Tricia, could you cooperate, please? I'll get you home as soon as I can."

Pouting, Tricia obeyed. She left with one of the newly arrived officers while Skip went with the other to check the building.

They knocked, got no answer, and entered to find a rented room with a few personal items, but no Reed, no Sally, and no obvious clues as to where they were. She needed a warrant to do a real search. She asked the district officers if one would stay to secure the room until she could return with it. Then she got Tricia off her hands.

"Where do you live?"

"It's okay; you can just drop me on a corner or something."

"Now you know I can't do that. Are you staying at your parents' house?"

"No, really, anywhere's all right."

Skip sighed. "All right. How about Darryl's?"

"Oh, no. I can't bother Darryl again. He'd kill me."

"What's wrong with just telling me where you live?"

"Well, I'm not going home yet."

So that was it. "You want to go to Maya's?"

"No! Uh . . . no, of course not. I was only at Maya's for you, Skippy. I wanted to find Dennis for you because I fucked up so bad the other night."

"Okay, where then?"

"Listen, really. That's the only reason I was hanging there. I'm going into treatment right away, I swear; I just wanted to do this one thing for you."

Well, ah ... no, of course not. I was only at Maya's for you. Skip; I
wanted to find Dennis for you because I looked under his bed the other
night.

"Okay, where then?"

"Listen, really, I hate the only reason I was hanging there. I'm going
into treatment right away. I wasn't I just wanted to do this one thing for
you.

Back in her car, her head beginning to clear, Skip realized she was barely
disappointed at all not to have found Reed and Sally. She hadn't expected
them. After Toni's story, she had known in her heart that Dennis was
traveling alone.

He was waiting for her at headquarters. She found one of the officers
on the night watch. "Is his lawyer on the way?"

"He says he doesn't want one."

"You're kidding."

"Looks like your lucky day."

"I'm way overdue for one."

Hours later, after she'd gotten her warrant and conducted her search,
she joined Dennis in an interview room. "I've been looking for you."

He didn't answer.

"I hear you don't want a lawyer."

"That's right. I just want to tell my story and go home."

"Go home? You really think you're going home?"

"I haven't done anything."

"Oh, no? As it happens, I just searched your room. I found some white
powder in there."

"Are you trying to bully me?"

"I'm trying to impress on you the seriousness of your position."

"I told you—I want to cooperate."

"Okay. First things first. Where are Reed and Sally?"

"I don't know."

"You don't know."

A sob came out of him. "I feel like shit. I just feel like shit."

"You kind of look that way too." He wasn't the Dennis of the photograph. He was thinner and he obviously hadn't shaved since he left home. Skip didn't think he'd bathed or changed clothes either. "And smell that way."

He looked surprised, as if personal grooming were something from a strange country that he could barely remember hearing about.

"Dennis, what happened the other night?"

He looked at her out of eyes that seemed surrounded by bruises, the skin around them was so dark. "Evie came. She took Sally."

"Evie? Who the hell is Evie?"

"Reed's sister."

"Wait a minute. You're telling me Reed has a sister?" *And nobody's mentioned it? Am I going crazy here?*

"Yeah. Evie. It's a long story."

"Well, in that case, maybe you could just tell me some other time. I got things to do, you know?"

"Huh?"

"Start talking, Dennis."

"She came in and tried to get Sally. Naturally, we resisted. I mean, Arthur did—he was closest to Sally. So Evie shot him."

"How'd she get in?"

"Rang the doorbell. Reed answered it, for some reason."

"What reason?"

He closed his eyes and thought. He opened them. "Arthur asked her to. He was always ordering her around."

"Then what?"

"Reed came in, with Evie behind her. Nobody'd seen her in more than a year. She said hello and Arthur didn't say anything—just went on eating as if she wasn't there. Then Reed asked her if she was hungry—and she said no, she just came to get Sally."

"Came to get Sally."

"Uh-huh."

"Was she going to take her to the playground or what?"

159

"Sugar didn't tell you any of this?"

"Sugar was there?"

"No. No. Sugar was gone. I mean, she didn't tell you about Evie?"

"You tell me."

"Well, she claimed Sally was hers."

"Claimed."

"She was Sally's biological mother."

"Ah. Maybe you'd better tell me all about Evie before you go any further."

He looked down at the table between them. "I should know. She used to be my girlfriend."

"Before you met Reed?"

"Oh, God yes. That's *how* I met Reed. See, Evie was the bad sister. She and I were junkies together, and when we ran out of money, she said she had this rich family we could get money from even though they hated her. So we went to see them, and I saw Reed and—" He stopped, his eyes filled with tears.

"She yelled at us. Both of us. She'd never seen me before in my life and she yelled at me. She really made me feel like shit." He shrugged. "But then I fell in love with her."

"Just like that?"

"Sometimes I think so. I mean, I was always attracted to her. She was healthy and beautiful, and Evie was wasted, you know? And so was I. But I got to know her over a long period and she got me to clean up. I mean, to *want* to clean up.

"So I did. She got me into treatment. And that was it for Evie and me. She was a junkie and I was clean and sober—what could we possibly have together? But now Reed—she was another matter. I sometimes think that's why I went into treatment in the first place—so she'd notice me; maybe she'd consider me."

"What happened?"

"We fell in love and got married." He laughed. "Just about over Arthur and Sugar's dead bodies. You know, I wasn't only a junkie. It wasn't only that. Half my family's black—did you know that? And then there's my accent."

He spoke with the trace of a working-class accent. He had probably worked hard to get rid of it.

He shook his head. "Mm mm mm. All that goddamn hard work. And now I'm a junkie again. Shit!" He looked completely dejected. When he spoke, his voice sounded as if he were about to cry: "One minute we were having dinner, and the next, there she was. With a gun."

Skip wanted him back on track. "She's Sally's biological mother."

"Yes. See, she cleaned up too—a couple of years later. She showed up at a time when we were kind of hoping for a baby, but we weren't bent out of shape because Reed wasn't pregnant—it wasn't like some big deal. But then Evie offered us this great opportunity—she was pregnant and she couldn't keep the baby. See, she'd gotten sober and converted to Christianity—she was in some group or other that she said was really different. Different from what, I never knew, but whatever keeps you sober. She was sober, she looked good, and she said she'd just gone back to school. But she wasn't going to be able to finish if she had to take care of a baby. So would her only sister and her ex-boyfriend like to adopt her baby? she said. Well, of course we would. Who wouldn't, in our position?

"But we made sure it was all legal and perfect—a real adoption, none of this messing around. So little Sally came and we fell in love with her; we gave Evie some money for school, and everybody was happy."

Skip remained silent.

"Till she walked in with a gun."

"Okay. She walked in, said she'd come for Sally, and then what?"

"Nothing at first, I guess. We all just stared at her. Then Reed said, 'What do you mean?' and she said, 'She's my baby and I'm taking her back.' About that time Arthur grabbed her."

"Evie or Sally?"

"Sally. And then she started yelling." For a moment his face arranged itself in a half smile. "She hates that shit."

Skip was quiet.

"So then Arthur's holding her face-out, like she's a bag of groceries or something, but real tight, so she's crying, and Evie holds out her arms, like 'come-to-Mommy,' and of course the kid's never seen her before in her life, so not only does she yell louder, she balls up her fist and hits Evie." He smiled again, just for a second.

"Then Evie says, 'Put her down, Daddy,' and he says, 'You leave this house, young lady,' or something pompous like that, and all of a sudden she's holding a gun. I never saw her take it out of a purse or anything— just all of a sudden she was holding it. Reed said, 'Daddy, put her down— now.' You could tell she was scared to death, and so was I." He stopped. "You wouldn't have a cigarette, would you?"

"There's no smoking in here."

"Shit."

Skip had a moment's sympathy for him. If his story was true, he'd been through hell. "Forget it; I'll get you one."

When she came back, having bummed one from another officer, Dennis was staring into space, as if trying to find his wife and child somewhere in the distance.

"Then what?"

"Arthur put her down. Evie reached for her hand, but she wouldn't take it. So there was nothing to do but pick the baby up, and while she was doing it was the perfect time to knock her off balance. I saw it, but I was too far away. I don't suppose Reed even thought of it. Arthur took a step forward and she looked up and shot him. Just like that. Like she didn't give it a second's thought. He was hit in the leg, I think. I don't know, she must have hit an artery—blood started spurting everywhere. You know what I remember? How furious he looked. Like he was going to kill her. He lunged for her, and somehow or other he pushed over the table. I guess it scared her, because she shot him again, and that time he went down.

"Then all hell broke loose. I don't know, I just sort of went on automatic pilot. I went and bent down by Arthur and tried to help him. Evie must have picked up Sally. I heard her say she'd kill us if we tried to follow, but I was holding Arthur's hand and he was making these weird moaning sounds. I was kind of paralyzed, I guess, but I couldn't look up, I couldn't let go, all I thought was that he was dying right then and I needed to help him through. I mean, I didn't consciously think that, but when I look back, I don't really remember being aware of anything except Arthur. Then I heard Reed leave. I guess Evie must have backed out of the dining room, then when she got to the front door, she turned around and ran. And Reed followed, I guess. It was all sort of in my peripheral vision. I didn't really know anything except what was going on with Arthur; I just held onto him and said things like 'Take it easy' until finally he closed his eyes and died. And even then I sat there awhile.

"By the time I realized I was alone, everybody was gone. And so was our car—Reed's and mine. I guess Reed followed her, but—" He stopped talking and took a puff of the cigarette. He held it for a long time, staring at the wall, as if trying to come to a conclusion.

"But what?"

"Well, she had her own car. If Reed followed her, why didn't she just call the police when they got there? I mean—where the hell is she now? This is what I can't get to the bottom of."

"Why did you leave the crime scene, Dennis?"

162

"The crime scene? Oh. You mean Arthur. Well, that's a real good question, officer. Why did I? Why did I do anything I've done in the last few days? Because all those years of being sober fell away, that's why. Because I couldn't think of anything at all except getting fucked up." He stopped and thought again. "No. No, I wouldn't put it that way. I don't remember thinking of a damn thing. It was like I was comatose. I just walked till I got to a bar, where I got drunk enough to make it to the next one. It was like wasting good booze on a dead person. But of course that wasn't the half of it. What I really wanted was to chase that ol' dragon."

"Are you back on heroin?"

"Yeah."

"Where'd you get it?"

He shrugged.

"You got it from Turan, didn't you?"

"Turan?" He looked so puzzled she thought he probably was.

"Turan."

"Never heard of him."

"Who then, Dennis—who'd you get it from?"

"I can't talk about that."

"You got it from Delavon."

"I got it from who? Are you speaking English, lady?"

● ●

Jesus shit, thought Evie, *I haven't had a drink in three days and I haven't hallucinated or convulsed. Maybe things aren't as out of hand as I thought.*

She realized, further, that despite her desperate circumstances, she was possessed of a suddenly optimistic spirit. The thought came to her that maybe there was a way out. But looking down at her handcuffed wrist, that seemed preposterous.

Shit. How'd I get into this?

Mo's face swam before her. The face of her lover.

It's always a man, isn't it?

That and alcohol.

This time you really blew it, toots. This has got to be your all-time dumbest.

Shit! I swear to God if I do get out of this I'll never touch another drop.

Even though she was sure she hadn't hallucinated, there were things about her current circumstance that could hardly be explained any other way.

The fact that her lover was holding her prisoner, for instance. Because it was Mo's house that she was in. He was a lawyer with a beautiful house; a perfect marriage candidate. . . .

Right.

Well, hell, I lied to him, maybe he lied too.

She had told him she was Yvette Johnson, a laborer's daughter from Mississippi. It was a persona she'd had for a long time; being Evie Hebert just hadn't worked out for her. She didn't like a single damn member of her family and she didn't see why she should use their name.

She'd looked pretty damn good the day she met him, wearing tight jeans and some sort of low-cut blouse, her hair in a ponytail like a kid's. Because of her private-school accent, she'd made her dad a carpenter this time—it was the kind of job that an educated man might do—and she'd said her mother was a schoolteacher and that she herself had gone a semester or two to Millsapps.

She knew he was hooked the minute she walked in that house. Before she left, he'd asked her to dinner, and before the date, he sent her a dress and shoes to wear; he had a thing about shoes.

She didn't know if she should wear the outfit, thinking he probably expected a quid pro quo, but then she figured, what the hell, who cared what he expected, she could still say no if she wanted.

But he didn't even hit on her.

It was a while before he brought her here, to the mansion. He'd treated her like a princess.

Of course, she did have to contend with Mrs. Garibaldi, the terrifying housekeeper, who acted more like she owned the place than like a servant, but that was the only bad thing.

That and the fact that Mo traveled a lot. Sometimes she wouldn't see him for a couple of weeks at a time, or even longer, though in the meantime he'd phone from whatever far-flung place he'd landed in. He could always make her laugh when he called, but then when she hung up, she got this empty feeling.

This sort of lonely, desperate, bouncing-off-the-walls kind of feeling. And what she'd do then was drink a lot to ease the melancholy.

Drink and fantasize about how her life ought to be. She ought to be with Mo in this house, for instance. With the man she loved, and who loved her.

And she ought to be with Sally. For some reason, Sally had loomed large in her thoughts lately.

Not the real Sally, whom she didn't know at all, but a kind of perfect, blond, laughing baby with the tiniest toenails anyone could imagine.

She

She loved babies' toenails.
She wanted her own baby.

If they were going to be together, she and Mo, she could have Sally.
They'd have enough money, and Sally would have a father, and there
would be no reason why not. Surely Dennis and Reed understood that
Sally was just sort of on loan to them until she could get her life together.

Well, actually, she hadn't really thought that would ever happen, but it
was about to, that was obvious. She was more or less Mo's hostess, and
that was only one step from being a wife. When he had parties at the
mansion, she was his date, and she did the hostess thing damn well.

Mo told her so all the time.

She ought to be good at it. As a little girl, she'd walk around Hebert's
with her dad, watching him welcome the guests, shaking hands with everyone, making small talk. Then later, she'd done all that preteen crap,
dancing lessons at Miggy's and everything. She ought to be able to handle
herself at a party.

She looked classy too, when she was dressed up. That was Mo's word.
She looked like her mother, when Sugar was thin.

But Mo didn't know that, he thought she was from Mississippi, and he
talked like he was from the Ninth Ward or something. But his friends
were pretty impressive. A lot of them were politicians whose names she
knew; plenty were businessmen and lawyers, from the looks of them.

Who knew who they all were? They seemed to have money.

For once, she'd fallen in love with a man who had it together. She kept
looking for flaws in him but she couldn't find any.

The guy was perfect.

Yeah, and I was drunk most of the time.

He was perfect and he loved her, he told her so all the time. It would
only be a matter of time till they were married, that was obvious.

She couldn't wait. It would be the perfect life, the three of them living
here together. Of course she'd fire Mrs. Garibaldi; that was going to be
the first thing she'd do.

Then she'd redecorate, get Sally in a good school, and then . . . then
she thought she'd travel. She and Mo. Maybe she'd go with him on some
of his business trips. And maybe she'd get him to go with her to some of
the places she wanted to see.

China.
The Amazon.
Lots of places.

Or maybe she'd just go alone. Whatever she wanted would be fine with

Mo. That was the way he treated her. He bought her clothes, he bought her shoes, he bought her underwear, and flowers. He took her to nice places. He always noticed if there was a draft blowing on her, or if she was tired, or if she wanted another drink. He knew things like that before she did, he was that carefully attuned to her.

He was far and away the most generous lover she'd ever had. That was the kind of man he was, and that was the way he felt about her.

What she wanted, he wanted for her.

Still, she didn't want to spring Sally on him.

He already knew she had a daughter who didn't live with her, and she'd told him how much she missed her.

"Maybe you should think about getting her back," he'd said.

As if he'd read her thoughts. As if his thoughts were her thoughts.

The plain fact was, three nights ago, she'd gotten drunk and gone to get her daughter.

Oh, man. Drunk doesn't begin to cover it. What the hell did I think I was doing?

It made her cringe to think of it. She'd thought she'd just go get Sally and bring her home and that would be that. And then, when things got out of control, she'd acted perfectly rationally, even in her polluted state. She'd gone right to Mo, her dependable helper and protector who always knew what to do.

The part that made her cringe wasn't that, though. It was the way she'd had visions of Sally crying, "Mommy!" and leaping into her arms.

The child had never even seen her, not since the day she was born.

The other thing that humiliated her was her surprise when they'd all been awful to her. They treated her like dirt. Like she was some distant relative who embarrassed them. They'd always been that way. Why had she imagined they'd be glad to see her, or even civil to her?

She didn't know exactly how or why, but she'd found herself holding the gun Mo had given her, that he insisted she carry because her neighborhood was so dangerous.

Within seconds, the world had cracked and split open.

18

• •

Sugar hated sitting still, it was unlike her to sit still; she was a woman of action. But there was nothing she could do right now except try to pick up the pieces. She had had a service come in and clean her house, but there were still grisly signs of what had happened. She had called painters. She was going to have the room painted another color—a peachy pink—so it would look completely different.

Grady had said, "Mom, why don't you move out? This place is too *big* for you and it has horrible memories. You don't need it, make a fresh start."

But she didn't want that. There were horrible memories, all right, but some of them were old and she'd been living with them a long time. She was going to go through everything and get rid of the garbage—get rid of everything that was Arthur's—and she was going to have the whole damned place painted, all in colors she loved that Arthur had vetoed. She might even get rid of all the furniture, piece by piece, and buy stuff Arthur would hate. Being a widow had its upbeat side.

But it scared her to death.

Now, when she should be mourning Arthur—and a piece of her was, she just didn't show it—she was also realizing how furious she was with him. It had been there for years—this smashed-down, walked-on, crumpled-up fury—and now she could no longer stamp it down.

She hoped she wouldn't get up at the funeral and deliver a diatribe. *The funeral! Jesus. Where are Reed and Sally?*

The question popped into her head every time she managed to distract herself from it, which was about once every six hours. Aside from these four (more or less) daily distractions, it was all she thought about. The worry was always just underneath whatever else she was doing, like some ferret or weasel gnawing at her vitals.

It was always there, but she felt better, she felt almost good, when she was acting; trying to solve it; working to get to the bottom of the problem. Two people so far had told her they thought she was "in denial," whatever that was, because she was keeping busy. And she had seen how that cop looked at her, that Ms. Langdon, a huge brute of a woman—as if she were heartless. But it wasn't that. She should be so lucky. She just didn't show her emotions like other people.

She was putting things away in her buffet, so the painters could move it, when she came upon the photo albums carelessly stored there after some family dinner or other. Without thinking, she opened one. It was an old one, put together when the children were young, when they were all happy together. Before Arthur started cheating on her.

There was Reed with her complete set of kiddie kitchen equipment she'd gotten one Christmas, and in another, all three of them holding up their Easter baskets. That was the year she and Arthur had been so foolish as to get Grady a baby duck, which had grown up and chased Reed around the backyard whenever she ventured out.

There they were in their Easter clothes, Grady in a little boys' shorts suit and the girls in matching pink dresses. Evie had hated hers and wrecked it, falling down; purposely, Sugar was sure. Reed, true to form, hadn't gotten so much as a smudge on hers.

They were unbearably adorable—how on earth could they have turned out so abysmally? Grady a worthless failure. Evie a drug addict. *Was I that bad a mother?*

No, that has nothing to do with it. Look at me—I had a dreadful childhood and I'm fine.

That was what she always came back to. She thought that a person had in her the seeds of ability to do and be anything she wanted, and she considered herself proof of the theory. She didn't think that you were shaped by your environment, and she wasn't even that sure about your genes. It was you. Your own character. Your own strength.

168

Sugar had been born the third child of an oil company executive and a professional mom. Georgina, her mother, had had to be a pro, because two more children came after Sugar. The stair steps were Michael, Patrice, Eugenie, Patrick, and Peter. Sugar had been nicknamed because the other kids couldn't say her name.

I didn't even get my own damn name.

Michael was the oldest, Peter was the youngest, Patrice was the first girl, and Patrick was a boy, which meant he outranked her.

Everyone made *that* perfectly obvious.

There were four years between Michael and Patrice. Georgina probably thought she was off the hook when Sugar came along.

She took it out on me too. But she was oh-so-glad to have two more boys.

There had never been anyone to play with. The two older kids had each other, and so did the two younger ones. Nobody ever even noticed Sugar; no one cared about her.

She should know. She used to stage crying jags and lock herself in the bathroom, just to get noticed.

It didn't work.

(But one thing, she knew what that was all about; Evie used to pull the same thing, always trying to get attention, and Sugar never let her get away with it.)

She got all A's. That didn't work either.

Once she wore the same clothes for a week. Nobody even said anything.

She had read that you spent your whole life fighting the patterns set early in life, and she'd certainly found it so.

I feel like I'm invisible; like I have to raise my hand and say, "Excuse me, I'm here. Would you look me in the eye now and then? Would you just pretend for one second I'm as important as my husband? Or even that you see me?"

That was the way things had been for her. Whereas nothing really awful had ever happened to any of her children.

At least until the Bad Day.

The pictures in this album had all been taken before that; back when the world was young and innocent.

That was the worst day of her life, or probably any of their lives. She would never forget the look on that poor child's face . . . or the wound, so angry, so inhuman-looking; or the sounds she made, later, during her therapy.

Sugar shook her body, willing the memory away.

But that was just one day in our whole lives; and in the end, it brought us closer together. We all had to rally around in the face of adversity. Arthur even dropped his current mistress. I'm pretty sure he did, anyway. He acted almost normal for a while.

Sugar closed the album and, to her intense surprise, found herself sinking to the floor, great, hopeless sobs escaping from her diaphragm.

When the phone rang, she thought, *Reed. It's Reed!* And she was almost right. It was Grady, with news of Dennis.

• •

Grady was trying to recover, somehow make sense out of Dennis's story. Dennis had phoned him to come bail him out. The police had found heroin in his room, and they were going to use it to keep him.

Grady didn't know what to do. His mother was at Dennis's house; he couldn't let her junkie son-in-law move in with her, and he certainly wasn't going to move her into his own house. On the other hand, Sugar really had no right to be in Dennis's house.

Sugar had settled the whole matter herself by saying she wanted to go home anyway. He'd found her there, cleaning up or something. "Tough old bird" was too mild a phrase.

Dennis was going to be a problem, though. No question he was using again, and Grady didn't see any signs that his brother-in-law was going to stop.

He should have left Dennis in jail—he'd have had to detox.

But in the end he couldn't do it. He liked Dennis, and even if he hadn't, it would have been too mean.

He believed his story too.

Oh, yes.

The ring of truth was more like a peal.

That was like Evie. Exactly like her. To get drunk and go nuts like that. That was Evie.

"She's bad! She's always been bad," his mother had blurted. She was a real *primitif*, his mother was.

But Evie—what was she?

This was the part of the story he was trying to make sense of, that he had struggled with for years. Who and what was Evie, and how did she come to be?

The Evie Phenomenon, he called it, and he thought it might be different from Evie herself, but he wasn't sure. His parents had considered her devil spawn without apparently seeing the irony of it.

The piece he was working on when he got the phone call was called "The House of Blues Before The Thing." Oddly enough, it was about her.

She was so far out of control.

So terrifying. Somehow, everything she did ended up being frightening, he didn't know why. "It was a Sunday afternoon," he had written, "and our cousins had come over . . ."

• •

Maybe it was Easter or something like that—we'd had some big family gathering and they were all there, Tante Patrice's kids and Tante Breezy-Ann and Uncle Patrick's. There must have been nine or ten of us, including a few grown-ups who'd been detailed to supervise, and we decided to play softball.

The grown-ups drifted away, all except for Uncle Michael, who was the black sheep, being gay, and probably didn't care much for the others his age.

We were doing fine, having a great time, when Evie hit a foul ball and it went through the kitchen window. That wouldn't have been so bad if Mama hadn't been standing at the sink, washing some crystal things she didn't want to put in the dishwasher. The ball whizzed by her ear, hit the refrigerator, ricocheted off it, and hit her smack in the middle of the back.

Holy shit, you'd have thought she'd been shot. From the shriek she let out, you'd have got the idea she was paralyzed. Well, poor thing, she was probably scared to death. It's not every day a flying missile doubles around and hits you in the back, chases you down like one of those vulgarly named pyrotechnical devices.

She started screaming, "You kids! You kids!" and someone said Evie did it—probably me—and she hollered, "Get in here, Evelyne Hebert. I'm going to knock you into the middle of next week."

Evie started crying and cringing—God, I was sorry for her! I don't think I've ever seen anyone look so scared in my life.

It wouldn't have occurred to me to be so scared of either of our parents. I don't know if Evie was just a natural victim or what. Maybe things happened to her that Reed and I don't know about. She's the oldest—she was there before we were. Maybe her life was different somehow.

For whatever reason, she was always different from us.

She was bad.

That wasn't news. We knew she was bad because that's what everyone

171

said—it was a given in our family. But until then I didn't know how scared she was.

She was cringing like some kind of pathetic dog—actually holding onto a tree and hiding behind it—and she said she didn't do it.

Mama said, "Mike. Did she do it?"

And Uncle Michael said, "She hit the ball, Sugar, but Elise pitched it, and anyway, I'm the adult here, I was—"

"She just lied to me—did you hear that? Did you hear her lie?"

All the other grown-ups were gathered in the kitchen by this time—all of them come to see if the person howling was their own dear little child, I guess, but Mama didn't seem to care how big a spectacle she made of herself. They were just kind of watching in various states of shock, mouths open, and Dad had his arm around her waist. He was probably saying, "Now, Sugar, honey," or something like that, but she was all alone in the world for all the attention she paid.

All alone except for Evie. She said, "You *lied* to me! You're just a little liar, aren't you? You come here to me. I'll show you what happens to liars."

By this time even I was getting scared, and so were the other kids, I think. We were just standing around like the grown-ups, sort of frozen in place. I don't know what we thought Mama was going to do to her, but there was something terrifying just in the way she was yelling.

And of course we knew that it was her fault. Because somehow or other Evie made things go wrong. We knew in our hearts that none of us was capable of making that ball hit Mama, that only Evie did things like that.

No one moved; not even Uncle Mike. Mama kept saying, "*You* come here to me. *Do* what I say, Evelyne Hebert," and slapping the kitchen counter with the flat of her hand. It made a noise like a gunshot.

Evie sort of whined, "No, Mama; no, Mama," like some pathetic baby animal, and then Mama said, "Don't make me have to come and get you," in a voice like the blade of a saber.

Evie started dancing. Jumping up and down and turning around and around, flinging her arms in the air, flailing them about. She was saying, "No! Noooo! I can't," and her hands looked like they were going to fly off her wrists.

Mama said, "You've got five to get over here." And she started counting. "One. Two. Three."

Evie was still dancing, still jumping up and down, but she was scratching the tree now, attacking it with her nails, which were probably bitten to the quick, but I guess she wished she could turn into a cat and climb it.

I don't know why she didn't run, though. She could have.

I saw that scene played out a lot, other times, in greater or lesser degrees, but she never did run.

I think I would have, I really do. I've wondered a lot why she didn't.

Mama reached five and she started walking toward her.

Slowly.

Drawing out the torture.

By the time she got there, Evie was standing still, braced against the onslaught. When Mama got to her, she raised her hand and kept it poised in the air, level with her face, the back of it facing Evie.

Then she swatted her.

Backhanded her as hard as she could.

I heard her hand hit Evie's face, and then Evie fell on the ground, sobbing like a little bitty kid who'd lost its mother somewhere in the jungle.

"*Get* in that house," Mama said, and her voice was napalm.

Evie didn't move, so Mama hit her again. "You *get* in there. I'm going to turn you over to your daddy."

Evie started crawling; sort of walking like a crab, except low to the ground, trying to get out of Mama's way, but Mama was chasing her, hitting her all the way in the house.

My cousin Andrew started laughing. "She looked just like Pooty when she did that, didn't she?" Pooty was their dog.

He started whining like Pooty, and barking a little, and some of the other kids joined in, howling and yipping, maybe to drown out the sound of whatever else was happening to Evie, I don't know. I went for a walk.

I walked around the block, and then I did it again. Then I finally walked to the Plum Street Sno-ball stand and got a strawberry Sno-ball, and then I walked back.

We were pretty young when that happened, and I think I forgot it until recently. At any rate, I don't ever remember thinking about it. It slithered back into my consciousness after Reed and Dennis disappeared.

Maybe it was triggered by that woman in the House of Blues who looked like Evie. Maybe there was something scared in her face that reminded me that Evie could be that way, because mostly what I remember about my sister is that she wasn't scared.

She was just bad.

When she'd do something bad, which was often, they'd yell at her— both of them. They yelled at me sometimes, and now and then at Reed, though really not often, but they yelled at Evie a lot.

And she'd do something neither Reed nor I would ever have thought of doing. She'd yell back.

She'd yell back.

Was she crazy?

Dad would say, "Evie, go upstairs and do your homework."

And she'd say, in some whiny teenage nasal voice, "I don't have to."

And he'd say, "What did you say, young lady?"

"I don't have to do my homework."

"What did I hear you say?"

Now, how smart did you have to be to know where that was going to lead? But nobody said Evie was dumb; she was just bad. So I guess I thought that's why she did it—not to make Dad and Mama mad, nothing so well thought out—just because it was her nature.

Our parents were pretty volatile when we were growing up, but of course we all knew that was Evie's fault.

Because she tried their patience.

Because she never thought about anybody but herself.

Because she just liked to cause trouble.

Those were the things they said.

Mama hated her, so I had to stay as far away from her as possible. I don't think it ever occurred to me to become her friend or ally, to think of her any way at all except as an outcast; an outcast within the family. She simply wasn't important.

Wasn't, in a way.

Was nobody.

Maybe I wasn't the world's most sensitive child, but I suspect this business of Mama hating her did more to form my opinion of her than anything else. The plain fact was, if I got close to Evie, she'd hate me too.

Hate me more, that is.

Mama wasn't all that fond of her baby boy either.

Let me rephrase that. I think she probably adored her *baby* boy. It was just that, the older I got, the less she liked me. She didn't like the way I used to chase the dog around the house; chase Reed around the house, for that matter.

She said I drank too much orange juice and too much milk.

I ate too much.

I ate standing up.

I was always dirty.

My pet duck pooped all over the flagstones.

I was noisy.

I got sticky fingerprints everywhere.

Do all mothers complain about such things? I'm sure they do, but somehow, perhaps in the *way* she complained, Mama gave me to understand that the trouble with me was that I was a boy.

She didn't like boys. She made that perfectly clear. So she didn't like me. The older I got, the bigger my feet got and the more they stank, the more milk and orange juice I drank, the more, in short, I grew to resemble a man. And the less she liked me.

I think all that was true, pretty much, throughout our childhood and adolescence, but all bets were off when The Thing happened.

Everyone was so miserable then, hardly anyone raised his voice for a long, long time. This was disconcerting, because we were a family that yelled.

The Thing was possibly the seminal event of my childhood; the single most important event in it. The reason, perhaps, that I am a poor scribe instead of a rich lawyer or banker. It is always in the back of my mind, or just under my skin, or crawling around in my belly. It is always there, whatever else I am doing.

The Thing is there when I go out to get my morning paper and wave to my neighbor.

It is there as I sip my coffee.

It is there as I make phone calls, trying to scare up a freelance gig, something to pay the rent for yet another month.

It is there if I have lunch with an old friend.

It is there if I have two drinks before dinner and two after.

It is there when I make love.

It is with me when I walk into the House of Blues, though often, while I listen to the music, I can forget it completely. It is with me when I walk out.

Increasingly, it is there when I write.

I cannot lose it, I cannot forget it. It wants to come out.

It is trying to worm its way onto the paper.

It is a beast inside me struggling to get out.

And I will let it out.

This means something. When something is this persistent, this strong inside oneself, it means a creative leap. I know that.

I don't know how I know it, but I do. If I can write about this, my writing will take a turn, I am sure of it. I've been nibbling at the edges of it for a long time, standing on a metaphorical precipice, and this stunning new fact may push me over. This grotesquely amazing thing.

The fact that Evie, my sister, has killed our father.

Is that possible?

It has occurred.

Now I have written it. If only I could assimilate it, could make myself believe it.

Events, thoughts, are turbid within me; old memories take on new meanings.

A funny thing, though. That softball thing, the thing where Evie flailed and jumped up and down, I *think* that was on Easter. The Thing certainly was.

We were all dressed up, I remember it well; we had been to church.

The girls and I fought in the car. Reed had a hat and I think I jerked it off her head and threatened to throw it out the window. She cried, and Mama slapped me.

It was a beautiful day, a perfect day, the reason pagans celebrate the spring, and I guess the reason Christians do too.

We had been to church . . .

● ●

Grady stopped, realizing he had already written that. He exed it out and wrote, "Reed had a hat . . ." before he stopped again. His skin felt prickly and the back of his neck was damp. His stomach crawled with venomous snakes. He felt a furrow in his forehead as deep as a ditch. His jaw locked so hard his teeth hurt.

Wait. Breathe deep.

He brushed sopping hair from his face.

It'll be okay.

Nausea roiled in his groin and began to travel to his solar plexus.

Get up and walk around.

As he got up, he began to flail the air, recognizing in the gesture something of what he'd written about his sister. He walked and flailed, stretched a few times, and then threw himself on his bed, still breathing deeply, until the terror and hatred had passed.

Can you be phobic about a day in your life?

Maybe.

But I don't think I am. This isn't a phobia, it's a parasite chewing on me.

It had to go, The Thing had to go.

And for the first time, he thought he could get it out, pull the worm

176

from beneath his skin, all twelve miles of it, or three thousand miles of it, whatever was in there.

He thought it would come out soon.

But not now.

As soon as he was breathing normally again, he would shower off the sweat and go to the House of Blues.

19

• •

Skip woke up to the sound of a yipping puppy. But the outside noise was nothing compared to what was going on in her head. This Dennis development had her reeling.

She had hoped that when she found Dennis, she'd find Reed, Sally, and all the answers. Instead it seemed she'd only opened a can of worms wriggling at something approaching the speed of light.

One of those wriggling worms was called Tricia, but she figured that was something she'd have to deal with later. Right now, life was throwing things at her like one of those machines that serves tennis balls.

Dennis, Dennis, Dennis, do I believe you?

She had no choice.

That was the practical consideration, but there was also another. Deep in her gut, she felt he was telling the truth.

The more time she spent as a police officer, the more she was coming to trust her intuition. It seemed a contradiction in terms that intuition should come with experience, but even the most grizzled cops talked about it. Guys without a metaphysical cell in their bodies. Who wouldn't be caught dead in a church, say, unless someone had died.

Her brain did a kind of mental "oof," and a black curtain dropped somewhere in her psyche as she remembered that someone had.

And yet, the curtain swung down and swung back in a few moments, more or less of its own accord. The loss of Jim was going to be a raw wound for a long time, perhaps would never completely heal. But it was starting to scab over.

She pulled on a pair of loose-fitting linen pants and an olive silk T-shirt, kissed Steve good-bye, and left in a coffeeless daze, thinking to get caffeined-up at work.

As she sipped, she considered her situation.

Oh, hell, she suddenly thought, and looked in the phone book for an Evie Hebert.

There wasn't one.

And of course, Evie could be calling herself Skip Langdon for all she knew. Nothing to do but start at the beginning, and that was Hebert's.

To her distress, Sugar was there; Skip had hoped to find Nina alone.

"Officer Langdon," said Sugar, "could you please tell me what's going on? Last night, Grady called me at my house and said Dennis was back and needed his house, could I please go home? Can you imagine? Not even offering to put me up. Not even thinking about my things, over at Dennis and Reed's.

"Now Dennis won't answer the phone, and I can't find anything *out*. What happened? What's going on?"

"Grady didn't tell you?" She thought Dennis had probably filled him in.

"Nobody tells me anything."

Skip considered. "Let's sit down," she said. "You have a right to know. But I'd appreciate it if you'd keep it to yourself."

When they were seated, she said, "First, let me tell you that we still don't know where Reed and Sally are."

With her right hand Sugar batted away the irrelevancy. "Grady told me *that*."

"Okay, here's what Dennis said. I'm afraid there's some very bad news —your daughter Evie is involved."

Sugar's mouth pulled tight at the corners and a furious look blazed in her eyes. Skip found the expression unnerving, wildly inappropriate for a person who was being told her oldest child had murdered her husband. It was so full of anger and hurt that they spilled over and filled the room.

"I'm sorry," Skip said when she had finished her story.

Sugar said nothing.

179

Skip made her voice businesslike. "I need to know anything you can tell me about how to find Evie."

"I don't know how to find Evie."

"This is important, Mrs. Hebert. Think back to the last time you saw her."

"Why are you making me do this?" Sugar's face turned ugly and liquid; her voice was harsh.

"I'm sorry. I know it's hard for you. But I think if you mull it over, you'll understand why it's important." She couldn't see trying to explain something so obvious. "Is Nina here?"

"Nina? What do you want Nina for?"

She stood up. "I'd like to talk to her. Excuse me, will you?"

She found Nina in her own office. "How come nobody told me about Evie?"

"Evie?" Nina sounded hurt and puzzled. "What does Evie have to do with anything?"

I guess that's my answer. "She may. It turns out she may."

"Oh?" Her face was a mask of curiosity.

"Do you have any idea where she is?"

Nina shrugged. "No. I don't think she's been heard from in a couple of years."

"Think back carefully to the last time you saw her. I need to know anything you can remember—"

Sugar barged in, interrupting: "I remembered something. She was born again—that must have meant she was a member of a church."

She looked extremely pleased with herself.

"Ah. Did she happen to say what church?"

"Why, no. She didn't."

Nina said, "Something with 'lamb' in it."

"Good. Mrs. Hebert, does that ring any bells?"

Sugar looked disconcerted. She spoke to Nina: "She told you that?"

"You mean the name of the church?" Nina shrugged. "She hardly talked about anything else."

Sugar said, "I don't believe you."

Nina didn't speak. She sat impassively waiting for more.

"If she'd talked to anyone, it would have been me. I mean, *I* am the girl's mother."

"Well, if I'm not mistaken, she did tell me." Her tone said: *This woman's going to drive me crazy if I don't kill her first.*

Skip said to Nina. "Do you remember anything at all about the church? What denomination, for instance?"

"Not really. I have the impression it was something kind of off-brand. I don't even know where it was."

"You mean, whether it was in New Orleans or somewhere else?"

"Uh-huh. I realize I don't even know."

And she was the one who knew the most.

Skip left, thinking it was a hell of a family she'd gotten involved with. *Oh, well. Mine's no great shakes either.*

Her dad hadn't spoken to her for nearly two years after she told her family she was going on the job; her brother Conrad sold her information in return for fixing his parking tickets (actually she paid them herself); and her mother judged herself, her husband, and every member of her family by what she thought other people thought of them.

Naturally, since Skip didn't have a high-status job, she was usually found wanting. On the other hand, whenever she got in the paper over some case or other, she enjoyed a brief flurry of maternal popularity.

But at least we don't murder each other.

● ●

She went back to headquarters and looked in the phone book. Dozens, probably hundreds of churches. She started scanning for "lamb" names.

In the end she had a list of five. She could call them, but a little background wouldn't hurt. She dialed the *Times-Picayune* and asked for Eileen Moreland.

"Skippy Langdon. You must want something." Moreland had the world-weary air of a reporter from Central Casting.

"You know me, Eileen. I'd never take advantage of our friendship."

"What friendship? You ask me for clips and I give them to you. You make me promises and you don't deliver."

"Let me say the magic word. 'Arthur Hebert.' "

"Arthur Hebert what?"

"I don't know yet. But something when the case breaks. Something for your column. I'll take notes."

"Oh, sure. Just like always."

"Lunch, then."

"How about fixing my parking tickets?"

"How about lunch?"

"Oh, forget it. You'd probably stand me up. What do you want any-way?"

181

"Clips on five churches."

Eileen sighed. "Shoot."

As it happened, there were clips on only one: Blood of the Lamb Baptist, which was renowned for its fine Gospel choir.

Skip said, "Maybe you could introduce me to the religion editor."

"Stanley? Oh, all right."

She could tell Eileen was done with her. One day she really would have to give her a decent news tip.

There were a few seconds of silence, then some rings, and finally a high male voice. "Detective Langdon, this is an honor. How may I assist you?"

A godly man indeed. I wish more people thought it was an honor.

She asked for a rundown on the five churches.

Three—including Blood of the Lamb—were established neighborhood churches. The other two he knew nothing about.

"But I've got a hunch about Great Mount Precious." (Full name: Great Mount Precious Lamb of God.) "Why don't you check it out?"

"Check it out for what?"

"What are you looking for?"

"A recent convert. A born-again who may have pretty much devoted her life to the group."

"Oh. That kind of church. More or less a cult."

"I'm not sure."

"Check out the Precious one. I don't think it's what you want, but it might be something you never saw before. Maybe they pray to St. Expedite." He chuckled delightedly. "I know I do."

"I'm going over right now and light a candle to him."

She hung up, thinking she would if she knew how. She could use a little help of the sort he was said to supply. St. Expedite, unknown to the Vatican, had arrived in New Orleans in a box, sometime long ago. That is, a statue in a saintly robe had, and the box was stamped "Expedite." The polytheists who passed for Catholics in New Orleans had clasped him joyously to their bosoms and the statue stood big as life, even now, in a church on North Rampart Street.

Having been brought up Episcopalian, Skip didn't quite know how to pay homage to him. In lieu of a candle, she wrote the word "expedite" over her list of lamb churches and started phoning them.

The first three were the ones Stanley had known about. At all three she talked with a nice machine that said its owner would call back.

At Great Mount Precious she got another machine: giving only the time of Sunday's service.

At the last one, Blood of the Lamb Divine Evangelical Following, she talked to a woman who said she'd get back to her.

By the end of the day, calls had been returned and she was singularly unimpressed, as Stanley had predicted, with the first three. Nice church ladies had looked up records and said no Evelyne Hebert had ever been a member, and furthermore, two out of the three had said they'd have known her if she had. The third one indicated that if Evelyne were white, she would probably have been pretty conspicuous and might not have even been welcome.

All three could have been lying, but the last two churches looked a great deal more promising.

She never did get anyone at Great Mount Precious. That made it attractive, like ice cream on a diet.

And the church lady at Blood of the Lamb Divine Evangelical Following hadn't been nice. That made *her* attractive.

Besides that, she wouldn't give out even the tiniest bit of information, would only make Skip an appointment to see the pastor—Sunday at three.

Skip went home feeling almost relaxed—it was Friday and she was about to have a day off. St. Expedite could take over for the next twenty-four hours. When she had sworn to learn to meditate (a task at which she'd been less than successful), she'd also tried her hand at visualizing. That was easier. In fact, she could do it with her eyes open and her mind on her driving. She tried it now, seeing the gentle saint's foot come slowly back, disappear behind his robe, then come forward quickly, displacing the robe, causing it to flip up unabashedly—delivering a good swift kick to the butt of her problem.

"Steve? Oh, Steve," she hollered, unlocking the door. She wanted some kicks of her own—dinner and some music, say. Or skip the music, maybe just a walk by the river.

No one answered. Maybe Steve was at the Big House.

Jimmy Dee answered the door. "Darling! Thank God. I've been dying of boredom. Your bear took the kids and the animal out for a romp. The quiet is piercing my eardrums."

"Shall I shriek and bark a little?"

"If I'd known you were into leashes, I'd have gotten you one with rhinestones."

"How about getting me some lovely white wine?"

"Well, aren't *we* the libertine." But he got it, and a glass for himself as well.

"Let's go in the front parlor, shall we? Geneese never dusts it, but on the other hand the monsters never enter it—an excellent trade-off in my opinion."

The curtains were drawn. It seemed almost gloomy, a word she'd never associated with the Big House. "It's deathly quiet."

Dee-Dee sighed. "How values change. I was actually lonely, can you fathom it? You'd think I would have been thrilled."

"Where's Layne?"

"Damn that man-mountain of yours! He's ruined my life."

"Oh, for heaven's sake, Dee-Dee."

"Well, he has. He brought that wretched animal into the house, and the minute he did, my whole world disintegrated."

"Oh, no. You mean the allergy."

"Kenny adores the dog. He's a new child—a dry child, I might add, if you take my meaning. Sheila adores the dog as well. For once they agree on something. They're almost civil to each other, they're so pathetically eager to feed the little thing and take care of it, no doubt proving themselves worthy so nasty old Uncle Jimmy doesn't send it back to the pound where I cordially wish it had met its demise."

"Dee-Dee!"

"It's ruining my house! All my beautiful renovations—gone. Chewed to rags and ribbons."

"Well, they were just for the kids anyway."

"I *am* a homosexual, in case you haven't heard. I need smothering, fussy decor, or I swoon."

Usually he only did the swish act when he thought Skip was depressed. Today it had a different quality—she thought he was avoiding something.

"I have this weird feeling there's more."

"You asked where Layne was?"

"Oh, no. I don't think I can stand it."

"Well, he hasn't dumped me yet. But he may—over that precious little Angel."

"He's really, really allergic?"

"Yes. He has to take about four pills even to come over here, and by then he's so loaded he falls asleep over dinner. Do you know how rare it is to be allergic to a dog? Cats, no surprises. But hardly anybody's allergic to dogs."

"You'd think he'd have noticed it before."

"Oh, he's not allergic to *dogs*. Never been allergic to dogs in his life. Only Angel."

"The name stuck, I guess."

"I guess. Nobody's come up with anything else."

"Oh my God, if *you* haven't, you must be depressed."

He grinned ever so slightly. "Well, Angel kind of fits her."

"How serious is this Layne thing?"

"I guess it's too soon to tell. We've only had the damn dog a couple of days. He's called an allergist, but he hasn't seen her yet."

"That wasn't what I meant."

"Oh. You mean Layne and me. Do I ask you personal questions?"

"Now and then. Whenever the laryngitis clears up."

"Remember that time I said you'd never seen me in love? I warned you, didn't I? It's not a pretty sight."

"Oh, don't be so dramatic. If it can't conquer an allergy, it's not love."

"Well, listen to the expert. Miss Give-Up-Your-Career-and-Come-to-Me-or-Else."

Skip felt the blood come to her cheeks. "Go ahead, Dee-Dee—bring up the stupidest thing I ever did in my life."

"You didn't do anything I'm not capable of. You were afraid you'd lose him—it's a feeling with which I'm familiar."

"So I dumped him so he couldn't hurt me first." Her face felt like a griddle. "Brilliant."

"Not to mention kind, understanding, and loyal."

She winced. "Dee-Dee, don't. The wound's too fresh."

"I'm sorry, Tiny One. I forget you're only tough on duty."

"Anyway, maybe I learned something from it."

"What? Not to be scared? Not to do anything stupid when you're scared? We all think we've learned that one, but it keeps coming back. I don't know if there's anything to compare with the fear that you might lose somebody you love."

He looked so miserable Skip wanted to hug him like he was Kenny's age.

"Well, I might have learned specific things not to do. Like try to replace him with somebody else just because I'm scared shitless."

"You're not going to say, 'even though men do that all the time'?"

"Come to think of it, I guess that's what Darryl was doing. Maybe not quite that—for him it was a rebound thing."

"There's fear in that too—the fear that never goes away. That you'll get sick and you'll be alone. That you'll die alone."

She felt her throat closing. She thought of Jim and his two wives and two sets of children.

At least he wasn't alone.

Yes, he was. When he died, he was alone.

I wasn't there.

"What is it, Venus? What's wrong?"

She shook her head. "Nothing. It's a sad thought, that's all. Dying alone."

"You've got me," he said, and she knew he wanted to take her hand but wouldn't.

"I know."

"And I've got you. I know that, you don't have to say it, but do you mind if I vent for a minute?"

"Sure." But she was puzzled, having no idea what was coming.

"Well, you *could* marry the man-mountain."

"What! And make you miserable?" Though things were better since Layne's arrival, the tension between Dee-Dee and Steve would always be there.

"It's just theoretical, darling. You could marry him. I mean, it's legal."

She was beginning to get his drift. "Dee-Dee, for Christ's sake—you're pining for a white wedding? Sheila as bridesmaid and Kenny as ring-bearer?"

"Cruel, cruel beast."

She could see he wasn't offended, but for form's sake she said she was sorry.

"Oh, I'm just carping. I'm not much into the politics of it all. If Layne and I wanted to own property together, we could. I could leave my oh-so-modest fortune to him—only now there are Sheila and Kenny.

"And you, of course. The city's so broke, you're going to need help even if you make chief." He got back to the original subject: "What I'm talking about is more an angst kind of thing."

"About being gay." He'd never expressed the slightest dissatisfaction with it, even though she knew he was in the closet at work.

"The truth is, I don't know if I'd feel comfortable living with Layne, even if I didn't have the kids. You know how I sometimes take a female date to parties? Like Your Tininess, for instance. And now with the kids, would it really be the best thing? I mean, would Kenny's little friends call him a queer and stuff?"

"Dee-Dee, Kenny's lost both parents. Compared to that, it doesn't seem all that important."

"But that's the point! His life's been hard, and now he's in an alien world—I don't want to make it any worse."

"Okay, so let's see if I'm getting this right. You're upset because Layne's allergic to Angel, and also because you can't marry him, but mostly because it wouldn't look too good to live with him. Does that about cover it?"

"Oh, Ming the Merciless. How can you?"

"I'm just trying to get the lay of the land."

Dee-Dee put a hand over his mouth. "I will *not* make any cheap jokes." She could see he was cheering up. "God, I'm unattractive when I get like this!"

"Oh, you are not, Dee-Dee."

"I don't know what comes over me, I just get these pathetic *longings*."

"Give yourself a break. The average person wants to be able to get married and have the same rights as anybody else—"

"God, you sound doctrinaire."

"Now you're going to trivialize it?"

"Hey! Let's hear it for queers. I'm certainly not going to trivialize it." He looked sheepish. "But about my pathetic longings—"

"What's pathetic about them?"

"I only get them when things are going great."

"So the truth comes out. Things are going great, are they?"

"Well, they were until the sneezes started. This could cause real baby-sitting problems, do you realize that? I mean, if I can only go over there."

"So take the kids. They can play some of Layne's games."

"Oh, enough. How's *your* love life?"

"You certainly have a short attention span."

"Cough it up."

A wave of regret broke over her. "Great, except he's leaving in a few days."

"Well, gather ye rosebuds and all that."

"The other night I saw Darryl with another woman. I had a pang, I have to admit it."

"Hussy."

"Hasn't it ever happened to you? Being with somebody you love, but attracted to someone else that you know wouldn't be right for you, and anyway the other one's the one you're committed to, but you sort of can't resist anyway? It's like you're hypnotized or something; or under some evil spell."

"You terrify me, darling. My bones are absolutely rattling with fear. No! I cannot do it again. When I think of what I just went through with you! The way you moped for weeks after you tossed aside your bear like a hamster—"

"I'm not going to do anything, Dee-Dee. I'm just talking about the way I feel."

"Let me tell you something, Thumbelina. It's damned dangerous talk."

She knew it was. Darryl exerted a powerful pull on her, she didn't know why. And he was around a lot. During that turbulent period, he'd gotten to know the kids and they adored him.

He flirted when he came around too.

20

• •

Reed heard a key in the lock. Her body stiffened. Anna Garibaldi again. Perhaps she could talk Anna into letting her have a minute with Sally, even letting her see Sally, just for a moment, even a moment.

Maybe she should offer her money.

It sounded as if Anna was fumbling; funny, she didn't seem the type. And then Evie, not Anna, fell into the room under a heavy weight.

Sally.

The child, struggling in Evie's arms, had apparently thrown her off balance. Evie had a hand clasped over Sally's mouth, which meant she had had to negotiate the lock with the hand that balanced Sally in her arms—no easy task. She closed the door quickly by banging her butt against it.

When she took her hand from Sally's mouth, Reed saw that the child's face was red with fingerprints, but it seemed trivial at the moment. Sally was here and unharmed.

"Mama. Mama." Evie released her and she ran to Reed, who had only one arm to pick her up, the other being handcuffed once again to her chair.

"Oh, baby. Baby, baby, baby."

189

Evie said, "Reed, I'm sorry."

Sorry!

Sally was cuddling like a monkey, trying to wrap herself around Reed tight enough to stick if anyone tried to pry her off. But like Reed, she had only one hand right now; her right thumb was in her mouth. And Sally didn't suck her thumb.

"I got drunk. I'm really sorry. I can't believe I could be so stupid."

Reed fought down all the ready answers to that one. She felt her hand on Sally's soft cheek, the pressure of the child's legs around her. "Evie. What's going on here?"

"I don't know what happened. I just—"

"Evie, work with me. Please!"

Evie glanced at the door. "You're right. I don't know how much time we have." She dropped her voice. "Anna's on the phone—she left her keys in my room when she went to take the call. Something's wrong with her; she's not acting normal. When the call came through, she kind of went berserk."

"You're involved with these people?"

She glanced at Reed's handcuffs. "Not really. But they know me here, so they let me out now and then—when they need a babysitter. Basically, I'm locked in a room most of the time, but, see, Anna's got this thing for Sally—it's like she's some frustrated grandma who just found something to love. I don't know—she's just gaga over the kid—so sometimes she lets me out to take care of her for a little while, if she has to go out for a few minutes."

"She's let you out before and this is the first time you've brought her to me?"

"You don't understand. This is the first time I haven't had somebody watching me like I was about to steal the silver. There's these guys—these real big guys."

"They're here now?"

"They're always here."

So much for any thoughts of making a break for it.

"What is this place?"

"My boyfriend's house."

"Well, who *is* your boyfriend? Gus Lozano?"

"He's this really nice man. A lawyer . . ." Her eyes filmed over and her voice dropped to a whisper. "But something's off; something's way off." Again she glanced at the door. "Let me just check something."

She opened the door and stepped out for a moment. She came back nodding. "She's still talking. I'd better take Sally back."

"No." Reed squeezed the child against her, and Sally, instinctively, hugged her tighter as well. "You took my baby for this frustrated grandmother? Did you sell her? Is that what's happening here?"

Evie looked horrified. "Oh, no. Oh, no, it wasn't that."

"Well what?"

"I was just . . ." She paused, apparently trying to get her thoughts together about what had happened. "I don't know, I was just incredibly stupid. That's all."

What kind of stupid, dammit? But she held her tongue, knowing nothing she could say would speed up the process.

Evie shrugged, obviously still trying to make sense of it. "I just got involved with somebody I didn't know that well. When I think back on it, I guess that's what happened. He seemed like a pillar of the community. You know. Lawyer. Nice house and everything"—she indicated the room surrounding them—"but I guess when you get down to it, I just . . . really didn't know him. I should have known. I never dated anybody that nice before. Men like that don't like me; why would they? But I thought, since I cleaned up and everything—"

Cleaned up. Right. "Evie, what happened?"

"I got drunk. I got drunk and kidnapped Sally so we could be a happy little family. . . ."

Reed couldn't help herself: "You must have been seriously loaded."

"Don't, Reed. Just don't, okay? Don't you think I feel bad enough?"

"Sorry." But she wasn't. She felt like a Stephen King character, the imprisoned writer in *Misery*, at the mercy of a lunatic.

Sally said, "Mama? Go home now? Daddy?"

"Soon, honey. Soon." Reed's conscience throbbed. She didn't believe in lying to children. But she didn't need an argument now.

For the moment, Evie had replaced her ditsiness with a look of determination. "When things went wrong—you know, at Mother and Daddy's —I came to Mo. My boyfriend. I mean, what else would you do? I thought he'd protect me. But he ordered both of us locked up; all three of us, I mean. I don't know why. I swear I don't. When he came to talk to me that night, all he said was, there was a huge meeting going on here and he'd have to get back to me. I didn't even realize I was locked in until I tried to leave the bedroom."

"Meeting," said Reed. "That explains what Barron Piggott was doing here. And Bruce Smallwood and Lafayette Goodyear." She looked up at her sister. "But the boyfriend, Evie. A thug named Mo!"

"His name is Maurice Gresham and he's a very nice—"

"Maurice Gresham?"

"You know him?"

"Very well. He and his wife are regulars at the restaurant. Every Tuesday night, just about."

"Wife! Did you say *wife*?" Evie's eyes flicked, panicky.

"Evie, he's no lawyer. And he couldn't possibly own this house. He's a cop—and not a chief or anything either. I don't know if he's even a sergeant."

Behind Evie the door flew open and the entrance was filled with one of the real big guys she'd mentioned, dressed in khakis and a polo shirt. Pointing a gun at the three of them.

He stepped into the room, the Dragon behind him.

Evie was right. There was something strange about the Dragon, if that's who Anna was; something shaky and slightly out of control. Her face was chalky and her skin drawn. She looked as if she'd had a horrible shock.

The big guy put his gun away and began the task of peeling Sally off her mother.

• •

Skip couldn't say when she'd last been to church on Sunday. She didn't know what to wear. Pants were just about all she had, so they'd have to be okay. Maybe with a silk blouse and some nice earrings. Showing respect was the thing. As if she'd taken care.

She was puttering around looking for something suitable when she heard Steve sit up in bed and stretch. He was a slow starter in the morning.

She said, "You like a little investigative jaunt. How about church?"

"I think I'll pass. I went once."

She had occasion later to wish he'd gone, so she'd have a reality check on what happened. She'd been a lot more than once, and it was always the same, except that day.

The church, in a part of the Ninth Ward to which not even she had ever been, was surprisingly affluent—meaning it was a small neat wooden building capable of holding about a hundred people, instead of a garage or someone's living room, which was what she'd imagined.

The neighborhood was one of tiny houses, quiet-looking, not slummy at all, but there were no sidewalks. Probably the families who lived here had been around for more than a generation.

The church was dim. After Skip's eyes had grown accustomed, she saw that it had two altars, one in front and one in back, each holding so many statues of saints she wondered how anyone dusted them all. If there were copies of the original St. Expedite, no doubt one was here.

Though the service had started, there were only a few people in the pews, fifteen or sixteen, she thought; mostly women. It looked like a poor black neighborhood church in the nineties, struggling to keep even a few old women in the congregation, not the sort that Evie would ever even find, let alone be persuaded to join. Skip thought of leaving, but didn't for two reasons.

One was that a woman turned around, saw her, and beamed. "Welcome," she whispered, and her face was so warm, so gentle, that it would have been churlish to leave after that.

The other was that there were three white people in a back pew, all young, and even though scrubbed-up for church, a little on the scruffy side. The sort of people she could picture Evie hanging with.

In fact, the one woman among them might almost have been Evie—she was blond and very pretty, but too thin, too pale, a little druggy-looking. But she was younger than Evie by five or ten years, Skip guessed.

Still. Perhaps there was something here—some ministry to addicts; free food after the service.

Something.

She sat down and looked around.

She needn't have worried about getting the uniform right. One woman —though not in the choir, which consisted of five or six people in street clothes—wore what appeared to be a pink choir robe.

Others had on respectable dresses with nylons and heels; generic church clothes. Two or three wore pantsuits.

Another, an older woman with huge dark-rimmed glasses, wore a long white robe and matching wrapped head garment. She was tall and looked like some elegant African elder, perhaps dressed for a party at the consulate of a struggling nation.

The men wore carefully pressed shirts tucked into clean dark pants, collars open; the building wasn't air-conditioned.

The clergyman who delivered the sermon—Skip never did catch his title—wore an elaborate robe, blue satin lined with pink, and a hat like a bishop's miter. She thought of an essay she had once read by Zora Neale Hurston praising black people, her own people, for their exuberance, and

Skip would have been happy to praise the minister's outfit instead of the Lord.

She wasn't sure what denomination she'd wandered into, but she was pretty sure it wasn't Lutheran or Presbyterian.

Though the congregation was tiny, there was not only a pianist, but a drummer, and the minuscule choir could rock out as if it were a hundred strong.

There was quite a lot of music and some readings, done by different church members, and there were a number of small rituals that Skip had never seen before. At one point the entire congregation got up and walked in a circle. Why, she couldn't have said.

There were anointings, with perfume, apparently. Once again she wasn't sure why.

People were given an opportunity to testify about the way their spiritual lives were shaping up. One woman got on a roll, speaking in a kind of rhythmic way, about the unfortunate way her husband had treated her and how Jesus had gotten her through it. She started to sway as she talked, and Skip had a premonition about what was going to happen: *She's going to flip out in some way and they're going to say she's "in the spirit" or some such.*

But she didn't. She cried through the last third of her testimony, which sounded as if it had been written and rehearsed, but she didn't flip out.

Most of the other testimony was a great deal more informal, involving thanks for simple things, mostly: good weather and a good night's sleep; food; family.

Skip wasn't too sure what moved people to get up and talk, if they had nothing more important to impart than that—the desire to participate, she thought, the need not to be left out.

One of the white people spoke. He said he had a plant that was growing well and he was enjoying the way God was tending it. Marijuana was Skip's guess.

At one point there was something called a "hand blessing," in which people lined up to put a hand on the Bible, it looked like, and say a private prayer. You put down a dollar bill at the time, if you wanted to be so blessed, which struck Skip as at least as good a deal as playing Lotto. She did it herself, praying for enlightenment on the subject of Evie, figuring it couldn't hurt.

Back in her seat, she thought: *What did I do that for?*

The service was long, but it built. Skip tried to explain it later, to Steve, but she couldn't. What she noticed about halfway through was that her hands tingled and her ears rang a little bit.

When the congregation was invited up to the altar to pray, in some sort of ritual that looked like communion without the bread and wine, she found herself going, though she knew she didn't have to, that it would have been perfectly acceptable to stay where she was.

She didn't especially believe in God, at least not this one, or at least didn't want any contact with him, after the way he ordered all that slaughter in the Old Testament and the way everyone spoiling to get in a war used his name as a rallying cry. But there she was, kneeling in some unknown and probably unheard-of neighborhood in the middle of nowhere that probably wasn't even on a map, with fifteen or sixteen strangers whose lives she probably couldn't begin to fathom if they spent the next three weeks telling her their family histories.

And something odd happened to her. Something came up through her bent knees—or perhaps it started in her feet, she couldn't be sure—and coursed through her body. It couldn't have been the famous "spirit" because surely that came down instead of up; but it was something. She felt an odd peace afterward, a curious fulfillment.

Holy shit. Maybe that was a religious experience.

Of course it was, stupid. You're in a church. Anything that happens here is one by definition.

Uh-uh. What about that woman with the little boy?

At the beginning of the service, a little boy had started to cry and his mother had hit him with a belt in the pew beside her, apparently brought especially for the purpose.

Watching her wasn't a religious experience.

But what the odd occurrence was, she couldn't decide. Perhaps because it was a small, very focused group, something was unleashed that she hadn't experienced before—some kind of directed energy.

This was why she thought later that she needed Steve for a reality check. She couldn't even really describe the thing, much less be sure it was real.

Afterward, she was about to go talk to the minister when a small woman tapped her on the back. "Aren't you Skip Langdon?"

She turned around, amazed. New Orleans was tiny in some ways—you always knew someone wherever you went—but this time it was not only unlikely, it was impossible. This neighborhood was probably unknown even to the census takers.

"I'm Emmaleen Boucree. Tyrone's mother? I saw you at a concert once, and Joel showed you to me."

She was from the family of musicians that had produced Darryl.

Skip blurted, "What on earth are you doing here?"

Emmaleen smiled. "This my old church. I went to this church years ago. My mama still live in the neighborhood, but she gettin' on now. Really gettin' on. She ain' really well enough to come to church. I just come over and bring her something to eat on Sundays and I drop in for services when I have time. We all go to Spiritual churches, all us Boucrees —didn't you know that?"

"Spiritual churches?" Weren't all churches spiritual?

"Oh, yeah. We kind of different." She cackled.

"It was—um, a beautiful service."

"Was, wasn't it? But kind of tame. You should see it when folks really get goin'—come sometime to the Friday evenin' healin' service; then you really see something. Now how can we help you?"

Well, I had this funny feeling when I was supposed to be praying, and I was just wondering—was that God or anything?

"You didn't come here to get touched by the spirit, did you? Miss Langdon, you with me?"

"Sorry, I guess I spaced out. I'm trying to find someone named Evelyne Hebert. Everyone calls her Evie. Do you know if she goes to this church?"

"Don' ring a bell. Which I think prob'ly means no." She waved an arm. "You can see it's kind of a shrinking deal anymore—Sunday mornin's at least. I think the Friday night healin's go a little better, probably. L'es go ask somebody who knows."

She took Skip to the fancifully dressed clergyman, who confirmed that no Evelyne or Evie Hebert, or anyone answering her description, was a member of the church or had been. But he said Skip was invited to come back any time she wanted to and bring all her friends.

"We glad to have you any time," he said. He shook her hand. "We glad to have you," he repeated. And he smiled so benignly that it made her wonder why smiles like that were missing from her life most of the time.

She had time to go home for lunch before her second appointment, and when she arrived, the kids were in the courtyard with Angel, Steve, Jimmy Dee, and Darryl Boucree, the men drinking coffee at a table under an umbrella. The smaller animals frolicked in the sun, and the day was so perfect it was as if Arthur Hebert were alive again and Sally was home with her parents, and Jim had never gone on that stakeout with her.

"Darryl. What are you doing here?"

He got up to kiss her, and she felt the current that was always there. She wondered if it was visible to the naked eye; Steve knew she'd been interested in someone last year, but he didn't know it was Darryl.

"I came to bring the new baby a toy." She saw that Angel had some kind of chew-thing, which the kids kept snatching and throwing.

"I saw your Aunt Emmaleen this morning. At least I guess Tyrone's mother's your aunt."

"Great-aunt, I think. Even I get it mixed up."

Steve said, "Where'd you see her?"

"Church. There were less than twenty people there and one of them was Emmaleen Boucree."

"Well, if it was church, that makes sense," said Darryl. "The Boucrees are very large on religion. That's why there's so much good music in those churches out there."

"What's a spiritual church?"

"You mean you just went to one and you don't know? Well, I been in 'em all my life—not sure I do either. We're big on statues, I'll tell you that. And you should see it when somebody gets baptized."

Skip was silent for a minute.

"What is it?" Steve put a hand over hers. Faintly embarrassed at the gesture, she glanced at Darryl out of the corner of her eye.

"I don't know. I was just feeling left out, I guess."

"Left out of what?"

"Oh, a culture worth having."

Darryl said, "You one of those white people wants to be black?"

Skip couldn't think of an answer.

"Quit looking sheepish," said Jimmy Dee.

"Well, if you are, I don't blame you," said Darryl, and he leaned over to tweak her cheek, with Steve sitting right there.

Absolutely undaunted, Steve kept beaming, still covering her hand with his.

I wonder what it would be like to trust somebody like that? Why can't I be like Steve?

From the first moment they'd met, Steve had never given her the slightest reason to think him other than utterly devoted to her, and more than once she'd nearly destroyed the relationship with her doubts.

He must have had a nice mama.

The thought made her glance over at Sheila and Kenny, who had no mama at all.

197

• JULIE SMITH •

I hope I can be decent to them. Just give them a little something they can use later. Something; just a little something.

"I'm hungry," said Kenny, and Jimmy Dee went off to make seafood salad.

They ate outside, Skip between Steve and Darryl, enjoying as great a sense of well-being as a baby in the womb.

Why can't I have them both? she thought, knowing she was a fool for thinking it; wondering if adolescence would ever end.

Before she left for the Blood of the Lamb Divine Evangelical Following, Layne dropped by and Steve and Darryl took the kids to find a park for Angel to romp in. It was a weird setup, she thought, not exactly Dan Quayle's notion of the ideal family. But for the moment, just for today, she felt completely happy.

The Following was in Metairie, in a freshly painted but modest building meant to be lived-in, but, like its owners, born again.

If the church lady who'd made the appointment had seemed slightly testy, the one who answered the door more than made up for it. She had on some kind of white summer dress that perfectly set off her chocolate skin, and she wore a yellow headband. Her smile was as wide as St. Charles Avenue and her voice sweet as a pound of pralines. In fact, she was so full of southern hospitality, you'd have thought she'd spent her whole life collecting beauty titles, which she probably had.

"Welcome to our home," she said in the voice of a docent at a museum. "I am Nikki Pigeon and I would like to say on behalf of the Reverend Mr. Errol Jacomine that we are delighted to have you here today."

She stepped away from the door so the honored guest could enter, and Skip found herself staring at a smallish white man in a guayabera shirt, sitting on a Victorian love seat upholstered in crimson velvet. Grouped around the love seat were six or eight wooden chairs, not turned to face each other for conversation, but also confronting the door. Each chair was occupied by a man or woman, black or white, young or old—it was an artfully mixed group that gave a peculiar impression of courtiers surrounding a king.

The king rose to greet her. When he did, so did everyone else, and Skip knew instantly there was something very wrong here.

The king stepped forward. "Hello, hello, Detective Langdon. I am Errol Jacomine. May I congratulate you on the wonderful job you did with the Kavanagh case and express my deepest sympathy about your partner."

"You seem to know a lot about me." *Way too much.*

"Why, you're a very famous young lady." When he smiled, they all did. He was average height, even a little short, and slight, with a bit of a bulge at the center. His face was some kind of crude cross between Cajun and redneck—dark hair, fine nose, but mean little eyes and sinewy neck. He parted his hair on the side, and it was a little curly, slightly unruly, which must have given him fits. He looked like the sort of person who'd expect every hair to toe the line.

Even if she hadn't felt she had to hose off the smarm after shaking hands with him, she couldn't see what could possibly make him a charismatic leader, though apparently he was to at least the eight people in this room.

"It's an honor to have you here. Please sit down and we'll have some tea."

"Oh, no thanks, I just have a question or two and then I'll be off."

He nudged a hand under her elbow and began to edge her toward the love seat. "Nikki will simply not have it. She's been baking all day." Indeed, there was a delicious bakery odor in the air.

One of the parishioners, if that's what they were, had closed the door behind her (Nikki having disappeared, presumably to fetch the tea). The others still stood stiffly.

"I really must be going." She sounded like a parody, but she liked it. It was properly distancing.

"You must certainly not be going. You must indulge us all—we've been curious about you."

"It sounds as if you've indulged your curiosity."

"How's that?"

"You know everything about me."

"Not everything, Detective. You still have some secrets. For instance, I don't know yet how I can help you."

She was disconcerted to find she was sitting on the love seat; she wasn't quite sure how he'd done it.

Instantly, someone held out a chair for the Reverend Mr. Jacomine, and in almost the same second, two more people wedged a small table between the two, so that Skip was facing the Reverend Mr. over the table.

And then all but two of the others sat down. The whole thing was so carefully orchestrated it frightened her to think what these people were capable of—what Jacomine was capable of, to have subdued them so completely.

"These are our people," he said, throwing his arm out in an arc that seemed to take in the world. "I thought you might like to meet some of

199

them so you'd know the kind of work we do. That's Ruby, who was addicted to painkillers when she came here.

"That's Fred; he had two convictions for armed robbery; he's been with us four years now and he has a good job. That's Mimi right behind Fred. She was a crack whore at this time last year. Ah, here's Nikki."

Nikki in the nick, Skip thought. She was embarrassed at knowing so much about perfect strangers.

Nikki had tied a black apron over her white dress, and had placed a black cupcake hat over her headband. The effect was ridiculous—pretentious in the nineteenth century, absolutely unacceptable, Skip would have thought, in a 1990s biracial organization.

Nikki set cups, saucers, and a tray of cookies on the table.

Skip was becoming increasingly uncomfortable. They had researched her and they were going to a lot of trouble for what should have been a five-minute interview. Something was wrong here. She wished she had some backup.

"Could I use the phone a second?"

"Ruby." Jacomine raised a hand and made a gesture so fast Skip couldn't follow it. It reminded her of a command for dogs.

Ruby disappeared, and as Skip watched her go, she felt her hand catch fire. "Ouch." She snatched it back, knocking over a lamp in the process, and saw that Nikki had spilled tea on her.

Her eyes swept back from the lamp to the room just in time to see Jacomine mouth something at Nikki. She couldn't tell what it was, but the expression in his eyes was controlled fury.

The back of her neck prickled.

This man is dangerous.

She took deep breaths to stay calm.

Ruby said, "Sidney's using the phone."

"It's all right. I only have a couple of questions anyway." She glanced at her watch. "So long as I call in in five minutes."

She wondered if Evie was in the house. It was seeming likelier and likelier.

She stared at the window. Behind her someone righted the lamp—not Jacomine, she was sure. He had probably activated one of his robots with a little hand command.

"Is something wrong?" said Jacomine.

"I just wanted to make sure my partner found a parking place."

"You got a partner out there? Why, bring him in. Bring him in right now and let's give him some tea."

"Mr. Jacomine—"

"Errol. Please."

"We really didn't come here to have tea—I'm trying hard to impress on you that I have a job to do." No way was she drinking a drop or eating a crumb.

"We didn't mean to do anything wrong. We meant to make you feel welcome." His eyes were hard, brown little pebbles.

"Thank you. I appreciate that. I'm wondering if you know a woman named Evelyne Hebert, nicknamed Evie."

Behind her, she heard the sound of breath being sucked in. Jacomine's face twitched ever so slightly.

"I do."

"Do you know where she is?"

"No, I don't. Evie was a member here for a while, but she left us about a year ago."

"Did she live here? In this house?"

"Another one. We have several for our people to live in. Especially those dealing with addictions."

"She must have left a forwarding address."

"No. Evie's departure was rather sudden."

"What happened, Errol?" Not strictly her business, but maybe he'd answer anyhow.

"She decided this wasn't the path for her."

"It sounds as if there were bad feelings around it."

"She's still one of our people and we still love her."

21

• •

Skip went immediately to the office and ran a records check on Jacomine. He had only minor traffic infractions, but she was willing to bet there was a sealed juvenile record somewhere. This was the kind of guy who chopped up his grandparents.

She needed to know more about him. She called Ramon, in Intelligence, and posed her question.

"Jacomine. Sure, I know about him, haven't met him personally. Good reports on him. He takes in people who're pretty desperate and cleans them up. Has a pretty good following. Mixed—black and white, a lot of families. Runs a day-care center, all the right civic liberal bleeding-heart bullshit."

"Something's funny with him. The guy's a creep."

"He does pretty good work for the community. That's all I know about him."

"He's got some kind of little fascist army going."

"I thought I was the expert."

"When he stands up, everybody stands. All the followers. You know what I mean?"

"What's wrong with that? That's just showing respect for their leader."

"He knew a lot of stuff about me; he'd researched me."

"Aw, you're famous. Don't be so paranoid."

It was curious, she thought, the way human beings never wanted to think ill of each other, the way they excused each other's misdeeds by professing to know someone else's intent—as if that mattered. It was a cliché the way relatives of a murderer said he was a good boy, he never did mean any harm.

Neighbors closed their eyes and ears. "Well, yes, we knew they beat their children, but they were good parents, the kids were always clean and well-fed. They were just doing what they thought was right."

She hated the word "good"; it was a license to kill. Cindy Lou was right: when people thought they were "good," they thought it was okay what they did, and so did their families and friends. At the latter, she wanted to shout: "Who cares what he meant? I don't give a shit what they thought. It's what they did that keeps me on the job."

To Ramon she wanted to say, *Open your eyes.*

But what was the point? Jacomine had no arrest record and hadn't committed any crimes in her presence.

He knew more about Evie than he'd told, though.

She arrived at the office Monday morning with a list of things to do: look up the property the Following owned; try to find disgruntled members; or better yet, ex-members.

She sat at her desk and thought.

Might as well talk to the ones I already know. She drove back to the little house in Metairie and knocked. The man who answered was a stranger, burly and face-tattooed, looking as if he'd just been released from Angola. Better not start with him.

"Is Nikki Pigeon in?" It was the one name she knew.

"She gone."

"When do you expect her?"

"You ain' got no bi'ness with Nikki."

Skip produced her badge.

The man was suddenly sullen. "I find you somebody," he mumbled, and was gone.

He came back with a middle-aged woman Skip knew—Ruby, she thought, the one addicted to painkillers. "Yes? Can I help you?"

She could have just questioned Ruby, but her curiosity was piqued. "I'm looking for Nikki Pigeon."

"Ms. Pigeon is not a member of our congregation."

"Is she an employee, then?"

"I'm afraid I really have no information. I'd be happy to refer your inquiry to Daddy, if you like."

"Daddy."

"The Reverend Mr. Jacomine."

"Thanks, it won't be necessary."

Something was up here. Yesterday Nikki had been a member.

She went back to the office and ran a records check on her. Nothing.

The DMV provided a two-year-old address, which hardly seemed worth checking out. Skip had the distinct impression Nikki'd been living at the Following house.

Sighing, she settled back with the phone book, open to P.

Eight Pigeons. Not bad. She dialed Tanya, on Baronne, and asked for Nikki.

Tanya didn't answer, just turned away and hollered, "Nikki! Phone."

A moment later she was back. "Nikki ain' home."

"Thanks."

Skip could hardly believe her good luck. Tanya's part of Baronne was only minutes away, in Central City, possibly the most depressed, decrepit neighborhood that wasn't actually a project. It was an area where it seemed as if every other building was abandoned, a place where hope was hard to hold on to. No wonder Nikki had left. She must have had a compelling reason for returning.

Nikki answered the door herself, in baggy jeans and T-shirt, mouth swollen, a sharp contrast to the neat, prim church lady of yesterday.

"I saw you comin' up the walk, said to my sister, tha's one lady I want to talk to. You call here earlier?"

"Yes—you weren't home."

"Ha! Thought those assholes tracked me down. How you find me?"

"Looked you up in the phone book." Skip smiled and shrugged.

Nikki laughed. "Did, did you? Whyn't you come in? I want to talk to you."

Skip stepped into a dark living room, curtains drawn, very little furniture, no rug. Though no one was in the room, the television was going full-blast. A photo of Martin Luther King stood on the mantel.

Nikki gestured for Skip to sit, and pointed to her injured mouth: "I'm gettin' mad about some stuff."

"Who did that to you?"

"Who you think? The Rev. Mr. High and Fuckin' Mighty, tha's who. I'm gon' git that bastard."

Go, Nikki! But she kept her face impassive. "Oh?"

"You know what they doin' over there? They plannin' somep'n. What, I don't know. But somep'n. Gotta be. Why else put together an army of zombies?"

"I beg your pardon?"

"Well, tha's just what I call 'em. They ain't killin' anybody and bringin' 'em back to life. But Daddy—tha's what we call him—"

"You mean Errol Jacomine?"

"Yeah, him. But that's not his real name."

Bingo.

"Oh, really? What is it?"

"I'm not sure. I jus' know it's not Errol Jacomine."

"How do you know that?"

"He talks about it. Talks about how he used to be somebody else, back before he was born again; how he did a lot of bad things and then he got saved and realized he needed to help people who were worse off than he was. Said he got a new name to go along with his new life. We'd be surprised, he said. Shee-it. I wouldn't be surprised at nothin'. The man's violent." She paused, fingering her split lip. "Evil. I honestly think he's evil. I don't know if I ever met anybody else I felt that way about."

"Why do you say that?"

"Because he gets people, like, under his control. And he makes 'em do stuff."

"What kind of stuff?"

Pigeon lowered her head. "Sex."

Of course. Guru-itis. "What else?"

"Work on, you know, whatever he wants us to. Causes and shit. Like work the phones for some politician he wants to get elected. You know? That kind of shit. Then, the politician gets elected, I bet he makes him do what he wants."

"Nikki, why'd you decide to leave?"

" 'Cause I've had enough of this shit. See this lip? You know why he hit me? 'Cause I spilled that tea on you, tha's why."

"Oh, my God. I'm so sorry."

"Well I'm not. Tha's what woke me up. All this time I've been takin' his shit, just takin' it and takin' it, sayin', 'He' a good man, he don't mean to hurt people, he just does it for their own good.' Can you believe I could be that dumb?"

"Everybody's that dumb about some things."

"See, what he does, he makes you be a maid if you transgress somehow

205

or other. I did somethin' he didn't like—oh, hell, you know what I did? When I look back on it now, I just can't believe I was so dumb, some of the things I put up with. What I did wrong, I didn't wear the right kind of perfume when it was my turn to go to bed with him."

Skip started. "Your turn? Do all the women have to go to bed with him?"

"Oh, no. Just the ones he wants. Guys too. He makes some of them do it too. And he's married! That's the worst part—he makes his wife get people ready for him—baths with special scents, nightgowns and shit, perfume. Shit! It wasn't even my fault about the perfume, it was Tourmaline's—that's his wife. *She* was supposed to know what kind of damn perfume he wanted. See, she has this back problem and can't have sex— tha's what *he* says—and he says a man has to have certain things and it's our duty to see that he's satisfied."

"So he got mad at you and made you be his maid."

"Not *his* maid, exactly. The church's. Like what I did yesterday. Servin' tea for dignitaries; that kind of shit."

"Speaking of that, how did he happen to know so much about me?"

She looked surprised. "I don't know. I just got a message to be over there at two-thirty, dressed in white and lookin' like a nice church lady. I used to be a stripper, you know. I was doin' fine—a lot better than before I met Daddy—but my boyfriend beat me up real bad and I couldn't dance, and then he kicked me out of the apartment, and by then I didn't have a penny and I was homeless.

"I had this girlfriend, Carla; her cousin was in the church; and she made a phone call and they said they'd take me in." She shrugged. "Simple as that. They took care of me while I healed, and then I was part of the church family. Tha's what they called it. Church family!" She stopped and thought about it. "Yeah. Incest is best."

Skip winced, but Pigeon emitted peals of wild, sharp laughter, evidently letting off steam.

"I bought it. I really did buy it for a while. I thought it was great to be a part of this community, you know? I never was a part of anything, never, you know, like *worked* toward anything. This was—you know, holy work. Cool. *Me.* Doin' holy work. I thought I was hot shit. Brought my sister's kids to church and everything. Tanya, she always said there was somethin' wrong—but I didn't see it. Said Daddy gave her the creeps.

"Then yesterday after you left, he called a house meeting—about fifty people were there—he called it for the sole purpose of humiliating me. 'Look at this girl! The white honky po-lice come, and she make us look like we ain't even out of the trees yet. There we are tryin' to look good in front of the community and Miss Nikki Pigeon pours hot tea all over 'em, jus' like she was drunk.'

"Then he falls in love with that one. He goes, 'Nikki, I b'leeve you *were* drunk. Were you drunk, Nikki? You were prob'ly on dope, weren't you? And now the whole community's gon' have to suffer for it. Everybody here's gon' have to do sixteen hours of work this week.

" 'Those who're employed.

" 'Those who aren't, you gon' do sixteen hours *over* what you normally do'—most of us do about forty-five. Either that, he says, or put in two hundred dollars. 'That's gon' be pretty hard on some of y'all, idn't it? Nikki Pigeon, I want you to be aware—I want you to be *aware* of the havoc you've caused.'

"And tha's when he slap me.

"In front of all those people—can you believe it? Even Joel, my ex-boyfriend who beat me up, never did it in *front* of nobody. And he say, you gon' have to wear sackcloth, like in the Bible, all week to atone for your sins.

" 'Wha's sackcloth, Daddy?' I say, and he say, 'Burlap, girl. And it's gon' hurt you. It's gon' make you itch real bad. And what's more, you gon' have to make your garments. I herewith order you to make yourself a pair o' underpants, one of those—you know, chemise things'—camisoles, somebody in the audience say, and he say, yeah, camisoles, and a burlap dress to go over it. Somebody say, 'Whoo, tha's gon' be hot,' and Daddy, he say, 'Yeah, gon' be hot. Hot and itchy too. Miss Nikki's gon' be sorry she *ever* disobey her daddy,' and I say, 'But Daddy, I didn't disobey; it was a accident,' and he slap me again.

"Well, I went back to my room and I just lay down on my bed and cried and cried, feelin' like the lowest worm in the world, thinkin' it wadn't fair, wadn't fair at all. Then I remembered pore Evie. And I thought, 'I don't have to take this shit.' And I called my sister to come get me.

"See, what they do, they get you dependent on 'em. You can't go do nothin' on your own. I thought about that when I was lyin' there. I wanted to go, but where was I gon' go? The church wouldn't let me go back to dancin', and tha's the only way I know to make a livin'. Tha's when I thought about Evie and how she left 'em—just flat-out up and left 'em—so she could do what she wanted.

"She's a real pretty girl, see? You ever seen her?"

Skip shook her head.

"Pore thing, I bet she had to get all perfumed for Daddy every now and then. Anyway, everybody said she should be a model, she was pretty enough, and that gave her the idea to go to a modeling agency. You know you can make good money that way? You don't even have to take your clothes off or nothin'. You get jobs like handin' out stuff at conventions, shit like that. No sex. No nothin'. Just handin' shit out." She shrugged, as if it were too much to fathom.

"Well, Evie did that, and he did the same damn thing to her."

"I don't follow you."

"Humiliated her; held her up as some terrible example of a hussy in front of everybody. So then she had no way to make a livin'—or she wouldn't of if she hadn't seen through it a lot faster than I did. She just went, 'I'm outta here,' and that was that. So I thought, 'I can do that.' And you know what? I'm outta there."

"I'm happy for you, Nikki, I really am." Skip smiled. "Tell me, do you have Evie's forwarding address?"

Pigeon looked surprised. "No. She didn't leave one."

"Oh. Well, do you know what agency she worked for?"

"Agency?"

"Didn't you say she worked for a modeling agency?"

"Oh, yeah. No, I guess I don't know. If I did, I'd go right down there myself."

"Okay. Do you want to file a complaint about the battery?"

"What battery?"

"Jacomine hitting you."

"Oh, no. No way. He'd kill me."

"Kill you? You really think he'd kill you?"

"I wouldn't put it past him."

"Nikki, are you trying to tell me something?"

"You mean, like, he kills people? Well, I don' know of any, but I'm just sayin' he could, tha's all. He's that evil."

Skip went back to her desk and started calling modeling agencies.

The fifth one, fancifully named Cygnet, said Evie Hebert no longer worked for them, and twenty minutes later she was in their office. Another ten minutes and she had Evie's address.

Just like that. St. Expedite was working overtime.

Or, she thought, every now and then things just go right.

Something shifted inside her, and she realized it was depression beginning to lift. She hadn't yet experienced it as depression, only as a heaviness; unnamed baggage she'd carried since that night in the Iberville project. There had been a sense, she realized, that nothing would ever go right again, a low-energy feeling that affected her self-esteem.

She had a sense now of victory, almost an elation, far out of proportion to the tiny fact she'd uncovered.

I'm going to get Sally back. She knew she hadn't really believed it for some time.

Things are going right. They really are. Tricia found Dennis; that fell into my lap. Though not really, she knew, because she had found Tricia and had set in motion Tricia's need to prove something to her.

And now this.

Evie lived near Claiborne, in a run-down building in a run-down neighborhood. Whether it was mostly black or mostly white, Skip didn't know; demographics changed from block to block. There were a few cars parked out front, but not the Heberts' beige Mercedes, the one Reed had left in. The place looked deserted.

She found a phone and called Cappello. "I got an address for Evie, but it looks like no one's home."

"I'll send you some backup."

"I think I might try the Avon lady routine. If I don't call back in twenty, assume the worst." She hung up before Cappello could answer.

She had no bag of cosmetics, but she always kept a clipboard handy, along with a copy of an opinion survey she'd picked up from a genuine surveyer, and some product brochures.

She rang Evie's doorbell and waited.

Nothing.

She rang it again, and stood there.

She was about to slip a brochure under the door, to discourage suspicion, when someone shouted down from upstairs. "Hey! You lookin' for Evie?"

Skip consulted her clipboard as if unsure. "Does Evelyne Hebert live here?"

"Yeah. I mean I guess that's her name—I call her Evie. She hasn't been home in days."

"Are you the building manager?"

The face leaning down was round, white, and surrounded by black hair; the voice was female. "No, uh-uh. Just the upstairs tenant. I'm gettin' a little worried. I thought maybe you were a relative or something."

"I wonder if I could come in for a minute? My company's offering free gifts for the first thirty-five—"

"Sorry. I've got to get back to work."

209

The face disappeared.

The building was a fourplex. Evie was in Apartment One, and this was the one above—Three, probably.

Suratt.

She rang Suratt's bell.

The face came back.

"Could I talk to you a minute?" Skip held up her badge, not wanting to shout her identity.

"Hey, what's that? Are you a—"

Skip nodded and held a finger to her lips, holding virtually no hope it would work. But Suratt nodded and disappeared from the window.

She appeared downstairs breathing hard.

She was about a hundred pounds overweight, with quite a lot of curly hair and the pretty face with which every fat girl is supposed to be blessed. She wore leggings, an oversized T-shirt, and sandals. She looked intelligent, and there was something else about her, a kind of joie de vivre.

"Diane Suratt," she said. "Could I see that again?"

Skip displayed the badge and introduced herself. "I wonder if we could talk inside?"

"Sure."

Diane led her into an airy apartment with very little furniture, mostly thrift-store stuff to which she'd applied various exotic paint jobs. Below the window she'd shouted from was a large white worktable covered with tiny fruits, airplanes, cars, flowers, birds, cats, fish, trees, cups, saucers—anything you could name—some painted, some awaiting paint.

On another table were pairs and pairs of earrings attached to little paper cards. All were large, dramatic, exuberantly painted, and made of the tiny objects. She'd seen them many times around town, both in stores and on ears. In fact, Dee-Dee had given her some, which were amusing but which she couldn't bring herself to wear.

She said, "You're the Slutsky lady. I've got a pair of your earrings with little revolvers and knives on them."

"I made those for Halloween one year." She frowned. "They didn't sell, though."

For a moment Skip didn't speak. She was trying to take it in—this woman's apparent poverty and the popularity of her work. Finally she said, "Do you have anyone helping you?"

A shadow passed over Diane's face. "I can't really afford it right now. But I might get a contract for a department store chain. . . ." She crossed her fingers. "Then I could get a couple of people. Evie never seemed to have any money; I always wanted to hire her. But lately she's been screwing up pretty bad."

"How's that?"

"Drinking too much. Maybe doing drugs, I don't know. And a *horrible* boyfriend. Manny.

"God! Rides a motorcycle, looks like a thug, and hollers at her all the time. Did I mention his tattoos?

"He hasn't been around lately, though. For about a month, I guess. In fact, things have been so quiet over there I thought maybe she'd gone back to AA—she used to be sober, did I say that? Nice girl when she's not loaded. But I don't know about her and men. That Manny was abusive as hell."

"How long has she been missing?"

Diane looked uncomfortable. "About a week, I think. I'm not sure when I first noticed she wasn't there. Tuesday or Wednesday, maybe.

"Her newspapers started piling up. I've been removing them so the neighborhood hooligans don't get the idea they can make off with the Picassos."

"Picassos?"

"Kidding. So far as I know, Evie hasn't got a dime. Supports herself with crummy little modeling jobs."

"Has she gone missing before?"

"When she was seeing Manny, she'd be gone a couple of days sometimes. But what's funny—she'd usually ask me to get her mail for her. And this time she didn't. Why are you here, by the way? Did someone report her missing?"

"Something like that."

"I don't even know where she's from. Must be Louisiana though; with a name like Hebert."

Skip asked if the building manager lived on the premises.

"There isn't one," said Diane, "but I can give you the owner's number. You can call her from here if you like."

● ●

She called Cappello first, to report that she was still in one piece.

The owner sounded young, as if she'd inherited the building but wasn't ready for the responsibility. When Skip told her the situation, her voice turned high and tense.

"Do you think we should go in and look? Is it legal?"

"It's legal in an emergency, and frankly, I think we've got one here. But if nobody's there—and I'm presuming Evie's not—I'll need a search warrant. I'll call you back when I've got it."

It took two hours to get the warrant delivered and another hour for the owner to bring the key, during which time Skip sat in her car and stared at the building as if her gaze was needed to keep its timbers together.

The owner was older than she'd thought, but still not much over thirty. Her name was Belinda Carbo, and she was worried about getting sued; for what, Skip wasn't sure.

She went through the apartment with Carbo behind her, finding an even mingier decorating job than she'd done herself on her first apartment at Dee-Dee's, before he'd taken it away from her and made the Big House big again.

Evie's place would have been depressing in any case, but right now it was dusty and lonely and a little mildewy.

Skip found little except some snapshots in a drawer, of a very pretty blonde with a young man who looked like the sort who gave white trash a bad name. He had a thick, nasty neck, too large a head, and tiny little eyes that probably had a mean glint in them, she couldn't tell from the photo. There was a Rolodex as well, but only a few of the cards had been used, which struck Skip as sad. She looked under "Hebert," and under "Foucher," but Evie hadn't recorded the phone numbers of any member of her family.

Skip gave Carbo a receipt for the Rolodex and snapshots, then knocked once again on Diane Suratt's door. "Sorry to bother you again, but do you know these people?" She proffered the snapshots.

"Sure, Evie and Manny. How'd you like to meet *him* in a dark alley?"

Skip went through the Rolodex in the car. A Manny Lanoux was listed, with no address.

She found a phone and called his number. No answer.

She turned over the snapshot, staring at it, willing it to release its secrets.

The more she stared, the more Manny looked familiar. As if she'd arrested him maybe; or should have.

Oh, well, at least I've got his name.

She went back to headquarters to look him up. And there he was, two years before—a domestic violence case with her name on it, back before she'd been in Homicide. She remembered the woman well, her nose smashed in, blood running down her chin. And she remembered Manny's voice—high and whiny.

The woman's jaw had been broken, as well as her nose. She'd pressed charges, and Manny was convicted of battery. He was now on probation, which meant it was only a matter of calling his probation officer for his address.

She also got a work address for him, but it was now going on five o'clock. Better to go to his apartment and hope to catch him as he was getting home from work.

She marched into Cappello's office. "Well, now I've got to see her ex-boyfriend. This time I better take somebody with me—I know the guy. He's a creep."

"Okay, Thuringer. But tomorrow I'll have somebody new and kind of great—we don't have Jim's replacement yet, but O'Donnell's getting transferred and we have his." O'Donnell was the other sergeant in their platoon. "I mean, nothing against Thuringer, but this is somebody you've worked with before."

"Who'd we get?"

"Adam Abasolo."

"You've got to be kidding."

"The movie star himself."

He wasn't a movie star, but he looked like one—tall, slender, and wiry, with dark hair and blue eyes. He also looked a little like a thug. He was one of the best policemen in the department—she'd worked with him on the Axeman case.

"Well, that cheers me up."

He was such a hotshot, she hadn't looked forward to working with him, afraid he'd be bossy and superior, her two least favorite qualities in a partner. But he was great. If she couldn't have Jim, Abasolo would do just fine. Her only regret was that, since he was a sergeant, she couldn't often partner up with him.

Today she had more than one reason to miss Jim. Thuringer, though a perfectly adequate policeman, could bore the pants off a naked person. He was a short detective with glasses and a kid in college, who was his only subject of conversation.

Manny wasn't home when they got there, which meant time in the car together; hours, as it turned out.

It was Steve's last night in town.

22

•   •

Manny never did turn up. By the time Skip staggered in, Steve was sleeping like a baby.

Oh, well. I'm way too tired for a night of passion anyway.

He rolled over and put an arm around her, which was what she did want and something she was going to miss when he left—the feel of his body; the comfort of it.

The morning was overcast, which matched her mood. It was not only the day of Steve's departure, it was the day of Jim's funeral.

Jim had been Catholic, but almost certainly not a member of St. Louis Cathedral, which was where the funeral was held. He had probably gone to a small church somewhere—but this was to be a big deal cop funeral.

The *Times-Picayune* had made a major event of Jim's death, and the chief had treated it as a personal affront. Everyone in the department who could would probably attend the funeral, and a number of politicians were expected.

Not to mention Jim's friends and family.

"Families," Steve reminded her as they walked over. "That means two sets of in-laws, aunts, uncles, every kind of thing—how the hell did he do it?"

214

"Reminds me of that country song."

"As you know, I would listen to country only if you tied me up and tortured me."

"If you ask me nice, I might."

"How does the song go?"

"Tryin' to love two women is like a ball and chain."

"I'd never attempt it." He wouldn't. She was sure of that.

"Funny thing, though, Jim didn't seem any more tired or distracted than anyone else."

"How could you even handle the logistics of having two families?"

"Well, I've been pondering that. You know the way our schedules change all the time? Like one month my platoon's on the first watch, which is eight to four, the next it's on the second, which is four to twelve, the next it's the third, which is midnight to eight. At first I thought maybe he could tell them it changed every day or something like that. But you know what? I couldn't figure a way in hell to make it work. The only thing I can imagine is he gave them some idea that being a policeman is like being a spy—he can't be called at work, he's out of pocket for days at a time. Lies upon lies upon lies."

"And think how small he'd have to tell them the pay is."

"Oh my God, I hadn't considered that—I hope he wasn't sending all those kids to Catholic school."

They were nearly at the church. Steve nuzzled her neck briefly. "Did I ever mention I like a woman in uniform?"

It was the right thing to say. She'd worn one for the occasion, along with her mourning band, the little black elastic sleeve that fit diagonally over her badge. But one of the great perks of being a detective was not having to wear a uniform; because if the truth were told, it was distinctly unflattering. She felt self-conscious today, too heavy in the boobs and butt.

Having arrived fairly early, they were shown to seats about midway to the altar, giving Skip a good view of the front pews. She had wondered if each of the two families would take a side, as at weddings, giving everyone a choice of Wife A's side or Wife B's.

But what she saw amazed her. The two families were sitting together, the women side by side, their children interspersed. They'd apparently bonded.

Skip felt tears come to her eyes, she wasn't quite sure why. *They were dealt a bad hand and they made the most of it; that's better than most people would have done.*

She tried to imagine it: overcoming your jealousy and sense of betrayal at a time like that.

It would take a bigger woman than me.

She watched the pols and dignitaries file into the church, and thought that Jim was a much more important person in death than he'd been in life. He would have shaken his head, she thought, and said, "Mm mm mm."

There would have been a lot here to puzzle him.

So much had been changed by his death. It wasn't merely that one second he'd been breathing, the next he hadn't.

It wasn't just that his death left a hole.

The department was different, his families' lives were different, her life was different. Even the climate of the city was different.

And who could have predicted it? He was only one man—a decent man, a good cop, a good friend—but the domino effect surprised her.

There was something here that bore thinking about; something larger; but she couldn't handle it now.

The service had begun. Sounds of quiet sniffling filled the church. When the eulogies were given, she joined in herself. When Joe Tarantino, her lieutenant, talked about what Jim had meant to the department, it came clear to her how much she was going to miss him, how much she'd depended on him.

She saw Adam Abasolo near the front of the church and wondered what a steady diet of him was going to be like. He'd come to Homicide from Sex Crimes, much against his will, she was sure. He'd once told her he liked Sex Crimes because the perps got more time, the cases were more interesting, and you were really doing something for the victim. He was right on count one, semi-right on count two—a lot of teenagers killed each other over drugs, but every now and then, Arthur Hebert's daughter shot him—and right again on count three. In Homicide the victim was past it.

Abasolo had been fine in the short term, but she didn't know how he'd wear. The fact that he was so attractive might be a problem. Would it be weird, riding in a police car with all that testosterone in the air?

Probably not, she thought. Police work was absorbing enough so you'd hardly notice. Unless his ego was so big he insisted you notice.

But she didn't think Abasolo was like that. She thought he was a good cop. More of a hot dog than Jim, maybe, but a little faster, probably, and a little trickier.

And that, she realized, was what bothered her. She was tricky herself. Were they the same kind of tricky? That was the question.

A hymn began, and that brought her back to the present.

Jim's barely cold, and I'm already thinking about working with someone else.

But I had to sometime. Life goes on.

It seemed immeasurably sad to her, that life would go on without Jim, and yet it did occur to her to consider the alternative.

What's wrong with me? I haven't got time for this crap, I'm a cop.

But she had a nagging feeling somewhere in the back of her brain that she wasn't done with it; that it wouldn't let her alone, whatever it was.

When the service was over, she and Steve walked back to her house, so she could change for lunch, but they were barely inside the door before they were all over each other like a couple of teenagers. They ended up making love on the living room rug, not even managing to climb the stairs, and they didn't make it to lunch either.

Because she had worked so late the night before, Skip had taken the morning off, but the case really couldn't wait while she took Steve to the airport, especially since the trip there involved a stop to get Napoleon. So she had called him a cab.

She made a couple of tuna sandwiches to eat while they waited for it. She was only able to nibble, pretending a little. She found the food wouldn't go down past the lump in her throat.

Steve said, "I don't know if I should say this, but I can't help worrying about you sometimes."

"When you're in L.A., you mean? Why?"

"Oh, I don't know, it's like a magic spell. If I'm here, nothing can happen to you. If I'm not—if I call you and you don't answer—my imagination runs wild."

"Look. What happened to Jim was a freak. I mean it; Homicide's one of the safest places a cop can work. Think about it. We get there *after* the shooting." She was trying hard to keep her voice from breaking. What she was saying was true, but at the moment not even she believed it.

She forced a smile. "Let's talk about you. The famous project that's going to bring you back to New Orleans."

"I wish I could meet Delavon."

"Delavon! Do you realize he probably set us up? I mean, Jim was probably killed on his orders. You can't mess with a creep like that."

"He must be a true psychopath. I'd love to get a psychopath on film."
"Forget it," she said. "Why don't you do kids with gay parents?"
"Whatever made you think of that?"
"Or French Quarter kids. On the one hand surrounded by drag queens and literary eccentrics, on the other, known by everyone in the neighborhood. Big-city, small-town life all rolled into one."
"Not bad. It's not exactly the heartland."
"Or just—you know—weird lifestyles; odd families."
"I can't think where I'd find any of those."
"Maybe Dee-Dee and Layne'll get married." She was babbling.
They were both babbling.
The taxi had honked once; it honked again.

● ●

Grady had been drinking all morning. He never drank to write. Couldn't focus, couldn't think, couldn't even stay awake. On the other hand, he hadn't been able to write about The Thing sober. The worst that could happen was he'd waste another day; he'd already wasted plenty of them.
He plunged in, as far back from the bad part as he could remember:

● ●

It was Easter, and Reed had awakened both of us early, Evie and me, so we could see what the Easter bunny brought. The Easter baskets varied from year to year. That year I got green and the girls got purple; that is, they were straw-colored with another color woven in—green for me and purple for them. They had that synthetic grass in them, the stuff that looks like shredded AstroTurf, and plenty of jelly beans in the bottom. Then there were chocolate bunnies and marshmallow chicks that tasted like cellophane, and chocolate-cream eggs. The Easter eggs weren't there, because we'd dyed them ourselves—so the bunny couldn't be expected to bring them.
We always got some little gift besides the candy. One year I got the duck that became the bane of all our lives, but it wasn't that year. That year I got a Mickey Mouse watch. Reed got what Dad insisted was a "bunny lady," a purple and white stuffed rabbit with short mouselike ears instead of long ones, red cheeks, and feminine features, pouty mouth included. Evie got some sort of jewelry-making kit, and frankly, I don't think she liked it much. She was in a horrible mood that day, cranky and snappy.
She even threw a tantrum before church.

"I don't want to go!"

"Quiet, Evie."

"You can't make me."

"I'm going to count to three . . ."

That sort of thing. At the time, I didn't know what it was about—no one paid any attention to Evie, except to tell her to shut up—but now that I think back, she was in a tomboy stage. She was probably pissed that the bunny hadn't noticed and brought her some boxing gloves or something.

She must have hated her dress too. It was some kind of light pink extravaganza; and Reed had white lace, I think, with a pink sash, those tiny little black shoes with straps (are they the ones called Mary Janes in books?), and white lace socks.

I'll never forget how she looked that day. I thought she was the cutest thing I ever saw. She had a neatness to her, a compactness, even as a tiny child, that I always admired. Evie on the other hand was all over the place.

I wonder what on earth I'm saying here. Perhaps I'm talking about energy, whatever that is. Reed's was contained, I think, just as it is now (too much so, I think). Evie's was full-out.

A child like that is an inconvenient child; a child who takes up a lot of space; space I felt should have been mine, I guess; space our parents would just as soon have had empty and peaceful.

Naturally, Mother and Dad won the fight, and Evie did go to church. It's worth noting here that she always seemed to think she'd win, and she never did. I never even tried, and I don't suppose Reed did either because we saw you *couldn't* win. But that never seemed to occur to Evie for a moment. What was wrong with her, I wonder?

Anyway, we did go to church, all five of us, and afterward we were supposed to go have lunch with our grandparents—Dad's parents, the ones who started the restaurant.

They were old even then, and had long since retired from running it. They lived in Covington, across the causeway, and the ride over always seemed endless to us, or perhaps only to me, if it's true that boys are noisier and more rambunctious. Anyone who's ever had Evie for a sister would doubt it, but there is only one such male and I did turn out to be a writer, a distinctly effeminate calling in my father's opinion.

We all knew the afternoon would hold no pleasures for us children. First there would be a lunch of ham, probably, with a million vegetables, followed, if we were lucky, by some passable dessert. The whole procedure would be far too formal for my taste, and none of the food appealing except the dessert. But with luck Ma Mère would make a peach pie, I thought (though I know now it was far too early for peaches).

The worst was that we wouldn't be permitted to remove our oppressive Sunday clothes until after lunch had been consumed and—tedium of tedium!—photographs taken. Hair would be combed and recombed. Then we'd have to stand still and squint endlessly into the sun, holding our Easter baskets and possibly the treasures brought by the seasonal rodent. With luck, Evie and I would be posed together and I could untie her sash, or hit her upper arm or something. Both girls had Easter bonnets that year. On the way to church I had jerked Reed's off her head and threatened to throw it out the window. She cried and Mama hit me, but I could probably attack Evie's with impunity. It was a sort of wide-brimmed straw affair with a pink velvet ribbon around it and a nosegay stuck in the ribbon. I might be able to pull the flowers off, or perhaps sail the entire hat into the neighbors' yard.

We had to make a stop first, and I remember thinking about that in the car—the little ways I could torture Evie. When I look back on it, it amazes me that I wasn't remotely worried about punishment. I am not quite sure why, but I have some ideas. There is the possibility that I was just dumb, unable to think that far ahead. But I have considered this a lot —I have had much occasion to ponder it, as the day's subsequent events will show—and I think not. I think that I believed I could do what I wanted with impunity, especially where Evie was concerned, and I think I had good reason for so believing.

Why, I really do not know.

I am over thirty now, and that was in the early sixties, before feminism got going, I think. I wonder if it was simply that I was male (a poor specimen in my father's opinion, but male nevertheless) and therefore privileged. It doesn't seem possible, and yet how else to explain it? Reed was self-censored, so far as I can tell. She never did anything wrong. Evie did everything wrong. But surely not *everything* because it is not she who would have sailed the hat, and then there was the other thing. The thing that I call The Thing.

The stop we had to make was at the restaurant. I don't know why we stopped that particular day, but it wasn't unusual for us all to stop there on a Sunday, or any other time when Dad had business to do. And Easter was a huge day, a day when all those who didn't have to go to their grandparents' got to have Shrimp Arnaud at Arnaud's, or Bananas Foster at Brennan's, or Oysters à la Foch at Antoine's, or Crab Hebert at Hebert's.

220

While we had to eat ham.

Not only that, we weren't about to get any ham for at least an hour.

We were starved. But when we went in the kitchen at Hebert's, the cooks made over us and gave us tidbits, especially one named Albert, an old black man, or maybe he wasn't so old, but his hair was starting to gray and he was slightly stooped.

Albert had a gentleness about him, a maternal quality, it seemed to me, though that sounds contradictory considering his sex. I felt—I don't know—*loved* (I guess I can say it, I'm half drunk) in his presence, in a way I never did in the presence of either of my parents. Albert simply was more gentle, there's no question, by temperament, but I think perhaps there might be more to the story.

All parents say they love their children, and no doubt they believe they are telling the truth (though I never saw the slightest evidence that either of our parents loved Evie, unless you count the fact that they took care of her in material ways). No doubt they would have felt bereft if their children had died (though Evie might as well have, and I am not sure that anyone missed her after she left, except for me, and I was always attracted to her. She was a sexy child, I think—can children be sexy?).

But I think that many parents, ours included, simply do not like children much. Do not like the noise they make, their high level of energy, the way they are always in perpetual motion—and the care that must be taken of them. In a word, they find children inconvenient, and an inconvenient child like Evie they particularly dislike, though they may "love" her in some vague way that probably has more to do with parental ego than otherwise. (I guess I must have thought of all this because Reed was so very convenient; so calculatedly convenient; so obedient and helpful, such a little volunteer. In short, being intelligent and being the youngest, in a perfect position to observe, she figured out what would fly.)

Albert, I think, actually did like children as a class, something I hadn't seen before. He was even nice to Evie, which was something of a taboo in our family. Whenever we saw him, it almost made me rethink her: If Albert liked her, could she really be so bad?

Mother always said the way he treated us was just his way of sucking up to her and Daddy, which hurt my feelings. But not for long because even in my seven-year-old heart I knew it said a great deal more about her worldview than about Albert.

The way Albert was, the way he felt, *the intuitive sense I got from him*— his vibe, his energy, his presence (I don't know what to call it because there isn't a word for it)—this feeling belied what she said.

Albert had the job in the restaurant of making the *pommes de terre soufflés*. This is a dish served at most of the great New Orleans restaurants as an hors d'oeuvre, sometimes, though not always, with béarnaise sauce. At Hebert's the *pommes* are always served plain.

Once, before the day of The Thing, Albert showed me the whole procedure. First he'd slice his potatoes thin, thin, thin with a tool called a mandolin, then dry them, then toss them in boiling oil, very hot. He'd let them float to the top, then take them out and pop them in another pan of boiling oil, even hotter than the first, smoking this time—450 degrees. I'll never forget how proud he looked when he told me that.

The thing I never could understand, and never *will* understand is that the flat slices miraculously puff up into little pillows, as if two pieces of potato have been glued together around a bubble of air. How one slice of potato can do this is beyond me.

The oil makes the *pommes* puff up, but they aren't perfect unless they're crisp, somewhere between french fries and potato chips; in other words, they don't crunch when you bite into them, but they aren't soft and soggy either. Only Albert could accomplish this miracle. I've had the potatoes at every restaurant in town, and nobody then or now can make them like Albert.

This is all Albert did—all day, every day, day in, day out. A lesser cook would have been bored to tears, but Albert took great pride in the perfection of each potato pillow he turned out. On his day off, Hebert's didn't even serve the *pommes*—nobody else's could come close to Albert's.

I could watch Albert do this for hours, and sometimes I did. The best part, of course, was that I was free to nibble now and then, especially when he spoiled one.

The day of The Thing, Albert barely had a word for any of us. The restaurant was working at full capacity, and two of the line cooks had the flu. Everyone was flying about looking like speeded-up film.

In fact, Albert was entirely out of character that day. Perhaps he was angry at Dad for some reason; perhaps it was just the heat and the pressure.

"Albert! How're ya doin'?" I shouted gleefully.

Without looking around, he said, "Grady? That you, boy? You chirren shouldn't be here today. Too much goin' on; you better get out of the way."

Crushed that my idol had spoken harshly to me, I withdrew against a wall. After a while I noticed Evil Evie picking cherry tomatoes from the salad plates. Reed, too young to know this was forbidden, was watching too. Next thing you know, she had joined her. They were systematically denuding all the salads, already made up and waiting to be ordered, of their round red fruit.

Wanting to strike out, I grabbed Dad's hand. "Daddy, Evie and Reed are stealing the tomatoes." At the time, he was in conversation with someone, I couldn't have said who—if it wasn't Albert, I didn't care much —and he shook my hand off.

I'm quite sure he didn't hear what I said, because to this day I believe he'd have minded that his salads were under attack. "Don't bother me now," he said, and then I had been rebuked twice.

There was nothing to do but charge.

I came up behind the girls and pinched each of their arms simultaneously, which so startled Evie that she knocked to the floor four or five of the nearest salads. Furious, she turned around to hit me, but I ran away.

"Reed! Get him!" she shouted, and tiny Reed, ever-obedient Reed, came after me. I looked over my shoulder, laughing, and ran smack into Albert, who fell forward, hitting the handle of his first pan of grease. Sensing disaster, he hurled himself toward Reed, but he wasn't fast enough. He landed on top of her, but she had already slipped on the oil and her legs had straightened as she went down. That in itself wouldn't have been so bad except that Albert, in his leap, had knocked over the second—and hottest—pan of grease, and its entire contents poured onto Reed's feet and legs.

I missed the first part, but turned around just in time to see the second pan of grease empty its contents on that tiny, innocent, inoffensive child. Evie, half crazed with fear, ran to our end of the kitchen, and I guess all our parents saw was that blur of motion.

But none of that is what is most horrible to me. It is two other things: first, what happened later—in the hospitals, the burn hospitals, before the skin grafts, and after them—knowing the way she suffered. And yet, I didn't know. Later, in that way that we are fascinated by what horrifies us, I read a magazine article by a man who'd been badly burned, and I really had had no idea. I threw up after reading it; I dreamed about it four days running.

I didn't know the details, but I knew what her face looked like. I saw the happy child replaced by that pinched little mask.

Her face, remembering her face, is why I could not write about this, could not think about it, and yet, that is only part of it.

There was the other thing, the thing that is worse. And that is remembering the sounds of that moment.

Albert's anguished emission of emotion—something like "Uhhhhhh," but full of tears. A vampire shriek from somewhere—I guess it was Evie. The clatter of the two pans hitting the floor. The manifold screams of the kitchen staff. Reed's whimper. That's all there was—a whimper.

And Dad beating Evie.

He spoke first. "Evie, I'm going to kill you," and he reached her in two quick strides. He struck her face with the back of his hand, and the noise it made is something that is with me still, in my dreams, in my sickest fear fantasies.

I didn't see what happened to Reed, who picked her up, who took care of her, I was too fascinated by the horrible, the unthinkable. Dad began hitting Evie with both hands, with his fists, and someone—several people, I think—finally pulled him off of her.

She didn't protest, didn't even try to explain what had happened, probably because she couldn't speak under the rain of blows. Nor did I, and no one ever brought it up, never even asked.

The loudest noise, the most terrifying, the one that is most debilitating today, was the sound of my silence.

But maybe it never mattered at all. Perhaps both parents knew perfectly well what had happened, had even seen it. Not long after, I asked my dad, timidly, why he had beaten Evie.

"She's the oldest," he said. "She should have been watching the younger kids."

23

• •

Skip got up an hour early on Wednesday and drove straight to Manny's, hoping she'd catch him before he left. But all was quiet at his apartment, a dump of a place on Jackson Avenue. She got out and walked around, even rang the bell, backup or no, thinking to play the Avon lady trick again. She had been in uniform when she arrested Manny; surely he wouldn't recognize her. But she didn't think it would come to that, and it didn't.

No one answered the door.

She'd gotten his motorcycle license number from her records check, and she saw no sign of the machine. She didn't see the point of hanging around.

She went to the work address she'd gotten from Manny's probation officer, without much hope of finding her quarry.

Manny was apparently a mechanic. He worked at a place called Rayson's Garage in Jefferson Parish, which appeared to be doing a hefty business. She asked for Rayson and was directed to a grimy, thickset man wearing round, heavy glasses, a baseball cap, and clean T-shirt. How he managed to keep the T-shirt clean and the rest of him dirty she could only speculate.

"You need an appointment? We're booked solid till a week from Friday." He had the air of one too harassed for humans; his business was with machines.

"No, thanks." She identified herself. "I'm looking for one of your employees. Manny Lanoux."

"Manny." He looked utterly mystified. "We ain't got no Manny here."

"No? You never did?"

"Well, now, I didn't say that." He rested an arm on a handy shelf, starting to relax; he'd caught her out and he was enjoying it. "Did you hear me say that?"

She had no patience with whatever petty game he was playing. "Are you saying he used to work here but he doesn't now?"

"No. Not saying that at all."

He was determined to drag it out. Skip stopped trying to cut to the chase. With or without patience, she was going to have to play this stupid game.

"May I ask what you *are* saying?"

"I'm saying I don't know."

She would truly have loved to kill him.

"Is there anybody here who would know?"

"Don't know."

That's it.

"Rayson. You're a horse's ass."

His face turned from smug to nasty. He took his arm off the shelf and moved toward her.

"Don't even think about it." She paused, feeling her feet dig into the earth beneath her; sure of her ground and loving it. "Or I'll have your fat ass thrown in jail so fast you won't remember the ride."

He stopped, hatred rampant on his heavy features.

Petty tyrant. He probably beats his kids and voted for David Duke.

"Now you stop playing your junior high games and start giving me straight answers."

"You gotta ask me a question first."

"I'm not asking you any more questions. I'm making a demand. You either tell me everything you know about Manny Lanoux in the next five seconds"—a stubborn look crept over his face; he opened his mouth to speak, but Skip headed him off—"or find me somebody who can."

"Orrin!" He roared so loud she nearly jumped. "Get your butt over here and talk to this cop."

He walked off, picking up a clipboard and roaring someone else's name. "Larry! What the fuck are you doing?"

Orrin appeared, a confused expression on his gentle features. He seemed a different breed of cat from Rayson.

Skip gave him her best smile, feeling guilty about bullying Rayson, wanting to leave that part of herself behind. If you were a cop, you didn't have to take any crap from anybody; that was the good news. The bad news was, if you pulled rank, if you did what she'd just done, it made you hate yourself. At least it did Skip.

O'Rourke probably loves it; he's Rayson in uniform, anyhow.

She also had a superstition about it. It was like marijuana leading to heroin. You started popping off at the Raysons of the world and you couldn't stop. Next thing you knew, you were beating up innocent people with your nightstick; then you started shooting them.

She believed this because she had seen it. She had seen perfectly good policemen start out slowly, mouthing off at jerks like Rayson, and end up suspended, even fired.

Then there was the toughness issue. She did not believe that nastiness was a charming quality in either sex, and she did not think it signified its owner was tough. Toughness, to her, was more like Hillary Clinton's quiet self-possession, her ability simply to stand firm. She had been mystified the first time she heard the joke about the meanest woman in the world— Tonya Rodham Bobbitt.

"What is that about?" she'd fumed at Jimmy Dee. "What does Hillary have in common with leg-breakers and dick-slicers?"

"Haven't you heard? Men are threatened by assertive women. Should make *your* job easier."

In fact it didn't. Instead, whatever personal power she had just made people like Rayson hostile. Which meant she eventually pulled out the stops, which in turn meant the whole thing was a self-fulfilling prophesy: *You want to see a bitch? Watch this.*

Why, she thought, *can't people just be nice to each other?*

"Orrin," she said, "I'm looking for a guy named Manny Lanoux."

Orrin was probably six-feet-four, and skinny, with a prominent Adam's apple. He would have been a dead ringer for Ichabod Crane if not for a pair of exceptionally broad shoulders. Skip was willing to bet he had a terrific chest and good biceps as well.

"Oh, Manny. Yeah, he used to work here. Left about six months ago." He had sun-bleached hair that looked fine as corn silk.

"What happened?"

"He got a better job. But I don't think it was working on cars—said he'd never have to get his hands dirty again."

"Do you know where he went?"

"Well, it wasn't a company, I don't think. Some kind of, like, assistant's job or something."

"Assistant to whom? Did he say?"

"He told me, but it was a while ago." He looked troubled. "Hey!"

"Beg your pardon?"

"Hey!" Orrin stared into space. "He gave me an address. See, I'm the one does the hirin' and firin'. I was s'posed to send his last check to the new place. He had some kind of problem with things getting stolen out of his mailbox." He started walking toward a cluttered office. "Come on. Let's see if I still got it."

Rayson was in the office, but thought of pressing matters elsewhere when he saw Skip bearing down. Orrin rummaged in a wooden box full of three-by-five cards.

"Here it is." He pulled one out in triumph. "Damn. It's only a P.O. box. Got a name, though. Think that'd help?"

"Might. What is it?"

"Larry Carlini."

"Did you say 'Carlini'?"

"Umm-hmm. Don't know him. Do you?"

"I don't think so."

But she did. Larry Carlini was a small-time creep with alleged mob connections, nobody important, but nobody you wanted to meet in a dark alley either.

He wasn't in the phone book, but she knew that was no problem, any more than locating Manny had been. He had a record the approximate length of a fishing pole—mostly minor offenses, but lots of them. A little research and she found he lived near the lake, in a new-money neighborhood that prided itself on its ostentation.

His house was of white-painted brick, originally a sort of two-story rectangle with a narrow balcony on its otherwise plain facade. It was a couple of decades old and therefore hadn't been built to take up every inch of its lot. Later owners, perhaps the Carlinis, had added a couple of wings that remedied that situation. The thing looked like three oversized building blocks piled together by some demented baby.

To Skip's delight, there was a motorcycle parked in front. Carlini must work out of his house.

A black maid answered the door, in uniform and looking cross about it. Skip didn't think being a cop was going to get her anywhere.

"I work for the mayor," she said, which was borderline true if you considered that he appointed the superintendent of police, for whom Skip could arguably be said to work. "There's something we need to speak to Mr. Carlini about."

The maid looked alarmed. "I'll get him," she said, and disappeared. She came back alone. "He says show you into the living room."

Was it safe? She thought so. He wasn't going to try anything in front of this woman.

She was shown into a living room that looked exactly like a Henredon ad in *Architectural Digest*. In fact, it was eerie, the sense of déjà vu it gave. Gold and burgundy print sofa, dark wood coffee table, even a phalaenopsis in a brass pot on a desk at the side, exactly as if a decorator had said, "Okay, let's do design 122. I'm going to the beach; wake me when the check's signed."

Or maybe there had been no decorator. Maybe Mrs. Carlini had simply torn the ad from the magazine and systematically set out to re-create it.

In a moment, a tall man who did nothing to dispel gangster stereotypes joined her. He had dark hair to which some sort of grease had been applied, a too-studied tan, white slacks, and white polo shirt. His arms looked as if he might work out now and then, but his waistline looked as if he ate out even more. He had probably been a looker ten years ago, but now he had pouches under his eyes, and a couple of chins; it wasn't so much a look of dissipation as of giving up, of saying good-bye to a piece of himself. If Skip had seen him in a lineup, she would have said he was depressed, but it seemed an odd description to apply to a gangster.

Behind Carlini—if that was who it was—was Manny Lanoux, as ornery as his picture, and twice as ornery as the last time Skip saw him. He wore jeans and a black T-shirt. He was too heavy, with a neck so thick mice could nest in its folds, but he looked powerful. Perhaps he was Carlini's bodyguard. He probably had an IQ about like Angel's, but in case he remembered her, Skip didn't want to say her name.

"Hello, Mr. Carlini," she said instead, and stuck out her hand. As Carlini gripped it and began pumping, Manny's face, over Carlini's shoulder, registered horror. He mouthed something: "Shit," Skip was pretty sure; and headed for the door.

Skip couldn't move. "What his problem?" she said to Carlini, hoping he'd turn around and let her hand go, but he did only the former.

Manners were no longer appropriate. She broke away and raced after Manny, who by this time was flinging a leg over his motorcycle.

"Manny! Stop!" she hollered, knowing he'd as soon send her a taped confession whenever he mugged an old lady.

She grabbed his arm, but he shook her off. However, she'd slowed him down enough that she was able to fling a leg over the hog herself. She attached herself to his back, arms around his neck, just as the chopper took off. She reached for footholds and tightened her grip on his neck, having no choice. He tried to shake her off, tried to get his speed up enough to unbalance her, and it worked.

The problem was, he unbalanced himself and the machine as well. Skip was thrown off, onto a grassy area. Manny wiped out on the street. Naturally, he hadn't stopped to put on a helmet.

Carlini rushed out. "What the fuck is going on?"

"Police. You better call an ambulance."

Skip was shaky, but in one piece. Manny was out cold, and she couldn't find a pulse.

● ●

It was a couple of hours before he was conscious and recovered enough to be interviewed. He had scrapes on his face and an IV in his arm, but otherwise he looked mean as ever.

"Manny, how's it going?"

"You're the bitch got me for that thing with Pam Kansco."

"Language, Manny. You're looking kind of helpless today."

"Bitch," he said again.

"Sticks and stones, big boy. Pam looked kind of bad when you got through with her."

"Fuck!" he yelled, "I don't have to take this shit."

Skip heard a scurrying outside, hospital personnel coming to quiet them. She reassured them and closed the door.

"Now we're alone and, like I said, you're kind of helpless. You gonna be good?"

Skip, you sadistic bully.

Yeah, I guess so. Second time today.

But she had no intention of stopping.

"I don't have to talk to you," he yelled again.

She smiled sweetly. It was delicious having a captive audience. "Oh, yeah? You got something better to do? Due at the White House or something?"

"What do you want?"

"I'm so glad you asked. Here are my non-negotiable demands. First, I'd like you to speak in a normal tone of voice. Second, apologize for calling me a bitch. Third—"

"You're full of shit."

"Now that's better." He had spoken in almost a normal tone. "I just want to ask you some questions, Manny boy. About another of your ex-girlfriends."

"They're all cunts."

"Now, now. That's not a nice word at all."

He was silent, eyes smoldering.

"Evie Hebert."

"Evie. Shit. Evie."

"Meaningful relationship, I gather?"

"Know what? That bitch is poison. You wouldn't have a cigarette, would you?" His tone was definitely conversational now. She had his attention.

"You can't smoke in hospitals."

"Evie fuckin' Hebert. Evie!"

"Piece of work, huh?" Skip was actually enjoying herself.

"God, I hope I never hear her name again."

"This is your lucky day, Manny boy. You can pour out your whole sentimental heart to Auntie Skip."

"You tryin' to be funny?"

"Uh-uh, it just comes natural."

"You're different from that other time."

"When I arrested you, you mean?"

"Yeah. You ain't half as mean. What's the matter, you in love or something?"

She had arrested him six months after graduating from the academy. She winced to think how nervous she'd been, how frightened that she'd do something wrong, blow the only thing she'd ever really wanted. She probably was different now.

"In love with you, Manny boy, if you tell me what I want to know. You cooperate and you're walking out of here."

"What the fuck! Why wouldn't I walk out of here? I haven't done anything."

"No? Then why'd you take off like that?"

He actually chuckled. "Force of habit, I guess."

But there was something. There had to be, and she could find it if she had to. Manny knew that.

"What you want to know about Evie?"

"Where she is."

"I don't know."

"Have you seen her lately?"

"Not for six months." He raised his eyes to the ceiling. "There *is* a god."

"Okay, then, start from the beginning."

"What do you mean?"

"Give me the whole Evie story. How you met her, how she dumped you, and everything in between."

His pig eyes turned ugly. "What makes you think she dumped me?"

"Manny boy, you're really going to have to quit shouting. This is a hospital."

"Okay, okay, she dumped me."

Skip waited.

"You sure you don't have a cigarette?"

"It's a great day to quit. You'll feel a hundred percent better."

He gave her a look of pure hatred. "I met her in a bar." He shrugged. "How does anybody meet anybody?"

"What bar?"

"Now how in the hell would I remember something like that?"

"It shouldn't be that hard. You probably have different bars you frequent. It must be one of those."

"Wait a minute. Yeah. Yeah, I was washing my clothes. It must have been Igor's."

"Igor's! You've got to be kidding." Somehow, she hadn't thought of Igor's as a preening place for the sexually available. It was a bar, all right, but it was also a Laundromat. In fact, there were two of them—the concept must have caught on.

Manny stroked his upper lip, maybe compensating for not smoking. "No. No, it was definitely Igor's. I remember I got up from the bar to go put some money in the dryer, and there was this babe, this incredible blond babe, sorting out her whites and her darks."

"Which Igor's was it?"

"The one on St. Charles. That's where I always go."

If I ever need to pick you up again, I'll know where to look.

"The babe was Evie?"

"Yeah. Yeah, that was her. She belonged to some crazy religious group and she wasn't supposed to drink. But she was in Igor's, you know? I mean, if you're just going to do your laundry, what do you need a bar for?"

"What happened next?"

He shrugged. "We had a drink. I think that's what she had in mind."

"And you got to know each other."

He laughed. "You could say that, lady. You want the details?"

"If they're relevant."

"Relevant to what? What the hell's going on here anyway?"

"You're shouting again."

"I don't give a shit."

"Doesn't it make your head hurt? You've got a concussion, you know."

"It's none of your damn business what I have!"

"Let's get back to your favorite subject."

"Evie's not *my* favorite subject. Oh, no. You can think again on that one."

"Sure she is. The girlfriend you love to hate."

He stroked his upper lip again, staring at the wall. For once, he made his voice low, almost too low to hear. "You know what that bitch did to me?"

"Dumped you. You already told me that."

"Jesus, shit, what a slut."

"Ah. I'm getting interested."

"I got this job with Larry, see. You know who I mean—Larry Carlini; the guy whose house I met you at."

"Actually, Manny, we met over that little matter of Pam Kansco. I wouldn't forget that if I were you."

"Okay, okay, what's the difference?"

But she noticed with pleasure that she'd made him uncomfortable.

"Anyway, I got this job with Larry—kind of, you know, taking care of things, you know what I mean?"

"Taking care of things."

"Like, you know—doin' stuff that needs to be done."

"Like what stuff?"

"Well, like deliverin' stuff. You know."

"Picking stuff up."

"Yeah."

"Sure. Running errands."

He turned his Genghis-Khan-Nazi-Blood-and-Crip-hate-look on her. "A lot you know about it."

"Listen, Manny, I'm glad you like your work. Congratulations on getting such a good job—that you didn't report to your probation officer."

"I was gonna tell him."

"Oh, sure. You're not supposed to consort with felons, right? Carlini's got at least one conviction I know of."

"Are we gettin' off the point here, or what?"

"So you got this good job."

"Yeah. I'd been goin' with Evie about three months at the time. Head over heels, I swear it. Swear to God; she really had me goin'. You know I'm really a sentimental guy?"

"So you'd known Evie about three months and then you got this great job."

"Well, I was supposed to take something to this house, see, and Larry said, 'Wait'll you see the joint. You think this one's something—you're going to a mansion, baby.' Well, I had a date with Evie and I thought she might like to see it, you know what I mean? So I took her over there."

"On the bike."

He looked at her as if she was crazy. "Yeah, on the bike."

"The package must have been kind of small."

"What package? You lost me."

"The thing you were delivering."

"Oh. Well. It was more of an envelope. A letter, maybe."

"Business size? Manila envelope? Eleven by fourteen? What kind of letter?"

"What do you care?"

"Okay, let's leave that for now. So you had Evie and the envelope on the bike. And you went to this mansion. Where?"

"Out near Bayou St. John. You ever been out there? Man, they got some *places*."

"Uh-huh."

"It was addressed to some woman, but this guy answered the door. See, I left Evie outside—I thought it looked more professional—and I just went to the door to take the thing, and this guy said come in. I said, I can't, I got my girlfriend with me, and he said fine, no problem, bring her on in and have a drink. So I looked around, kind of automatically, you know how you do, and Evie was standing by the bike holding her helmet. She always hated the damn helmet—took it off every chance she got. She had on these pants I got her—I got her black leather pants for the bike, can you believe that? Turkey! Major turkey.

"She had on these pants, see, and they kind of fit like the skin of a tomato or something, and her blond hair was hangin' down, all shiny in the sun, and she had on shades. She looked like a movie star, I swear to God. Well, naturally, I wanted to impress her by askin' her to have a drink in this amazing Hollywood mansion. This guy was really slick, you know, with some hundred-dollar tie and all that shit—"

"What was his name?"

"Well, now that *is* a question."

"Why?"

"I didn't pay attention to it." He slammed his fist on his bedside table. "Do you believe that shit? I just didn't goddamn listen." He rubbed his lip. "Or maybe he never said. I mean he said 'Maurice,' that much I know, but what else did he fuckin' say? You know how many times I've asked myself that?"

"Couldn't you just ask Larry?"

He shook his head. "Not cool. Definitely not cool."

"Why does it matter so much anyway?"

" 'Cause he took Evie, that's why. I never even fuckin' saw her again."

"What do you mean he took her?"

"He fuckin' swept her off her feet, right there in front of me. He talked to her and not me, you know how a person can do that? Like make you feel like you don't exist? And *she* acted like I didn't exist. She just fuckin' forgot about me. I'd try to say somethin', like join in the conversation, you know, and they wouldn't even answer. It was just the two of them alone in the world. After a while he asked her if she'd like to look around the house, and she said sure and they both just left me sittin' there. Can you imagine what that felt like? Just me, sitting all alone in that big ol' house."

"You're right, Manny. You're a real sensitive guy."

"So I left."

"That was it? You cut her out of your life, just like that, because she flirted with another guy?"

"Flirted! She was fuckin' all over him."

"That was really the last time you saw her?" Skip was sorely disappointed. She couldn't find one useful fact in this story.

"Hey. I was in love with her. Did I mention that? You think a guy like me can't fall in love? You think love doesn't happen for people you don't like? I walked out 'cause I was mad, but I tried to get her back. I wasn't gonna leave it like that, I just wanted her to see how bad she acted. I wanted her to really unnerstand it, can you get to the bottom of that, or is that too much for you?"

235

"Go on."

"So when I called her, she wouldn't talk to me."

"No! After you acted like such a gentleman and all?"

His tiny eyes turned into dangerous slits. "You enjoy bein' a bitch or what?"

"She wouldn't talk to you ever again, have I got it right? Hung up when you called?"

"No, she didn't hang up. She told me she was only gone for five minutes, and said why couldn't I act like a gentleman, and I said—oh, never mind what I said, but then she did hang up. So I let about a week go by—lettin' her stew, see? I mean, that's what I thought. But when I called, she said she was involved with someone else and wouldn't be seein' me again."

"Did she say who?"

"Well, it was him. Who else would it be?"

"I don't know. Aaron Neville, maybe."

He sighed. "God, I wish I had a cigarette."

"Did you ask her?"

"Yeah, I asked her. You could say that, I guess. I said, it's that slick asshole, right? Maurice. And she said, 'It's a pleasure to be around a gentleman for a change.'

"Well, I thought she should give me the damn pants back, so one day I went over there, and there he was. Answered the door at her house just like he did at Anna's."

"Anna? Who's Anna?"

"What does it matter, dammit? You're ruinin' my timin'."

"*Sorry*. Then what happened?"

"He pulled a gun on me."

"And threatened you?"

"Yeah. If I ever bothered his precious Evie again."

"Was that the last time you saw her?"

"I didn't even see her that time. But trust me, it was the last time I even thought about tryin'. I know you don't think Larry's all that savory a character, but I never seen him point a gun at nobody. That Maurice—now there's a piece of work."

"Back to this Anna for a minute. I get the feeling that's the woman the letter was addressed to. Did you meet her?"

"No. Didn't see a soul but Maurice. He said he'd give her the letter."

"You said it was Anna's house—how do you know that?"

A puzzled look settled on his features. "I just assumed. I mean, because it was her letter."

"What was her last name?"

"It was . . ." He closed his eyes. "Oh, shit, I know it. Leonardo. No, Dante. Shit, that's not it. Something long; some dago name you've heard before. You know, some dude that, like, *did* something. Like that guy who invented the telescope. Some name like that."

"Galileo?"

"Yes! No. Let me think—is it Galileo? Garibaldi! It's fuckin' Garibaldi! He was something too, I swear to God—he didn't invent the telescope?"

"You sure?"

"I swear. It's Gari-fuckin-baldi."

"Great, Manny. I'm impressed."

"That I knew who invented the telescope? I graduated high school, you know. I'm not as dumb as you think." He looked hurt; maybe he was sensitive.

"No, impressed you remembered who the envelope was addressed to."

"Well, that's why, see. Because of the telescope. Gari-fuckin-baldi—I'll never forget it again."

"Now here's another one. Can you remember the address of the mansion?"

"Hell, no. How the fuck I'm supposed to remember something like that?"

Skip shrugged. "Just a thought." She was silent a moment, trying to figure out where to go next.

Manny said, "Jesus fuckin' Christ, I need a cigarette." He sat up and began working at his IV, tearing the tape off his arm. "Come on, let's get out of here."

"What?" was all she could say. *What am I? His chauffeur?*

"I'll take you there. To the mansion."

"Manny, it's okay. Just give me the name of the street and tell me what it looks like."

"No way. I'm outta here."

"Manny. Hey. Look, you got hurt out there. You can't just go racing around with a concussion."

"Watch me."

He had the needle out of his arm by now and had flung the covers aside. He was wearing only a hospital gown that exposed his legs, and if he turned around, she knew she was going to see a lot more of Manny than she really wanted to.

"Throw me my pants, will you?"

Instead, she pressed the button for a nurse, and opened the door to the corridor. "Got to go, Manny. Stay out of trouble."

She went to the nurses' desk and told them Manny was about to run out on the bill, hoping that would qualify as an emergency. "And by the way," she added, "may I see a phone book?"

Anna wouldn't be listed, but she had to look.

There was a John Garibaldi. She dialed and a child answered.

"Is your mama home?"

"No."

"Is her name Anna?"

"No, that's my auntie. She's really nice. She takes me to get ice cream and things."

"Ah. Well, I have a special present for your auntie. Can you tell me where she lives?"

"In the house with the wall."

Not four walls? "On what street?"

"On our street."

"She lives near you?"

"Uh-huh. I have to go now."

Skip noted the street name. It was near Bayou St. John. She sighed. Just to make sure, she really should check the reverse directory.

Manny was racing down the hall, chased by four nurses.

"Hey, Manny, would you say it was a house with a wall?"

He stopped in the middle of the hall. "How the hell did you know that?"

"I'm psychic." The nurses were starting to swarm over him. "Go back to bed, okay? I'll bring you some cigarettes."

But she wouldn't. She knew it even as she said it.

The *City Directory* was irrelevant now. She went to find Anna's, thinking just to drive by, to get the feel of it. Anna might be "really nice" to her little niece, but Maurice had been there the only time Manny had, and when next seen, he'd had a gun. She'd need backup to approach.

The wall, she thought, must separate the house from the street.

And sure enough, when she got to the John Garibaldi address and drove another block, there was such a house. And there was a gardener trimming the ivy that grew on the wall. She got out of the car with her clipboard. "Is this the Garibaldi home?"

"Who wants to know?"

"I do. Why?"

238

"Why you want to know?"

"I'm conducting a survey." She rummaged in her purse and pulled out a ten.

He took the ten and shrugged. "She's home."

But Skip didn't want to knock on the door, not without backup.

"What you waitin' for? She's home."

"I have a free gift for her."

Funny term, free gift. Is there any other kind?

She opened her trunk and pretended to look for it. The gift wouldn't be there, of course, and she'd say she had to go back to her office to get it. Still, she wished she'd never spoken to the gardener.

She thought she heard something behind her, and she was conscious of a blur, something in motion. And then a searing pain at the back of her skull, the thin part, she had been told.

24

• •

Her hands wouldn't move. When she tried to wiggle her fingers, make a fist, anything, she couldn't. Worse, she had no feeling in them. She was alive, though, because her head was killing her.

It must be a nightmare. She willed herself to wake up.

Her eyes flew open.

She was in a room she'd never seen before, a hotel room perhaps, but a very fancy one, so well done it looked almost like a real room in someone's house.

She wasn't alone. Another woman sat in a chair in the middle of the room, reading a magazine, facing away from her.

She tried to sit up but she couldn't. Her hands were above her head, attached to the bed, like Jesus on the cross. This was no nightmare, except metaphorically. She could see them if she looked up, secured to the headboard with duct tape.

She remembered the name, "Anna Garibaldi." Could that be Garibaldi in the chair?

"Anna? Are you Anna Garibaldi?"

The woman turned toward her. "You're awake. I was worried about you."

Skip recognized her face. "Reed Hebert."

"Reed Foucher, actually. How do you know me?"

"Jesus shit." Skip had just realized the import of the situation. "What's happening here?"

"Do your hands hurt? I wish I could help you." She twisted so Skip could see that she was handcuffed.

Okay, so she was Reed Hebert and she was a prisoner. "Sally!" Frantically, she swiveled her head, looking for the little girl she knew wasn't there.

"You know me, and you know Sally, but you're not one of them. What are you?"

"A cop."

"Oh, shit."

"Yeah. Not exactly the cavalry. Where's Sally?"

"Here somewhere. She's fine, but we're all prisoners."

"Who is we?"

"Sally, me, and my sister Evie."

Skip nodded. "I know about Evie."

Reed's face was suddenly alarmed. She'd apparently realized Skip probably had news. "My dad! You must know—"

"I'm sorry, Reed. He didn't make it."

She looked away. "I knew that. I don't know why I asked."

"How did you know?"

"I felt it." Reed turned toward her again, her moment of mourning past. "How's my mom? And Dennis?"

"Your mom's okay, and Grady's okay."

"You know Grady?"

"At this point I know just about everybody you do. I'm Skip Langdon, by the way."

"Oh. Don Langdon's daughter. Your parents are regulars at Hebert's."

Skip realized that if she had met Arthur, he would have known her too. She had been in the paper more than once since she got transferred to Homicide; New Orleans being a village of about half a million, and her dad being a popular doctor among the Uptown set, she had a certain dubious fame. It made her uncomfortable, but she was used to it.

Reed said, "You didn't say how Dennis is."

"He isn't hurt, it isn't that. It's, uh . . ." She didn't know how to break it to Reed.

"He's using again."

"I'm afraid so."

She looked away, and when she turned back, her face was wet. "Oh, Evie, why did you do this?" she asked the wall.

"Look, Reed, I know about Evie coming to your parents' house and taking Sally. I know about you following. But that's all I know. Where are we? Who's holding us prisoner?"

"We're near Bayou St. John."

"I know that. I meant, what is this place?"

"All I know is I followed Evie here, and some people were leaving. I called to them to help me, but they didn't, although Lafayette Goodyear looked like he was going to."

"Wait a minute. You knew these people?"

"Sure, they're all members of the casino board. You know, Hebert's is going to run the restaurant in the casino."

"Yes." The whole city knew that.

"Well, when we were trying to get the concession, I had to appear before the board a lot—and then go talk to everybody and have lunch, all that kind of thing too. So, yes, I know them.

"I know them well.

"And they just stood there and watched me and my daughter get kidnapped."

Skip felt an icy hand clutch at her insides.

"Maybe they didn't recognize me." She paused, staring into space. "But I did call them by name. I guess they didn't realize what was happening."

I cannot believe the lengths to which the civilized human will go to make excuses.

Anything to avoid the all-too-obvious conclusion.

She didn't find it a charming quality. "What happened next?"

"People grabbed both of us; and Sally. Evie was holding Sally. They brought me here, and a very scary woman came in and asked me some questions, but I couldn't answer any of them."

"Who was the woman?"

"I think of her as the Dragon. She didn't say her name, but she was like no one I ever saw. Dark, but she didn't have an accent. I mean, she looked foreign, but she wasn't. A long face; older."

"Why did you say she was like no one you ever saw? What was different?"

"There was something regal about her—something commanding. Women aren't usually like that." She sighed. "I wish I were, though. Don't you?"

Especially now.

"But something else. There was something very sad about her, lines around her mouth or something; as if she hadn't gotten what she wanted out of life." She paused, apparently trying to reconcile the two impressions. "I don't know, though. I saw her again, and she didn't seem that way at all. I mean . . . regal, larger than life. She seemed scared or something. Off balance. I don't know what."

"You saw her again?"

"Yes. You see, they locked me in here, handcuffed to a chair in the daytime and to one of the beds at night. So I can't move. Also, I can't hear anything. Do you think this place could be soundproofed? I never hear a phone ringing or footsteps, or anything. I never hear—you know—Sally. But Evie brought her in once. I mean, just like—I don't how to say this—just like a sister. She's never done anything like that in her life."

"She brought her in? Why?"

"That's what I mean. So I could see her, I think. So Sally could see me. It was a kindness."

"How does the woman fit into this? Anna Garibaldi." The name slipped out unconsciously.

"Anna Garibaldi?" Reed looked supremely puzzled.

"That may be who the Dragon is."

"That's somebody we do business with. My father knows her well."

Skip was interested. "Tell me more."

"Well, she owns the fish company we order from, but I think she has some connection with the casino as well—that would explain why half the board was here the other night. I always dealt with Mr. Daroca at the fish place, but Mrs. Garibaldi's been calling the restaurant a lot lately—for Dad. They've been having all these long, whispered conversations over the last few weeks.

"In fact, I think it's something to do with our getting the concession. He negotiated with her, I'm pretty sure of that, I heard him. But I don't know what her job is."

"Tell me about the second time you saw her."

"While Evie and I were talking, she came with some of her henchmen. And took them both away." Her eyes moistened. "I hope they don't beat Evie or anything. She actually did something for Sally and me. I think she realized the baby needed to see her mother—that's really something after what she did. But then she was drunk."

"When she kidnapped Sally?"

"Yes. She told me. She told me everything about it. She did it because a guy she met had told her a lot of lies and given her false hope. So she thought she could get Sally back and they could all be a family."

"That's why she kidnapped Sally?"

Reed shrugged. "Evie was never all that clear a thinker."

"I'm still confused. Why did she come here?"

"Once things went wrong, all she could think of was to ask her boyfriend for help. But when she got here, he locked her up. She doesn't know what's going on either. She says this is his house, but he's a cop. That doesn't make any sense. How could a cop have a house like this? I mean, no offense, but does that seem likely? And why would a cop hold three people prisoner, including his own girlfriend and a baby?" She stopped talking and remembered Skip. "Four."

The back of Skip's neck prickled; her scalp crawled. She felt cold all over. "A cop? This is a cop's house?" Had she been recognized? Was that why she'd been captured?

"Well, he told Evie he was a lawyer, but I know him from the restaurant and I know he's a cop. Married too." She sighed. "Poor Evie; she always gets in the worst kind of scrapes."

"You don't know his name, do you?"

"Sure. Maurice Gresham."

Bingo.

He wasn't just a cop, he was a detective in Skip's platoon. He was the one Cappello thought was dirty.

"I always did wonder how he could afford to eat at the restaurant so often. Maybe he has family money."

Right. Marcello family money. The Marcellos were the celebrated South Louisiana arm of the mob.

This is some kind of mob deal. It's some kind of clubhouse; a meeting place. Maybe Gresham owns it or maybe Garibaldi does—on paper. That's a fine point—the issue here is that a dirty cop and a Dragon have got me taped to a bed. And I'm only one of four.

She shook her head.

Reed said, "What's wrong?"

"Nothing. Just thinking."

Just lying. Something's badly wrong. Whoever heard of the mob taking prisoners, one of them a Homicide cop? Whatever's going on here is plain crazy. It's not mob stuff, it's something else.

Something worse.

But what?

Okay, think.

We're locked up because we know too much. It must be the casino board members. They must be in deep with the mob, and Reed saw them here. So maybe Anna stowed her away till she could think what to do with her, and she had to stow Evie because she knew about Reed.

Then there's me. I tracked them here, so I'm even more dangerous than they are right now. But how did they know I'm a cop?

Her mind answered the question almost immediately: *The gardener saw the gun in my purse. When I opened it to give him the money.*

Damn the kid with the ice cream! I wasn't even a little bit nervous about Auntie Anna.

So what's the deal with her? Reed said Anna had lost some of her self-possession the second time she saw her.

But who wouldn't? Boy, are we a hot potato!

Why don't they just kill us?

She knew the answer to that. It wasn't the mob's way to kill, except for revenge or over money. But they might if they had to. The real reason they'd done nothing probably was that they were waiting for orders. Gresham probably didn't count at all, was just an errand boy at the cop shop.

That left Anna.

Who was she?

One thing, she was a woman; that meant she wouldn't have any real power in the mob. But who did?

The answer hit her like a thunderbolt:

Gus Lozano.

The missing Gus Lozano.

Suppose he was the one whose answer they awaited? What was it likely to be?

At this point, what could it be?

Depends how important Gresham is to them. If they let us go, Anna goes down, so does he, and very likely so do their three tame casino boarders.

But maybe the casino guys don't go. Sure, Reed recognized them, sure there'd be an investigation, but they could probably ride it out—while remaining voting members of the board. Very Louisiana.

Anna's probably expendable as hell.

Being a woman.

So no big deal there.

Gresham's the problem. Cappello's testimony alone could do him in once his connection came out. If it does, he's a goner.

So the question is, how much do they need him? Because the answer to that probably determines whether we live or die.

25

I have to get us out of this.

The realization was about a nine and a half on the terror scale.

But there was no one else.

No one outside the house knew where she'd gone, and everyone inside was either another victim or an enemy.

And something was screwy.

The setup just wasn't logical. The mob was nothing if not professional. And there was nothing professional about locking up two civilians, a child, and a police officer.

But since somebody had—Gresham and Anna Garibaldi, it would seem—the prognosis was pathetic.

Skip had a headache and didn't want to think about it. She felt like drowsing off again, but she knew that wasn't wise. A compromise, then. She'd close her eyes for just a few minutes. . . .

To her horror, she was awakened by a door slamming. The woman who entered was old enough to be commanding, and she had the longish face Reed had described. But she wasn't a Dragon.

She was an older woman in a blue silk robe, a very nice robe, but soft and luxurious, the last thing a Dragon would wear for terrifying the prisoners.

She was wearing full makeup, and her hair was neat. She looked as if she planned to go somewhere. And she trailed some kind of citrusy scent, as if she were fresh from the shower.

She crossed the room and began opening drawers, not even glancing at Skip. There was something frail about her.

Skip caught Reed's eye. "The Dragon?" she mouthed.

Reed nodded.

To speak or keep quiet?

It was a vain hope, but maybe if Garibaldi didn't know she knew her name . . . ?

Reed said, "What's happening?" but the Dragon didn't deign to answer. She continued to open drawers, not bothering to close them, until she pulled out Skip's purse.

As they watched, she rifled it.

Skip said, "Can I help you with something?" half in sarcasm, mainly just wanting to get Garibaldi's attention. The Dragon's hands shook as she found Skip's wallet and removed money first, then credit cards; then paused, and took out her driver's license. Her face was intent, but Skip could see worry there. She had a sense of ruin, as if the Dragon, scale by scale, were falling apart before her eyes.

When she had what she wanted, Garibaldi dropped the purse on the floor and left, closing the door behind her, locking it with a key.

The purse, falling on soft carpet, failed to make much of a thud, so that there was really no way to tell, but Skip had the impression her gun had been removed. She herself usually had to take it out to find anything, and Garibaldi had rifled freely, as if there were plenty of room in there.

So probably no gun, and maybe no badge, but there were other things in the purse. Skip went through a mental inventory: pens, cosmetics—lipstick, blusher, that was about it—a notebook, a hairbrush, a tiny manicure kit in a leather case, keys, sunglasses, maybe some tissues with lipstick on them, aspirin, handcuffs—no, they'd probably taken the handcuffs. But there was an extra key, and they probably hadn't found it. Skip kept it in a compartment of her wallet. If she could get it, she could uncuff Reed.

And there were cuticle scissors in the manicure kit.

Maybe Reed could reach the purse.

But she couldn't even see it—she had her back to it, and anyway, Skip couldn't stand to watch if she asked her to try for it. Even if it seemed harder—even if it seemed impossible—Skip had to do it herself.

She remembered what she had told Steve, about the rarity of detective deaths. She felt far from heroic, but statistics were on her side. Jim had just died, so what were the chances of another Homicide detective getting killed so soon afterward?

Good.

Well, it'll certainly happen if you just lie here.

And yet, what was the choice, given the circumstances?

Think of something.

Because they had left her legs free, there was a way to get up, she was pretty sure of it. But it was going to be hugely uncomfortable.

She swung her legs toward the floor. They didn't reach. She tensed her muscles and gave a mighty heave. One foot of the bed, at her head on the right, lifted a little. She tried again, and thought she felt it lift a little farther. She kept trying, and each time got her legs closer to the floor.

How could she get the bed to come up?

I don't think I can.

Truly, it seemed like a losing battle, but she kept trying.

Finally, with a great creaking, it came up enough for her to touch the floor. On the next heave, the whole thing began to upend itself.

Reed watched with eyes like coasters, apparently trying to gauge whether it was going to hit her on the way over.

It didn't, however. After about twenty minutes of heaving and wrenching, Skip found herself on the floor with a bed on top of her—mattress, box springs, and frame.

"Skip, are you all right?"

"I think so."

She was a little dazed. It had hit her hard. She hadn't thought it would be so heavy.

Okay. I did it. Now the question is, can I move?

I don't have far to go. Four or five feet, probably. Piece of cake.

She took a deep breath, and as she did, she smelled smoke.

Oh, shit.

She hoped Reed hadn't yet noticed the smell; she'd panic, not knowing where her child was.

Only one thing to do. Same thing I'd do if there wasn't smoke.

Like a hermit crab, its house many times its size on its back, Skip began to make her way toward her own discarded property.

She had to move on her elbows, like a soldier slithering through trenches, but it was much harder than it should have been, not only because of the weight, but because her arms were so far apart, taped as they were.

The carpet smelled of feet, and cigarettes, and some kind of chemical, a cleaner, probably, and the fabric itself. Yet she could smell smoke as well, and it wasn't the sharp scent of tobacco burning.

Reed said, "Skip, do you smell anything?" and there was a tremor in her voice.

Skip didn't answer. She was drenched with sweat, she must have blisters on her elbows, and she thought perhaps her back was wrenched beyond usefulness.

She caught the leather handle of her purse in her teeth and began the painful business of turning toward Reed. If she could just make the turn, she'd only have about three feet to go.

About half as many as I just went. About as many as I could cover in three centuries. By which time we'll be ashes.

Still, slowly, like the snail that carries its house, she twisted her body and, with it, the bed. She rested a moment, forehead on the carpet, before beginning the endless slither toward Reed. Sweat poured into the fabric. She gagged against the purse strap.

"Skip? I think we're on fire."

Now she not only had no inclination to speak, she could not; or she would have dropped the purse strap.

Finally, every muscle in her body shaking, most of the liquid in her left on the carpet, she judged she was close enough to attempt the vast problem of upheaval. Reed, being cuffed, couldn't lean down to get the purse; but if Skip could maneuver it close enough to her open hand, she might, in about three or four hours, be able to extract something from it.

Skip got up on her knees, the bed like a boulder on top of her. Reed stretched her fingers toward the purse. Finally, sweat dripping from Skip, Reed's eyes nearly popping with the effort, they maneuvered the trade.

Skip made a decision.

"Cuticle scissors," she managed to gasp. "In the leather case. Cut my tape."

She heaved onto her right side, which meant slamming the bed onto the floor, on its side, which, judging by the way it felt, probably broke her back.

Is it my imagination or is it getting hotter in here?

She really couldn't know, feeling as she did—as if she'd just run a marathon.

Using her whole body, legs more than arms this time, she slithered toward Reed, close enough for her to cut the tape; but she stayed there a very long time while Reed held the purse awkwardly in one cuffed hand and felt for the case with the other.

Smoke was beginning to enter the room, curling under the door, only a wisp at first.

"Goddamn motherfucker. Asshole cocksucker." Reed kept up an impressive litany of swear words while she worked. Finally she had the tape of one hand cut deeply enough for Skip to wrench her hand free. It was dodgy work because she had almost no feeling in the hand.

She bent her fingers a few times, waiting for the sensation to return, but her body would not cooperate. Nevertheless, there was no time for recovery.

She began the operation of freeing her left hand, more sweat pouring. *I'll die of dehydration if I live long enough.*

"Skip?" said Reed again. "I really think we're on fire."

One thing at a time, dammit.

When she had freed her hand, she took no more than a few seconds to rub it. Fumbling, still numb, she found her extra cuff key and freed Reed.

For which she received only abuse. "You knew that was in there all the time! Why didn't you tell me to get that first? I could have gotten you loose a lot quicker with my hands free."

"Yes. But would you have?"

All she knew about these people was what they'd told her—first Dennis, then Reed. She was not about to make herself, immobile in a burning building, vulnerable to yet another stranger.

She let Reed chew on that a few minutes while she pulled futilely at the locked door, her throat starting to burn from the smoke. Since it opened from the inside, she couldn't kick it in.

Reed was starting to lose it. She was standing in the middle of the room, wringing her freed hands. "Sally," she said. "Please be safe. Please God, let her be safe."

Her eyes were wild.

And Skip felt something more than smoke clutch at her throat. If she did get the door open, she might find an inferno behind it—flames that would race through this room, killing her and Reed in minutes. The door might be the only reason she and Reed had survived this long—she'd once heard a fireman call hollow doors "twenty-minute doors"; solid ones would last about an hour, and from what she knew about this place, with its soundproofing, this was probably a solid one.

She battled the thing in her throat. *I can't lose it. This is no fucking time to lose it.*

She pulled the heavy gold curtains.

Light flooded the room. The window was huge, a single pane of glass set into the wall, not meant to be opened. Since the house appeared to be soundproofed, it was probably freakishly thick.

They were on the second floor. There was grass below, but they were too high up to jump. The smoke showed up much better in the light. There was a thickening cloud in the room.

Skip realized there was an advantage to the unbroken expanse of glass with no tiny panes, no sliding mechanism.

Reed said, "Oh, God. Sally. What are we going to do?"

Skip picked up a chair. "Stand back." She swung the chair at the window, but nothing happened.

What was heavier?

She wished she had her gun.

The television might work, she realized. She tried to pick it up, didn't succeed.

"Reed, help me throw this at the window."

Reed was beyond arguing. She picked up an end. It sagged, but that wouldn't matter much.

"Now let's go. Heave."

Reed coughed from the smoke, and dropped her end.

That caused Skip to drop hers. It landed on her foot.

"Owwww. Goddamn, motherfucker."

The outburst calmed Reed, somehow brought her to her senses. "Come on. Let's try it again."

Sweat popped out on Skip's forehead, from the pain. But she managed to hoist the machine once again, and Reed got her end in the air.

The television crashed through, sending glass splinters back into the room. One caught Reed on the arm. Blood ran.

Skip picked up the chair again and bashed out the rest of the window, but the glass was very thick. It was maddeningly slow work.

Reed tried to tear a sheet, to tie up her wound. "What are we going to do?" she said. "It's too high to jump."

The smoke was getting worse. Skip was starting to cough. She wished she had some water, to wet down a sheet or something.

"Come on. Help me pick up this mattress." The one on the bed that was still standing.

Once again she thought she felt the room getting hotter, but there was no way to tell. The air from outside was hotter than inside, and anyway, the fire could have caused the AC to go off long ago.

As they worked the mattress off the bed and onto the windowsill, Skip wondered why the firemen weren't there, why there were no sirens in the distance.

Maybe it's just a small fire.

But she knew better.

They let the mattress go, and it landed well, spread out under the window, one end on top of the television set, but that was the breaks. It was as good a cushion as they were going to get.

"Let's go," said Skip. "You first."

"Let's push the other mattress out." For a double cushion. Skip had thought of it, but discarded the idea as frivolous. They were going to die of smoke inhalation if they stayed much longer, and so were Evie and Sally.

There was something else as well.

If Reed wanted to, she could remove both mattresses after she jumped, effectively trapping Skip in the burning house.

She said, "No. Go."

Reed glanced wistfully at the other mattress.

"Think of Sally."

She climbed up on the sill and hung there.

Skip pushed her.

She wasn't quite ready, and landed slightly short, half off the mattress.

"Are you okay?"

"I don't know." Her voice was small and panicky.

"Well, roll to the side. I'm coming."

"I think my ankle's broken."

Shit!

"Reed, get up, go next door and call 911. Sally's in here."

No answer.

"Crawl if you have to."

Reed began to crawl, propelling herself on her elbows.

As soon as she had clearance, Skip climbed up on the sill, but she didn't jump right away. It occurred to her at the last second to gather up her purse and its contents. She climbed down and then back up.

She jumped.

She landed hard, her system shocked. She'd been taught how to fall, but it hadn't worked quite right. And no one had told her her teeth were going to bang together with a crash that rattled her skull.

Reed was still trying to maneuver on her elbows, but at least she'd thought to start screaming.

"Help! Fire! Help!"

The window looked out on a huge backyard, and beyond it, on the bayou itself. From inside, Skip hadn't seen the houses on either side. But now she saw that they weren't far away. The Dragon's house simply seemed isolated because of its wall and the soundproofing.

Someone leaned out the window of a huge Tudor on the left. "Are you all right?"

"The house is on fire. Call 911."

There was still apparently no smoke outside. The peeker, a white-haired woman, craned to see some.

Skip hollered, "Police! It's an emergency." She got up and made sure nothing was broken. Every muscle in her body shook; she was a human chihuahua.

But she forced herself to move, to try to find a way back in. She found a garden hose and wet herself down. From Reed, who was now lying crumpled, moaning her daughter's name, she demanded her shirt.

Reed was clutching her ankle, as if to keep it attached. "My shirt?"

"Goddammit, give it to me. I'm going in to get Sally."

Reed didn't question the sense of that. She simply took off her shirt and handed it over. Skip wet it and draped it around her neck, to be used to cover her face.

She could see thick, curling smoke through the kitchen window, but at least she didn't see flames. She held onto the porch rail and kicked the door as hard as she could. It didn't budge, but the pain in her ankle was so excruciating she had to sit a moment while it subsided. She'd once sprained an ankle that way, but this time she recovered fast: it wasn't a sprain.

She could no longer use the TV as a bludgeon, but found a heavy flower pot, containing several colors of impatiens. She heaved it through the window, unwittingly feeding the blaze a giant meal of fresh oxygen. Fierce, scorching, almost yellow-white flames leapt to the trough, a savage fireball that made her suck in her breath, searing her throat. But suddenly she was cooler, and she realized she'd jerked back reflexively and fallen to the ground, under the flames, which had begun to retreat after their first ravenous surge.

She rolled out of the way and sat up. The shriek of sirens mixed with the roar.

"Omigod," said Reed, "your eyebrows."

Skip touched a hand to her forehead and felt the crumbling of singed hair.

26

• •

Reed had struggled to her feet, and now turned the garden hose on the blaze, which produced only a pathetic sputtering under its thunder. The sight and sound seemed to Skip unbearably sad.

"Come on. Let's get out of here." Gently, she put an arm around Reed's waist and helped her to the front of the house. Reed's ankle didn't seem broken, hadn't started swelling much, but it had gotten a nasty twist.

The white-haired woman from next door offered ice. While they waited for that and the firemen, Skip looked for her car.

She found it in a garage on the right side of the house, and as the firemen arrived, she radioed headquarters, saying only that she was okay and would call back from a land line.

Then, mind racing, she asked the white-haired woman if she could use her phone.

Anna Garibaldi had taken her money, credit cards, and driver's license. Then she had probably pulled on a designer dress, stepped into a pair of Italian shoes, and set the house on fire, endangering the lives of one police officer and at least one citizen, probably two.

Skip could not bring herself to think about Sally, to consider the kind of woman who'd burn a baby alive.

Since there was no bridge to burn, the house was the next best thing.

Surely no one who did such a thing, or series of things, intended to stick around. Anna had to be smart enough to know the cards and license were good for one day only, if that. But if she was desperate, she could use them once, at least the cards. To buy an airline ticket, for instance.

She had to be leaving town.

Skip didn't know how much time had elapsed, but maybe not that much —maybe there was a good chance of catching her at the airport.

How could she be anywhere else?

She thought it through again, trying to make any other sense out of what Anna had done, or, assuming it was true, imagine how she'd travel if not by plane.

But nothing else added up.

She called the airport police before she called Cappello. "This is Detective Skip Langdon, NOPD. I need help on an attempted murder."

She gave them Anna's description, had a bad moment explaining that the suspect might claim to be Detective Skip Langdon, and said she'd call back soon.

Looking out the window, she saw that firemen were hacking apart the house next door and drowning it. Two climbed ladders at the back, apparently trying to find signs of life.

She called Cappello.

More bad moments. No police officer wants to admit being surprised, overpowered, and imprisoned.

But Cappello was so glad to get her back alive she didn't make any remarks, just listened, alert as always.

"Okay, fine," she said, as if this were a routine report. Skip could see her nodding. "You need to come in and give me your statement."

God, she's unflappable. "I hope that isn't an order. I've got to go to the airport."

Cappello sighed, and for a moment there was silence on the line. Finally she said, "I'll see you when you get here."

Skip let out her breath; she hadn't realized she'd been holding it. "Can you call Jefferson Parish?"

"Sure."

Though the city owned the airport, it was technically out of her jurisdiction—she needed sheriff's deputies to meet her there.

Outside again, she saw firemen working to resuscitate someone.

Evie.

Reed was nearly hysterical. "They didn't find Sally. They went through every single room. Not a sign of her."

The hard thoughts that Skip had put off, about the kind of woman who'd try to burn up a baby, took a ninety-degree turn.

"She must have taken Sally with her."

"But why?"

The answer wasn't pretty. "Reed, I need you for something. Are you up to going to the airport? We could probably get you a wheelchair once we get there."

"You think that's where they are?"

"Maybe. I think you need to be there for Sally—if Anna sees her crying for you, it might do something." She shrugged. "It's a shot in the dark, but it's all we've got to work with. But here's the thing—you have to agree in advance: You take orders from me. Don't do anything unless I tell you to; don't interfere with me or any other officer in any way. Understood?"

Reed nodded. "Of course."

They got in the car, put the light in place, turned on the siren and burned rubber.

Skip radioed the airport police, saying she was en route—and that the description had changed. They were now looking for a woman with an eighteen-month-old child.

They were nearly there when the airport police radioed back: They had found Anna and Sally. Anna was holding a gun to Sally's head, demanding a plane to New York.

Skip made a fist and slammed the steering wheel. "Shit! I knew it!" Horrified at herself for losing it, she sneaked a glance at Reed, whose head lolled back against the seat, whose eyes closed briefly, then opened again.

At least she's still conscious.

"Reed, I'm sorry. I shouldn't have done that."

She'd been through a lot, but there was a lot more to get through. If her mind stayed clear, she'd be fine. She was worried her control was slipping.

"It's okay," said Reed. "The Dragon won't hurt her."

Skip said nothing, wishing she believed it, marveling at the relentless power of the human mind to detour around disaster.

"Evie told me she loves Sally. I've been thinking about it. She said the Dragon was like some grandmother who'd finally found someone to love."

Skip remembered the child to whom she'd talked on the phone, the one who must have been the Dragon's niece, who had spoken so lovingly of her Auntie Anna. But she didn't dare to hope.

They were talking about a woman who was holding a gun to a baby's head.

The airport was closed to all except emergency traffic, of which there seemed enough to control a prison riot, and more was converging. Sirens and red lights were coming out of nowhere.

It didn't seem to Skip the best way to handle a hostage situation with a woman who'd seemed unstable and shaky before she even went into action.

She radioed again: "Langdon here. Arriving with the child's mother. Could someone meet us with a wheelchair?"

A female officer met them, apparently pissed at missing out on the action. "Dietrich, Jefferson. We gals do the fetchin' and carryin' here."

Skip raised an eyebrow. "Thanks for your help," she said coldly, thinking Reed didn't need Dietrich's problems.

She was itching to get there herself, but she took her time helping Reed get settled, making sure she was comfortable. As she opened the footrest on the folding chair, helped Reed balance her injured leg, she noticed for the first time that her feet and legs were horribly scarred.

Dietrich's cheeks were pink, with embarrassment perhaps, for her faux pas. "Come, I'll take you there. It's not far. Apparently she didn't want to go through the metal detector till the last minute, because then she'd have had to dump her gun. At least that's what we think. She bought a ticket on the next plane to New York and waited for her flight outside the search area even though she only had ten minutes before it took off. She was playing with the little girl when we found her." Dietrich shook her head. "She looked up and saw us, and that was that. It's like she's a multiple personality, you know? All of a sudden everything changed. Like she became a different person.

"Just put her hand in her purse, came out with the gun, and stuck it to the kid's head. Must have gone to Plan B is what we figure."

What was she thinking of? Is she nuts?

Maybe not, but something. Under pressure, maybe.

Not maybe—certainly. She had three prisoners that she didn't know what to do with.

So why'd she try to burn us up? It doesn't make sense.

It does if she was desperate.

Which she must be, but I wonder why. What's up with her? Where'd she get off thinking she could just kidnap a child and get away with it?

There's the human mind, doing it again.

Don't you remember you and Reed nearly burned to death? If we hadn't escaped, she would have been in fat city. Once on that plane, no problems. Nobody would have known where she'd gone, and by the time some bright person figured it out, she'd have been engulfed by the city.

And she got caught only ten minutes away.

Skip's fingertips felt cold.

There were still things that didn't fit—the apparent irrationality of taking Sally, of burning the house—contrasted with the coldness of Plan B, making Sally her hostage. But the Dragon was emerging as a very intelligent woman, someone who planned for contingencies.

Still. She was a wreck when she came in that room.

That could be good or bad, Skip knew. It might mean she was vulnerable; it might signal instability.

She said to Dietrich, "Did they call the hostage negotiators?"

"Hell, I think they called everybody but the governor. But the hostage guys aren't here yet."

A semicircle of police with drawn guns separated mother from child, Anna from Skip.

A man on the sidelines approached. "Johnson, Jefferson. I'm in charge of this operation."

"Skip Langdon. And this is Sally's mother, Reed Foucher. I thought she might be able to help. May we talk to the suspect?"

"I'd rather wait till the negotiators come." He was a redhead with freckles over very white skin. Skip wondered if he was always so pale. He was twitching from nervousness.

"I wouldn't," said Reed, and hollered, "Sally! Mommy's here."

A snake of fury raced up Skip's spine. *Damn her!*

There was an intake of breath, and a tremor went through the semicircle. Peering through, Skip could see Anna holding Sally and Sally struggling, pushing futilely against Anna's confining arm.

"Mama! Mama!"

Reed said, "Oh, God. Ohgodohgod. *Sally!*"

Skip whispered to Johnson, "Let Anna see us, at least."

He nodded, deep lines between his eyes.

Two men stepped aside, clearing a path for Skip and Reed. Skip pushed the wheelchair very slowly, as nonthreatening as possible.

Anna said, "Stop or I'll blow her head off."

Skip stopped. "Anna, you wouldn't do that."

"Don't push me."

Sally was struggling so hard Anna had to hold her way too tight. Her screams were the forlorn howls of babies in hell, noises that took Skip back to childhood, to pediatricians' offices, emergency rooms, places where a child howled in the distance and you knew it was undergoing unspeakable torture.

Sally's torture was psychic, but it was torture nonetheless. Each policeman's face was a discrete, personal study in tension and misery.

Skip knew what was in all their heads: *I twitch my little finger wrong and the baby's dead.*

She whispered to Johnson, "I'm going to talk to her a minute, and then I'm going to walk toward her."

He started to shake his head, but didn't. Indecision played on his features.

Skip turned back to Anna, knowing that for the moment she was in charge. "Anna, you wouldn't hurt Sally."

"I'll kill her, and then I'll kill myself."

Skip could feel sweat flowing at her hairline. She hadn't gotten that far yet—hadn't thought of that one. "Life seems hard right now because you're going through something. I don't know what, but I know you are. That's why you left your home in a hurry. That's why you feel so desperate. But you're a strong woman, Anna. You've been through a lot and you can get through this one too. You're not going to kill yourself."

She was making it up as she went along, going on the way Anna looked and on Reed's description of her—if she'd been a dragon, she had to be a strong woman.

Skip took a step forward. "I knew you wouldn't kill Sally. You know, before I came to your house, when I was trying to find you, I called your brother's house."

"My brother?"

Skip took another step. "Yeah, John Garibaldi."

"My husband's brother. My *late* husband."

"I talked to his little girl. What a sweet child!"

I can't believe the stuff I'm saying. I sound like I'm at a tea party.

But it was working. Anna was quiet; something seemed different about her. And she was sufficiently distracted to discuss her relatives.

Skip took two more steps, keeping her eyes on Anna's face. She couldn't see Johnson, but that was just as well. He had no choice now except to let her handle it.

Anna was looking at her, not Sally. But Sally lurched in her arms, squealing, and Anna's attention turned back to the child.

"Little Kathy. Isn't that her name?" *It had to be* something *ending in a Y.*

Anna didn't answer.

"She told me how you take her to get ice cream cones. Did you know you're her favorite aunt? She told me that. Did she ever tell you that?

"Do you know how disappointed that little girl would be if she never saw you again?"

"You're just trying to manipulate me." Anna's voice was thick; full of tears.

"Look, we can work this out. Whatever trouble you're in, it can't be as bad as leaving Kathy alone. Really think about that. Weigh it. What's the shock going to be like for that little girl?" Skip came closer and held out her hand, slowly, as if trying to make friends with a dog. "Why don't you give me the gun?"

"Leave me alone, goddamn it!" It came out as half a sob, half a scream. Sally lurched again, and the Dragon cooed, "Oh, baby, did I hurt your ears? Poor little Sally-wally. Nonna didn't mean to."

Skip saw what Dietrich meant about dual personalities. She said, "You love Sally, don't you? You love her very much." She paused. "Let her go to her mama."

Hearing a familiar word, Sally screamed, "Mama! Mama!"

"Anna. You know you're not going to kill her. A beautiful, sweet child like that. You love her. You just can't do it. Go ahead. Let her go."

Anna stared straight at Skip. She began to bend from the knees.

Omigod, she's going to do it.

Skip started to panic, realizing that the minute Sally was on the ground, Anna would turn the gun on herself.

She ran the last few steps, knowing Anna's decision was made. No way was she going to shoot Sally. She grabbed the other woman's gun hand and twisted till she felt the fingers relax, heard the gun drop.

After that, it was a blur. Other officers piled on and separated the three of them—Sally, Anna, and Skip. Then Sally was running, shouting, "Mama! Mama! Mama!"

Skip was sorry that Reed couldn't run as well.

● ●

It was hell getting out of the airport. Once Skip had fought her way through the thicket of reporters that now bristled through the corridors, she had to give her report to the Jefferson Parish guys. By the time that was done, some of the arguing was over about who got Anna, and the news wasn't too bad from Skip's point of view: the FBI claimed her for the federal crime of taking a gun into the airport.

The good part was, since the airport was the city's property, she'd be in federal custody in Orleans Parish prison—not Jefferson.

Cappello met her at her desk. "Great job. I'd say go home, but there's news."

"I couldn't anyway. I've got to figure a way to sit in when the feds question Anna." As one of Anna's victims, she couldn't be involved in the questioning, but it was one show she didn't want to miss.

"Who is she, anyway?"

"Damned if I know. Piece of work, though. What's the news?"

"O'Rourke identified his attacker."

"Yeah?"

Skip could barely comprehend, her head was so full of Anna.

"From mug shots. Look at this." She tossed a snapshot on Skip's desk.

"Jesus."

"Not exactly."

It was the same picture Skip had picked after Jim's murder, the one of the man she'd failed to identify in the lineup.

"Augustine Melancon. We meet again."

"He's coming in for a lineup in an hour."

Skip sighed. "I guess I'd better go." She was exhausted.

She went home, took a shower, and thought about calling Jimmy Dee to tell him about her narrow escape. But that was a longer talk than she had time for.

She grabbed a Diet Coke, found her spare .38, and returned to an interesting message on her desk—from a Turner Shellmire at the FBI. But no time to call him—she barely had time to get to the lineup.

One man stuck out—all but hooked her with a finger and begged to be arrested. It was the same one O'Rourke had picked.

Augustine Melancon.

I wonder what I was thinking before?

This time the pressure was off; days had passed; she was clearer-headed. Or so she told herself.

Melancon, of course, didn't know why he'd been picked up. Skip, O'Rourke, and Cappello tackled him together, the better to scare the bejesus out of him.

"Remember me?" said O'Rourke. "You have fun beating me up?"

He didn't answer.

His lawyer, public defender Alfonso Green, advised him to zip his lip and keep it that way.

Skip said, "Look, Augustine, that's your right, but you have other rights that aren't covered by Miranda. You have the right to explain what happened if you want to. Nobody's saying you have only one option."

Melancon looked hopefully at Green, but got no help. Finally he said, "Asshole set me up. I think I want to tell her."

Green shrugged. "You can always waive."

"Shit." Melancon turned to Skip. "I'm gon' talk to you. I want to keep my lawyer here, but I'm gon' waive that silence shit. Why the fuck should I go down alone?"

"No reason," said Skip. "No reason at all. You work for Delavon, don't you?"

Melancon said nothing.

"I was out in Gentilly Thursday, seeing Delavon. The night before, I was in the Conti Breezeway, at Delavon's suggestion. You were there both times. Therefore, you work for Delavon."

"I don't know no shit 'bout no Conti Breezeway."

"Come on. Delavon set you up—you just said so. I saw you there, and you know it, 'cause you saw me. Sergeant O'Rourke saw you beating him up. That's one police officer you killed and one you assaulted. You really think we're gonna let you get away with any of that? You think Mr. Green can just make you a deal, get you out of this after two, three years—five-ten years maybe? You think it's that easy? You killed a cop, didn't you?

"Didn't you, Augustine?"

Melancon glowered, but Skip was pretty sure she saw fear below the beetling brows.

"You killed my partner, didn't you?"

"Shit, no."

"Well, I think you did. You know what, though? I'm gonna cut you some slack. Because I don't think it'd be very easy working for Delavon. I bet he threatens you sometimes. I bet he threatens your wife and your—"

"Ain't got no wife."

"He kill her already? That Delavon, he's one dangerous dude."

Melancon didn't answer.

"Maybe you got a girlfriend. Maybe he threatened her. Maybe there's a reason you did what you did."

Did she see hope on his face?

"I didn't do nothin'!"

"You killed my partner."

"That shithead Delavon, he tol' me if I didn't go over there, watch Jermaine's back, he gon' kill me. See, I owe Delavon a bunch of money—"

"How much?"

"Bunch."

"How much?"

" 'Bout ten thousand dollars. Deal went wrong once; and then there's the interest. Mr. Green, I got to tell 'em. Cain't I tell 'em what I tol' you?"

Slowly, Green nodded.

"I didn't kill nobody. I swear I didn't. But I know who did."

"Who did, Augustine?"

Green pointed a finger. "You answer that one and I kill *you*, boy." He turned to the three officers and smiled: "Deal time."

In another twenty minutes they had it hammered out: Melancon would testify against one Jermaine St. Jacques and one Desmond Lavon Bourgeois, in return for which he'd be permitted to plead guilty to battery.

The best part was, he gave them Delavon's address.

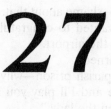

27

• •

It was Cappello's job, as Jim's sergeant, to investigate his death. Skip was beside herself, desperate to get to Delavon, yet dying to know what was happening with Anna.

"Sylvia, one thing you should know. I've got to go with you when you pick him up."

Cappello was preoccupied. She brushed at the hair in her eyes and glanced at her watch. "No way. You're too tired. Anyway, I don't even know if I'm going—Joe asked me to sit in when the feds question Anna, and my babysitter's got to go home sometime. I was going to see if Abasolo would do it."

"Tell him he has to wait until I can get free." She held her breath. Cappello would be perfectly within her rights to say, "I give the orders."

Instead she managed a tired half smile. "Are you saying a woman's got to do what a woman's got to do?"

Skip knew she had won.

She went back to her desk and called Agent Shellmire.

"Ah," he said. "The lady of the hour. Hear you got Anna Garibaldi."

"I hear you've got her now."

"Int'restin' lady."

265

"Fine hostess, anyhow. I had a lovely rest in her stately home."

He chuckled. "So we heard. Listen, I got a bigger case on her than this piddly airport shit, but I don't think I can make it now—and you folks still got to handle the arson and false imprisonment and all that—so I thought I might as well give you what I have. It's somethin' I think you'll be pretty interested in."

There is a God. She said: "We'd be delighted. But as you know, it's not my case anymore."

"Yeah, you bein' a victim—shame about that. But I knew your name, so I thought I'd call. Also I wanted to congratulate you—that was pretty impressive, what you did at the airport."

"Thanks." Her cheeks burned.

"Listen, I'm over at the parish prison—why don't you come on over with whoever's got the case and I'll play you a kind of int'restin' tape. Then maybe we can question the lady."

She rounded up Cappello and Joe Tarantino.

Shellmire was a tall man with a fruit-and-vegetable look—potato face, seaweed hair, pear-shaped body. When they had shaken hands, he said, "Let's wait a minute on that tape. I do b'lieve Ms. Garibaldi's lawyer just turned up. Y'all want to meet him?"

"By all means."

Anna's lawyer was waiting for Shellmire, huffing and puffing, dressed in a suit that had probably cost more than the combined furnishings of Skip's apartment. He was furious.

"I thought you were ready to question Mrs. Garibaldi. I hope you don't think I have time just to sit around inhaling institutional odors." He curled his lip.

"Hey, Mr. Delmonico. Haven't seen you in a while." Bobby Delmonico's presence confirmed things Skip already thought. He represented biggish drug dealers; people involved in video poker; random thugs up for assault and sometimes murder. A lot of them had Italian names.

Whoever the Dragon was, she was connected.

"Don't think I know you," Delmonico said.

"Shellmire. Agent Turner Shellmire. This is Detective Langdon, Lieutenant Tarantino, and Sergeant Cappello, NOPD."

He kept his face impassive. Though Shellmire held out a hand, he didn't shake.

"Have you talked to your client yet?"

"Yes. She's a little upset."

"I don't blame her. She's in big-league trouble."

"I think she might have a medical problem."

"I beg your pardon?"

He spread his hands, just a well-dressed dummy trying to comprehend a vast and confusing universe. "She seems to think she doesn't need a lawyer."

"That's her prerogative." Skip thought, *There has to be a catch: we couldn't be that lucky.*

"I've known her family all my life. Anna's always . . . well, always been unstable."

"Mr. Delmonico, do you see a jury in here? Don't you think it's a little early for this kind of thing?"

"Look, she needs legal representation and she won't listen right now— how about letting her have a good night's sleep? We can do this tomorrow."

"A good night's sleep? Sure. We'll break out the satin sheets."

"I just thought . . ." Apparently, he couldn't finish the sentence.

Skip realized he was desperate, and she liked that. "Look," said Shellmire, "I'm going to question the prisoner. Are you coming?"

He shrugged and followed them to the room where Anna had been taken. She was sitting, head in her left hand, back bent, looking forlorn and a little bit old. She raised her head, marshaled her fury, and aimed it at her lawyer. "I told you to get out of here."

There was fire enough in her voice to fuel a whole herd of dragons.

Delmonico looked beseechingly at Shellmire, who only stared at him, probably trying to figure out why he was still hanging around. Finally, the agent shrugged. "Sounds like you're fired."

When he had gone, Anna said, "I called someone to get me another lawyer. But so far no one's turned up."

Shellmire led the others away. "Got a real treat for y'all."

The tape began with a male voice.

"Hello?"

Another answered.

"Eddie, it's Gus. Lemme speak to Anna."

There was a pause and Anna's voice said, "Gustavo?"

"Anna, are you all right?"

"Why wouldn't I be all right? Why haven't I heard from you?"

Skip thought the words sounded fuzzy, as if Anna had just awakened from a deep sleep.

"Anna, something bad happened. You know what these people are like."

"These people, these people." She was slurring her words. "You were the one—"

"Don't start, Anna. I haven't got much time."

"Where are you, Gustavo?"

"I'm in another country, do you understand? I can't come back to America."

Anna gasped.

"Anna, listen. They think I cheated them. If they find me, they kill me."

Another gasp.

"You need to join me."

"What are you saying?"

"I want you to come to New York, and stay with our friend. You know who I mean?"

"Yes."

"He'll have a ticket for you. You'll love it here; it's beautiful."

"Gustavo, what do you mean? What are you talking about?"

"I mean, Anna, that we both have to leave the country. They're trying to kill me, do you understand that?"

"They won't kill me."

"First of all, they'll take everything you own. Because you don't really own it, you remember that? When they've done that, they'll try to get to me through you."

"Pfah. They'd have done it already."

"No. I bought you some protection. Pray God only the FBI's listening, because you're dead and so's somebody else if they find out. I bought you some protection, Anna. Do you understand that? Do you know what I had to pay for it? You don't want to. Believe me you don't."

Anna emitted some sort of sound—whether another gasp or a sob, Skip couldn't tell.

"But it's running out. It's only good for a few days. It's information that won't be passed, do you understand? And then when it is, everything's over."

"I don't follow."

"You don't need to follow. What you need to know is that you need to get out of there today. You need to get to New York and talk to our friend."

"I can never come back, can I? That's what you're saying."

"I'm sorry, Anna."

"I have to leave everything—" She was shouting so loud Shellmire had to turn the volume down.

The caller interrupted, shouting louder: "Shut up, Anna! This isn't for Eddie and Mike to hear."

"Omigod! Are they going to be all right?"

"Don't worry about them. Worry about yourself." Shellmire turned up the volume. "You've been drinking, haven't you?"

"I've been out of my mind. You disappear for days, I don't hear from you, you leave everything for me, and I don't know how to do anything—"

"Anna, shut up and listen, will you? I'm telling you what to do now. Are you listening? Can you hear me?"

"Yes."

"Pack a suitcase, and call the bank—have your money transferred to New York. You know where I mean?"

"Yes."

"The money's all you'll need. That and a few clothes."

"You're telling me to leave everything I have?"

"For Christ's sake, bring the family pictures. Nothing else is yours, can't you understand that? It's theirs. It's always been theirs. You had it on loan."

"The fish company's mine."

"They let you run it for 'em because you look respectable. And because you're my sister. You were their front, that's it. Face it. It's over now."

The silence of loss filled the room, of a life slipping away.

The caller said, "Send Mike and Eddie home. Then go into the safe in the closet, take out all the records and burn them. After that, go to the airport and if there isn't a plane to New York within the hour, take the next plane to anywhere and go from there to New York."

"It has to be done that fast?"

"Yes. It does."

"I can't just leave like that."

"You can and you will."

"You don't understand, Gustavo. I've been holding things together for you. Everything fell apart when you left like that, and I had to do what I could. I've been waiting for you to call and tell me what to do. I've been out of my depth here."

"What are you talking about?"

"I'm holding four prisoners, one of them a cop. And one's a baby."

"*You what?*" This time Shellmire didn't bother to turn the thing down. He watched the others jump and seemed to enjoy it.

"I had to, Gus, I—"

269

"You crazy bitch. I can't fucking believe you could be so fucking incompetent. I swear to fucking God I can't—"

"Everything fell apart, Gustavo. What was I *supposed* to do?" The question was a wail.

"Okay, okay, keep quiet. Eddie and Mike, okay? Look. Let me talk to Eddie. I'll send 'em home now—tell 'em their checks are in the mail."

Shellmire said, "I'm going to fast-forward to the place where Anna picks up again."

He didn't judge it quite right, and Skip heard the end of what the caller said to Eddie, speaking in a perfectly reasonable, well-modulated voice. He asked for Anna again, and when she was on, he continued his tirade as if he hadn't been interrupted.

"I don't care what the fuck happened. Who the fuck authorized you to lock people up, for God's sake? When the fuck have we *ever* done anything so crazy? And a cop. A cop! You are the craziest goddamn broad in the entire benighted state of Louisiana."

"If you'll let me talk, I'll tell you what happened."

"I don't care what happened. Why would I want to know what happened? I'm out of the fucking country and out of the fucking game. You want to live, Anna, you better get here too."

"Gustavo, what am I supposed to do with these people?"

"I don't care if you burn the whole fucking place down with all of them in it."

"What did you say?" The words were spoken more in incredulity than inquiry.

"I said fry 'em, I don't care. What the hell else are you going to do? Let 'em go? Then the cop arrests you. You can't let 'em go."

"Leave 'em tied up? If one of 'em gets loose, it's your ass. You're dead, do you understand? You want to get out alive? Kill 'em. I swear to God it's your only chance."

"But Gustavo, you can't just—"

"I can't what? I been dodging bullets all week, and now this. You don't know what my stomach feels like. You just don't know."

"I can't do what you say."

"So die, Anna. That's your alternative. Just burn the records before you do, okay?"

He hung up.

Shellmire turned the machine off. "What do you think?"

Cappello said, "Was that who I think it was?"

He nodded. "Gus Lozano. Who we'll now never touch. He's gone back to the fatherland or some place. But we might get some of his pals if we work together on this."

Cappello and Tarantino murmured assent. Skip said, "I need to know something."

"You mean, are we going to let you sit in when we interview her?"

"How'd you guess?"

The others laughed.

●   ●

Anna's new lawyer was a young woman named Dina Roth. She had shiny shoulder-length hair and the clear eyes of a teetotaler, something you didn't see that much in New Orleans. She wore jeans and a blazer, and she was smiling.

"My client," she said, "has something to tell you before you begin. I advise you to hear her out. It could save you a lot of time and trouble."

"Sure," said Shellmire. "Just let me remind Ms. Garibaldi of her rights." Anna scowled as he spoke, and when he had finished, she nodded impatiently.

"I want to tell you why I changed lawyers," she said. "I never called Bobby Delmonico. Someone called him for me. I was so arrogant, I didn't call a lawyer at all—just phoned a few of my influential 'friends' to get me out of this.

"First I called Maurice Gresham, who, I think, works with the three of you. He's a very special friend of mine, or he was, until he refused to take my call.

"After that, I called my friends on the casino board and my friends in the governor's office; every single one of them couldn't wait to get me off the phone. I called ten in all, and I'll be glad to give you all their names and a list of the crimes I personally know they've committed because I've been a witness to them.

"One of them, apparently, sent me that horse's ass, Delmonico, who advised me not to say a word, although so far as I could tell, this had little to do with helping my case and everything to do with protecting my 'friends.'

"I am fed up, ladies and gentlemen. I am the sister of Gus Lozano, who as you know was the mob boss of New Orleans until a few days ago. Our longtime employers have now tried to kill my brother and caused him to seek exile in another country. I locked up four people and kept them prisoner trying to protect our employers and their 'friends,' and then I thought I had no choice except to kill them to protect myself. I am

271

informed by my brother that our friends in the dear brotherhood are gunning for me as well as him, though I doubt that, because they usually only kill if you've cheated them or they think you have.

"But in any case, I would like to see them all die horrible deaths. Therefore I'm prepared to sing like the proverbial canary not only about my own case, but about everything I know about the Mafia in New Orleans. And all our dear 'friends,' of course." She stopped, hands in lap, smiling like one of the nice church ladies Skip had recently met. "I do this more in hopes of revenge than leniency."

"Okay, Anna," said Roth. "Let's stop there." She turned to the others. "She'll be happy to tell her story tonight. When we start dealing, we'll talk about the other stuff. The canary songs."

Shellmire looked like he'd died and gone to heaven. Skip thought: *The D.A.'s going to be pinching himself as well. I hope I'm maintaining my usual poker face.*

Shellmire said, "Mind if we tape this?"

Roth shook her head. "Not at all."

Once again he reminded Anna of her rights. "Okay, Ms. Garibaldi, why don't you tell us what happened?"

Anna looked pretty good for someone who'd been through what she had. Some criminals probably did want to be caught—especially those fleeing their country and a burning house for an unknown life in an unknown land. To Anna, a prison might be preferable.

That and revenge.

She said, "Where shall I start?" She seemed a different person from the frightened, shaky wraith who had rifled Skip's purse.

Sobered up probably. And not only in a physical sense.

"Wherever you like."

"I guess in a way I've always been involved because of the fish business, although I didn't know it. Gus set my husband up in the business when we were very young, and of course they didn't tell me any of the details because I was a woman. Women have no role in the mob except to produce children. Then when Phil died, he left the business to me, and I found out it was a money laundry. Well, I knew what my brother did for a living, and our father before him; that didn't surprise me. But I'd never heard anyone talk about it before. I wasn't really one of them, do you understand that? Because I'm a woman.

"I think Gus probably had to fight pretty hard to get them to let me keep running the business, but he wanted that, because he didn't have time to do it himself. He could trust me, you see—he knew I was the one person who wouldn't cheat him. Not only that, I'd been running it since Phil got sick, and I had an aptitude.

"I was happy doing it.

"We've always been close, Gustavo and I. His wife left him a few years ago. I don't blame her—who wants a husband who's never home and never talks about anything important? I had one like that. But it's different with brother and sister—Gustavo and I could talk; he respects me as much as he can respect a woman.

"So when he got the idea of buying the house—the one where Detective Langdon was my guest—he asked me if I'd like to be his hostess. The idea was a meeting place, a place where we could impress people we needed, do you know what I mean?"

Tarantino said, "Not exactly."

"I mean politicians. People on the casino board. People who control things that affected us.

"People like Arthur Hebert—he's been to parties there. He's worked with us for years. A restaurant owner's ideal for passing messages—he goes around, shakes hands with the customers, he talks to everybody. Nobody sees anything, you understand? Of *course* he got the casino restaurant concession—why wouldn't he?"

Skip realized that Sugar's mysterious "Ann" had probably been the Dragon herself. She said, "Was Reed in on it?"

"God, no. But she had to go before the casino board as a formality. Poor thing; I hear she worked her little butt off trying to get what was already in the bag."

Shellmire said, "Could we get back to the house, please? What did you use it for?"

Anna settled back, looking as if she were used to an audience. "We'd invite these people to parties there, and let them throw their own parties." She shrugged. "We'd even get them bimbos if they wanted them. Of course I didn't have to do that. Gustavo always tried to protect me. . . ." She blinked and paused for a moment. "It worked two ways. If they were already in, it was just a clubhouse for them. We've got a pool and a gym, billiard room—all that kind of stuff. Your Sergeant Gresham, for instance —he liked to bring his women there.

"If they weren't in, they'd come and meet people who seemed respectable, and they wouldn't know what they were into till it was too late, and then we could blackmail them.

"Anyway, what I did—I ran the house. I guess you could say I was literally a housekeeper. I hired the staff, gave the parties, took care of the caterers, all that kind of stuff; I did all the scheduling, took care of the laundry—everything except procuring the bimbos. Also, I kept running the fish company. If you looked in Maurice Gresham's records, you'd see that he did a whole lot of 'private security work' for us."

"Which he didn't really do."

"Are you kidding? Why would a fish company need security? He just did us the kind of favors a guy with the run of the cop shop can do."

Cappello caught Skip's eye. Skip raised an eyebrow, acknowledging their previous conversation.

"So that was the setup," she said. "What happened last Monday?"

"Monday?"

"Were you having a meeting at the clubhouse?"

"Oh, the night Mo's bimbo showed up pursued by the mother of the baby she'd kidnapped. What a piece of work, huh? Can you believe anybody could be so stupid? And can you believe she's Arthur Hebert's daughter? God, I have some bad luck.

"Reed comes running up to the gate, trying to get in, and yelling everyone's name. We had three casino board members there—did the neighbors need to know that? They'd just left the meeting, but it was still in progress and I had to do something with this crazy woman. I didn't have any choice about it."

She was momentarily fiery, no doubt the Anna that Reed had seen when she named her the Dragon, the one who was probably good in business and who ran the mob clubhouse like a four-star hotel.

There are women like that. They're great in business, do their jobs well, they make a terrific impression, but they're completely submissive to men. Twofers.

"Why not just tell her to go home?"

"She saw those casino board people—don't you understand? Do you know what that means? Then it turns out she's Reed Hebert. Not only does she know them, but they know her. She's seen them at the mob clubhouse. That tries and convicts them in their own minds—and who knows where it might have led? I certainly didn't, and I didn't know what to do. Except contain the damage. That much I knew.

"So I had Eddie and Mike bring her in, along with the bimbo, who was out of her mind drunk—or something—and couldn't be reasoned with. And the little girl. Sally." In the midst of it all, Anna smiled. As soon as she said the name, her face was transformed.

She looked at Skip, possibly because she'd known her the longest by a couple of hours. "Is Sally all right?" Her voice was different too, high and too light; worried.

"She's fine."

"I took good care of her. I'd never have hurt her. You know that, don't you? The gun was empty."

That was true: there were no bullets in the gun she had held to Sally's head.

Shellmire said, "So you took the three of them prisoner."

"I had no idea what to do. Nothing like this had ever happened before —first of all, decisions to make; second, Gustavo out of action. He had gone to New York for a day or two. I faxed him immediately, thinking to hear back in an hour or two, like always. Thinking he'd be back in the morning. He'd left no one in charge, you see. No one.

"So that meant me. I knew that if I didn't hear from him, I was supposed to pretend I had, I wasn't to let anyone know he couldn't be reached."

"You had that agreement with him?"

Anna looked at him coldly. "When you've spent your whole life in the mob, you're expected to have a minimum of street smarts. You don't need agreements."

"I see."

"I kept thinking I'd hear from him any second, but I also knew that if I didn't, something was badly wrong. I was crazy with worry, and I couldn't help it, I started drinking and couldn't stop. I don't usually do that." She sounded surprised.

"I mean, I've never done that in my life." She looked at each of them in turn. "But I've never—I've never had a problem like this. Could I have some coffee, please?"

"Of course. Let's take a ten-minute break."

Shellmire was probably happy to get her some coffee. He wanted her to stay alert, stay focused. Keep talking.

When they had reconvened, Anna seemed to have gotten a second wind. "I don't think any of you can understand how panicked I was and how the panic increased minute by minute, hour by hour, day by day. I'm not trying to excuse what I did—I am deeply sorry and I know I'll be punished. I just want you to know that you can't know how crazy I was."

She stopped and didn't speak for a few minutes, apparently making up her mind about something. She stared at a spot on the wall, perhaps projecting on it her own private movie.

She said, "I lied when I said I've never done that. When my son died, the same thing happened." Tears flowed freely down her aristocratic cheeks. "I started drinking and I couldn't stop. It was like that for two weeks. And then—I did.

"I'm not an alcoholic. I don't do this periodically. I guess—" She stopped and stared again for a while, working it out. "I guess I must do it when I just can't face something. I thought Gustavo was dead. I thought I was alone in the world. I mean, I see now that was what I was trying not to think. And you see, it happened at the same time Sally came. I had all those same feelings—of loss, of the most excruciating despair—that I had when I lost my son, and yet, here was something filling me up again. Here was this wonderful little girl I kept falling in love with a little bit more every day.

"I would never have hurt her. You have to believe me. I thought it was the only way I could get to spend time with her—to pretend like that. I just wanted to be with her."

Skip thought of the way she had held Sally too tight, the terrified look on the child's face, the way Sally had screamed for her mother.

We do such odd things in the name of love.

Shellmire said, "Your son was Frankie Garibaldi."

Anna looked surprised. "Francis, yes. They killed him."

"But it didn't happen here—it happened in New York."

"They set him up."

"Why?"

"They sent him there. They could have sent Johnny. Or Carlos or Martin. Any of them were more experienced. They didn't have to send Francis."

Shellmire spread his hands. "It sounds more like they gave him a chance and he blew it."

"The bastards set him up."

28

• •

Skip had drunk coffee along with Anna, enough to get her through a long night. She still had to talk to Reed, but that could wait. Cappello had told her Abasolo was waiting for her call.

She got some peanut butter cookies from a machine in the basement and ate them mechanically, not tasting, not wanting to, just needing fuel.

She got Abasolo's machine. "Oh, well, out at a bar, I expect." It wasn't likely—Abasolo was a staunch member of AA—so staunch that was his sometime nickname.

He picked up. "Officer Langdon, I presume."

"Thanks for waiting for me, Adam. I really appreciate it."

"I couldn't resist—it was so much fun the last time we partnered up."

"Some backup you were then." He had watched her fight off a suspect who was also an unwelcome suitor.

"I thought you wanted to handle it yourself." She had, as a matter of fact. "Anyway, it gave me new respect for tall, dangerous female officers. You have Delavon's address?"

"Does the pope wear dresses?"

"Okay. Get some uniforms to meet us there. And pick me up in twenty."

• •

Abasolo lived in a small, neat house in mid-city, newly painted, but spoiled by a cluttered porch. "What do you think?" he said. "I just moved in. Still moving—guess you can tell."

"Nice."

He got in the car. "Gonna be nicer. I'm going to dig up those awful azaleas and put in some roses, for one thing. Then I'm gonna get some nice annuals, just for now, while I'm trying to figure out what I really want."

"I never figured you for a gardener, AA. You're a man of hidden depths."

"All of them murky."

He was wearing the requisite dark clothes—jeans and a black T-shirt. He seemed about as tightly wound as a guy on his way to a Saints game.

"Where are we going?"

"Beautiful New Orleans East. Did Cappello tell you the story? Here's the deal—Delavon's the gangster who sent me out to the Iberville, where Jim got shot."

"You think he set you up?"

"Not really. He couldn't have known when I'd be going there, and I don't think his guys would have made Jim—I think he probably just got in the way. But Delavon made sure I knew about this heroin dealer working out of the project. He must have got tired of waiting for us to pop him and decided to take him out himself. Anyway, I saw someone there that night, and the same dude beat up O'Rourke while I was talking to De-lavon a few days later."

"He works for Delavon."

"And he made a deal with us. Hence, tonight's adventure."

"So what do you think the setup is?"

Skip shook her head, vaguely aware that she was biting her lip as well. "I've got a real bad feeling about this dude."

"Like a premonition?"

"I wish to hell I did get those. I've spent a little time with him now." She shook her head again. "I don't know. I just don't know."

"Hey, you're fadin'; talk to me."

"It's some black, dark feeling, like the worst has already happened. I get it when I'm around him. I even get it when I think about him."

"Ah. Depression."

"Not depression. More like pure evil."

Abasolo gave her a squinty-eyed look and didn't speak for a while. Finally he said, "Maybe we should go back to gardening."

She felt slightly betrayed. "You asked."

They were getting near New Orleans East now. This was where she thought Delavon had met her the time he had her kidnapped. But they weren't on the way to the pleasure dome, or whatever it was. Augustine Melancon had specifically said it was a house, the house in which Delavon lived. Probably he had a stash house somewhere as well.

Skip had asked questions about the house—who lived there, how big it was—but Melancon didn't know. He said when he picked up Delavon, he waited in the car. That was all he knew.

The part of New Orleans East where they were going was a neighborhood in decline. It boasted blocks and blocks of scuzzy condos and lots of brick fourplexes with barred windows. Some of the condos were so poorly constructed they were literally falling apart. In some cases, trim that had fallen off lay on the ground; in others, gutters hung down.

The condos were disheartening, but downright heartbreaking were the tiny, neat little houses that were also falling apart—and also barred. It was hard to picture Delavon in one of these. Skip imagined the occupants as honest, hardworking people—postal employees perhaps, laborers, hospital workers—beset by neighborhood conditions they could do nothing about.

Drug dealers in the Superstore parking lot, and in the doorways of the condos.

The flash of gunfire at night.

Terror that the kids would end up in gangs, or on drugs. Dead.

But the fact that Delavon lived in one put a different light on it. Maybe they were all the tidy, prim lairs of vicious criminals who emanated the evil that had so spooked her in Delavon's presence.

In that case, who watered the lawns and took care of the flowers?

She pulled up in front of a red brick one, so tiny it looked like the prototype for the one in the three pigs story, snug and impervious to lupine huffing and puffing.

It had a well-kept lawn and beds in which zinnias and marigolds flaunted themselves like drag queens. In the back there were very likely sweet peas and vegetables. Probably the lady of the house sent one of the kids out every Sunday to get a couple of ripe tomatoes, maybe some cucumbers as well, to slice up for lunch, to go with the chicken and the rice and the fresh peas and the fresh corn, and all the other vegetables she'd prepared.

279

What lady? What am I thinking?

It was as if she'd fallen into a trance, forgotten what she'd come for. Abasolo said, "How do you want to play it?"

"It's your call."

He shook his head. "You're the one who knows him."

"Okay. We should use that. I'll knock. You stay a little behind me. If he comes to the door, we take him. If he doesn't, we play it by ear."

"By ear's fine. Love by ear to death." She glanced at him to see if he was being sarcastic, but she saw only a long-legged, languid, utterly relaxed, precision-tuned cop. The sight made her feel better. She removed her gun from her purse and put it in her pocket.

The uniforms were waiting for them. Abasolo sent one to the back, told the other to stay in front.

It was nearly ten o'clock. The house was well-lit and she could hear the drone of a television.

She banged on the door.

A little girl opened it, smiling. Her face fell when she saw Skip. She was about seven, wearing pink jeans, a Little Mermaid T-shirt, and rubber thongs. "I thought you were Uncle Eric," she said.

"I'm here to see your daddy."

"My daddy don't know you." Good smells wafted out the door—dinner smells, a couple of hours old.

"Shavonne. Shavonne, who's that?" called a female voice, and then an older woman stepped into view.

She was overweight and her hair had a white streak in it, but her skin was unlined, her face round and strong, her heavy breasts waiting pillows for anyone needing a hug. She held herself with dignity, and could have been the model for a statue of an African deity; Yemaya perhaps.

Skip felt a tug in her chest. This woman looked as if she taught Sunday school. More women's voices fluttered softly on the air, probably from the kitchen.

"We're here to see Delavon."

"Delavon?" The woman's head swiveled. "He on the phone. Y'all come in, won't you?" She opened the door.

Something was wrong here. This was not a home where pure evil could flourish.

Skip could see a room full of kids, eyes glued to the tube. She glanced at Abasolo. He looked a lot more nervous now, his neck practically a swivel, checking out everything and then some.

"I'm Martha Redmann—here from Illinois, visitin' my daughter. Used to live here, though—still miss it, can you imagine? We havin' a big family reunion this week. Y'all want some gumbo?"

Skip stepped inside, Abasolo following. Martha Redmann turned toward the kitchen, but Abasolo didn't. He walked around Skip into the room where the kids were.

Skip turned to follow their hostess. Behind Redmann, against a wall of the living room, was an old-fashioned secretary, shelves above a fold-down desk. The shelves were glass-enclosed, and in the glass Skip saw a man reflected.

He was wearing a T-shirt and baggy, bright print pants. He was pointing a gun at her.

She couldn't tell if it was Delavon or not, and it didn't occur to her to wonder. She dropped into a deep crouch, a squat almost at floor level, and whirled, pulling the gun from her pocket.

The secretary exploded behind her, and Martha Redmann screamed. Glass rained on Skip's head. She fired.

The man fell, dropping the gun, blood spewing onto his white T-shirt. Skip tried to stand but couldn't. She ended up sitting on the floor, watching Abasolo fly into the hall, feeling Redmann come from behind her. For a moment she thought the two were going to collide, but each managed to stop in time.

"Police," said Abasolo, gun drawn. More women were pouring from the kitchen, keening. To her left the children, the tube hounds, were frozen; not screaming, not moving.

"My baby, my baby," said one of the women, Delavon's mother perhaps, or maybe the mother of one of the children.

And then Shavonne, the little girl in the pink jeans, stood up and screamed, "Mama!"

Skip got only a glimpse of her face before Shavonne began to run toward the women, but she could see that the child, in her Little Mermaid T-shirt, her impossibly tiny jeans, knew that her world lay about her in shards. She tripped on her clumsy thongs almost as soon as she was in motion, and fell with a noise like a brick dropped from above.

She seemed not to notice that she had fallen.

"Mama! Mama!" she cried again, and she began to crawl, very fast, as if a wolf pack were chasing her. Skip didn't understand why her mother didn't run to her; later remembered Abasolo's gun pointed at the women, pinning them in place.

She finally managed to stand.

"You okay?" asked Abasolo.

"I think so." She looked around, reorienting herself. In the kitchen behind the women stood one of the uniformed officers, gun drawn. The other was just inside the doorway, radio at his mouth.

Abasolo said, "Everybody be still. Just be still for a minute and everything's going to be all right." He spoke to Skip: "You want me to make the check?"

Someone had to see if there was anyone else in the house. Skip's legs had about as much starch as a pair of rubber bands, but she wasn't about to say so.

"I'll do it."

Shavonne had reached her mother, who was holding her and crooning to her: "You fine, baby, you fine. Everything gon' be okay now."

Skip turned to the room full of children. "Everybody stay still a minute. I'll be right back."

"I'll be right back." Like I'm their mama, gone to fetch a glass of water.

One of the uniforms went with her, the other went to the fallen man.

The shooter was the only man in the house. Everywhere else she found open suitcases, children's dirty clothes, in piles and simply strewn, suitcases—all the appurtenances of the family reunion Martha Redmann had mentioned.

She went to the man on the floor. She knew as soon as she knelt that he was dead. That she had killed him.

He was Delavon. Delavon the Evil. Lying on the floor in a pool of blood surrounded by women and children, at a family reunion.

Presumably one of the women was his wife. Skip had shot him dead in front of her; in front of his own children, and their cousins, and their aunts and their grandmother.

The room started to blur.

"Langdon!" Abasolo called sharply. "Sit down and lower your head."

She obeyed and in a few moments began to feel sharper. She must have been swaying.

Oh, great. First, you kill somebody and then you almost faint.

First day with a new sergeant. Terrific impression you're making.

Later, when she talked about it, she couldn't believe those thoughts had gone through her mind.

When she could stand again, and once again began to act like a cop, she worked mechanically, now thinking only one thought: *It happened so fast. How could it do that?*

She knew that her life was forever changed.

As the shock began to wear off, and the children to cry, she and

Abasolo let them go to the women, but Abasolo kept his gun trained on them until the district cars began to arrive.

First on the scene was a grinning man with a bag full of ice cream. Uncle Eric, for whom Shavonne had mistaken Skip.

Abasolo took Skip outside. "You all right?"

She shrugged. "Sure."

Happens every day. I shoot somebody's daddy and then watch her crawl across the floor.

"You know what color you are?"

It felt like an attack, like he was telling her she hadn't measured up, she wasn't good enough, she'd almost fainted and couldn't be trusted. "Leave me alone, goddammit!"

She turned away, but he grabbed her arm.

"I'm up on my colors these days. You're Navajo white."

"I'm fine. Could we get back to work, please? It's not like there's nothing to do in there."

"Hey. You're the cop who got the guy who killed Jim. You're a hero. Don't you think you get a five-minute break?"

"Oh, bullshit. You don't even know what happened."

"I hear two shots, I spin around, you've got glass in your hair, and the other guy's lying on the floor with a gun in his hand. The story kind of tells itself."

"I've got glass in my hair?"

"Uh-huh, but let's don't take it out yet. I want a lot of witnesses to this."

"That's where I saw him—in the glass. He was already pointing the gun."

"Shit."

"So I ducked. What would you do?" She started to laugh.

"Probably freeze and get shot." He laughed as well, a little uneasily, as if he didn't know where Skip's laughter was going. He put a hand on her shoulder, to steady her, she thought, and she found that she was profoundly grateful.

She had been numb before; dazed. But when Abasolo mentioned the glass in her hair, and witnesses, she had felt the leap in her chest that meant fear.

"Nobody saw what happened," she said. "But they could say they did. They could say anything they want."

Awkwardly, Abasolo stroked her arm. "You forget I was there. Two other cops were there. It'll be okay. Believe me. It's going to be okay."

That's what you told those women when their husband and son and son-in-law and brother was lying there dead. That's what Shavonne's mama said.

She turned in her gun for evidence, then went back to headquarters and gave her statements to someone from Internal Affairs, someone from OMI—the Office of Municipal Investigation—and Cappello, who'd been called back to take it. It was hours before they let her go.

But she found that Abasolo had waited for her, to drive her home. She was annoyed. "I'm okay to drive."

"Take it easy, will you? I want to talk to you."

"What about?"

"Come on. Let's get in the car."

"This is ridiculous. I brought my car, which means I really have to drop *you* off."

"Oh, quit bitching. I'll take you home and get a taxi from the Quarter. Okay?"

She didn't speak again, until they got to her car, ashamed of herself for snapping at him, not sure why she had. When she spoke, it was only more of the same. "I can drive."

"You're nuts, you know that? This is an honor for me. To be able to drive the hero of the day."

"Quit trying to flatter me."

They were alone in the dark now, the two of them sitting side by side. He didn't start the car, didn't even put the key in the ignition.

He said, "Look, I feel bad about this."

She felt the fear-leap again. "About what? What's going to happen to me?"

He touched her arm, and once again she found it reassuring. "Will you stop it? Everything's going to be okay. I meant I feel for you; I feel bad because you feel bad."

That got to her. She felt blood suffuse her face, felt her cheeks heat up and the muscles move into a smile of sorts. "That's the sweetest thing a cop's ever said to me."

"I've been through it before."

"You shot somebody?"

"My partner did. It was like tonight—God, this was déjà vu. We were at somebody's house and there were a bunch of screaming kids. We couldn't hear anything, so he went into another room to question the suspect. The next thing I knew I heard shots." He hesitated. "I was destroyed because I couldn't do anything."

He stopped and sighed. She could feel his body shift in the dark, and realized he had demons of his own about tonight. "But that's neither here nor there. What I want to tell you about is what happened to him. He went into a frenzy of work; he got all snappish and nasty like you did."

"Sorry. I don't know what's wrong with me."

"And I realized it was all a way of keeping the way he was feeling at bay. I didn't get it; I really didn't get it at first. But tell me if this is right— you don't feel like a hero, or even like you're in control. You feel vulnerable."

She stared at the lightish circle that was all she could see of his face. "How did you know that?"

"I'm right, aren't I? I'm right." He sounded triumphant.

"How do you *know?*"

"Well, that's how I get when I feel that way. Snappy. Like everybody's intruding." He inserted the key and turned it, apparently satisfied that he'd made contact.

When they were out of the garage, abroad in the soft night, he said, "I finally figured that out. But I never figured out why."

"I'm not sure. I guess—it's such a huge thing—you don't want to think about it. Anyone who comes around and says, 'How do you feel' or something makes you think about it. And that's the last thing you want to do."

He nodded. "You want a drink?"

She did. She wanted two or three. "No. I mean . . ."

"No," she said again. "I'm fine."

"No, you're not. But I am—on that one. I could watch you drink until six A.M. and not even be tempted."

"Mr. Macho."

"No. It's just not an issue."

"Maybe not tempted. Repelled."

"I like drunks. I've spent a lot of time with them."

She knew he couldn't possibly—even drunks don't like drunks—but she went with him to the Blacksmith Shop and had two beers while she talked to him. Mostly, she talked, not him. She told him every detail of what had happened at Delavon's house and everything that led up to it, even about being kidnapped by Delavon's thugs.

"Okay, that's it," he said. "Now even I don't believe you. He didn't shoot first. You just had to kill him, right?"

"What do you mean, 'even' you?"

"Oh, no, I forgot to tell you. The IA guys won't say so till it's official, but you're in the clear. That gorgeous woman—Martha something—said she saw it and it happened like you said."

"She couldn't have seen it. She had her back turned."

"She says she turned around to say something to you."

"I don't think so. I didn't see her."

"You were looking in the glass."

"Yeah, but you feel things. Motion. I think she was already in the kitchen."

"Would you want your daughter to marry Delavon? She'll probably send you flowers."

She knew he was making a giant effort for her, and she was grateful. She wondered if she would have done it for him, for Jim, for any partner in trouble.

Probably not. I get my feelings hurt when people snap.

She was grateful that he had not; that he had known what was wrong, and cared enough to wait for her, to sit with her while she talked it out. Tomorrow was his second day in Homicide, and it was only a few hours away; he would want to be rested, and he wasn't going to be.

She thought: *I could love this man*, and knew that it was only partly the beer. He reminded her of Steve.

When she was home, in bed alone, she found that the tears finally came. They surprised her, and not the least of her surprise was realizing she had kept them back, she hadn't cried, she had behaved with dignity.

She missed Steve so much her whole body hurt, and it was all she could do not to reach for the phone. There was a time when she'd have called Jimmy Dee, no matter how late the hour, but with the kids there, she could no longer do that.

After a while she slept, but she awoke early, leaking tears onto the pillow. The image of Shavonne tripping on her shoe, crawling to her widowed mama, wouldn't leave her.

29

•••

She got out of bed, sat on the floor, and tried to meditate. This was something she did every time she felt stressed out, and she always failed. She simply couldn't sit still long enough to empty her mind.

This time it was like a waking sleep.

She had the sense that it wouldn't lead to spiritual enlightenment, was somehow not what was meant by the empty-mind concept, but, oddly, it felt safe.

She had no idea how long she sat there, legs folded, back straight, hands open on her knees, but when her alarm rang, it penetrated her peace like a gunshot. She opened her eyes and made to get up, but her knees hurt and she had to straighten them slowly, which made her realize she had been sitting this way for a very long time.

What she had been doing, she didn't know, but she was faintly alarmed by it. It wasn't quite sleep and she didn't think it was really meditation; it seemed instead to be some kind of shadow state, brought about by shock.

Her phone rang. "Baby, you okay?" It was Cindy Lou, who never called her "baby" and never, ever sounded frightened, though she did now.

"Lou-Lou. What's wrong?"

"I heard what happened last night. Cappello called me."

"It was pretty grim."

"Why in the hell didn't you call me? Just tell me that?"

"I should have. You're the person I should have called."

"Damn right you should have. I'm your best girlfriend and I'm a shrink and I care about you. Call, hell! You should have just come over."

"Well, it was late and I didn't—"

"Late! Late! Honey, you were in trouble, weren't you? Couldn't have been feeling okay; no way. And don't try to tell me different—you aren't the first one who's ever been there."

Skip started to cry. "You really mean it, don't you? You wouldn't have minded, no matter how late it was."

"What kind of friend do you think I am? Besides, I'm the cop-shop shrink. They'd have probably paid me for it—hey. I'm kiddin' about that. I shouldn't have said it—I don't want to be flip at a time like this. I want you to know I'm there for you—do you get that?"

For some reason, this seemed too much to take in. Skip felt overwhelmed for what seemed to her all the wrong reasons—it seemed inexpressibly sad that she hadn't felt connected enough to the human race to call Cindy Lou last night, even to realize she was there to call. Her body began exploding sobs in quick rhythmic succession, a bazooka launching shells.

"Okay, baby. It's okay." Lou-Lou didn't sound like herself. She sounded like a mother soothing a child. "Now, look—I'm coming right over, okay? You just stay there a few minutes and I'll come make you some coffee. Maybe some toast too. Does that sound good?"

"I've got to go to work."

"Are you kidding? Cappello told me to tell you to bag it."

"Uh-uh, I've got to talk to Reed."

"Huh? Reed?"

"Oh, she didn't tell you everything."

"Just that you got Delavon and you felt pretty down about it."

"Well, a few other things happened too. The upshot is, Sally's back and so's Reed."

"Skip. That's wonderful."

"It was a hell of a day." Skip sighed. "Anyway, it's my case and I'm not leaving the interview to someone else."

"Okay, baby. Okay. You sound fine for now. You just call me when you're done, you promise?"

"I promise if I can stay awake. I may just pass out."

"Just give me a call and let me know. Promise, okay?"

"Okay." She felt slightly annoyed at having to answer to someone, but at the same time, Cindy Lou's concern was touching.

She really meant it. I could have called her in the middle of the night.

Suddenly, Skip understood that she could have called Jimmy Dee or Steve as well, never mind the time difference or the kids; they'd have wanted her to call.

She felt better, not quite so desolate as the night had left her.

She dressed carefully for work, not wanting to look the worse for wear, sure that eyes would be on her. But she wasn't prepared for what happened when she walked into the detective bureau. "Hey, Langdon," said someone; she never knew who. And then she was aware that everyone was on their feet, applauding.

She was confused. "What's going on?" she murmured, head swiveling.

Joe Tarantino came out of his office. "Nice going, Skip. Good job." He shook her hand.

When she had made her way to her desk, she saw that O'Rourke was at his, deep in paperwork. She hadn't noticed him when everyone stood, but she was sure she would have seen him if he'd been sitting down. Had he really stood and applauded her?

Impossible.

But if not, where was he?

She had too much pride to ask anyone, even Cappello. She'd never know.

Abasolo came by and gave her shoulder a squeeze.

"You okay?"

"Great." *Liar, liar, pants on fire.* She gave him a big insincere smile. He squeezed a little harder, as if to show he appreciated the effort.

Because Reed and Sally had been through a week-long ordeal, and because all hell was breaking loose, Reed had been sent home with her child rather than questioned. She'd been asked to return at nine-thirty to give her statement.

By then Skip had had coffee and talked to Jimmy Dee, who said, "Tiny, precious darling, why didn't you come over to Dee-Dee's and cuddle up with a little white puppy? Whatever were you thinking of, trying to go through a thing like that alone?"

"I must have been crazy, Dee-Dee. Never again."

"Certainly not, my angel. Certainly not. Come tonight; now promise!" His voice was so stern she didn't dare argue.

Reed arrived looking like the restaurant queen of New Orleans, in a wheat silk suit with cream blouse, silver Thomas Mann pendant set with a carnelian, and matching earrings. She seemed to have made quite a recovery. Skip wondered what it must have been like coming home to a husband who'd become a heroin addict; a mother who'd apparently decided to take over the job Reed had worked for her whole life. She wondered if Dennis would clean up again.

"Let's go to an interview room. I'll just get us some privacy and we can do it pretty fast."

"I'm sorry. I'm afraid I'm not going to be able to."

"I beg your pardon?"

"On advice of my attorney."

Oh, boy. Here we go. "I see. Is he meeting you here?"

"Do I need him? He said just to say—"

Skip didn't wait to hear the rest of the sentence. She said: "You'd better call him."

In the end it shook down this way: Reed was perfectly prepared to tell the story of the Dragon's lair, and adamantly unwilling to talk about her father's death.

Dennis must have done it. He laid it off on Evie, and Reed wouldn't go along with it. But she won't incriminate her husband.

Still, there was another witness.

Evie had been taken to Baptist, rather than Charity Hospital, probably at Reed's behest. Skip rounded up Abasolo—she wasn't doing this without a witness—and paid her a visit.

Evie had on no makeup, and her hair was matted, but she must have gotten a night's sleep. She was pale and thin, but Skip could see the beauty that had captured Dennis, and Maurice Gresham, and Manny Lanoux.

She introduced herself and Abasolo.

"You're the one Anna locked up."

"Don't remind me."

"You saved us—Reed and me. And Sally too, I heard. You know what? Anna Garibaldi always did scare the shit out of me. Long before this happened. She fell for the kid, though—I never saw anything like it. She was all gloppy and goopy around her—like caramel sauce or something. You could throw up."

Abasolo gave Skip an amused glance.

"Is Sally okay?" Evie asked.

Skip nodded. "Fine. How about you?"

"My throat hurts like a son of a bitch. The smoke, they said. I can talk, though, as long as I keep sucking ice." She pointed to a glass of ice chips, and helped herself to one.

"We want to talk to you, but I need to tell you a few things first." Skip gave her the Miranda warning.

"Am I under arrest?" Evie asked calmly.

"Yes. Do you want an attorney?"

Evie waved a hand, pursing her lips impatiently. "Hell, no."

"You're waiving your right to an attorney?"

"Yeah. Later for that crap."

Skip wasn't going to argue. "Tell us what happened a week ago Monday night."

Evie sat back and sighed, and blew out her cheeks. "Do I have to? It's too embarrassing."

That's the least of it. "I think you'd better."

"That's the night I got drunk and decided to reclaim my long-lost child. Pretty brilliant, huh?"

Abasolo smiled. He had a way about him.

"I don't know what got into me. I swear to God I don't."

"I do," said Abasolo. "I'm a drunk from way back."

"Oh, no. You're not going to give me that Twelve Step crap, are you?"

He shook his head. "Uh-uh. I mean, unless you want me to."

She hesitated, once again waved a hand. "Ehhhh, save it."

"What happened, Evie?"

"They let me in, and I demanded my fucking maternal rights." Skip could have sworn Evie's cheeks got slightly pinker, as if she were blushing at the memory. "What was I thinking of? I know less about children than W.C. Fields."

I don't care what you were thinking of. Just tell the story, goddammit. Skip thought she was going to pop, but Abasolo nodded and gave Evie a polite smile.

Like he's flirting, Skip thought. *God, he's good.*

She shrugged. "Dennis tried to get the gun away from me. Do you blame him?"

Very deliberately, Evie made eye contact with Abasolo, who shook his head this time.

"We struggled—little me and great big Dennis. I mean, I was commode-huggin'. I probably thought I could win. And to tell you the truth, I almost did." She hesitated. "It gets a little fuzzy. Anyway, I thought I was winning, but somehow or other, the gun flew across the room. I mean, *flew.* Like it was shot out of a cannon.

291

"Then it got really weird. When I think back on it, it doesn't make sense. Reed picked the gun up, and Daddy tried to get it from her. I mean, that's not the part I don't get—that was just like Daddy. A hundred percent like him." Her face twisted with dislike. "Controlling goddamn bastard. You know how bad he is? When I was in high school, we got this new electric can opener. So I came home one day and said, 'How do you work this?' Grady showed me—he was always handy with stuff like that. You know I have a brother, Grady?"

Skip nodded.

"But Daddy was in the kitchen, see. Getting some iced tea or something. I started doing it, and I was a little slow catching on. I didn't put the can in right and it was opening crooked or something. I took it out and put it in again, but it still wasn't quite right. Grady said, 'That's right, you've just got to move it a little to the left.' So I reached up to do that, and I felt someone come up behind me, cover my body entirely with his body, so I couldn't move, and just take the can out of my hand.

"It was Daddy, of course. He said, 'Neither one of you can do a damn thing right,' and he stood there, with me trapped between him and the kitchen counter, and opened the damn can. What do you think of a man like that?"

Abasolo said, "Ummm." Skip shook her head, as if in disbelief. She thought: *How awful to have spent thirty-odd years being a father and have nothing more to show for it.*

"Back to Monday night," she said.

"Well, I've had pretty much time to think about it, see it from Reed's point of view, and I swear to God I know how she felt. I swear to God I'd have done the same thing if it had been me."

Skip waited, heart pounding.

"Anyway, he said, 'Give me the gun,' and he reached for it, but she kind of waves it and says, 'I'll handle it, Dad. Keep out of the way.' So he yells at her: 'Give it to me, Reed!' and she turns to him for a minute, which is good for me—I'm thinking maybe I can make some progress while she's distracted.

"What happened was, she says, 'It's my kid. Get out of the way.' I mean, she yells it, actually. Let's face it, we were all getting pretty excited.

"So what do I do, I take advantage of the situation, get to Sally, grab her, and then I hear the gun go off. I think I'm dead, right? And Sally starts in like somebody's tearing her apart. But I don't feel a thing and I look over there, and blood's coming out of Daddy's leg like a fountain— way high up—I mean, like right at the crotch. And he looks—I can't even describe it—he's just got the most surprised look I've ever seen on a human being. Somehow—I'm not sure what happened exactly—but the table went over, and then I heard another shot. And Daddy went down."

She stopped, but Skip prompted. "Then what?"

"Well, something weird. Dennis said, 'Reed!' in a weird voice. You know what voice I mean? Like when a kid's done something wrong. You know, like you say, 'Sally!' if she throws her supper on the floor. You know what I mean? Like Reed was a real bad little girl.

"Anyhow, he said that, and then Reed yelled back, 'Goddammit, he should have gotten out of the way.' I figured they were going to argue for a while, so I took Sally and split."

"Taking the gun, of course."

"Are you kidding? What did I need the gun for? And how the hell was I going to get it? I just turned around and ran. Wouldn't you have?"

"Who shot your father, Evie?"

"What?" Evie looked bewildered.

"You're lying. What really happened?"

Comprehension dawned in her eyes, but puzzlement came out of her mouth. "Goddamn, motherfucker." It was an expression of amazement, not an epithet. "You don't believe me."

"Why should I believe you? You're a drunk, you're a junkie, you're a kidnapper—you're a murderer too, aren't you?"

"I haven't been a junkie in years, goddammit!"

"But you are a murderer."

"You're trying to fuck me, aren't you?"

"Get real, Evie. You weren't the only one in that room."

"Oh." Evie let that sink in a minute. "That bitch Reed wants to let me take the rap. Just when I thought—goddammit! Of course they'd play it that way. Of course. I was always dirt to them and I still am." A tear formed at the corner of her eye. "Fucking Dennis too, I guess."

Skip felt unbearably sorry for her. She almost didn't blame her for snatching Sally: *A baby doesn't judge and doesn't betray. As long as you feed it, it has to love you. There's nothing else in its world.*

Evie didn't speak for a while, obviously making an effort to pull herself together. When she did, she said, "I want a lawyer."

● ●

On the way back to headquarters, Abasolo did his best to be consoling: "Maybe the gun'll turn up in the debris of Anna's house."

But it didn't.

Nor was it in the car Evie had driven, or the one Reed had driven.

Anna denied that either she or her thugs had taken a gun from either of the women. Maurice Gresham—now in the throes of a massive Internal Affairs investigation—also denied it.

Dennis had undoubtedly disposed of it—either sold it to buy drugs or chucked it to protect Reed.

In the ensuing days, Skip brought him in repeatedly for questioning, and she brought Reed back as well. Still Dennis insisted Evie had shot her father—though Skip could swear he now looked sheepish when he said it—and still Reed said nothing, though she became red in the face and she sweated under questioning. Her foot tapped the floor and she shredded more than one tissue.

One day, when Skip was spending an unproductive hour with her, she caught an expression, a set of her mouth, that reminded her of Anna Garibaldi, and she realized something that astonished her:

They're practically the same person.

They both went into the family business, where they were totally subservient to the men.

They're both good little girls who never for a second stepped out of line; just conformed to the prevailing culture and waited for pats on the head.

Did what they were supposed to do, and volunteered for more. Suffered put-downs every day and worked all the harder to be a credit to their sex.

Probably built up a storehouse of resentment someone like me couldn't begin to comprehend. I'd have blown up the damned fish company. Burned the restaurant down. They just bowed a little lower, and scraped a little deeper.

Then one day they both rebelled.

Big-time.

Evie, under further questioning, only grew more rocklike, though a sullenness entered her demeanor, especially on days when she seemed to be suffering a hangover.

Susan Belvedere, the Deputy D.A. assigned to the case, was married to a man who had dated Reed in tenth grade and said she wouldn't hurt a fly—she'd be too sure she was going to hell for it. Yet Susan believed Evie's story with the fervor of Skip herself.

Long before she began her aggressive questioning of Evie, before Evie even got as far as the can opener, Skip had had a feeling. Evie was too relaxed, too easily waived her right to an attorney, to be worried about a murder charge.

Then there was her story.

As Evie told it, Skip had felt the tightening in her stomach that meant she was hearing an unpleasant truth—not what she expected to hear, or what she wanted to hear, but what every cell in her body told her was true.

"What do you think?" she asked Abasolo.

"I don't blame her. I'd have done it too."

"Who, goddamn it? Who don't you blame?"

"For Christ's sake, Skip, if Evie shot her dad, why the hell would Reed clam up?"

"To protect Evie?"

"Uh-uh. Not Little Miss Goody Two-Shoes. She'd get her the best legal counsel, all that kind of crap, but she'd feel deep, deep in her little civics-lesson heart that her sister, 'though still my sister and I love her, must Pay her Debt to Society.' Believe me, I know the type."

"Why, AA, I wouldn't have thought a rogue like yourself would go in for those babes."

"I don't. They go in for me—they all want to reform me."

"That makes sense. Reed reformed Dennis."

"I guarantee you it makes sense. It's why I'm single today."

Despite her best efforts and those of Susan Belvedere, and all the support Abasolo could muster, they still had no physical evidence and two witnesses with different stories.

There was simply no way to take the case to court. But they could at least take it to the grand jury.

Or so Skip thought until Belvedere showed up shaking her head one day. "Sugar got to my boss."

"Sugar! What are you talking about?"

"The Heberts are pretty damned influential in this town, did you know that?"

"I know they were connected. Is that what you mean?"

"I don't know if that entered into it. All I know is, yesterday Sugar turned up and had a conference behind closed doors. The next thing I knew I was told to drop the grand jury investigation."

"No!" Skip couldn't take it in.

"I'm sorry, Skip. I'm just as sorry as I can be." Belvedere looked as if someone had died.

"It happens," said Cappello. "You've got to let it go, Skip. The old fart had it coming."

She didn't mean it, of course.

Skip knew her: Though she had small children like Reed, though she knew that if Reed were convicted, Sally might be left to the tender mercies of Dennis and Sugar, Cappello would have locked Reed up and thrown away the key if she could have. She was trying to make Skip feel better.

But nobody could these days.

30

• •

She came home from work and fell immediately into bed, unable to read or even watch television. She tried spending time with Dee-Dee and the kids, but they didn't cheer her up, she brought them down. The kids didn't need that; they had enough trouble.

Sometimes she'd see Angel after a few days—or was it weeks?—and she'd have tripled in size. She'd panic: *I'm missing it. She's growing up, the kids are growing up, and I'm not even there for it.*

Still, she could do nothing. She couldn't stay awake. And when she was awake, she didn't want to be.

She dreamed sometimes of the night in the Conti Breezeway, saw Jim's face as he lay wounded on the ground, and when she saw Augustine Melancon's face, it was not the terrified baby face of a teenager caught in a nightmare, it was a Satan mask and it spoke to her, droning and much too slow, like a record played at the wrong speed.

"Your turn now," it said, and she would wake up sweating.

In the dream, she thought the figure was predicting her death, and sometimes she would tremble afterward, unable to go back to sleep.

But in daylight she'd remember what she knew it meant, what she always forgot when she dreamed it: It meant it was her turn to kill.

It was funny. For the longest time she was afraid to go to sleep for fear of dreaming. Yet she never dreamed the thing she feared, never saw tiny Shavonne crawling across that floor to her mama.

She did all the time in her conscious hours. Every time she saw a pair of pink jeans or a pair of flip-flops, or even, sometimes, just a small black girl with braids, Shavonne came to her like an acid flashback.

Sometimes when that happened, she would very deliberately switch channels—take her camera across the room to Delavon lying dead of her own bullet. She wanted to avoid hiding behind his daughter, to break the denial she knew was there, to understand, deep in her belly, that she had taken a human life.

And yet the image of Shavonne hurt her more deeply than that of Delavon. Indeed, she found it almost unbearable, and sometimes, in the office, brushed at her head when it came, as if a swarm of bees surrounded her. People stared. Cappello brought her coffee and asked if she were all right.

She said she was, she always said she was, because she knew the job was the only thing holding her together right now, and she could not risk being transferred. The pressure to perform was enormous.

The funny thing was, at work she was a hero. The round of applause the day after the shooting was just the beginning. She got a Medal of Merit, a little gold button shaped like a badge. She got congratulations from people whose names she didn't even know, strangers who stopped her in the hall. She finally gave Eileen Moreland an interview.

Eileen didn't ask her, she asked the superintendent, and he all but ordered her to do it. "Heroic Female Cop" was great publicity for a department that sorely needed some.

"Oh, Skippy, don't be such a pill," said Eileen. "It's a chance to get things off your mind."

Sure. Heroic Female Cop's supposed to tell the whole city about her depression. About the recurring nightmares. The superintendent would love that one.

She ended up saying, more or less, that she did what she had to.

As if it were original.

As if it were the end of the story.

As if police officers were automatons.

And then she had to deal with a second round of congratulations.

Joe Tarantino, her lieutenant, encouraged her to take the sergeant's test, saying she was "ready" now; she'd "matured." She was "seasoned." All words that mocked her.

You're mature if you shoot somebody? A seasoned cop is a killer?
What the hell am I doing here?

She was there because it was her job and it was the only identity she felt she had right now; she needed it to maintain contact with the Earth. But even at headquarters she couldn't check her hopelessness at the door.

Cindy Lou told her she should be in therapy, but she couldn't seem to get around to finding a therapist and making an appointment. She certainly wasn't going to do it at work, where everyone, including O'Rourke, could hear.

And when she wasn't at work, she was either asleep or just couldn't get up the energy to find the phone book. She couldn't shop or cook either. She ordered greasy po' boys from the Verti Marte or the Quarter Master, and her clothes got tighter.

Her appetite was erratic, but she never lost it completely. Mostly, she ate because she was hungry, not because it gave her pleasure.

Steve Steinman, worried and sure he could cure her, came for a weekend and went home more worried. She did with him what she did with her other friends, with Cindy Lou and Jimmy Dee, even with the kids and Darryl—she listened politely, ate and drank at appropriate times, even laughed at the proper places, but didn't contribute much.

"Darling, the sparkle is gone," wailed Dee-Dee. "You do not shine and glitter from twenty paces. You are no longer a walking Christmas tree, a spinning Ferris wheel, a revolving klieg light. Quite simply, you are not Margaret Langdon. You are a pathetic and flagrant impostor." He was begging her to take a little time off.

Everybody knew how to save her.

But weeks went by and she didn't get better.

• •

Her doorbell rang one Saturday.

Convinced it was one of the drunks who prowl the Quarter pushing bells for amusement, she ignored it. But it rang again and she came alert —the pranksters didn't break stride when they rang, much less waited for an answer.

She was sleeping as usual, but thought it might be one of the kids, locked out or something. She roused herself: "Who is it?"

"Tricia. Back from the dead."

She was too disoriented to answer right away.

Tricia said, "Are you speaking to me?"

I can barely remember who you are.

But she said, "Of course. I'll be right out," and remembered too late that Tricia was a drunk.

Well, if she's drunk I'll send her away. It's the middle of the day, she'll be fine.

But she knew she wouldn't. She would take care of Tricia if she needed her; caretaking was one of the few things for which she could still find energy.

Something about guilt, probably.

"I brought you something." Tricia was holding a beribboned package.

Probably a peace offering.

She looked good in a T-shirt and shorts that showed legs shiny gold from the sun. Her eyes were bright and clear.

Now she has her sparkle, Skip thought. *She does glitter at twenty paces.*

"You look wonderful." Feeling a surge of warmth for her old friend, she held out her arms for a hug.

"I do, don't I? I'm on a pink cloud."

"What does that mean? You're in love?"

"It's something we say in AA."

"Oh. AA." Skip let it hang there.

They walked back to the courtyard, where, for once, there were no kids and no puppy. "Want to sit out here?"

"Perfect."

Skip left and came back with a couple of Diet Cokes. "Tell me about the pink cloud."

"It's that great feeling you get when you get all the toxins out of your body." She spread her hands, as if displaying her purified form. "And your life is going somewhere again, and you're surrounded by nice, supportive people. Of course, it doesn't last—we all know that—but it feels great for a while.

"Clean and sober for a month. Congratulate me."

"Tricia, that's wonderful."

"I went through a seven-day treatment program. On the streets three weeks—I'm a new person." She saluted with her Coke. "And you were there when I hit bottom."

"You mean the scene in front of Maya's?"

"Oh, God, that was nothing. I bet I've thrown ten of those fits in the last six months. I mean having you see me—you know, in that place."

"Maya's?"

"I thought I'd die. I swear I did."

"I don't get it."

300

"You wouldn't think embarrassment would do it, would you? You'd think having a wreck or beating your kid—now that would sober you up. But there you were, my oldest friend, and you thought I was sober and doing great, and there I was, holding onto the chandelier for dear life." She shook her head. "I can't explain it. All I know is, I thought, 'What the fuck has become of me?' "

Skip laughed. "Rather unseemly for a McGehee's girl."

Tricia covered her head with her hands, as if to hide. "Life is too silly, isn't it?"

Skip was unconvinced; it had seemed deadly serious lately.

"Anyway, it was all your doing." Tricia handed her the package. "So I brought you a present."

It contained a framed picture, a pen-and-ink drawing of a large, proud, black woman. With very few strokes, the artist had captured a state of mind that said, "I am a goddess and don't you forget it."

In spite of herself, Skip was touched. "Carol Leake. I have one of her watercolors."

"You're kidding."

"I'll show you." She realized that her oldest friend had never been inside her home.

Tricia exclaimed appropriately over its adorableness, the tastefulness of its decor, and the beauty of its artwork, including the aforementioned Carol Leake, which, upon inspection, proved to be a study of the same model who'd sat for the drawing.

The warmth she felt for Tricia was increasing by the moment, as the broken bond mended itself, as she remembered the things they'd been through together, over so many years. Somehow the fact that Tricia had picked this drawing by this artist, whom Tricia couldn't possibly have known she admired, made her feel known.

Understood.

Part of something ongoing; something that might last.

But it wore off.

They hung the picture, Tricia advising on the exact right spot, and settled themselves once more. And after a while Tricia began to annoy her.

She's so pleased with herself, so damn smug, so thrilled with her little achievement.

Skip remembered her screaming, out of control in front of Maya's, and thought, *What the hell is she thinking? This is never going to last.*

She was so out of sorts, her nerves so frayed and raw, that she blurted it out: "Come on, Tricia, you've done this before. What makes you think it'll stick?"

And then she thought, *She'll go right out and score drugs. She'll get strung out and it'll be all my fault.*

"God, Tricia—I'm sorry. I don't know why I said that."

But Tricia smiled, apparently unoffended. "It's okay. I ask myself that all the time." She leaned over and patted Skip's hand. "Don't look so miserable. It's okay. Really."

Skip was still mortified. "Want another Coke?"

Tricia didn't acknowledge that she'd spoken. "It's worse than you think, Skip. I've done it *twice* before. But to answer your question, I have no idea whether I can make it stick. You know what we say in my religion— one day at a time."

It's so fucking pat.

"You want to know what? I'm hanging by a thread here. But today I'm okay.

"If I get loaded tomorrow, so be it. But *today* I'm okay." She shrugged. "And I feel like I've got my life back."

Skip felt a surge of envy. "You seem . . . almost happy."

"I'm delirious. I'm trying to be a writer, but I don't write because I've been so out of it lately. Instead, I'm a cocktail waitress. I haven't had a date in two years that you could actually call 'a date.' I mean I might have slept with a few guys whose names I can't remember, but nothing—you know—resembling a relationship. I've only got a month's sobriety and I'm already a two-time loser—in short, I'm a mess. But I'm thrilled out of my mind. I'm beside myself with delight. Life's crazy, huh?"

Skip thought of the night, weeks ago, when Steve had been with her and they were at dinner with Cindy Lou and Layne and Jimmy Dee, and she had been so happy she wanted to preserve the moment in amber. It was the same night Toni had read her palm; the night before Jim was shot.

"Yeah. Life's crazy." Skip tried to keep the bite out of her voice.

"Uh-oh. Something's wrong."

"You don't know, do you?" Tricia must have been in rehab when Skip was front page news. Skip didn't feel like dancing around it: "Somebody killed my partner, and I ended up killing him."

Tricia was quiet. Finally, she said, "How are you handling it?"

"Poorly. Damn badly." Here was someone she'd known her whole life, who probably wouldn't think she was nuts if she mentioned that she herself was hanging by a thread. She told her everything, ending with the part that was consuming her. "The worst part is, I feel like it's all a big zero. I can't figure out what the fuck it means."

"What it means?"

"Did I have to go through this for nothing? Isn't there something to be learned from it? There's got to be something. But so far no. Everyone tells me I'm a hero and I did a great job. And I know I did a great job. He'd already tried to kill me by the time I shot. He fired first, and he probably would have got me if I hadn't seen his reflection—so see, I did a good job, and not only that, I was lucky." She threw out her arms in frustration. "So I'm here and he's not. What the hell does it mean?"

"Why was he trying to kill you?"

"You know, you're the first person to ask that? Even Cindy Lou never asked. I don't have the least idea why he was trying to kill me. I didn't stop to ask him."

Tricia sat back on Skip's striped sofa. "It's got to give you a different take on things—someone trying to kill you."

Skip shrugged. "He's not the first one."

"Oh, God, I'd be depressed too."

Skip clasped her hands, sunk once more in despair. "Yeah."

Tricia said, "I've got to think for a minute." She closed her eyes and rubbed her head. Then she got up and walked to the window.

When she came back, she said. "Well, there's *got* to be something to be learned from this."

"That's my line."

"Here's the thing: It will come clear. But I have to warn you of something. It may take years. You can't sit around waiting for a sign from heaven. You could go to a shrink—or are you seeing one already?"

Skip shook her head.

"I thought not. This doesn't feel like it's something in you. The answer, I mean. In you yet, anyway. When it comes, it'll come."

"What will come?"

"The lesson; the justification. I don't know—the knowledge. The thing that puts it in perspective."

"What makes you so sure?"

Tricia laughed. "Nobody can prove me wrong, can they? I love predicting the future—who's going to disagree?"

It's too facile. But her mind began to chew on it.

Even when you're a kid, when you're in school, you don't get the point of anything. You don't see why you have to learn to add or know the parts of speech, and then one day you're trying to balance your checkbook or write

*some damn case report, and you never think, "Oh, so that's it." You've just
learned it and you use it.*

Maybe this is like that.

She was suddenly unbearably tired, couldn't wait for Tricia to leave.
The instant she could, she threw off her clothes and flung herself down.
The taste of tears warmed her tongue as she fell asleep.